Yakuza Courage

H.J. BRUES

Dreamspinner Press

Published by
DREAMSPINNER PRESS

5032 Capital Circle SW, Suite 2, PMB# 279, Tallahassee, FL 32305-7886 USA
http://www.dreamspinnerpress.com/

Yakuza Courage
© 2014 H.J. Brues.

Cover Art
© 2014 Reese Dante.
http://www.reesedante.com
Cover content is for illustrative purposes only and any person depicted on the cover is a model.

ISBN: 978-1-62798-865-0
Digital ISBN: 978-1-62798-866-7
Library of Congress Control Number: 2014943205
First Edition August 2014

Printed in the United States of America
∞
This paper meets the requirements of
ANSI/NISO Z39.48-1992 (Permanence of Paper).

To Marta and Victor, my own team of indefatigable friends on sea, air, or land.

CHAPTER 1

BRENDAN O'FARRIHY forced himself to stop checking the altitude on his watch. After two years he still wasn't used to flying in a commercial airliner without expecting to perform a perfect "D. B. Cooper" to insert into a hostile country.

He sighed as he let his head fall back against the headrest. He was a regular passenger on a regular commercial flight to Oahu—he wouldn't jump with his shooters in midflight because he didn't command an assault element anymore. Now he was something undefined between a government gofer, a security guard, and—on his best days—a private investigator. *A glorified dick*, his leading petty officer would have called him.

He smiled. Tyrell "Otter" Hayes had called him far worse, always flashing his teeth in that manic grin he used to compensate for his twin's forbidding seriousness. Not that John Burka was his biological twin, but they were more or less the same height—about five ten—both long-legged and swimmer slim, both with the same Southern drawl, but one African American and the other so pale and blond you could see his hair glowing when you looked at him through night-vision goggles. That was why John had to cover his head with an extralarge bandana that the guys started calling his burka, and that was why the same witty guys would ask Tyrell whenever he was on his own, "Hey bro, where have you left your albino twin?"

The truth was that Brendan missed the easy camaraderie among his men. The teams were not so much about military protocol as about results, and you couldn't get results from people you didn't trust. That had ultimately been the reason for their demise—that some politician back in Washington had decided they couldn't be trusted with their nation's safety.

He heard the racket of the beverage cart as the stewardess pushed it down the aisle, and thought briefly about ordering one of those tiny bottles of Scotch. But even after all that had happened, he still considered alcohol to be the refuge of cowards. Defeated he might be, lost even, but he'd kill himself the day he had reason to be called a coward. Besides, Big Brudda would be waiting for him at Honolulu International, and he didn't want his former engineman to smell alcohol on his breath.

It had probably been a mistake, telling his man that he was coming over to Hawaii. What was the likelihood of a chance encounter in a place flooded daily with thousands of tourists, come summer or winter? In any case, at six-two and 177 pounds, it should have been easy to spot Big Brudda and duck out of his way, even if Brendan hadn't been trained as a Navy SEAL. But the big man was also a good friend—every single one of them was—and Brendan would have felt like a traitor hiding behind corners to avoid the bitter memories.

It'd be the first time that he actually visited the home island of one of the Islanders too. He smiled. The other assault elements hadn't lost a moment to give them the moniker once they discovered all of them came from one island or another. Brendan himself was of Irish ancestry, and he led two Cuban Americans, a Hawaiian, a

Manhattanite, and two Floridians—the Twins—one from Marco Island and the other from… Hialeah, which was no island at all, but Otter, being an African American in the SEALs, was as close as anyone could get to becoming an island unto himself.

Brendan checked his watch one more time. Still half an hour to reach his destination. He wasn't looking forward to this assignment, and having to explain to Big Brudda what his job was like nowadays didn't help in the least. Not that Big B would scoff at him like Otter would surely have done. Nahele "Big Brudda" Fernandes had been born and raised in a place where the concept of saving face was first and foremost among the values taught to every child, and from his point of view, if Brendan had been recommended for a job by his former Navy employers, he'd fulfilled his duty by accepting it.

Yet Big B was also a fundamentally honest man who'd never learned how to keep a poker face, and Brendan was sure he'd see his expressive native features show his disgust as soon as he understood that his former commander was just following around politicians' cheating spouses, digging up dirt on electoral competitors, investigating lobbyists' financial sources, and generally keeping Washington's dirty laundry inside its sealed hamper.

Brendan felt disgusted with himself. How did one travel all the way down from proud officer in a naval elite force to garbageman? Well, he guessed the explanation was rather simple. As Senior Chief Blake put it, "When the high brass screw up, shit falls on the guy holdin' the M16."

At least he'd taken the shit and avoided the shrapnel. Not all of the Islanders had been that lucky.

BRENDAN FELT a little odd descending from a bus with big hibiscus flowers painted on the sides, but at least nobody was going to hang a garland around his neck as soon as he set foot in the terminal—Big B would know better than that.

He strode purposefully toward the baggage claim, noticing the looks his lightweight wool suit was earning him. His trained eyes noticed everything in their search for possible threats, but it had taken a very different sort of training to discern between the oh-my looks directed at him and the oh-wow ones. Yeah, it had taken the Craig crash course on style to have guys turning their heads at him to check out his clothes.

Now he knew enough to realize that he was slightly overdressed for Honolulu International Airport—and likely for the whole island—but he also knew the people doing a double take would soon forget about the too many layers for the local weather factor and focus instead on the nice fit of his slim pants and tailored jacket. They made him look taller and more confident in a sense that didn't scream military smugness, and that was one of the greatest ways to go unnoticed: be right in the spotlight and have people think his measured movements were runway trained, the hard look behind the sunglasses an action-flick-star pose.

Before Craig, every time he'd donned a suit, people would immediately peg him for some sort of special agent—he'd simply switched one uniform for another. Now it would only take one look at the leather bag he was shouldering to put him on the other side of the District's fence—the one inhabited by lawyers, lobbyists, and politicians. And he didn't even want to consider what that said about him.

The expensive Danish bag was a present from Craig, and Brendan hadn't failed to notice the blatant looks of envy from the guys carrying the more popular Tumi luggage. His competitive streak soared at that, but some very tiny voice in the back of his mind kept telling him he never used to notice the quality of people's luggage, much less know the difference between brands.

Not that it mattered much, what he had turned into. He wasn't a link in a chain of command anymore, and nobody depended on him. He was just a civilian with short-term contractual responsibilities—whatever he did with his so-called life was his own business. And yet he knew it should irk him, the way Craig displayed him as he would a pedigree guard dog, but Brendan was past caring. Once he'd accepted being a government whore, it didn't take much effort to slip into the boy-toy role. In fact, if he should take the time to really consider it, he might come to the conclusion that it'd been a step up from the kind of anonymous sex he'd indulged in whenever the need overtook his common sense. Now he had nothing to lose, no reputation to keep, and there was this comfortable numbness where his feelings used to be. Definitely a step up.

The racket of the luggage carousel brought his mind back into focus, and it didn't take him much to spot Big B among the crowd. Tall, broad-shouldered, his thick black eyebrows drawing a perfect V as he frowned at the tourists gathering around the conveyor belt, Big B was the epitome of the Polynesian warrior of old, fierce and unyielding, right until the moment he spotted Brendan. As soon as their eyes met, the warrior mask dissolved into what had to be a full-body grin.

Brendan shook his head, his own smile almost making his mouth ache he was so unused to smiling anymore. Geez. He couldn't remember the last time someone had looked so honestly happy to see him.

"Aloha, Boss Man," Big B's voice resonated across the terminal, and Brendan surprised himself by chuckling. People were looking at them, but he didn't care; in fact, the warm welcome was making the tension in his shoulders slip down a notch. It felt like returning to a place where he didn't have to prove himself every step of the way, where he didn't have to feel ashamed, not even embarrassed to be what he was.

"What's up, Brudda?" he said when he was in front of Big B, actually having to crane his neck to look into smiling brown eyes. He extended his hand, but when Big B took it in his big tanned fingers, Brendan was pulled into a bear hug.

"*E komo mai*, sir," Big B said softly, and Brendan felt as if someone had used his sternum for underwater knot tying practice. The last time he'd been called *sir*, he'd been shopping at Macy's.

"*Mahalo*, Petty Officer Fernandes," Brendan answered with the only Hawaiian word he'd ever learned apart from the hackneyed "aloha."

Big B let go of him and waved a dismissive hand. "I'm just a private contractor to the Navy now, Boss."

"You'll never be *just* anything, B. And that's what I am too—a private contractor." Though in his new environment being called a *mechanic* didn't exactly mean repairing Zodiac outboard engines like Big B did.

"Yeah, I sort of noticed," Nahele said, giving him an amused once-over.

Brendan smirked. "You did? And what gave me away, the relaxed grooming standards?"

"That's anything but *relaxed*, man. You look like some hotshot corporate executive about to conduct a hostile takeover."

He laughed. It felt surprisingly good to be embarrassed about dressing too well. "I didn't want my only suit to get wrinkled inside the bag."

Big B eyed his leather bag with something close to apprehension. "Is that all your luggage?"

"Yeah. Anything else I need, I'll buy here."

"Good. Shall we go to a clothing store first?"

Brendan laughed again. He didn't remember the last time he'd laughed so easily. Maybe calling his former engineman hadn't been a mistake after all.

CHAPTER 2

"*MATAKU*," KINOSUKE Yonekawa mumbled under his breath. For the second time this week, Kotarō was late, and Kinosuke knew exactly where the kid would be right now. Not that he couldn't understand the attraction of the beach, but Kotarō had some duties that should stand before everything else—surfing included.

The real problem was that Kinosuke had lost the authority his former lieutenant rank had given him, and now he only had his seniority to depend on for Kotarō's respect, should the kid choose to show him any.

They had left the Shinagawa-gumi with their boss, Shigure Matsunaga, and were no longer yakuza. None of them—certainly not Kotarō, who had been a mere apprentice—answered to their former superiors in the Shinagawa chain of command.

Still, they may have left the yakuza, and even Japan, but they were honor-bound to the man who had given them a way to earn their living, a place to call home, and the pride of belonging to a respected family. Shigure Matsunaga had been one of the top Shinagawa *wakagashira*. His house, a renowned training center for new recruits, was where Kinosuke had learned how to use a katana and, most importantly, how to take orders without chafing at the thought of someone having any kind of authority over him.

That was the problem with Kotarō, he believed. While Kinosuke had dropped out of school to join a *bōsōzoku* biker gang and had been well on his way to becoming the kind of petty criminal who'd lived his sorry life in and out of the can, Kotarō was a small-town boy who'd been sent to Tokyo the same way people throw nasty stuff in the ocean, hoping the tide won't ever bring it back.

And so Matsunaga had played a different role for each of them. The imposing underboss had grabbed Kinosuke by the ear and taught him how to be a man. He'd been the first person in Kinosuke's life who cared enough to slap him out of his stupidity—and the boss hadn't even had to use his hands for it; the man could stare you down until you felt like the cockroach you'd never wanted to admit you were.

For Kotarō, though, Matsunaga had meant comfort and security. The little boy had been about to be swallowed by the merciless city, and the yakuza had pulled him out of the killing waters and wrapped him in a blanket of affection. The boss had given him a family when he'd desperately needed one, but Kotarō was fast outgrowing that need now. Like every other teenager, he had reached that point where he needed to prove he could live out of the protective net of family ties. And he had definitely reached that point in the worst place and at the worst possible time.

"*Chikushō*," he cursed as he paced up and down the narrow reception area of the dojo.

"What's wrong, Kinosuke?"

Shit. Of all people.

"Nothing, Kenshin-san." He didn't need to turn around to know that Kenshin-san was rolling his eyes at the honorific attached to his name, but Kinosuke wasn't backing down. How could he stop showing his respect to the man who'd saved his life?

"Nothing? So, what is it that you're doing? Carving a path on the floor for visitors to follow?"

"I'm just—" Kinosuke made the mistake of turning to face Kenshin-san while he was speaking. He should know better by now. Their favorite gaijin's clothes could hit like a jab under the ribcage and leave you breathless.

"What? You don't like Hawaiian shirts?" Kenshin-san asked innocently.

"That's not Hawaiian," Kinosuke countered. "That's... that's fucking insane, man."

Kenshin-san frowned as he studied the print on the shirt he wore unbuttoned over a black tank top. "Look, it's got big flowers all over it. In bright colors too."

Kinosuke snorted. "Yeah, big *thorny* red roses on a *black* background."

"Like I said, big flowers in bright colors," Kenshin-san insisted.

"And what about the skulls, huh?" Kinosuke pointed. "What are they, aloha *spirits*?"

Kenshin-san shrugged. "They're smiling, aren't they?"

They looked at each other for all of two seconds before cracking up.

"Shit, man," Kinosuke said, shaking his head. "Laughing skulls. That's too much even for you."

"I just asked for something with friendly faces on it. And they sure gave me some toothy grins."

Kinosuke laughed. If he'd thought Kenshin-san would stand out less in his own homeland, he'd been clearly mistaken. As pretty as he was, Kenneth Harris would stand out anywhere, what with that slim body, those full lips, and those big—weird—eyes. Yeah. He might have been too pretty, if it wasn't for the shocking effect his eyes had on people; everyone did a double take to make sure the man really had one green eye and the other brown.

That would have made him different enough, but there were other reasons for him to draw attention. He wore his hair bleached white, most of the time gelled into spikes, and in the land of Bermuda shorts and flip-flops, he still managed to find clothes that appeared summery and breezy until you looked twice at them and the wacky details jumped out at you like booby traps.

And of course, he had the tattoos. Kenshin-san had been kidnapped, and the bastard who'd kept him and Kinosuke locked in a basement had carved the kanji for "dog" all over Kenshin-san's skin. When the boss had suggested a tattoo in the old *irezumi* style to cover the marks, the crazy gaijin hadn't even hesitated to place his body in the hands of Maedasaki-sensei, the tattoo master who'd done the artwork on Matsunaga and most of his men.

So there he was, a gaijin with eyes in two different colors, white spiked hair, and Japanese tattoos showing from under the short-sleeved clothes the local weather required.

"What?" Kenshin-san asked, still smiling.

Kinosuke shook his head. "I was thinking you're a crazy gaijin, but now that we're in America, I guess I'll have to stop calling you that."

"Nah. I kind of like it."

Kinosuke smirked. He'd been afraid of having the tables turned on him and becoming the gaijin as soon as they entered the United States, but a bunch of Japanese were as inconspicuous in Hawaii as they'd been in Japan, or even more, because this was a relaxed land where people lived on the beach and didn't pay much attention to the way you dressed or talked or bowed.

That was probably why Kotarō acted the way he did. He'd gone from the suffocating rules of life in small-town Japan to yakuza discipline, and now he found himself in what must be the most laid-back place in America, where nobody had anything to worry about but how many feet the surf would build to.

It wasn't the best place to set a teenager loose, and Kinosuke knew one or two things about loose teens. He happened to be a fucking expert, in fact.

"Shouldn't Kotarō be manning the reception desk?" Kenshin-san asked.

Kinosuke groaned. The kid should be there, behind the simple bamboo desk, three afternoons a week, substituting for Tachibana's wife. It wasn't much to ask, seeing that he was fed, clothed, housed, and provided with an education in return.

"Oh," Kenshin-san said. He looked at his watch and added, "I'm free now. I can sit there until Kotarō returns; it won't be long enough for me to make a mess."

Kinosuke didn't even smile. It was a familiar joke with them, the one about the gaijin's frequent episodes of woolgathering, but however true it might be, Kenshin-san still had his priorities straight and never let anyone down.

"You have to give him some time, Kinosuke. This is all new for him."

"This is new for me too, and you won't see me ducking my duties to go play the ukulele or some shit like that."

He saw Kenshin-san's lips twitch and pointed a finger at him. "And don't you dare laugh, you damn gaijin."

"Sorry," Kenshin-san said, raising his hands in surrender. "I just had a vision of you playing the ukulele in your *hakama* pants. But I won't laugh. I promise."

"Shut up." He tried to sound stern, but it was very difficult to keep a serious face around Kenshin-san. "And go change into something decent if you want to play receptionist for a while."

"*Hai, hai*," Kenshin-san said as he pushed the sliding door to the garden open and walked out of sight of the dojo.

Kinosuke shook his head. After all that had happened to him, Kenshin-san still kept too much trust in people for his own good. This place and all its trappings posed a great danger for Kotarō, and not because he was in any way a bad kid, but because he was just a kid, easy to lead in a direction that could bring the danger they had fled from right to their doorstep.

"Kotarō's missing again?"

Kinosuke turned to meet Shinya's concerned frown. Yeah. Here was a man who understood the danger perfectly well, as the nasty scar running all the length of his left cheek testified. "He was supposed to be here half an hour ago, and I'm not sure if I'd rather he were at Kalaeloa Beach with all those firefighters from the Fire Surf School keeping an eye on him, or at Kuhio, where he can get in trouble without a bunch of firemen asking him which hotel he's staying in."

Shinya nodded gravely. "I don't like the crowd he's hanging out with."

Kinosuke huffed and started pacing. "Weaselly lowlifes the whole lot of them, in a country where any fuckwit can get his hands on a gun. And our little dunderhead can't wait to at least have the fucking green card in his wallet before he goes out with a gaggle of scumbags who are sure to draw all sorts of unwanted attention. Shit. What the hell is Kotarō thinking?"

Shinya didn't give the obvious answer, but after a while of listening to Kinosuke's furious steps, he asked, "You haven't told the boss, have you?"

Kinosuke stopped in his tracks. He hadn't told anyone because he still felt Kotarō was his responsibility, but if the silly kid managed to stop them from getting their residence granted and they had to leave the United Sates, the least of his problems would be the boss yelling at him. If they had to leave, Kenshin-san would have no one to defend him against his father's shenanigans.

Kenneth Harris was the son of a senator, and the senator was a first-rate jerk, which wouldn't have mattered at all if the bastard hadn't been a powerful jerk too. The man only cared about his political career, and he had the means to suppress anything that threatened to affect it—namely, his son being involved with the yakuza, or getting kidnapped, or being queer, or simply breathing. He had already tried to commit Kenshin-san to a mental hospital, and the fact that they hadn't heard from him didn't mean he'd decided to let his son be.

Shinya nodded as if Kinosuke had already answered. "I'll keep an eye on Kotarō, but you better have a word with the boss. You know he's not blind. He must be waiting for you to mention the problem."

Kinosuke almost said that the boss was blind to anything that wasn't Kenshin-san, but he kept his mouth shut. It wasn't fair—and it wasn't even true.

Everything had changed so fast that Kinosuke felt completely disoriented about everybody's place in the scheme of things, and he hated it. He still called the boss "boss," but in truth, Matsunaga wasn't even the owner of the dojo—Kenshin-san was. Kinosuke knew they'd done it that way so they all had an American employer who could file a green card petition for them, but he still resented the confusion it created.

Being a kendo instructor was a nice job, and he couldn't complain, but he had grown up in the yakuza, and the yakuza was more than a job. He felt naked without the Shinagawa badge. It had marked him as a member of a group, given him respect. Now he walked the streets of this alien place and all people saw was a Japanese man, or worse, some kind of Asian who only had to open his mouth to betray his immigrant status.

Even sharing a house with the men he'd known forever felt strange now. Why were they living together when they didn't share blood ties? It might be all right for Kotarō, but what about him? Shouldn't he move out, live his own life?

Tachibana had met Alma, a Filipino woman, and moved to their own little house as soon as they married, and maybe it was time for Kinosuke to do the same. But then again, why would he want to do that? When they'd adapted the old warehouse that was their home now, Kenshin-san had made sure Kinosuke and Shinya had their private spaces, and Kinosuke doubted he could find something finer that he could afford.

Shit. Who was he kidding? He liked sharing his meals with these men, liked talking and joking with them, liked seeing Tachibana's wife restocking their fridge with adobo and *longaniza*, liked knowing he could find Kenshin-san drawing in that crazy greenhouse in the middle of the garden, liked having a bunch of kids calling him sensei.

The problem came when he left the sanctuary of their home and found himself a precarious alien in an alien land, no more the proud member of a respected yakuza family.

He heard Shinya laugh and then Kenshin-san's voice. "What? He told me to change into something decent."

The smile started to form on his lips even before he turned around, and then he had to ask Shinya, "Is he really wearing a skirt?"

While Shinya nodded, Kenshin-san said indignantly, "It's not a skirt! It's a lavalava!"

"A what?"

"A lavalava. It's the decent thing for men to wear on the Pacific islands," Kenshin-san explained, his hands smoothing down the beautiful blue cloth wrapped around his slender body from waist to ankles. A simple dark blue T-shirt and sandals completed the outfit.

"There are dolphins on his skirt," Shinya said, and Kinosuke felt his smile widening as he stepped closer to Kenshin-san to study the small pattern on the fabric.

"It's not a skirt!"

"Shit, man, look at this," Kinosuke said, and Shinya bent to take a closer look, ignoring Kenshin-san's protests. It wasn't hard to see the cute smiling dolphins, jumping in pairs and plunging back into the blue ocean waters of the background, but it was harder to spot the few sharks and their big wicked smiles. Shinya and Kinosuke exchanged a look, then looked up at Kenshin-san as he stood there with his arms crossed in front of his chest, and lost it.

"Laugh all you want," Kenshin-san said, pouting, "but next time you guys wear your *yukatas*, I'm going to tell you that you're wearing dresses; see how that feels."

"Yeah, you try telling the boss that he's wearing a dress," Kinosuke retorted.

"Who's wearing a dress?" came a grave voice from inside the dojo, and Shigure Matsunaga strode into the reception hall in his practice uniform, the white *uwagi* jacket tucked into dark blue hakama pants that rippled around his legs as he moved closer. He looked at them questioningly, his narrowed eyes traveling from them to Kenshin-san and then stopping short. "Why are you wearing a sheet, Kenshin?"

It was a sight to see, Kenshin-san's face, his eyes sending sparks in two different colors, and Kinosuke had to put his hand over his mouth to stop from laughing. For a moment there, the boss and Kenshin-san stood facing each other—one the picture of a dignified samurai with his wooden sword still in his hand, the other the picture of a very angry whatever it was that warriors from another galaxy were called, both trying to stare each other down, both dressed in the most exotic outfits that, strangely enough, seemed to belong on them, making them look formidable in their own opposite ways.

And then Kinosuke saw the exact moment their looks went from challenging to appraising, and he had to swallow hard. Shit. He wished someone would look at him the way those two men looked at each other, as if they were the first men on earth to discover fire all over again.

"We better get ready for the next class, Kinosuke," Shinya said, nodding toward the dojo none too subtly.

With a smile, Kinosuke followed Shinya. He lived in an old sprawling warehouse-turned-dojo, with a crazy American artist, two tough ex-yakuza, and a rebelling teenager. On an island where men wore sheets around their legs and rode the waves on ironing boards. Why would he want to change his life?

CHAPTER 3

BRENDAN STUDIED the photos one more time and grunted. Surveillance was always boring, but this particular job was getting on his nerves.

What on earth was he really looking for? The dojo didn't look like a façade for any yakuza operation, unless the whole thing was based on the petty scams of a bunch of juvies. That was all the suspicious activity he'd gotten on film: the youngest Japanese in the group hooking up with what appeared to be a gang of rejects of such mixed ancestry Brendan had difficulty identifying them as Filipinos or Chinese or Korean or what they disparagingly called *hapa* around here, people with mixed Hawaiian and Caucasian blood.

Geez. He'd thought that serving with Latinos, African Americans, Native Americans, and Pacific Islanders would have made him an expert in ethnicity, but the mainland and its tidy ethnic pigeonholes had nothing to do with Hawaii's racial cocktail. Even Big B, who Brendan had always considered the stereotypical Native Hawaiian, had Portuguese ancestry, and his Chinese wife had given him two beautiful kids who Brendan couldn't have placed in any known ethnicity if his life depended on it.

The truth was, the most easily identified people were whites like him, universally—and not always kindly—known as *haole*. And even then there was this whole list of qualifiers; you could be a local haole, or a mainland haole, or a military haole, or you could simply be the most common variety of Caucasian, your everyday *fucking haole*.

Brendan would have found it funny—being for once on the minority side of things—if it wasn't interfering with his work. In spite of the racial mix, people still flocked together in ethnic neighborhoods, and he was too conspicuously white loitering about the too Japanese Upper Manoa. Of course Kenneth Harris stood out even more.

Sitting in his car with only Harris's graduation photo for reference, Brendan had had trouble recognizing the white-haired, tattooed young man as the senator's son. Maybe he'd had this preconception about illustrators of children's books being the nerdy type, but he couldn't begin to imagine how a guy who wore black cargo shorts with metal eyelets, D-rings, and chains, would go about drawing Little Red Riding Hood. Well, he couldn't imagine what a senator's son was doing with a bunch of yakuza either, but he'd found that rich kids tended to go to great lengths to shock their parents, maybe to get even for stifling childhoods, or most probably just for the thrill of it.

So not much about spoiled Washington brats surprised Brendan anymore, but there was something else about this particular case he was finding difficult to chew.

He'd grown used to his employers lying or telling half-baked truths; it'd become a given in his profession—or rather in *their* profession, since they were all politicians or government officials of one sort or another—and he always double-checked all the information he got from them. The problem was that now, the more he checked, the blurrier the picture became.

According to Senator Harris, his youngest son had been visiting a friend in Japan when members of the Shinagawa-gumi, one of the two most powerful yakuza families, kidnapped him. As the Japanese police began to close in on them, the yakuza picked out a plausible scapegoat from their ranks and conned—or bribed—police investigators into nabbing some small-fry secretary who would take the blame for the underboss who planned the whole thing.

Since Brendan had never heard anything good about Japanese police, he didn't find the story surprising, except for that little detail about Kenneth sticking with his alleged kidnappers even after being liberated. Senator Harris insisted that the yakuza had snared his son and brainwashed or threatened him into staying with them, maybe hoping for another try at getting the money the kidnapping scheme had failed to extract from his father. But if that was true, Kenneth hadn't only stuck to his kidnappers' side, but had also traveled with them to the United States and made sure they were on their way to getting their green cards by financing a dojo and employing his former torturers as kendo instructors. That was a hell of a Stockholm syndrome.

To compound things further, not a single one of the Japanese men living with Kenneth had a criminal record. It might not be surprising for the youngest among them, but how did you become a yakuza underboss without being implicated in any kind of criminal activity? Of course yakuza were renowned for their loyalty to their superiors, and that could involve taking the fall for them and keeping them out of jail, but if that had been the case, some of Matsunaga's men had to have rap sheets as long as Nimitz class aircraft carriers. Otherwise, getting their records swept clean might have implied a huge amount of bribing, or the kind of leverage only the most powerful among the most powerful gangs could boast about, and those kinds of first-class criminals didn't flee their countries to spread martial arts traditions.

Senator Harris would insist that Matsunaga was using his son to expand Shinagawa business interests into the United States. And that had made a lot of sense to Brendan before he took a look at the unpretentious dojo and its occupants. Gangs, like any other corporation, were internationalizing at a fast pace, but they did so with the bold moves that fierce competition demanded; they didn't start transnational branches based on the amateurish swindling of teenage surfers.

At least the men in the dojo *did* have the yakuza look to them. Brendan had no trouble recognizing the hardness about the eyes that singled out men familiar with violent death, no matter which side of the law they stood. Even someone as fundamentally kindhearted as Big B had a toughened core that showed in the little details only a combat-trained person like Brendan might see, such as the subtle way the big Hawaiian scanned every room he entered for possible threats, or the way he looked at cars *and* their drivers in the rearview mirror. And Shigure Matsunaga, in spite of his elegant, dignified manners, had the eyes of a tough son of a bitch.

Brendan shook his head. He was sure Craig would have approved of Matsunaga's style, with his impeccable linen slacks and the nice touch of the rolled up sleeves on his always expensive-looking shirts, never suspecting that those designer clothes probably hid a full-body tattoo of the same kind that his less fashion-conscious men had no trouble showing.

Yeah, the others—Kenneth Harris included—might give Craig a heart attack. Shinya Nakatani looked like a poster boy for the underworld: crew cut, scarred face, and alternating dark suits with unbuttoned shirt collars and wifebeaters that displayed more or less of an intricate Japanese tattoo.

Yoshinori Tachibana was by far the worst. He had embraced the aloha shirt with a fervor not shown by locals and had no trouble baring his skinny, heavily tattooed legs—never failing to wear white socks with his sandals.

Then came the kid, Kotarō Fuwa, who blended in nicely with the beach crowd in his surfer T-shirts, boardies, and thongs. And last but not least, Kinosuke Yonekawa. That one intrigued Brendan in a way that he found slightly irritating.

Brendan had never reconciled himself with the fact that he liked pretty faces—it seemed unmanly to appreciate male beauty when he was an elite soldier; he should have been attracted to muscled, hairy, men's men, but he went unerringly for the pretty twinks every time he was desperate enough to go cruising, and every single time afterward, it felt like a weakness, a character flaw.

Even being with Craig now, with the obvious difference in age and status between them and all its implications, didn't feel as demeaning as Brendan's taste in bed partners had always been. Standing beside Craig at one of the posh receptions the lawyer liked to take his ex-SEAL to, Brendan felt the power of the older man rubbing off on him, as if just by being associated with the predatory attorney could gain him scraps of the respect—the fear in some cases—his lover had collected along his career. It almost made Brendan feel proud by proxy.

He shook his head. He'd texted Craig upon reaching Oahu, and Craig had answered with an equally short, equally inane text. Neither of them had tried to call the other in the two weeks he'd been in Hawaii. Yeah, they were both busy men with important missions—they didn't have the time or the stomach for chitchat.

Brendan put Craig out of his mind and concentrated on Yonekawa's picture. The young man had beautiful Asian features, with high cheekbones and dark eyes; his thick black hair fell in longish layers all over his face and made him look like one of those rail-thin manga characters. He had the body for that too—slender and long-legged as he was, though not as impossibly tall as his fictional counterparts.

Like Brendan, Yonekawa seemed to be in the five-eight, five-ten range. Brendan was exactly five-ten, the average SEAL height. People visualized SEALs as some sort of Conan the Barbarian in camo gear, but the truth was men like Big B were the exception in the teams. In fact, when the time came to haul ass, Big B tended to be on the slow side—as the rest of the squad had no trouble reminding him, competitive bastards that they were.

Those were the things Brendan liked about the Japanese punk, that and his given name—Kinosuke. It tasted nicely in his mouth, the strong Ks softened by the U near the end—a short, bittersweet morsel like the man himself. Because Kinosuke had a lot of bitter to compensate for the sweet face. Boy, did he.

Brendan could almost tell the days Kinosuke had woken on the wrong side of the bed by the way he styled his hair. Even without bugs in place, Brendan was sure there'd be a lot of cursing in Japanese every time the zoom in his camera caught Kinosuke's black mane plastered to his skull with an unholy amount of gel.

The transformation happened often enough for Brendan not to know which of the two was in costume, the cute Asian boy trying to hide behind his long bangs every time he left the all-Japanese neighborhood, or the cocky little shit who scowled openly at everyone crossing his path, be it man, elderly woman, toy poodle, or bawling toddler.

Every way Brendan looked at it, the youngster was a handful—and it seemed Brendan had been looking at it every other way, seeing as Kinosuke's side of the corkboard was the most crowded, with a bunch of photos capturing every single one of his quicksilver moods, from openmouthed astonishment at one of Harris's outfits to hell-fire, boiling rage. Brendan's favorite, though, was the one he'd caught of Kinosuke smoking by the door to the dojo in one of those Japanese outfits that looked like a cross between a kimono and a Victorian riding skirt.

Kinosuke's face carried all the mischief of a schoolboy playing truant as he raised the cigarette to his sensual lips, but the traditional gear gave him a timeless aplomb that made him look confident without being churlish, and the playful mixture of princely dignity and impish youth never failed to make Brendan's mouth go dry. Yeah. Kinosuke was one sexy son of a bitch.

CHAPTER 4

"ALOHA, BOSS."

To say that Big B was darkening his doorway wasn't even a figure of speech, given the relative sizes of the Hawaiian and said doorway. Brendan stepped aside with a sweeping gesture. "*Mi casa es tu casa*," he said, "and literally too."

Big B laughed his deep belly laughter. "Nope, not mine. My wife always follows the wiser Chinese traditions and keeps what's hers to herself."

"Smart girl."

Big B gave him a smug smile. "Yeah. I chose right."

"She chose right too—she married a Navy SEAL."

"And then had to put up with me," the big man said, shrugging, and Brendan chuckled at his contrite expression.

He motioned Big B into the living room and watched in amusement as the sharp brown eyes automatically checked his own wife's property for anything slightly more dangerous than dust bunnies—a clear symptom of combat withdrawal if there was one. And now of course Big B's eyes were unerringly drifting toward the open door to Brendan's improvised war room.

He knew it would be rude—and foolish—to keep his investigation from his former comrade; for junkies like them, there was nothing like an ongoing op, no matter how small or boring. And it wouldn't do to antagonize his landlord in a place where apartments vied with the best in Manhattan only as far as rent was concerned.

"You mind taking a look at my case?" he asked in a studiously nonchalant way. "I could use your input."

"Sure," Big B answered with the same degree of indifference, but a suspicious glint lit his eyes as they walked into the den and stood in front of the corkboard covered with pictures, house plans, and street maps.

"This is the senator's son I told you about." Brendan pointed to Kenneth Harris's picture. "And these are the alleged yakuza who are allegedly retaining him against his will."

Big B studied the photos carefully and then raised his expressive eyebrows. "Doesn't look too unwilling to me."

Brendan nodded. Beside the photos of each individual yakuza, he had tacked at least one that showed the same guy laughing or smiling with an obviously relaxed Harris.

"The overdressed dude over here's the boss?"

"Yeah. That's Shigure Matsunaga. To believe Senator Harris, he's top brass in the Shinagawa yakuza gang." Brendan smiled. "And he's not overdressed, just elegant."

"Whatever you say."

"See those rolled-up sleeves he pulls off so well?" Brendan pointed at the pictures to a skeptical Big B. "There's probably a full-body tattoo under them."

"Ah, that makes more sense. He and the guy with the scar look like the real thing to me, though I'm not so sure about this dude with the Filipino woman. The punk with the attitude looks like one of those bōsōzoku hot-rodders, and I'd bet the boy in here is about to drop school to join this mix of Filipino and Japanese bullies, but to tell you the truth, teenagers these days all look like gangbangers to me. I must be getting old."

Brendan chuckled, both at Big B's quick assessment of the situation and at his comment on getting old at thirty. "Yeah. I know the feeling. It took me some time to believe the guy carrying more skulls than a grave robber could be an illustrator of children's bedtime stories."

"Shit," Big B cursed under his breath. "Remind me never to buy his books. I don't want my kids to have nightmares."

"I don't know, Brudda. He seems to have quite a following among the lads. You wouldn't believe the number of times his name pops up in Google, or the way his agent acts as if he were a hotshot rock star."

"So he makes a good buck."

Brendan nodded, waiting for Big B to reach the logical conclusion to that statement.

"And they could have made him cough up some cash instead of asking daddy for ransom money," Big B finally said.

"Exactly. I don't expect the yakuza to be familiar with Washington politics, but they ran the risk of Senator Harris becoming too prissy and giving them the usual bullshit about not negotiating with terrorists, which I have from good sources that he actually did."

Big B looked at him as if he'd gone nuts, and Brendan had to smile bitterly at the thought that once he would have reacted with the same outraged astonishment. "Yeah, you heard it right, buddy. The good old senator wouldn't be parted with his money even when he learned that his son was being tortured."

"Jesus." Big B's eyes drifted back to the photos on the corkboard, that bit of information giving him a whole new perspective. Brendan was sure his former engineman was now taking in Kenneth's missing pinkie, the sometimes lost look in his freakish eyes, the particular postures the other men adopted around the senator's son.

"Those thugs are protective of him," Big B mumbled in surprise, his eyes still on the pictures. When Brendan didn't say anything, Big B started pointing at each of the photos in turn. "Look here. Every single time any of them is on the street with the American, the Japanese always end up on the outer, unprotected area of the sidewalk. If they go as a group, the American is always dead center. And look at that scarred goon—he's holding the car door open for Harris, but he's scanning the street, not looking down at the man. And here, check this out. The biggest meanie in the group has his hands on the American in every picture you've taken of them, and I can tell you, Japanese don't even hug their sons when they return home after years in the mainland."

Brendan nodded. He had the suspicion Matsunaga was not so much being protective as possessive, but he didn't voice his thoughts; he didn't want Big B wondering where that suspicion had come from.

"If the American didn't look that chummy with the toughies," Big B concluded, "I'd say they were keeping him hostage and protecting their investment, but as things are, he might as well have been the emperor's heir with his imperial guard."

"Yeah. That's my impression too."

Big B turned to look at Brendan. "What are they protecting him from?"

"Hell if I know," Brendan answered. "The Shinagawa-gumi has this big rival Korean gang—the Daitō-kai—but they have some sort of agreement between them, a truce that has been in place for years, so I don't think they're expecting any attack from that side, and even if that'd been the case, I don't see what the Harris kid would have to do with anything."

Brendan started pacing as he went on. "Maybe Senator Harris is right and Matsunaga is trying to expand his business and keeping Kenneth as insurance should things go south. And maybe he's waiting to get his green card before he sets anything in motion, but then the senator's son has to be in cahoots with the yakuza; there's no other way he'd be acting so at home with them."

Big B frowned. "It'd make sense if the man was trying to get back at his father for not paying the ransom, but didn't you say these guys tortured him? You think that was all staged from the beginning?"

"That's what I thought at first," Brendan answered, "but I have Kenneth's medical report, and let's just say no one in his sane mind would go through what he endured willingly."

"You've lost me there," Big B said. "If these guys really kidnapped and tortured him, why would he be with them at all? If he wanted to get even with his father, there's no lack of hired hands with the right expertise for that in Hawaii; he didn't need to pay his kidnappers the airfare."

"No, I think that's what the senator got wrong," Brendan explained. "I think the guy who was charged with the kidnapping was not Matsunaga's puppet, but the real perpetrator. According to the official version, he wasn't even a yakuza, but a rich kid who'd been forced to work for the Shinagawa as Matsunaga's secretary to cover his father's gambling debts. I believe he *did* use the kidnapping to try to frame Matsunaga, and that's why the yakuza even helped the police locate Harris, and, most of all, I believe that's why Matsunaga's secretary was 'accidentally' killed by one of Matsunaga's men. It stands to reason that it should be a question of honor for the underboss."

Big B nodded. "I can buy that. The Japanese would do anything to avoid losing face, but it seems to me killing the guy settled the grudge well enough. So if they're here, where the police will treat the yakuza as any other gang of lowlifes, it must be because there's something big for them here."

"That's what I think," Brendan said. "My contact in the Department of Labor tells me Kenneth Harris figures as the employer of three of the men in the dojo, as well as a Mrs. Alma Tachibana, who happens to be the Filipino-American wife of this guy here"— Brendan pointed at one of the pictures of the thug in white socks—"Harris has filed a petition for Matsunaga, Nakatani, and Yonekawa to get permanent residence as his employees, and Tachibana will get it through his wife. Matsunaga is Kotarō Fuwa's legal guardian, so Fuwa will get the residence as his dependent."

"So," Big B said, "except for that Tachibana guy, all of them will be legal residents thanks to Harris. But what does the American get out of this?"

"Harris's medical report said he was suffering from PTSD—"

Big B snorted. "No kidding."

Brendan smiled. His shooters had never cared much for the fancy name of what they simply called *having your head fucked up after a tour in the sand box.*

"So," he continued, "I got this idea that after what happened to him, Harris might feel paranoid enough to have his own security detail. And these yakuza seem accountable enough, especially if it's true they helped free Harris in the first place."

And the more so if Matsunaga and Harris were lovers, as Brendan suspected.

"Makes sense to me," Big B said, "but I guess you're gonna need a lot more intel on this to be sure one way or the other. You got any bugs in place?"

"No. This dojo is a fucking reconnaissance nightmare," Brendan explained as he pointed at the plan taped to the board. "It used to be an auto parts store and warehouse, so it's got all these isolated structures that they seem to have turned into three individual apartments, plus the actual dojo, plus this construction in here that I can't figure out for the life of me."

Big B stepped closer to the board to study the small construction in the center of the plan. "Looks like a tool shack to me. The plan is up-to-date?"

Brendan nodded. "Yeah. I got it from a friend in the Department of Assessments and Taxation. But I don't think it's a tool shack; the building permit says it's a glass-paned structure, and I don't know any guy crazy enough about his tools to showcase them in a glass shed."

Big B chuckled. "Oh, I know a few guys who would, believe me—it's just the fear of the wives' mighty rage that stops them. But how did you get your hands on the building permit, anyway?"

"I know someone in Honolulu Department of Planning and Permitting," Brendan explained.

"Shit, Boss. You got more contacts than a navy scrounger."

Brendan's smile was bitter. "You can't get anything done in Washington without contacts, especially if you're just an outsourced contractor and you lack the security clearance to access certain data." He forced himself to steer the conversation back before he revealed too much of his job's misery to his former boat crewman. He'd thought he was even past that point, but he had found he still cared about keeping Big B's respect. "So what do you think they need an all-glass room for?"

"Well, you know how the joke goes."

Brendan looked up at Big B. The Hawaiian turned to him and asked, "What do you call a group of Japanese goons making waves in the tub?"

At Brendan's raised brow, Big B answered, "The Jacuzzi."

That surprised a laugh out of him. "Geez, B, that's the worst joke I've heard in a while."

The Hawaiian reached out and punched Brendan's arm playfully. "Made you laugh, didn't it?"

Brendan shook his head, smiling. Until he'd put a few thousand miles between Craig and himself, he hadn't even realized how tight a rein he'd kept on his every reaction. Around his lover's high-class friends, Brendan thought twice before opening his mouth, even if it was to laugh at a joke—he'd rather be seen as dull than betray himself as the unsophisticated ex-soldier he really was.

He returned the punch to B's iron-hard biceps. "I have to suck up to my landlord and laugh at his bad jokes lest he put me out on the street. And so you know, that glass shed has no plumbing to it, so no Jacuzzi for the yakuza."

"No plumbing? Then what about a greenhouse? Wouldn't be the first to grow weed in the backyard."

"I'd peg them more for the meth-lab type," Brendan said, shrugging, "but maybe they're bonsai-growing buffs."

"Man, I don't know why they call it *growing* bonsais when it looks to me all they do is try to *ungrow* them."

Brendan shoved ineffectually at the big man. "Focus, B. We have to solve the glass-house mystery."

"Can't see how we're gonna do it without taking a look at it, Boss."

He sighed. "Yeah, you're right, Brudda. I'll have to go in there and get the place wired for good."

Big B gave him a fiendish grin. "Want some help?"

CHAPTER 5

KOTARŌ FUWA looked from his open homework to the old *wadokei* clock Kenshin-san had found at a yard sale.

Kotarō couldn't understand the zodiac symbols on the ancient clock face, didn't know what the sign for monkey meant in actual hours, and Aniki had taken away his wristwatch in one of his tempers, saying that he didn't need a watch if he was going to be late anyway.

Of course he was late. Hell, who wouldn't be late to this receptionist shit? His friends said it was wahine work, but nobody in this madhouse seemed to understand Kotarō's shame.

"Shit," he cursed aloud, delighting in the foreign echo of the word. He liked the sound of American curses, and he used them as much as he dared inside the dojo—and between every two words outside the boss's dominions. It was the only way he knew to avoid appearing like an F.O.B. Japanese hick, that and getting good at riding the surf, which he couldn't very well do if he had to stay put behind this ridiculous bamboo desk for three frigging afternoons every frigging week.

And what for? Parents took one look at Kotarō and decided he was too young to be trusted with any accurate information about the dojo workings; kids didn't consider him old enough to order them about; deliveries were never for him; and repairmen had to be directed to Shinya, or Aniki, or the boss, or even Kenshin-san, because nobody told him shit around here.

He flipped the pages of his textbook angrily. They'd told him he was lucky to have a chance at completing his education, and then enrolled him in a shitty public school where he didn't understand much of what was said, and couldn't read half his books, and didn't know how to take notes if it wasn't in the sloppy katakana that he had to hide from his fellow students because they'd sure laugh at him if they saw.

He had managed to avoid becoming a total loser by dint of paying attention in class, but not exactly to the teacher. He'd taken to observing which kids didn't take notes or were absent more often or kept texting each other all through class. Then, in the most casual of ways, he'd let them catch glimpses of the Shinagawa badge the boss had given him before leaving Japan, mentioning the boss's rank of wakagashira as if it had slipped his tongue.

He'd also borrowed the coolest clothes and jewelry from Kenshin-san, and had badgered Shinya for days on end until he'd agreed to pick up Kotarō once in the boss's new Acura MDX.

Hah. That had been a masterful touch, if he said so himself. It'd been difficult to keep the smug smile from his lips as he watched the other kids stare at Shinya, the big man leaning casually against the sleek SUV's door, his dark glasses highlighting the scar on his face.

After that day, some of the Filipino students had approached Kotarō, and the few words he'd learned from Tachibana's wife, Alma, had served to impress the kids further and secure him a place in a group that also included a few Japanese like him.

The Hawaiian lowlifes who had tried to bully him before had stopped right away after he started hanging out with his new friends, but he had to tread carefully around them. He'd more or less made them believe that the boss was still part of the Shinagawa, posing as a kendo instructor as he waited for the Japanese police to lose interest in him.

It was almost the truth, as it was almost true that Kenshin-san was a *mangaka* the rival Daitō-kai had had in their hit list since he'd portrayed them as fools in one of his comics. How else could he explain Kenshin-san's presence in his boss's house?

Their whole frigging situation was difficult to explain. For once in his life, Kotarō found himself surrounded by kids whose parents had abandoned them, had gone through shitty divorces, or were shadowy figures without a name to them. But now that his own family situation was even lucky by comparison, the fact that Kotarō was living with four adult men who weren't relatives of his or part of the foster system would look really weird if he couldn't explain it by their yakuza bond.

Some days Kotarō wished Kenshin-san had never showed up in their lives and they could all still be part of the Shinagawa, but then Kenshin-san would smile at him and Kotarō would feel ashamed to have forgotten what was there under his tattoos. So he spent half his time feeling mad at the boss for bringing them to this stupid place where they'd become nobodies, and the other half feeling like shit for having thought that in the first place.

"Aloha, Brah."

Kotarō almost jumped off the chair. He hadn't heard the man coming into the dojo, and he must have been really distracted because the guy was this frigging huge Hawaiian dude in yellow coveralls that sure was difficult to miss.

"Aloha, sir," he said as he stood and bowed awkwardly. He still hadn't learned to stop bowing to people and only remembered halfway through the bow, his hesitation making him look even dumber.

"No need fo' dat, little bruddah," the big guy said, giving him a bright smile. Kotarō knew he was staring, but the man was impressive, especially because his size didn't look as if it was mostly made up of fat, as was often the case with many big people around here. "Where da bugs stay?"

"Huh?"

The big man laughed and pointed to the black letters on his uniform that read *Kokua Pest Control*. "We make bugs, yeah?"

Kotarō's eyes went wide. "You make bags?"

"Fo' real," the man said, nodding fiercely, and Kotarō didn't know what to do. The boss and Kenshin-san were out, Shinya driving them, and Aniki was teaching some kids in the training hall; he couldn't go in there and interrupt him to ask what he should do about a man from a bag-making company.

The Hawaiian tilted his head to study Kotarō. "Japanee, yeah? Da kine inglish boddah you?"

Kotarō wasn't sure what he was nodding to, but he did anyway, because disagreeing with people was another American trait he hadn't yet caught up with.

"Sorry, man. My wife—she's from China, you know—didn't understand a word I said for months. Guess that's why she married me," the man said, chuckling, and Kotarō found himself smiling back. The guy was friendly enough, but there was also something familiar about him, something maybe about the way he stood or moved his body, that made Kotarō think about the Shinagawa men.

"So, where are those bugs that've been pestering you?"

Kotarō blinked. Now that he more or less understood the man, he still had no idea what he was talking about. Fortunately, the man kept talking before Kotarō had time to say anything. "I can't remember if they were cockroaches, or termites, or—" He rummaged in the tool bag he was carrying and retrieved a smartphone. His big fingers were surprisingly agile on the touch screen. "Kenneth Harris, right?"

Well, that one was easy. "Kenshin-san is not home now, sir."

"Kenshin?"

Kotarō blushed. He still had trouble pronouncing Kenshin-san's gaijin name. "Uh... Harrisu-san. The boss, um, we call him Kenshin-san. He lives here, I mean, he's the... owner." He couldn't have sounded any dumber if he'd tried.

"He's the boss, huh?"

"The boss is Matsunaga-wakagashira," Kotarō blurted, immediately wishing he could take it back. "I mean, Matsunaga-san is the boss. Kenshin-san is his, uh—" And now he wished one of those Hawaiian volcanoes would open right under his feet and swallow him. What the hell was he doing telling this stranger about Kenshin-san and the boss? He could picture Aniki's face when he learned about this. But what could he possibly say now, that they were roommates? At their age?

"His partner?" the man supplied, and Kotarō racked his brain for a negative meaning to the word. Since he couldn't find any and the big guy seemed cool about it, Kotarō gave the smallest nod in answer.

"'Kay, den. It says here you have ants," the man said after checking his cell. "Those are easy, but I'll have to find the nest."

Typical. Why should anyone bother to tell Kotarō that their home was full of ants? And then, of course, they all expected him to act responsibly and carry his own weight.

He nodded to himself. "I can show you around the house." See, he was being responsible. He'd fix the problem without saying a word to them, and when they started wondering how the ants had disappeared all of a sudden, he'd simply tell them, "Oh, I helped the exterminator get rid of them. Piece of cake." Yeah, that was exactly what he was going to do—see how they liked a taste of their own medicine.

CHAPTER 6

BRENDAN LAUGHED. That was priceless—Big Brudda in yellow coveralls overwhelming the Fuwa kid with his pidgin. "Da kine inglish" had become a sort of code language for the Islanders, especially when they had to share watering holes with the marines and wanted to keep the grunts in the dark, and hearing it again made Brendan feel nostalgic.

Funny how he was remembering more of the good times since he'd arrived in Hawaii. Big B's positive personality must be catching, and it certainly seemed to be working its magic with the Japanese kid.

Brendan studied the images appearing on his laptop screen as Big B moved this way and that, pretending to check the information on his cell phone. The high-resolution camera on his lapel had been worth the money; the images were neat in spite of the interior lighting in the reception area.

"The boss is Matsunaga-wakagashira," Kotarō was saying. "I mean, Matsunaga-san is the boss. Kenshin-san is his… uh—"

Wakagashira. Brendan whistled. That was top rank in the yakuza files; only a few counselors and top bosses stood between each gang's *oyabun*—the Japanese blend of godfathers—and these so-called *young leaders*. So maybe the senator was right and Matsunaga was setting up a branch of the organization on Oahu, though Brendan would have thought such a powerful gang would have established itself in Hawaii a long time ago, given the thriving *batu*—crystal meth—market on the islands.

Also, Kotarō was blushing and stammering so hard that Brendan was sure his suspicions about Kenneth and Matsunaga's relationship were true. And by now Big B must have caught on to it.

"His partner?" Yeah, Big B had surely connected the dots, or would now when he saw Kotarō's relieved nod at the—apparently—neutral word. Teens were a great source of information, their faces still transparent no matter what their mouths said, and this kid even had trouble filtering what came out of his lips. They'd done the right thing by waiting until Kotarō was alone manning the front desk.

"'Kay, den. It says here you have ants. Those are easy, but I'll have to find the nest."

This was the crucial moment. If Kotarō chose to ask Kinosuke Yonekawa, they'd be screwed. Brendan could only hope he'd been right in thinking the Japanese would be too polite and too martial-arts respectful to interrupt an ongoing kendo class.

"I can show you around the house," Kotarō finally said, and Brendan pumped his fist in the air; they were in.

Kotarō started walking without a single backward glance, and Big B seized the chance to quickly turn and give Brendan a full view of the unlocked, unmanned entrance. Yeah. They were both thinking along the same lines—no security to speak of, not even a camera, just a front desk with either a kid or a woman behind it.

"Watch your *kamae*, Seiji-kun! What are you, a hula girl?"

Brendan chuckled. That voice coming from inside the dojo had to belong to the infamous Kinosuke. He seemed to have the teaching subtlety of a gunny.

"We can't go in there now," Kotarō whispered, "but I've never seen ants in the dojo."

He led Big B along a hallway flanked by one of those beautiful wood-and-paper screens. Kotarō slid open one of the panels and stepped out into what had to be the backyard.

"Spock um out!" Big B said in shocked pidgin.

Oh yeah, Brendan was sure as hell checking it all out, the images flicking quickly as Big B moved around to take in as much as he could of the weird landscape in front of him. Small wonder the plans made no sense; Brendan had never seen a cross between a Japanese garden and a Martian colony before.

The camera showed Kotarō's shy smile. "It looked like a junkyard when we came here, but Kenshin-san changed it all."

"Wow. He an architect?"

"He's a mangaka.... I mean, he draws these things for children's books and so."

"Cool, Brah."

In a way, it made sense that the place had been created by an illustrator of children's stories. The practicality of many features was obvious, but there was this crazy touch about it all that could only have come from an unrestrained—nightmarish—imagination.

As Big B moved slowly around, Brendan saw three stand-alone structures forming the rectangle the dojo closed on one side. They must have been warehouses at one time, but the once-flat roofs had been completely reshaped, with mirrorlike solar panels cascading at a steep angle and an open gap between walls and roofs making it look as if gigantic spaceships were floating on air cushions above the walls.

The whole design was intended to keep the interiors cool—the inclination of the solar panels deflecting direct sunlight off the roofs, breeze flowing everywhere through the open space on top of the walls, louvered sliding doors closing the old warehouses' façades and most likely turning the front rooms into improvised lanais when open.

And then there was the garden. Or rather, everything would have been just fancy modern design until a whole tropical garden erupted through every crack. Climbing hibiscus seemed to pour down from the gap on top of every lateral wall, what looked like moss covered the roofs in the shade of the solar panels, and only big black limestone slabs allowed dwellers to set foot on anything solid among the studiously chaotic jungle growing on the yard soil.

When Big B stopped moving around, Brendan got a clear view of the structure right in the middle of the yard that he'd been wondering about for days. And Big B expressed his own thoughts word by word. "What the hell's that?"

Kotarō giggled. "You like it? It's Kenshin-san's studio."

A studio. Hence the glass walls. But only Kenneth Harris would have built a glass house around an araucaria tree, with galvanized metal louvers cascading down to block direct sunlight and make the araucaria look like the craziest Christmas tree on earth.

"Killahz studio, man," Big B said. "Great place for ants too—they're gonna love it that there's a tree and all inside."

"Oh, you think the nest is in there? Kenshin-san has never said anything about ants," Kotarō said, the camera catching his face as it went from pensive to grinning. "But he never notices anything when he's drawing—you can yell at him all the way from the door to his desk and he'll rip you a new one for *sneaking* up on him."

Brendan chuckled at the same time that Big B did. Kotarō probably didn't even realize the kind of expressions he'd picked up from his classmates, and he obviously had no clue he was revealing too much to a complete stranger. Then again, it might only mean that Kenneth's presence in the house was no secret at all.

"I have a friend like that. He gets so focused he even forgets to eat," Big B said as they moved toward the studio door.

"Kenshin-san always forgets. The boss has to come for him every time."

"He's a good friend, then, if he comes all the way from work to remind him."

Kotarō turned to look at Big B. "They all work in the dojo. It's just there." He pointed behind them.

"Ah, must be nice skipping morning traffic—I always get jammed up on the H-1. So what you all teach, kung fu or something?"

Brendan shook his head. In spite of his intimidating appearance, Big B knew how to make people comfortable, how to make them talk, though he wasn't sure Kotarō wouldn't have babbled away with almost anyone else. Now the kid was puffing up as he explained. "Kung fu is just Chinese boxing. What we teach here is the Japanese way of the sword, the warrior way."

"Fo' real? With katanas and all?"

Kotarō nodded as he slid the studio door open.

"Cool, Brah. You teach Mr. Harris too?"

The kid snorted. "Kenshin-san? He's better than all of us together. He even saved Aniki that time, picked a katana and slashed this thick rope that Atsushi had put around his neck for him to—"

Brendan listened intently. It looked like the senator had forgotten to tell him about his son being a sword master and saving one of the yakuza's lives—he wondered what other details might have slipped the senator's mind.

"You have to use any nasty stuff to kill the ants? Because I don't want to spoil Kenshin-san's drawings."

Crap. The kid must have realized he was tattling, if his sudden blush and change of topic were any indication.

"Nah. I'll just check out for the nest, won't make any mess," Big B answered. "When I find it, I'll send my bruddah back to kill the bastards."

Brendan smiled. Just like that Big B had paved the way for Brendan to visit the house as another pest control worker. Nice.

"You have a brah too, yeah?" Big B asked.

Kotarō ducked his head and stepped inside the studio. Not a topic he enjoyed talking about, then. "My brother's in Japan."

As Big B entered the glass house, Brendan got a view of the amazing light inside, the tree creating random patches of shade that crept near the carts full of art supplies, the flat files with myriad thin drawers, and the huge drafting table, all in stark white steel.

"Oh, I thought he was here, thought I heard you say Mr. Harris saved him or something."

Smart man. That bit of information was worth exploring, and Big B was doing it in the most casual of ways.

"That's Aniki, I mean, Kinosuke… um… he's not my brother-brother, he's my…."

"Your senior? I had dis younger Japanee pal who was always going aniki dis and aniki dat."

Kotarō gave him a grateful smile. "I always call him Aniki too. He yells a lot, but he's cool. You should see him when he rides his new bike; dude, he leaves all the cars behind and just keeps on like a bullet through all the frigging jams."

Big B had started moving about, pretending to be doing his job while unobtrusively placing a bug behind a file. "I hear you, Brah. My pal used to be in one of these bōsōzoku gangs, so he was killahz on two wheels. It was classic when we wen riding together."

"Aniki was a bōsōzoku too! The boss told him if he wore all his hair up like a *yankī*, he was gonna use the cattle clippers on him, so Aniki let it all fall down and the boss said now he looked as if he was gonna sing anytime and get the Shinagawa a platinum album and Aniki got so mad that he shaved his head, and then the boss said he couldn't go about with his head naked and got Maedasaki-sensei to give him a tattoo."

Geez. The lad could talk, and Brendan couldn't help laughing at the picture of Kinosuke the kid was painting. The young punk must have been a handful, all gelled hair and attitude, though Matsunaga sounded like the right kind of man to deal with the likes of Kinosuke—he wouldn't have made it to wakagashira if he couldn't handle a bunch of biker toughies.

"A tattoo on his head? Man, dat must have hurt," Big B was saying now as they moved out of the studio. "It felt like the old man was stabbing me when he reached my spine."

Kotarō stopped pushing the sliding door on one of the former warehouses to look at Big B. "You got a tattoo? One of those Hawaiian tattoos with shark teeth and spears and waves and stuff?"

Brendan chuckled. Kotarō was practically bouncing, his eyes gleaming with excitement.

"Yep," Big B said, the smile obvious in the sound of his voice. "Wanna see?"

"*Hai*! I mean, yes, please, sir."

The image shook with Big B's laughter, and the big lump of a man started unzipping his coveralls, the screen catching weird angles of the door, the walls, a fleeting glimpse of the sky, and the stone slabs on the floor. He was going to kill his engineman if the camera got a single scratch. Showy bastard.

"*Kakkoī*!"

Yeah. Brendan didn't need to see the convoluted black tattoo to know how cool it was. Damn, he could close his eyes right now and draw it to the last of its swirling symbols, he'd seen it so many times. And for a moment, the static image on his laptop disappeared, and all Brendan could see was exactly that, Big B's front torso as it was that day, neatly divided in two areas, the one with the impressive black warrior tattoo spreading from his left nipple to his forearm, and the other half of his body, the one decorated in the meaningless red patterns of shrapnel. And Brendan could see yet another tattoo, the naïve rendering of a Virgin and Child as it was quickly drowned in bright rivulets of red, the deep-water silence after the detonation swallowing Torres's last words and making every Islander a mute, slow-moving alien replica of himself as he tried uselessly to make sense of the surrounding chaos.

Brendan had thought he was being honest when he'd told the navy shrinks he remembered everything that happened, but as the images flooded his mind, he knew he'd been lying for two years. His smart-assed brain had been keeping the visuals carefully locked away, because the little shit knew Brendan would break if he so much as got a glimpse of John Burka's silver hair streaked red, Otter's black hand pressing against his twin's pale neck as he convulsed, Bobcat's wild eyes as they held Brendan's and saw reflected in them what he couldn't afford to look down to see—his whole body covered from head to toe in the thousand pieces of what had been only one second before a fellow Islander, a brother, a friend.

CHAPTER 7

KOTARŌ GIGGLED. Now it was the big man's turn to gawk like a ninnyhammer. Shinya's house was all decorated in *washitsu* style, so he supposed it looked pretty empty and boring to a gaijin, until you reached the *taiko* room, that is. Not that it was cluttered or anything, but there was this frigging huge reddish-brown drum on a tall stand and three smaller ones around it looking like fat daddy and his chubby kids having a luau in the middle of the room.

Nobody knew that Shinya had been a *taiko* drummer when he was young, but right before Kenshin-san and the boss bought the house, all of them had been checking the neighborhood to see what they were getting into, and Shinya had found this amazing music shop with all kinds of Japanese instruments. He had tried the drums in the shop, and the owner had told him he'd give Shinya a good price for them since he was the first customer he'd ever got who knew what the *taiko* were all about.

"Wow. Dat one must make plenny o' noise," the Hawaiian said. "My cuz plays the pahu, but, Brah, it stay tiny beside dat monster."

Kotarō nodded. "Kenshin-san made them put lots of the foamy stuff on the walls, so we don't hear it when Shinya bangs them, but he's very good anyway—used to play in *matsuris* and all."

They were all frigging good at something or another, all but Kotarō. As he led the big gaijin through the place, he realized they each had something special: Kenshin-san with his art, Shinya with his drums, Kinosuke with that bike he was always fiddling with, and the boss with… being the boss. Kotarō was only glad Tachibana didn't live with them, because he might have asked Kenshin-san to design one of those shooting ranges for him, and Kotarō didn't think it'd have been a good idea to have the big Hawaiian searching for ants among Tachibana's weapons.

It felt wrong to see the stranger in the boss and Kenshin-san's bedroom, but the man hadn't yet found the nest, and he didn't have to know who slept in here.

"Killahz tattoos, Brah."

Sure. And they all had the frigging tattoos, all but Kotarō. The boss had told him he'd have time to decide what he wanted when he was old enough to know what he wanted, but shit, he wasn't a child anymore, and Maedasaki-sensei wasn't moving to Hawaii anytime soon.

"Yeah, that's Kenshin-san and the boss. Maedasaki-sensei's very good."

Kotarō looked at the big picture on the wall and blushed. The Hawaiian didn't need to know who the men in it were since their faces didn't show, but it seemed weird to have a photo of two naked dudes in your bedroom if it wasn't one of those artsy portraits of yourself.

He could only begin to imagine what his classmates would say if they saw the boss's big hand placed that way on top of Kenshin-san's butt. "Mahu" and "faggots" were probably the least offensive they'd come up with.

Kotarō had never thought of the boss and Kenshin-san that way—they weren't like those guys his mates called fags—but there was only one bed for the two of them, and it sure had to mean something.

"Cool. Dat a lion?" the big man asked, pointing at the picture. Kotarō tilted his head to study the guy; he didn't seem to be finding anything weird about the photo, and he looked really interested in the tattoos, maybe because he had one himself.

"It's a… um… baby lion," Kotarō said.

"A cub? What's dat fo'?"

Kotarō looked at Kenshin-san's back in the picture. "See this water here?" The Hawaiian looked at the blue-and-white foaming water on Kenshin-san's skin and nodded. "It's supposed to be this… um… small river at the bottom of a cliff."

"A ravine?"

Kotarō shrugged. "I guess. It's from this Chinese story about a mother lion throwing her baby down the cliff to make him climb back up to her."

"Ah, fo' da little cub to show he's tough, yeah no?"

"Yeah. Kenshin-san let Maedasaki-sensei choose his tattoo, and Sensei went right for this one when the boss told him how Kenshin-san had fought for his life and saved Aniki even though he was hurt and couldn't use his right hand."

Kotarō felt he was blushing again. He didn't know why he was telling the man all this, but it seemed he couldn't stop himself. Aniki was going to have a hissy fit.

"Tough buggah, yeah? Have some bruddahs like dat from my time in the Navy. The other dude's tattoo's classic, too, with da big dragon on his arm and shit."

"That's the boss," Kotarō said, feeling strangely proud now. The Hawaiian had been a soldier, and he wasn't finding anything wrong with the picture—seemed to be admiring it, even. "He's very good with the *bokken*."

"*Bokken*?"

"Yeah, it's this wooden sword you use for practice, but you don't want to face the boss when he's using his. They say it was Musashi's favorite weapon too, and he won a lot of duels with it; the man took this piece of wood and carved a bokken out of it and then went to face his enemy with it and ended up killing him even when the other dude had this fine katana and all."

The Hawaiian smiled at him, and Kotarō realized he'd been frigging babbling one more time.

"You know a lot o' stuff. You teach in the dojo too?"

Kotarō puffed up a little. "I help with the beginners. I'm not that good to teach the others."

"Bet you'd beat the shit out o' me, Brah."

He had to duck his head to hide his blush; it was so nice to be praised that way. He quickly changed the subject, embarrassed. "Uh… there's only the bathroom left, and then there's the garage and my… um… place."

The man nodded and went about his business checking under and behind the furniture, inside the closets, in the line between the floor and the walls—wherever he thought the ants would have their house. Then Kotarō took him to the garage.

Kenshin-san hadn't done here that cool thing he'd done in Aniki's house, where you could see Aniki's big bike from the living room because the garage had this glass wall on it. The boss had said he didn't like his car so much that he had to look at it while he had dinner, and Kotarō was glad. This way the garage was this space splitting the house in two—the big house for the boss and Kenshin-san, and the little house for Kotarō. Not that it was really a house like Aniki's or Shinya's, but he had this nice room and his own bathroom too. He could also get to the street outside through the garage door, so he didn't have to tell them where he was going all the time.

Of course the man didn't comment on Kotarō's boards stacked on a rack there in the back of the garage. The dude was Hawaiian; he must have noticed the egg and the fun board were the only ones Kotarō used, frigging rookie that he was, the gun only there for show since Kotarō couldn't handle it for shit.

And Kenshin-san hadn't designed one of those cool rooms for his boards because Kotarō hadn't even known he'd start surfing until they'd been living here for two months and he'd had to go to that frigging school and find out only the losers couldn't ride the waves.

So there it was, his silly little room—well, not exactly little, but still silly since he'd done a poor job of choosing his furniture and sticking these posters to the walls. And worse still, he'd wanted his room to be different and pestered Kenshin-san to get a window on the street side. Kenshin-san had patiently explained that he'd have too much sun and noise coming through that window when he could get all the light he wanted by opening the sliding panels that made the other side of the room, the one facing the yard, but Kotarō had wanted something special, something different even if it was just the one window.

"Sorry, Brah, but the nest's out there."

Figured. Nobody had told him the house was full of ants, but Kotarō had the frigging nest right outside the wall of his room, the ants using his window to climb inside. And why could they do that? Because Kotarō had made them build the only window in the whole frigging house that faced the street. It sure made his room special.

CHAPTER 8

"BREN? IS that you?"

Craig's voice sounded hoarse over the phone. Brendan knew he'd be in bed, but he'd called anyway—he didn't want to be allotted a few harried minutes between one meeting and another.

"Yeah. Sorry to wake you up."

There was some rustling on the other end, and Brendan could almost see the dark silk sheets sliding down Craig's body as he sat up. That body, Brendan knew pretty well—the toned muscles belying Craig's age, the elegance of the long limbs, the tan he kept perfect all year round, the graceful movements that only self-confidence could produce.

"You okay?"

Brendan choked down a bout of hysterical laughter. He would tell Craig how peachy he was if only he knew which words to use for him to understand. How did you tell a corporate lawyer that you'd just remembered the way a guy looked when he was blown up to high heaven and then rained down in a thousand fleshy pieces on a fellow crewman?

"Yeah, just missing you."

In the silence that followed Brendan had time to feel stupid. They didn't have that kind of relationship, and neither of them were the type to blabber about their feelings.

"How's the job going?" Craig finally asked, and Brendan felt like laughing again. Trust a lawyer to drive the conversation away from touchy topics. It was a relief to pretend Brendan had never said that embarrassing piece, but in a way, it was also a disappointment, another proof that Craig always made sure things went the way *he* wanted them.

Brendan was about to answer something inane when he heard more rustling on the other end and then a male voice he didn't recognize calling Craig's name.

Brendan's own voice came out harsher than he intended. "Who's that?"

"Nobody."

He took a deep breath and counted to ten, but still his heart kept pounding as if he'd run a marathon.

"Bren, you know we talked about this. We agreed to—"

He clicked the disconnect button and hurled the phone against the nearest wall. He hated it when Craig got all patient with him like he would with a child, or a dog, or a retarded ex-SEAL who had to have everything explained about civilian life, silk ties, and open relationships.

Nobody. Was that how Craig referred to Brendan when he wasn't around? And what did Brendan expect? True, they'd talked, and sure, they had agreed to fuck other people if the need arose, but Brendan couldn't find it in him to act on their agreement. He hadn't so much as sat down to think about it, and he probably wouldn't have been up to the effort of cruising for some extra entertainment anyway, but he knew himself. Maybe it was a soldier thing—or one more in the list of his flaws—but it would have felt disloyal, and disloyal was a word that didn't exist in the O'Farrihy vocabulary since the time they had actually lived on an island.

Brendan stood and grabbed his wallet from the foyer table. *Fuck that.* Craig wanted open? He'd show him open.

He didn't even stop to check his looks in the mirror; he put on his hiking boots and slammed the door closed, his lips lifting in a wry smile as he thought Craig would have never approved of either the clothes or the boots he'd bought with Big B. Yeah. The cargo pants, plain black T-shirt, and Wolverine boots screamed working man, maybe because that was exactly what he was—a fucking plain working man that SEAL training had turned into something flashy, some sort of soldier Ken to its corresponding Barbie superstar lawyer.

He scanned the street for a taxi. It wasn't easy to spot one, since cabs in Honolulu weren't even the same color, not to speak of the variety of models that only a yellow dome with the name of the company identified as taxis, so he kept walking purposefully down the street. He almost smiled when the few people he crossed in the quiet night quickly averted their eyes, as if Brendan might attack them.

That was another thing SEAL had given him—the look. He knew that even at a party, with a crystal snifter between his fingers and a smile on his lips, his eyes still retained that hard quality that was branded on every man, woman, or child who faced—or caused—violent death.

The clothes Craig had chosen for him somehow softened that edge, turning it into some kind of role-play, but tonight Brendan didn't feel like playing. Tonight he was a man on a mission, and he didn't give a damn about looking harmless.

He took a left turn into a wider avenue and managed to flag down a cab.

"Aloha. Where you like go?"

Geez. He'd have to get on the only taxi in the whole city driven by a Chinese, or probably Korean, granny. That explained why there was so much room at the back, because the driver's seat was almost touching the wheel to allow her skinny arms to reach.

Still, he wasn't in the mood for politeness or even subtlety, so he went for brutal. "You know any gay clubs?"

The cabbie turned to look at him, and Brendan held her stare without blinking. Tonight he would have engaged Gandhi in a fight; he wasn't about to back down because an ancient Asian woman gave him the evil eye.

"Can take you to Max's Gym. Military Day today."

Brendan almost laughed, but the diminutive lady behind the wheel was still looking at him, her face serious as the grave. He was about to answer when the cabbie waved and shook her head. "Ai yah, no can. Dat's Military Mondays; Tuesday's Black Out Night, and you no want go deah fo' dat."

He raised an eyebrow—Blackout Night sounded just right for him, dark and dirty as he was feeling. "I don't?"

"Nah. Wanna get all buss? Take you to Bacchus on Kuhio—Two Dollar Tuesday today. Or Hula's on Kapahulu—classic prices. Wanna have one good fun time? Take you to my cuz's."

He had to shake his head at that. It seemed Hawaii was all about connections, very much like Washington. He might have felt right at home if the District had ever been anything resembling a home. "So what's this place of your cousin's? A club?"

"No club, spa. Give you lomi-lomi massage. No dark—you can see wot you get."

Did he really want to see? He had set out for results, hadn't given much consideration to the process because, in truth, he wasn't looking for a good time. And he didn't need a Navy shrink to tell him that he was projecting his need for vengeance on a smaller, reachable target like Craig, or that his repressed guilt made him believe he didn't deserve to enjoy himself.

"Good prices. No charge you fo' da towel as if it can sing. I no kid you."

And why not take the bait? He might be acting on all the wrong reasons, and Granny Lee could be part of a scam to rob the haole blind, but what the fuck—he was a SEAL, and a mad SEAL at that; he could handle anything they brought on.

"Okay. Let's see this place of your cousin's," he finally said, and the little woman nodded at him as if he'd made the right business decision.

CHAPTER 9

BRENDAN STOOD at the door to the spa, or rather, he stood in front of a big red Chinese gate with a curved tiled roof and a bunch of dragons floating over the golden letters that read "Forbidden City." And in case someone hadn't gotten the hint, there were smaller, less impressive letters with the explanation "Da kine place." As if the mating *male* dragons weren't obvious enough.

For a moment he thought this was stupid. He was looking for quick and dirty. He didn't need to pretend he wanted to be given a massage or have his skin problems taken care of. All he needed was the simplest, stress-relieving satisfaction of payback.

But then the door slammed open, the metal dragon knocker crashing against the wall and sending bits of plaster onto the sidewalk, and a string of angry Chinese-sounding words rent the silence of the quiet street.

A man stood at the door, his body turned so he could keep yelling at someone inside. Brendan took in his slender profile, the long blue gown hugging his torso and floating loose from the waist down, two long slits at the sides letting the tight black pants underneath show. The gown had no sleeves, and the arm Brendan could see holding the door open was long and tanned, the skin looking deliciously smooth over well-toned muscles.

Whatever argument the man was having didn't seem likely to end anytime soon, and Brendan took the chance to move closer, so much closer that he could have touched the man's thick black hair if he'd reached out.

He'd always liked dark-haired guys, always gone for tanned skin, hairless chests, everything that made a man his exact opposite. It might be a cliché about opposites and all that crap, but Brendan didn't find much to be attracted to in his Irish ancestry.

His milky skin had him hooked on sunblock and always threatened with the freckles that had made it into a temporary nickname until he commanded his first combat element. Then he'd become "Boss," "Sir," or "Mr. O'Farrihy," though he knew he was also called "Brendan the Bold," since he'd turned down an invitation from a Marine commander to send his shooters in a suicidal mission. "Red" he'd simply avoided by wearing his reddish hair shorn as close to the skull as he could manage and never sporting any facial hair—not that a red beard would've amounted to much in terms of camouflage anyway. And still he had to put up with the light red fuzz covering his body, another nuisance that he only found masculine in the slouch sense.

In truth, the only redeeming feature he'd inherited was the green of his eyes. It wasn't any extraordinary hue—just plain grass green—but it gave his otherwise blunt features an edge. That didn't make him a fan of light eyes, though; he found them as unemotional as frozen glass, and the Navy had made sure he got his fill of cold-eyed fuckers. Now all he wanted was the warmth of dark eyes untouched by the ugly miseries of warring men.

Brendan cleared his throat, and the man at the door almost jumped out of his skin. It was what Craig called a nasty habit, his sneaking up on people, but one that he wasn't about to let go anytime soon, especially if it granted him hot black looks like the one he was receiving right now.

"Someone told me this was the place to get the best lomi-lomi massage in Honolulu," Brendan said, trying not to appear too predatory.

The man gave Brendan the once-over, and his eyes went from angry to calculating in a heartbeat. "Need some stress relief, huh?"

The young man's whole posture changed visibly—his arm now holding the door invitingly, tense muscles going soft, his hip tilting in a seductive move that Brendan found too overplayed to be sexy.

"Just wanted to take a look inside the Forbidden City, see what the fuss was all about," he forced himself to answer, though he didn't quite pull the smile that should've gone with the lame wisecrack.

"Oh no, buddy, you won't just be taking a look, an action man like you," the Asian young man said, pushing the flirty tones until they reached kiss-ass level. "Green-eyed stud that you are, you cross this gate and you'll really get *inside* the Forbidden City, if you catch my drift."

Now Brendan wished he'd stuck to his District, Craig-styled wardrobe. Being around Big B had made him want to go back to his military looks, but being pegged as a military haole in a place like this didn't exactly help his pride. In fact, he was considering turning around and making a run for it, when the Asian stepped back and made a sweeping gesture with his bare arm.

"Please come inside," he said, and then winked, "You'll get a chance at that too."

Brendan took a deep breath and stepped into the dimly lit hallway. The walls were painted red, and a red-and-gold lantern cascaded down in a flurry of silk laces from what looked like a decorative rafter in the ceiling. The place looked deserted, no trace left of the person the young man had been arguing with.

"This way, buddy."

Brendan glared at the thin back preceding him all along the red dim corridor. If the man called him *buddy* one more time, he was going to do something he'd no doubt regret later. Much later.

"Here we are."

At least the corridor had been dark enough to ignore the decoration, but the room Brendan walked into was so unfortunately well lit that his eyes hurt.

The walls were wrapped up in some kind of yellow fabric that tried to look like golden brocade and failed miserably, the ceiling a mass of convoluted plaster appearing like the sort of stalactites toxic waste would produce, and big red lanterns everywhere tried to conceal the raw LED lights pouring down on baroque, plastic-looking, carved furniture.

Instead of the typical massage table, there was this strange bed with short, curved legs and railings on three sides that made Brendan feel claustrophobic even from where he stood—maybe more from the deep burgundy of the shiny comforter than from the crib-like enclosure.

"Wanna try it, baby?"

Anger didn't even register in his mind before Brendan found himself spinning around in a flash, his forearm shooting up to press against the man's windpipe and send him crashing against one of the yellow walls.

"I'm not your baby, or your buddy, or your chum; I'm not even your pen pal, so put a lid on it. You hear me, mate?"

This close, the man wasn't even good-looking. His cheekbones were too broad, making his face square and flat; his eyes were too round, showing so much white that he looked permanently freaked out—the more so now that he was panicking at having a client attack him. And yet, when Brendan was about to pull off, some flicker crossed those eyes, and the man looked down with a false modesty that made Brendan feel sick.

"Yes, sir," the man whispered, his body going almost limp against Brendan's forearm.

Christ. He thought Brendan liked it rough, thought he could control his anger and make it into a sex accessory.

He pulled away, anger melting into a pool of shame. "I don't think this is going to work, sorry. I'll pay for your time."

The dark head shot up. "No, no, no, please. Tell me what you like, let me make it right for you."

Brendan studied the eager face once again and realized this was not what he needed tonight. For some reason he couldn't fathom, he wasn't looking for the willingness to share a good time—he was spoiling for a fight.

The man mistook his evaluating stare for interest and flashed what he probably thought was a seductive smile.

"See something you can use?" he said, sliding his palms down the silk gown as if he was smoothing down a ruffled dress.

Brendan managed to contain the laughter bubbling up in his throat, but he couldn't help the crooked smile that—of course—the man understood as a come-on. The thin, tanned hand was only halfway to Brendan's zipper when his own hand shot out to grab the bony wrist and squeeze.

"Do. Not. Touch. Me," he said, enunciating each syllable as if he expected the man to read his lips.

And even then, the man tried to push his wares. "It's okay. If you're straight, I can give you a true lomi-lomi massage. It's very relaxing, and I'll be completely professional—I'm a certified masseur, you know."

Brendan let go of the man's hand with a weary sigh. "How much?"

Just two words and that dull face flashed as bright as a danger buoy. "Oh, it's quite cheap. You can get this week's special for eighty bucks. Of course if you prefer the deep tissue massage, it's one fifty, but it's really worth it, believe me. We also have the aromatherapy—"

Brendan stopped listening to retrieve his wallet and pulled out a hundred-dollar bill.

"Keep the change," he said, grabbing one of the fluttering hands to slap the bill against a very long life line.

He had almost reached the door when the man said, "You're leaving?"

He didn't even bother to roll his eyes, he was already out of there, his mind calculating how long it'd take him to get back to his apartment. But of course the man had to try one more fucking time.

"It's really okay if you're straight. I'm serious. Come on, buddy, I'll make it worth your while."

Brendan's feet took him to the man's side so fast that he found himself looking into frightened eyes with no obvious transition. And this time the fear he could see and smell in the man was the real thing—the deep animal fear of death, the knowledge that he was facing someone with the ability and the will to snuff out a life with a simple flicker of his hand.

And the worst of all was that Brendan felt his anger flaring even more at the man's reaction, adrenaline pumping in his veins with the urge to carry out the threat, to finally let the world know that you didn't train a dog to kill and then expected it to behave at dog shows.

It had been years. He had followed orders, stuck to procedures, toed the line so many times that he could draw it in the dark, that thin chalk line that separated what ought to be done from what you had to do. And he'd gone with it, every single time, swallowing his good sense, his frustration, his remorse even. He'd put up with everything, pushed his men forward, fought for something he believed in no matter how blurred it had become when the bullets started ringing. And then they considered that he was fighting maybe a tad too much, that, maybe, he might be too noisy for the new approach to international relations they were trying this month and that luckily would last them for a whole fiscal year. So they'd sent him packing, gave him a medal for putting his men in a position where the enemy could blow them to pieces, and recommended him for a profitable job in the District, where he got all the respect conferred to a club bouncer, the hulking guy with half a brain that you pretended to be chummy with only when the crowd got too thick.

Brendan spoke two inches away from the man's face, the urge to cause damage so strong that his voice came out in a hoarse whisper. "I'm not straight, buddy. It's just that you are so ugly I wouldn't fuck you even if you paid me to."

The man's eyes widened even more, and Brendan knew that he would hit him if the man so much as opened his mouth. And the guy must have seen it in Brendan's expression, because he kept his lips tightly pressed, as if he was trying to raise a quick dam against the flood of insults threatening to push out.

And then the moment passed, and Brendan's anger disappeared. He felt immensely tired as he started to move away, his feet shuffling across the red-and-black linoleum floor, his hand pushing the door open with trembling fingers, with that sudden, hard letdown that follows every adrenaline rush.

He couldn't even pull the energy to smirk at the yells in Chinese that started as soon as he reached the hallway, as if he was being barked at by one of those Pekingese dogs that only made a racket when you were a safe distance away.

Outside, everything looked drab and lonely, deserted streets he couldn't name turning into wide, brightly lit avenues that only a few scattered palm trees tried in vain to make different from every other avenue in any mainland city. And Brendan would have felt the same any place he went—the outsider watching everyday life from the cold perspective of the anthropologist, the man studying rites, customs, and ceremonies from the emotionless side of the nonparticipant.

Somewhere he flagged a cab and kept his eyes closed to ward off conversation. He didn't feel up to handling human language right now, didn't feel very human right now.

When he finally closed the door of the little house, it took all his willpower to turn on the lights and take one step after the other in the general direction of his bedroom, but his feet seemed to have their own agenda, and he walked into his den instead, his hand automatically flicking the switch that illuminated the corkboard with the photos he'd taken these last days.

He didn't have to search for it; his eyes knew where to look to find that face, and something like relief flooded Brendan as he studied the high cheekbones, the thick, expressive brows, the fiery black eyes, the sensual lips. Kinosuke Yonekawa was as gorgeous as he remembered—nothing bland or venal in the way the yakuza held his ground, his attitude one of defiance even in the few shots that had caught a rare unguarded smile. This man would never invite or even beg for sex; this man would take what he wanted and challenge you to try the same, that sensual mouth going straight for the bite, those sword-calloused hands with no time or will for tenderness.

Brendan felt a tightening in his groin that almost made him chuckle. What a total dud this night was turning into. How in all hell was he going to get back at Craig when he was so picky his cock only reacted to men he couldn't have? And why did it matter to get even anyway if Craig wouldn't raise a brow about it? In the end, it all came down to that; Craig didn't give a damn, but Brendan, in spite of all his tough-guy shit, did give a fucking damn, always had and always would.

"So sue me," he said aloud, anger filling him again and guiding his movements to his desk, where he flung himself into the chair in front of his laptop. He powered it up as if he were setting the timer on a bomb, and put on the earphones, hardly waiting to have them in place before checking the connections to the bugs Big B had planted in the yakuza house.

Everything worked fucking fine but, to Brendan's frustration, all the buildings were silent as the grave. Until he reached Matsunaga's house, that is. There, it was like suddenly opening the door to a crowded chow hall, with a dozen conversations going on at once, laughter here and there, the clatter of tableware, the clinking of glasses and bottles, the unidentifiable myriad noises of bodies moving this way and that.

Brendan felt it like a punch to his guts, the easy camaraderie pouring into his startled ears, the way those men were obviously a family of sorts, even though they didn't share bloodlines or even birthplaces—just like a perfectly adjusted team of shooters.

He'd had something like this, a group of men who couldn't be more different and yet fitted together nicely, worked together better than alone, knew each other's reactions and quirks so well that they moved like a single unicellular organism.

Brendan tried to push down the ugly mixture of envy and resentment that threatened to choke him, his ears straining to focus on any of the conversations that floated around him in the maddening swirl of his own thoughts. Maybe if he could just catch a whole sentence he'd stop needing to break something or scream at the top of his lungs, but he couldn't make sense of a single word, and it was driving him out of his fucking mind.

And then, finally, he understood his confusion was not a product of his messed-up head, and laughter poured out of him like an eruption of cleansing lava.

Geez. It was the perfect closure for a perfect clusterfuck of an evening, for all of his stupid careful planning, for Big B's mighty efforts, for the whole FUBAR of a job Brendan had accepted like the fool that he was.

It seemed Senator Harris had failed to comment on his son's ability to speak Japanese like a native, and now Brendan had a 24-7, perfectly clear connection to a *Japanese* radio broadcast. And it might have been great if Brendan knew any words in that language other than samurai, sake, kamikaze, geisha, and, of course, fucking yakuza.

CHAPTER 10

THE WOODEN floor resonated like Shinya's drums as Kinosuke stomped up and down the length of the empty training hall.

"*Mattaku*," he groused under his breath.

Kenshin-san had warned him that setting an adults' class during working hours was not such a good idea, but Kinosuke had wanted so badly to get rid of the brats that he'd gone ahead with it anyway, and now he never knew when any of his occasional students would deign to attend his class.

It was a beginners' class, too, and he'd found that people in America didn't have the patience to repeat the same stances and strikes until they could perform them in their sleep, not even the Japanese-American, or especially not them. That bunch spoke like characters from *Genji Monogatari* but behaved like American high school kids, addressing their *shishō* as if he were there to discuss with them his teaching methods and change them to suit his students' preferences.

The advanced classes the boss taught were doing all right because students there knew what they wanted, were committed to practice, and tended to take the boss's instruction without comment—they could see why their sensei was their sensei instead of another one of their practice buddies. Beginners, though, took one look at Kinosuke and started trying to chat him up, a disrespectful "Why?" always about to fall off their lips when Kinosuke told them to do something.

At least Japanese-Americans tended to be punctual, their background bringing a sense of shame that didn't allow them to interrupt a class once it started. The others, those arrogant whites, every time something came up in their offices, they stayed late, and still felt it was their prerogative to attend any fraction of a class they'd paid for.

Not today. Kinosuke had put up with enough waiting. He'd just go check on Kenshin-san and maybe even replace him behind the reception desk, since Kotarō was—again—missing and he couldn't help feeling it was his fault somehow.

He nodded at himself and strode out of the dojo hall, then stopped by the door to retrieve his *zōri* sandals from the antique *getabako* Kenshin-san had found in one of his aimless rambles about the neighborhood.

Voices came from the reception area, one obviously Kenshin-san's, but the other he hadn't heard before, clearly American too, probably mainland—Kinosuke was slowly catching on to the different hues to what used to be just this uniform nasal drone until he started learning the language himself. Now he could tell Hawaiians had a more singsong accent, probably because most of them had influences from at least another, usually Asian, language.

He approached the reception warily. Maybe he was a little paranoid, but he got a little suspicious about nonlocals coming to the dojo. They weren't even near any tourist or popular neighborhood, so people didn't happen to find the place by chance on their way to somewhere else. They either lived nearby or had been searching for a training facility through the kendo sites they were listed in, and no temporary visitor matched either criteria, unless he was one of the military stationed in Oahu, which would be even more problematic—Kinosuke hadn't forgotten the marines from the US Embassy in Tokyo who'd tried to take Kenshin-san away from them.

He reached the end of the hallway and stood there watching, searching intently for signs of trouble. Kenshin-san was explaining the class schedule, his voice betraying nothing, but Kinosuke knew Kenshin-san well enough to see the tension keeping the thin body stiff as he addressed the man in front of his desk.

The stranger had an air of studied nonchalance, but Kinosuke sensed the threat anyway. Something in the way the man stood hinted at tightly coiled muscles under the casual clothes, and the cropped hair didn't quite manage to look like a style statement.

From this distance, Kinosuke guessed the man was about five-ten, one hundred fifty—so nothing too imposing about his size, really, but Kinosuke looked at him and saw a crouching cat, ready to lunge claws-first if anyone made the wrong move, never mind the friendly kitty attitude. And to make matters worse, even though Kinosuke hadn't made a sound, the stranger's head turned to look straight at him, some kind of mocking recognition in the light eyes, as if the guy were thinking, "Oh, you're still there, are you?"

Kenshin-san followed the direction of the stranger's gaze, and Kinosuke felt his hands ball into fists as he saw the relief in those bi-colored eyes. He was going to kick that fucker's ass all the way back to his fucking mainland home.

"There's Yonekawa-sensei. He teaches a beginners' class right at this time. Maybe you can discuss your situation with him."

Kinosuke approached the desk, not bothering to answer the stranger's smile with one of his own. He simply bowed his head to a polite minimum and stood there staring at the man.

"Hi. I'm Brendan O'Farrihy," the guy said, nodding to him with that infuriating smirk, green eyes twinkling as he held back his hand, somehow guessing correctly that Kinosuke wouldn't shake it if he thrust it at him in the usual American way. "I did some fencing in college, but I don't suppose it'll help much with learning kendo, will it?"

Kinosuke bit back a snort. He always saw Western fencing as trying to stick needles on a doll when you could cut off its head with a single slash. "Different techniques. You ever held a katana, a bokken, a *shinai*, or a *suburitō*?"

He knew he was bragging, but he wanted to impress on the stranger who the master in this relationship would be. Brendan-Whatshisname seemed unfazed, though, that impervious smile showing even more teeth as he answered, "No, but I usually carry a tantō when I go, um, hunting."

The dramatic hesitation before he said *hunting* was so overplayed that Kinosuke would have rolled his eyes if he hadn't felt so peeved. The little shit was enjoying himself, taunting and prodding to see if he could get a rise out of the inexperienced sensei.

Tough luck. Kinosuke might be young, but he dealt with obnoxious teenagers on a daily basis—nothing like an ex-bōsōzoku gang leader to understand unruly behavior— and he'd been taught by the best.

He did his own rendering of the signature Matsunaga glower and said, "I am free right now, if you want to try it before you decide."

"Oh, I've already made my decision, but I definitely want to try *it*."

Kuso. He was going to break a *shinai* on the man's head and see if he liked *it*, exactly with that same mocking, suggestive inflection. Fucking smirking bastard. He exchanged a look with Kenshin-san and almost cracked up when his favorite gaijin put on a serious face and said, "*Namaiki da nē. Chotto shigoitaro ka.*"

"*Honto desu yo*," he answered in the same vein, as if they were discussing kendo moves, when Kenshin-san had really asked him to give the smartass a lesson. Oh, that he would, no doubt about it.

He turned toward Brendan and found the man still smirking, but Kinosuke wasn't deceived. Now Brendan looked like a wary cat, wondering whether he should trust the fish being offered, and that was how Kinosuke intended to keep him, right on his toes like a fucking ballerina.

CHAPTER 11

THERE HAD been a moment when Brendan thought Kinosuke might punch his lights out, but then Harris said something in Japanese, and they both acted like two Zen monks discussing a complex koan on a mountaintop. Brendan wasn't fooled, though; the joke had been on him as sure as his name was Brendan.

Kinosuke's mood had lifted, too, and now that handsome face almost smiled as he asked, "Have you brought some comfortable clothes?"

Oh no, he wasn't having any of this sudden preoccupation about his comfort.

"Yes," he simply answered, schooling his eyes not to look down at the clothes he was wearing. As he expected, Kinosuke stared at him for two heartbeats, waiting for him to add something, and then, when Brendan didn't, gave him the glower that had to be Kinosuke's most natural—and gorgeous—expression.

Those black eyes sent sparks in Brendan's direction. Kinosuke's thick eyebrows formed a perfect V as his brow furrowed, and his full lips pressed together in the sexiest pout Brendan had ever seen. Finally Kinosuke turned away from him, a rustle of fabric accompanying his movements as his pleated pants flowed about him like an evening dress.

Brendan didn't notice the decoration in the hallway, or the absence of it, since his eyes were focused on Kinosuke as he strode ahead of him. Those bulky clothes Kinosuke was wearing were strangely appealing because he didn't seem encumbered by them, didn't act as if he had to adjust his movements to an unusual outfit, a disguise he only wore on occasion. And, in spite of the way the sheer amount of fabric hid Kinosuke's body, it also invested him with an air of command, a sober dignity that belied his age— very much the same kind of magic Brendan had seen transforming young punks into accountable men as soon as they put on a uniform.

"Leave your shoes there," Kinosuke said, pointing at the floor near a wall.

Brendan took off his hiking boots and noticed that Kinosuke was carefully placing his flip-flops inside a tall wooden chest with simply decorated sliding panels. He didn't know much about furniture, but being around Craig had taught him to appreciate the quality of the materials, and that piece, with its cedar wood and bamboo finishing touches was something he guessed Craig would have bought on sight—it was minimalist enough to suit the man, since everything around him had to be reduced to a minimum to enhance his phenomenal presence.

"Socks too, if you don't want to learn figure skating instead of kendo."

He came back from his bitter memories with a start. Kinosuke had made a joke? His sullen, glowering Kinosuke? There was nothing minimalist about the young yakuza who strode past him into the training hall, the man's reactions immediate and visceral, as impossible to predict as the next wave in a squall.

Brendan couldn't help smiling as he got rid of his socks—he hadn't felt this excited since the first time he'd jumped off a plane in midflight.

The wooden floor felt nice under his bare soles, making his usually stealthy steps even more inaudible, but he didn't manage to surprise Kinosuke.

"What are you, five-seven?" the yakuza asked without turning from where he stood studying a rack with wooden swords.

"Five-ten," he answered immediately, realizing as he spoke that Kinosuke had miscalculated on purpose to make him feel belittled—classic gunny instruction technique. "Four inches over you, I guess."

Oh yeah, he could miscalculate too. Kinosuke didn't say a word, but murder flashed in his eyes as he handed Brendan a polished wooden stick. That was what it looked like, at least—nothing resembling the bamboo straight swords he'd seen in kendo tournaments; a few of those also rested on the wall racks.

This sword was hefty, slightly curved, with no hilt to speak of, or at least not one signaled by a guard. The polished surface felt smooth to the touch, and as Brendan held the piece as he would a foil, he noticed the weight was a little excessive, clearly calling for a two-handed grip.

"Stop that," Kinosuke said, and Brendan looked at him with a raised eyebrow that earned him a hiss from his impromptu sensei. "Yes, I mean all that fancy-assed fencing posturing."

Brendan let out a surprised laugh. Kinosuke might speak with a strong foreign accent, but someone had taught him a wealth of *expressive* vocabulary—and Brendan could bet he knew who that someone was.

He had unconsciously stepped into the en garde position, his feet perpendicular to each other in a wide stance that allowed his knees to bend comfortably, his left arm raised behind him and making his hips and torso rotate to one side to present a smaller target.

As he lowered both arms and stood straight, he noticed Kinosuke was looking at him differently, his head slightly cocked to one side, a young pup trying to identify the strange animal in front of him. He guessed his laughter had surprised the yakuza, maybe because Kinosuke expected Brendan to glare at every criticism he received from his instructor. Well, the Navy had cured him of those knee-jerk reactions, and anyway he'd always been too competitive to consider digs anything but a spur to try harder.

Now he stood silent, open to whatever Kinosuke wanted to teach him, eager to take on the challenge to learn something new and, why deny it, learn more—everything he could—about this hot-tempered, stunning sensei.

"YOUR FEET were almost right, just keep them both facing forward and don't spread your legs that much," Kinosuke said, a little disconcerted by Brendan's expectant silence. Even his smirk had changed, his features softened, right on the brink of a smile but not quite, the kind of expression someone would keep on a first date, when everything about the other person is still new and interesting.

Shit. Kinosuke blinked. Where had that thought come from?

"Move your left foot a little so the angle is not so open," he said, watching Brendan's legs easily click into the right position, knees bending immediately to a comfortable stance that lowered the body's gravity center to offer more stability. That was the first lesson any martial arts practitioner learned, and the fact that it seemed second nature to Brendan told Kinosuke it was probably much more than fencing that had kept the American fit.

Kinosuke didn't even need to tell him to keep his upper body straight and centered; Brendan had obvious muscle control, his abdomen and buttocks tightening as automatically as his knees had bent to the right angle. It was easy to see, too, because the cargo pants he was wearing instead of the usual hakama molded to the strong legs and allowed Kinosuke a clear view of the muscle play at work. Maybe too clear a view, in fact, because he suddenly realized he'd been staring for more than two seconds at Brendan's firm, round ass.

He cleared his throat loudly, moving closer to Brendan. "Now, about the proper grip."

Brendan looked at him, the light filtering through the shoji screens illuminating his face, and Kinosuke saw that the green in his eyes was not a solid color, but rather two concentric rings of an increasingly dark hue, the ring closer to the pupil in a yellowish grass green, while the outer ring had a touch of blue, something closer to bottle green.

"Um—"

"The proper grip," Brendan offered, and Kinosuke felt himself blushing embarrassingly. He was losing his focus and, though the man was behaving so far, he wouldn't put it past the obnoxious American to start laughing at him anytime soon.

"*Hai*. The proper way to hold a bokken is this," he said, mirroring Brendan's *sankakudai* stance and raising his left hand with the sword. "You place the extreme of the handle against your left palm and wrap your fingers around it, leaving your pinkie beneath the wood."

Brendan copied his movements carefully, thick fingers surprisingly nimble as they closed around the bokken.

"Now you imagine where the guard would be on a katana and place your right hand below, in a slight angle." He made sure Brendan got it before going on. "*Hai*. Like that. Now close your hand, but leave the index finger resting as it is on the wood, don't curl it like the others."

Brendan nodded and moved the bokken up and down experimentally, testing the comfort of the grip. It was obvious that he'd had some practice with swords, because, unlike most beginners, he wasn't trying to squeeze the life out of the wood, but holding it lightly, like a crystal goblet he didn't want to either drop or break. Still, the way he angled the bokken, almost parallel to the floor, betrayed a completely different style of attack.

Kinosuke moved to stand in front of Brendan, one step away from striking distance, his bokken lowered so he offered an open target.

"If you wanted to attack me now," he said, "what would you do?"

He expected Brendan to move slowly, explaining how he would attack, but before Kinosuke had time to brace himself, Brendan stepped forward, his right foot kicking out to cover the whole distance in a mighty lunge as his arms thrust the bokken at Kinosuke's left side, pressing the tip against a spot too dangerously close to his heart to be the product of chance.

"*Chikushō!*" Kinosuke cursed, his hand shoving Brendan's bokken away. He supposed a good *shishō* would have shown no emotion, patiently explaining to his student what he'd done wrong, but the American drove him out of his mind. There he was, stepping back from the lunge in a single graceful move, looking so smug that Kinosuke almost expected to spot yellow feathers peeking out of his mouth. "What the hell did you think you were doing? Skewering a marshmallow?"

Oh fuck. Now the bastard was laughing his head off, and Kinosuke couldn't help wanting to throttle him, though the more he looked at the irritating American, the more he wanted to laugh with him, sharing this emotion that made the unremarkable face glow from the inside, pour out a lot of what the man seemed to hide under a dull mask.

Kinosuke's lips twitched a little as he shook his head to resume what he thought about Brendan. "*Mendō kusai na—*"

Brendan looked at him, green eyes sparkling with mirth. "Sorry, Sensei, but I don't understand." And before Kinosuke could reply, he said, "I get the meaning, though. The way you said it, I guess it was something between stupid haole and dickhead."

Kinosuke waved a dismissive hand at him. "Nah, not that bad."

When he didn't offer anything else, Brendan chuckled, and Kinosuke found himself smiling.

"Okay," Brendan said. "I had that one coming. But would you at least tell me what I did wrong? I mean," he added at Kinosuke's raised brow, "of course I did everything wrong, but could you be more specific, so I can learn from my mistakes?"

The American was shameless, but his will to learn seemed genuine, and he listened eagerly while Kinosuke explained that the katana had a single-edged blade, designed for cutting, not thrusting, and so the legitimate cuts in kendo were located in areas that could be struck with vertical or lateral slashes: the upper part of the head, the throat, both wrists, and the lower part of the abdomen.

"Hmm, I get it," Brendan said. "Katanas are more like sabers than like foils."

Kinosuke understood Brendan was mostly talking to himself, so he went on explaining the basics about fighting distance, footwork, and the apparently simple down cut. To his surprise, Brendan started practicing and kept on doing it, relentlessly, swinging his bokken up over his head as he stepped forward, then bringing the sword down while returning to the sankakudai, the initial stance, and then starting all over again.

He was correcting things as Kinosuke mentioned them, pushing the bokken outward with his left hand instead of pulling it inward with his right hand, keeping it parallel to the floor when he held it over his head, making it move up and down in a straight line along the center or his body, heeding Kinosuke's admonitions to the letter, and getting it right after only a few repetitions.

For the first time since he'd started giving kendo and suburi lessons, Kinosuke understood how rewarding teaching could be. It was a heady feeling, watching Brendan's technique improve exponentially with every little detail that Kinosuke corrected for him. The way Brendan kept at it, with unwavering focus, made Kinosuke focus too, the world outside the dojo receding back, his worries, his insecurities and frustrations disappearing, replaced by a confidence Kinosuke didn't even have to consider or convince himself of— his knowledge, his experience, simply flowing out of him whenever Brendan needed them, in the seamless give-and-take of a true master-student relation.

They were so focused, in fact, that time stopped being a factor, only space existing around them as they redesigned it with their movements, the tips of their bokken creating an elastic circle where a potent spell kept them isolated from the solid constrictions of everyday, clockwork life.

And inside that magic bubble, Kinosuke noticed things he had overlooked before, like the tiny freckles spattered over Brendan's nose and under his eyes, the strikingly red highlights on his buzz cut, the flush that pinked his milky cheeks, the way he unconsciously pursed his lips in concentration, all the little details that, coupled with his tireless agility, made the American look like one of those cute *yōkai* that appeared in manga for girls—cocky little fellows with vibrant vermilion hair and pointy ears.

But then the door to the dojo slid open and the boss stepped cautiously in and bowed to Kinosuke. "Yonekawa-sensei, would you mind if my students came in to watch?"

Shit. He'd never, ever been late leaving the hall on time for the next class, especially since it was the boss who came to teach right after him.

Kinosuke bowed deeply. He wished he had the boss's easy manners as he scrambled for an answer that could be at least a third as elegant as Matsunaga's way to remind him of the time without making him lose face in front of the students.

"*Sumimasen*, Matsunaga-wa... sensei, but we were already finishing. I'd rather leave the dojo to you."

Shit. What a total dud. And he'd almost given the boss his yakuza title. Kinosuke couldn't imagine things getting worse, until he looked Brendan's way and saw the change in him.

The American was standing straight, alert as an alley cat on garbage night, the bokken lowered but held in a single-handed grip that turned it into a sort of billy club, and Brendan's sharp green eyes stared intently at the boss as if he didn't want to miss a single breath the boss took.

Nobody who looked from Kinosuke to Matsunaga would have any doubt as to which of the two was the alpha male of the pride, but it still rankled, so much so that Kinosuke felt a strong mixture of anger and betrayal choking him.

And the fact that he felt betrayed by some annoying, brash, rude, ignorant piece of shit made him so angry with Brendan, the world in general, and his own stupid self in particular, that he bowed stiffly to the boss and left the dojo in big furious strides, not even stopping to retrieve his sandals from the getabako outside.

As he crossed the garden to his place, he chewed the words *fucking haole* in his mouth, tasting their sour tang, understanding why Hawaiians used them and why they were perfect for Brendan and his kind. Brendan didn't even deserve to be called gaijin when that put him on a par with the likes of Kenshin-san.

"Aniki?"

He looked up to find a sheepish-looking Kotarō, standing a prudent distance away, obviously caught in the act of sneaking in from the boss's garage door. As well he might look chastised, the little shit.

"*Kuso gaki!*" Kinosuke exploded. "Why don't you keep to the streets if that's where you'd rather be, uh? Why don't you go ahead and destroy everything we're breaking our backs to build here? And why do you even try to pretend that you give a rat's ass about the people who've given you everything, who still worry about you as if you were worth the trouble? You know what would happen if the police found out what we used to be? No, you wouldn't know, because you don't care who you put in danger just to enjoy yourself with your scumbag friends."

Now Kotarō looked about to cry, but Kinosuke couldn't find it in him to empathize. Not today, not anymore. This was neither the place nor the time to pamper anyone, so when it seemed that the kid was going to speak up, Kinosuke raised a hand in warning.

"I don't want to hear any of your lame excuses. Act like a man for once and do what you have to do, or fucking leave us all alone."

And with that he stomped the little distance left to his place and disappeared inside, only regretting that sliding doors didn't slam as satisfactorily loud as Western doors did.

CHAPTER 12

KOTARŌ STOOD in the middle of the garden, shaking with rage, fear, and humiliation.

Nobody knew what he was going through; nobody asked. Well, Kenshin-san did—from time to time he would approach the matter casually, tell Kotarō some funny story about his days in high school, and then, even more casually, ask him how things were going, how he was adapting to new faces, new customs, new rules.

Yes, Kenshin-san cared. But he was the only one in the whole house Kotarō would never go to for advice. Aniki might see him as a useless brat, but he was old enough to know how much their gaijin had done for them all, how much of the money they spent came from Kenshin-san's books, how they were allowed to remain in the country because they were supposed to be working for him. And Kotarō knew better than to add to their debt with his own problems.

The rest of them were too busy with their lives to see Kotarō. They had jobs, appointments to keep, paperwork to fill, budgets, schedules, and a bunch of other frigging important things to do. Kotarō? He only had to choose between letting himself be bullied for being an FOB or joining the bullies and become a fully integrated local good-for-nothing. Easy as pie.

It might have been different if he'd gone to a private school, but his education had been so haphazard up until then that only special schools would admit him, and Kenshin-san had said there was no fucking way Kotarō was going to one of those correctional facilities—whatever he meant by that.

Not that he minded, anyway, because he'd never been bright to begin with, and he kept hearing that Japanese kids here were the geekiest geeks on earth, so they'd probably have treated him like a nonlocal retard all the same.

At least kids in his school were mostly average or straight dumb like him, the nerd factor reduced to one or two cases who were at best ignored or, more often, shoved back into their natural place in the scheme of things—under someone else's boot.

So Kotarō had taken one look at his classmates and known right away the only safe place for him to be was the back row. If he sat up front, people would mistake him for another Japanese nerd. He was too obviously out of it to go unnoticed if he chose the middle rows. His eyes were too slanted to even pretend he wasn't Asian, and if he was an Asian dude and went to a public school, that could only mean he was either Filipino, Korean, a freshly arrived immigrant or—worst of the worst—any of the first *and* the second.

For some time he'd felt proud that his plan to be accepted by the tough guys in his class was working great. Then he'd started to fear it was working too frigging great.

Maybe if he'd been in a biker gang like Kinosuke, he might have known what to expect, but growing up with the yakuza hadn't prepared him to face this mishmash of contrary dudes who never had a clear plan until someone suggested to do the opposite.

Of course he knew some of the old guys in the Shinagawa were way uncool—he had a close-to-home example in Tachibana—but even someone who'd wear white socks and shoulder pads with everything had a clear notion of honor, loyalty, and that other thing the boss had tried to hammer into Kotarō's thick skull without much success until he'd seen what it was like to do without: purpose.

Shit. The yakuza had rules, for crying out loud. You always knew what you were doing, where you stood. If you screwed up, you were frigging well aware why and what your punishment would be.

His classmates, they were a mess. They acted on impulse, said one thing and did another, might get mad if you commented on their hairstyle and laugh if you slurred their ancestry, or the other way round, depending on the weather or what they'd had for breakfast, the same way they would love something one day and hate it the next, so you never knew what to say or do around them to keep in their good graces.

Frigging *chinpira*, that was all they amounted to. Of course they believed they were the coolest, but even a clueless old dude like Tachibana would give them a run for their money without breaking a sweat. Aniki? He was in a whole different league from those lowly pissants—frigging light years away from them.

Kotarō felt his eyes fill with tears. Problem was, these days, Aniki seemed light years away from Kotarō too. And he didn't know what to do, who to turn to. Tachibana was too busy trying to become an honorary Filipino to show his face around the house, Shinya would look at him as if Kotarō had sprouted another head if he tried to talk to him about school problems, and the boss…. Kotarō couldn't run to the boss like a first-grader to his mama's arms; he would die if he felt he was disappointing the man who had taken him in when nobody else wanted to.

Though maybe he already was disappointing them all. Maybe Aniki was right and he was nothing but a burden, a crybaby who could never get anything done by himself. And maybe he should stay away, where they wouldn't have to see him, worry about his next fuckup, try to hide what they thought of him.

Kotarō sniffled and turned the way he had come, keeping his head down as he sneaked out of the garage, feeling like an unskilled burglar in a mansion, too afraid of being discovered to stay long enough, too ashamed of leaving empty-handed to keep away for long.

BRENDAN DIALED the number, his mind going over the conversation with Big B.

He'd asked his engineman if he knew someone who spoke Japanese to sort through the growing pile of recorded conversations that was stuffing the memory of his desktop, and the big man had told him he did, adding casually that Brendan did too.

"I do?" Brendan asked. "I thought your wife was Chinese."

"Oh, it's not me. I can't even get my mother-in-law's name straight, no matter that she believes I do it on purpose."

Brendan chuckled. "Yeah, it's very much like you to find convoluted ways to vex the old ladies."

"Very funny, especially considering I've had to call her 'Mother' to avoid the embarrassment."

Now Brendan laughed openly, imagining a diminutive Chinese woman being called "Mother" by a huge Hawaiian like Big B.

"It's Bobcat."

"What?" Brendan asked, sobering fast.

"Bobcat. He can speak Japanese."

"Bobcat? As in Roberto Catalán?" Brendan thought his eyebrows would reach his hairline. "Our Bobcat?"

Now it was Big B's turn to chuckle. "Yep, Boss. The one and only Cuban-American Bobcat."

"Damn. That's—"

"Yeah. I know," B said, his expression turning grave. "They told him he needed some quiet activity to get his mind off… things, and he took on Japanese calligraphy. He says it's soothing."

It seemed Brendan was going from surprise to surprise. "He talks to you?" he asked, bewildered. He'd thought the last thing Bobcat would want was to hear from any of them.

When Big B didn't answer, a funny feeling settled in the pit of Brendan's stomach. "Oh," he said. "It's only me he doesn't talk to, isn't it?"

"It's nothing personal, Boss. It's just that you are—"

"A cold-hearted bastard, yeah, I know."

Big B's eyes widened. "Jesus. You really believe that crap?"

Brendan blinked, not certain that he understood. He hadn't tried to contact any of his former boat crew, thinking they wouldn't want to hear from the man who'd led them into the worst nightmare of their careers.

Big B was shaking his head now. "Don't you see? Bobcat hasn't looked you up because you're the boss. If he mentioned something about what happened, it'd feel as if he was accusing you—"

"I would never—" Brendan interrupted, but Big B raised a hand to silence him.

"Even if you managed to convince him that was not the case, he'd still feel he was disappointing you by not getting over it soon enough. And now that they've retired him, well, he'd hide in a hole if we let him."

Brendan didn't know what to ask first. "They've retired him? And why on earth would he feel ashamed? He's the best communications specialist I've ever met, and nothing in that FUBAR operation was remotely his fault."

"Yeah, well, good luck trying to get that into his thick skull."

"They've retired him," Brendan repeated, the words *retired* and *Bobcat* not merging well in his mind.

Big B shrugged. "The shrinks declared him disabled, that's all we know. He'd die before revealing at what level of disability they placed him."

The noise of an answering machine picking up his call brought Brendan back to the present. There was no welcome message, though, simply the beep that signaled it was your turn to say something, and it caught Brendan so unprepared that he hit the disconnect button as if he'd been stung.

He took a deep breath and called again. Big B had told him Bobcat didn't always pick up the phone, even if he was right there beside it, and even though caller ID showed it was someone he knew, so Brendan needed to leave a message for Bobcat to at least have an idea of who was calling.

"Hi, Bobcat. This is Brendan," he said after the signal. "Um, Brendan O'Farrihy, that is. I was wondering if, um, you could—"

The dial tone cut his ramblings short. He guessed Bobcat had so many messages piled up that there was no space left on the tape for new ones. That would have to do, then.

He chanced a last call, in case Bobcat had been by the phone all the time, and he pumped his fist in the air when he heard a different sort of click on the other side.

There was only silence, though, and Brendan called Bobcat's name tentatively.

Still nothing. Maybe this hadn't been such a great idea. It took a lot for the Navy to declare someone disabled on mental health grounds when you had to be a little insane already to join the military with a war going on; to do so by joining the SEALs meant you were either a sports buff, a weapons fiend, an adrenaline junkie, or a lethal combination of the three on top of everything else. So maybe his former crewman wasn't really suited for the simplest tasks of everyday life—like answering the phone.

"Bobcat?" he tried again. "This is Brendan O'Farrihy. Are you there?"

"Yes, Boss. I'm here."

It was difficult to associate this gruff voice with the upbeat personality that Brendan remembered, but he felt relieved that his man would at least engage in conversation. And it never failed to make his chest swell a little when any of his shooters called him *boss* after all this time, after all that had happened.

"Hi, Bobcat. It's good to hear you," he said honestly and rushed ahead, not waiting for a reply. "I'm calling because I'm in Honolulu for a surveillance job, and I need someone who can translate Japanese for me. It's a sensitive matter, so I'd rather hire someone I can trust, and Big Brudda told me you speak Japanese."

"I can write it. I don't speak it."

Brendan smiled. Bobcat had always been a stickler for precise meanings, and he was glad to confirm that hadn't changed.

"You don't have to speak it. I just need you to sort through these recorded conversations and tell me whether there's anything suspicious coming up."

There was no answer, so Brendan decided to tell Bobcat about Kenneth Harris and his circumstances. His shooter had never been one to blab things he was told in confidence, and Brendan guessed his present state would only have made his self-isolation even more pronounced, if anything.

"The senator is paying me lavishly enough that you can name the price," he went on. "And of course the airfare is on me. Also, I'm renting this nice apartment from Big B, and it has a spare room you can use—if you don't want to stay in a hotel—and I'm sure you've heard about the waves around here."

Geez. He sounded like a used-car salesman, but Bobcat's silences were driving him crazy. He wished he could at least see his man's face.

"You know they've retired me, don't you?" Bobcat finally said, the complete absence of intonation making him sound as gloomy as a Seattle weathercast.

"I don't care what the Navy has to say. I know you, and I know I can trust you."

This time Brendan could almost feel the silence crackling with something noxious, something too complex and concentrated to be called anger.

"You don't have to save me from myself. You're not my parish priest."

"No. I'm not your priest," Brendan said, keeping his tone steady. "The church is still suspicious of redheads."

There was a surprised snort on the other side. "That doesn't even qualify as a bad joke, Boss Man."

Brendan smiled. His men always called him *boss man* when they wanted to make fun of him—with all due respect.

"Yeah, that's why I enlisted. Nobody would hire me as a stand-up comedian."

The silence was back, but this time it was different, comfortable almost, the silence you could share with someone you'd known forever, and because that was exactly the case, Brendan knew the best strategy was to put his cards on the table, offer the naked truth.

"I'm not going to pretend that I know what you're going through, Bobcat," he said, "and I won't even try to understand it—you know empathy is not my strong suit. I'm still the same selfish, ruthless bastard you were familiar with. I need someone for a job and I want the best, so I don't care if you are on antidepressants or have to follow the Mediterranean diet as long as you don't screw up. Are we clear?"

"Aye aye, sir."

Brendan tried to keep the smile out of his voice. "Okay, then. How soon will you be ready to travel?"

"It depends, Boss."

"On what?"

Bobcat paused. "Is there olive oil in Honolulu?"

"Huh?"

"So that I can keep on my Mediterranean diet."

Brendan laughed. There was still hope if Bobcat was up to lame jokes.

CHAPTER 13

"WHAT ARE you doing, Kinosuke?"

He almost banged his head against the getabako door, his sandals hitting the wooden panels with a loud thud.

"Just getting my zōri, Boss."

For the first two months since their arrival, the boss had tried to convince them to stop calling him *boss*—because he wasn't their superior anymore—but he'd soon had to desist, seeing that it was hopeless, and now he simply used subtler methods to show them they were his equals.

Kinosuke put the damned sandals on and stood, only to find Matsunaga looking at him with a raised brow. Yeah, well; Kinosuke could pretend to be his equal as much as he liked, but the boss would always be a step ahead.

It was obvious Kinosuke was retrieving his sandals now because he'd been in too much of a hurry to remember them after his class. And the hurry was always due to a desperate need to put distance between him and the obnoxious redhead who kept coming back to his classes like a single-minded, mulish, annoying dog after a bone.

"Is that gaijin giving you trouble?"

Shit. Kinosuke's shoulders slumped. How could he think it would have escaped the boss's attention? The man noticed everything, and it was silly of Kinosuke to pretend otherwise. He felt like an awkward teenager all over again. "He just gets on my nerves, that's all."

The boss nodded and started walking, knowing Kinosuke would follow him like a clueless puppy. That's what he was these days anyway—one moment a dignified sensei, and the next a runt with a mental age not that far from Kotarō's—and all it took was a single, even-toothed, mocking smirk to throw him over the edge.

They went into the garden and behind Kenshin-san's study, where a wooden bench sat under the araucaria shade. The shady spot was right in the middle of everything, but it had an air of quiet isolation that turned it into a sanctuary where you could see but not be seen, as if you had donned an invisibility cloak simply by sitting under a tree. It always made Kinosuke suspect Kenshin-san had a long history of hiding in plain view.

For a moment he just sat there, enjoying the peace. He knew the boss wouldn't say anything if Kinosuke didn't, and it was a nice contrast to the American way of prodding. Still, he sure as hell could do with a little piece of advice, even if it shamed him to expose his problems to the boss.

"He's a good student," Kinosuke said, "but sometimes—"

He didn't know how to explain it. One moment Brendan was the perfect student, drinking Kinosuke's words in and immediately putting them to practice, and the next he would look at Kinosuke in a knowing way, or give him that smug grin, or just stand there full of attitude, and Kinosuke would lose it.

"Sometimes he forgets he's a student," Matsunaga finished for him. "They all do."

Kinosuke turned to look at the boss. "Oh, come on. I'm sure your students respect you." All they had to do was look at Matsunaga, get that commanding vibe that poured out of him, and they'd had no doubt who the sensei was—even Brendan had straightened up on seeing the boss. "It's my age that makes them think I'm just one of them fools."

"It's not you, Kinosuke; it's the American way," the boss said with no little sarcasm. "As soon as they learn what they believe is a lot, they feel entitled to a familiarity with their sensei no student in Japan would ever dream of."

Kinosuke nodded. "Even if you manage to get better than your sensei, it'll be because of him. You should only show it off to make him proud, not to embarrass him as if he were an old buddy you left behind on your way to the top." He lifted his hands. "I can't understand this people, Boss. Don't they feel any gratitude, any respect for the ones who've taught them?"

Matsunaga seemed to consider his question for a moment. "As far as I can tell, I think their problem is they're in love with the sound of certain words."

"Words?"

"Yes, just words. Take *equality*, for instance. It's in the papers, on TV, and constantly on their lips. If you ask them, they swear they believe in it."

Kinosuke frowned. "They don't?"

"It's their favorite excuse, but they don't even know what it means. If they did, they wouldn't have different laws in each state, and their courts wouldn't have to be constantly deciding on its limits."

He didn't quite get it, and the boss must have seen it in his face.

"Look at these islands," Matsunaga said. "How many times have you heard about the melting pot, the aloha spirit, and all that gibberish?"

Kinosuke rolled his eyes. He'd even seen some shit about that on the wrapping of Kotarō's granola bars.

"The words are everywhere," Matsunaga went on, "but you'd have to be blind—or drunk—to believe them. Or do you think most Hawaiians get construction work because they like using their hands? And what about Filipino waiters, or Samoan security guards? Do they love their jobs? And why are there so many Japanese and Chinese CEOs? Did they get equal chances to be what they wanted and simply chose?"

Kinosuke snorted. "Not even whites get to choose here. If you're a mainland haole or a military haole you're screwed."

"That's what I mean," the boss said. "Nobody's equal in America, but they still act as if they were because it's a good justification to step on some heads on your way up. If everybody has the same chances, you don't have to feel guilty on behalf of those who don't make it like you do—they are either less skilled or simply lazier. At least in Japan they don't bother pretending the opportunities are equal for everyone, and that makes it easy to know exactly where you are and what you can aspire to. If your place in the whole scheme of things sucks, nobody will insult you by telling you it's your fault."

Kinosuke looked at the boss in wonder. The man was—had been—a yakuza, a simple, uneducated, old-style yakuza, and yet he was smart enough to look around him and understand what he was seeing. Kinosuke just got disturbing impressions and glimpses of reality he couldn't really thread together in a string of sensible words.

The boss laughed. "Don't look at me that way, Kinosuke. I'm just blabbering."

"Yeah, well. I wish I could blabber like that. I'm sure Brendan would stop mocking me if I did."

Matsunaga raised an eyebrow. "Don't tell me you call him by his given name."

Kinosuke felt himself blush. "What can I do if I can't pronounce his damn surname? The first time I called him Brendan-san he told me he hadn't been canonized yet—whatever that means—and if I call him Brendan-kun, it feels like I'm challenging him, because he's older than me, so unless I call him 'fucking haole,' I'm stuck with Brendan."

He gave the boss a defiant look. He wasn't encouraging the American's familiarity, damn it. He was trying his best to be a respectable, dignified sensei, and he managed quite well—except for the times he left the dojo, stomping barefoot across this very garden and didn't realize he'd left his sandals behind and taken the bokken home instead until he stepped on the cool tiles of his front room. Then he slammed the bokken against the floor and imagined how it would sound hitting a certain red-haired skull.

"Are you?" the boss asked, ignoring Kinosuke's irritation.

"Am I what?" he almost barked.

Matsunaga's face didn't change, his voice low and even, and Kinosuke knew he wasn't going to like his next words. "Challenging him. Are you?"

He felt it like a punch to his gut, because his anger was so immediate and extreme that he was sure only fear could have pushed it forth, and he was helpless to contain either feeling. "Are you crazy? Why the fuck would I challenge one of my students?"

Kinosuke felt a childish satisfaction when a muscle twitched in Matsunaga's jaw. Didn't he want to be treated as an equal? There, see how good *that* felt when things weren't smooth.

"Well, I guess you do it because he's older than you and you feel at a disadvantage. So you lash at him before he does, thinking you can affirm your authority that way. Or maybe you do it because he's stronger than you and you fear he might overpower you soon enough—so you try to make him lose his nerve to prove he has no self-control and is therefore no better than you. Or maybe you do it because you *want* him to actually overpower you. And so you act like an immature whelp in the hopes that his alpha nature won't stand it for long and take charge of things, leaving you without any responsibility to struggle against."

Oh shit. Kinosuke didn't know where to look, how to disappear from the face of the earth without leaving his usual muddied trail that cried out loud, *Kinosuke the fuckwit was here and did this stupid thing of underestimating his boss for the umpteenth time.*

The silence went on for so long that Kinosuke felt he had really dropped off the face of the earth. Problem was, shame had an even stronger pull than gravity when it came to bringing you down.

"I'm never gonna make a good sensei," he finally said, more as a statement than an apology, because he was well past the point of apologies with Matsunaga. He had once tried to kill the man's lover, so whatever lame-brained thing he did after that was a minor offense the boss could easily shrug off.

"You will, when you acknowledge what moves you."

He fought the urge to huff. Of course the boss would go all Zen on him and leave him as clueless as he'd been at the start, just feeling ten times worse about it.

"You like him that much, uh?"

His head shot up to look at the boss. "What?"

Now it was Matsunaga who let out a huff. "Kinosuke," he said as if he were reaching the limit of his patience. "If you're ready to admit you act on all these petty reasons before admitting you're attracted to him, it can only mean you don't even want to admit it to yourself in the first place. And how can you be clear about your teaching when your head is so muddled up?"

Kinosuke blinked. "Boss? I don't—"

Matsunaga got up and started pacing away from him, but on his way back, he looked through the glass panes into Kenshin-san's study and shook his head. "Who am I kidding? I acted the same way with my own personal gaijin."

Kinosuke swallowed. He had no idea what the boss was talking about, but his whole body seemed to dread learning about it, so maybe he had an idea after all, and maybe it was true he didn't want to acknowledge it. "Are you saying—"

"Yes, Kinosuke. I'm saying you're usually a good sensei, and if you can't be with this guy, it is simply because you're afraid of being attracted to him."

He jumped off the bench as if someone had lit a fire under his ass. "I'm not attracted to him! How could I, when he makes me so mad I have to leave the dojo in the middle of a lesson?"

The boss faced him. "Exactly. You have to leave because you fear he'll see what he does to you and act on it."

His eyes felt about to pop out of their sockets. "But, Boss, he's not even handsome. He's just this pasty-faced, freckled redhead!"

"You don't like his blue eyes?"

"Green. They're green." Kinosuke understood his mistake as soon as he closed his big mouth—he didn't need Matsunaga's knowing smile to confirm it.

"So you've noticed the color of his eyes," the bastard said. "And his freckles."

"I teach him every Wednesday and Friday, I can't help seeing his fucking face."

"Before or after he puts on his *men*?" the boss countered and Kinosuke felt the heat rising in his cheeks.

"We don't use the helmets much. Brendan, um, likes suburi training, and we're sort of sticking to it."

"Uh-huh. He prefers suburi. And what do the other students have to say about that?"

If Kinosuke blushed any more, he was going to look like one of Miyazaki's anime characters. The girl characters. "They don't come very often. I guess the time is wrong for most people here."

"So you're giving this Brendan private lessons twice a week for the price of a group class. Do I need to remind you that we're supposed to live on the profits of the dojo?"

Shit. He unconsciously straightened his back while he lowered his eyes. He'd assumed that position—the fuckup position—so many times that it came automatically to him. "I know, Boss. I was just waiting a little more, seeing if I could salvage the class before having to cancel it." Waiting a little in the hopes he didn't have to admit to another failure.

"So he's either such a good student that you enjoy teaching him, even if you're losing money, or teaching him is the only way you have to see him on a regular basis."

There it was. The anger. Again. Immediate and unstoppable, so mixed up in a confusing cocktail of surprise, hurt, and fear that Kinosuke didn't know where to start pouring it all out. "I don't give a damn about seeing that fucking redhead ever again, and I couldn't care less about the money. But if we're so hard-pressed that we can't wait to see if a class works before canceling it, fine by me. I'll keep teaching stupid brats who never want to learn anything that needs the slightest effort on their part but whose parents are ready to cough up a satisfactory monthly payment for their little show-offs."

"Don't you raise your voice at me, Kinosuke."

Oh, now that was rich. He snorted. "Why not? You're not my boss anymore. You're not even the owner of this dojo. You're just the owner's lover, and that doesn't give you any authority over me. And as for the money, let's not kid ourselves; we're living off your lover's money. We can pretend to be these dignified sensei all we want, but the truth is we're just a bunch of kept boys—or at least you are; we don't even get to fuck a pretty gaijin."

Kinosuke saw Matsunaga's face change, but it wasn't until he finished his tirade that he realized the outrage had been replaced by something very different, something that made Kinosuke belatedly turn his head to catch a glimpse of a retreating back he would recognize anywhere.

He didn't quite see Matsunaga as he passed by Kinosuke's side and ran after Kenshin-san.

Kinosuke slumped to the ground and covered his face with his hands. Fuck. What was wrong with him? Why did he have to hurt everyone he cared about?

CHAPTER 14

BRENDAN BROUGHT his bokken down awkwardly. Geez. Could he do it any worse?

His mind wasn't in it today. Seeing Bobcat had been a shock, no matter that he'd expected it after talking so much about it with Big Brudda. The man simply looked like a ghost—thin, numb, and haunted, showing the most distressful combination of a dejected attitude and an über-alert body language.

Big B had suggested they dress in gaudy aloha shirts to avoid looking military, but that was exactly how they'd dressed when deployed in Central and South America—trying to look like clueless tourists—so Bobcat could still make the connection with their past.

It was difficult, trying to avoid any reference to what they'd shared, so they opted for a pair of those half-finished-looking beachcomber straw hats, because they believed clownish would be less threatening than serious or—God forbid—sympathetic.

Not that it'd worked, anyway. Bobcat had taken a harried look at them and quickly gone back to scanning the baggage claim for threats. Well, Big B and he had done exactly the same, but just the one time, just keeping their eyes open, not their whole bodies tense and their heads swiveling this way and that like heroin addicts in need.

In truth, that was what Bobcat looked like—way under the correct dose of medication, but obviously medicated. And not even Big B's dazzling grin nor his bear hug had helped ease the man into something remotely close to normality.

Christ. To think that Bobcat and Paul "Pablito" Herrera had once been proud of showing every Cuban American stereotype with their expansive, loud, touchy-feely immediateness. Now Brendan hadn't tried to go further than a handshake, and even then hadn't managed to keep those once-warm eyes on him for more than a second at a time.

His shooter was a wreck, and Brendan wasn't sure he should have trusted him with this job. He had started it all right, carefully studying the pictures Brendan had taken of Kenneth Harris and the yakuza, and sitting for hours with his headphones on and a notebook always at hand to scribble quick memos, but he seemed to have taken it too seriously, almost insanely so, when the last thing this job needed was someone even more paranoid than the senator himself.

Brendan caught his reflection in the mirror and saw the awful angle his bokken had taken as he held it over his head. Geez. Kinosuke would start yelling at him in a second. As soon as he thought it, he realized he'd been screwing up every single move, from his stance to the direction of the cuts, without his sensei remarking on it in the most *subtle* way he usually reserved for the—frequent—times they were alone in the dojo.

Brendan lowered the bokken and observed his instructor. Those black eyes were unfocused, lost in some thought that didn't look to be especially cheerful, the young man's whole posture so listless that Brendan felt a pang of concern.

"You all right there, Sensei?" he asked, lowering his bokken and taking a few steps toward Kinosuke before he realized what he was doing.

Kinosuke looked startled, as if Brendan had suddenly popped into existence in front of him. "Hai," he almost squealed, "I mean, yes. Why are you not practicing?"

"I was, but you looked a little… sick," Brendan said, noticing even as he spoke that Kinosuke did look somewhat sick—his face pale, dark circles under his eyes and a weariness that made him move as if he found it difficult to carry his own weight. Of course as soon as Brendan mentioned it, his proud sensei bristled and glared, but even his reaction had less heat in it than usual.

"I'm not ill. Go back there and get that bokken swinging," Kinosuke said, pointing to the place on the wooden floor where Brendan should be standing. But Brendan didn't move, his eyes narrowing at the despondency that tinted even Kinosuke's voice.

"You might not be ill, but you're worried sick about something," Brendan stated, moving closer still to his sensei.

Kinosuke frowned and looked at Brendan's feet as if their movements were a conundrum that had him deeply puzzled. "What are you doing?"

He didn't even look up, and Brendan wondered if Kinosuke was drunk. His reactions had that delayed timing that drunks usually showed, but otherwise he didn't look drugged in any way. He looked numb, and it was such a contrast with Kinosuke's usual high-strung self that Brendan reached out to lift his chin and feel his forehead for a fever.

Surprisingly enough Kinosuke let him, dark eyes meeting Brendan's and blinking so slowly that Brendan had time to measure the length of every thick curved lash.

"What are you doing?" Kinosuke repeated, and Brendan ignored it. The skin under his fingers didn't feel overly warm, but he was reluctant to break a contact he hadn't expected to come so naturally, so soon, so much without a fight. As things were going, he more or less expected to be butting heads with his instructor already—in the literal sense too—but this unresisting Kinosuke, as much as he tugged at his concern, was an unexpected delight, something Brendan was not ready to give up in a hurry.

He moved his hand to smooth the longish black hair off Kinosuke's face. "What's wrong?" he whispered, too aware of the silent emptiness of the dojo.

Kinosuke closed his eyes and shook his head, the movement so light it almost looked as if he was afraid to dislodge Brendan's hand.

Brendan dropped the bokken to hold Kinosuke's head with his two hands. The clatter startled the young man, and his eyes shot open.

"Tell me," Brendan murmured, so close to Kinosuke now that he could smell him, a light cedar soapy scent, warmed and turned into something darker by Kinosuke's body heat, almost like stepping into a thick, subtly dangerous evergreen forest.

Kinosuke looked at him, really looked at him, dark eyes studying Brendan's face carefully, his gaze sliding over Brendan's hair, down to his reddish eyebrows, following the line of his nose, counting the freckles on his cheeks, tracing the curved lines of his lips, and finally moving up to linger on his eyes.

Brendan kept still under the scrutiny, barely breathing as he felt the trail of that gaze on his skin, hot and heavy as a hand molding his features in clay.

Kinosuke searched his eyes for a moment longer, a look of defeat creeping into his open expression. "*Honto da*," he finally said, the words thick with a mixture of emotions Brendan couldn't begin to make sense of.

"I can't understand you," Brendan said, desperate to know.

"I can't either," Kinosuke replied without a trace of humor. He looked as lost as Brendan felt, but Brendan had always been a problem solver, a man of action, the kid who couldn't wait for the flakes to actually pile up before he was outside gathering them into lethal snowballs, and so he stopped thinking about the things he couldn't understand and simply pulled Kinosuke's face closer until their lips touched.

Kinosuke didn't jerk away, but he didn't return the kiss either; he stood there motionless, as if his lips were involuntarily glued to a sticky surface, making Brendan groan in frustration. He stuck his tongue out and licked the seam of Kinosuke's lips, gently but insistently, pushing until he felt a small crack in Kinosuke's defenses and then letting his teeth take advantage by catching Kinosuke's lower lip and pulling a little.

That sure got a reaction, the young man making a weird sound—half-annoyed, half-aroused. His strong fingers grabbed a handful of Brendan's jacket and pulled, but Brendan didn't let go of his catch even as he moved forward.

Brendan's lips stretched over his teeth in what he knew was a feral smile, and his whole body tingled with the excitement of a good challenge.

Kinosuke didn't disappoint, as one hand came up to close around Brendan's nape and squeeze hard—as if he expected Brendan to go limp like a cub in the clutch of his mother's jaws—and the other hand did something with Brendan's jacket he didn't understand until pain flashed off his right nipple, forcing his mouth open in a shocked gasp.

That little distraction was all it took for Kinosuke to slip free and watch him with a feline smile of his own, Brendan's hands still keeping his face close enough to see the glint in his eyes. Yeah, much better. This Kinosuke was someone he knew how to deal with.

"You cheated," he said, his grin somehow spoiling the overall effect of his complaint.

"You bit me," Kinosuke countered, looking at Brendan's mouth as if to prevent a new attack. The tip of a pink tongue came out to wet Kinosuke's lips.

"Hmm. Don't show me that tongue if you want to keep it."

That sexy smile turned into the cocky grin of a streetwise urchin, and Kinosuke defiantly stuck out his tongue at him.

It made Brendan laugh, made him study the lines around Kinosuke's eyes as his grin widened, his sensei's tongue lolling out like that of an overheated dog.

"Tsk-tsk. You shouldn't taunt the beast."

Oh yeah. He knew Kinosuke was as competitive as him; once he snapped the safety off his weapon, there was no way to put it back on. So now the little shit was folding his tongue into a U shape, and Brendan chuckled, but he kept his dominant eye trained on his target, and the moment Kinosuke blinked, he struck like a cobra, his mouth closing swiftly around the tender bait.

A groan vibrated in his mouth, and Brendan fought the urge to smile as his tongue played with Kinosuke's, torturing its prisoner with heated touches and swirls, showing a hint of teeth when the young man tried to pull away.

As he expected, Kinosuke fought him, and not because he wanted to end the contact, but because he wanted control over it, wanted to come out on top. Tough luck. Brendan hadn't been a commanding officer for nothing—he enjoyed the view from the top too much to let go, and he enjoyed a good fight almost as much, so Kinosuke had a long way to go to regain the authority of a sensei.

Strong fingers tried to grasp his hair, his crew cut making it rather difficult and more painful for Brendan, who shuddered and grunted every time Kinosuke pulled.

Kinosuke made a sound suspiciously close to a chuckle, so Brendan stopped playing nice and stepped forward, his body pressing into Kinosuke's space and pushing until the cotton of their uniforms rubbed together, chest to chest, hip to hip, both men groaning at the same time when their erections bumped into each other.

And then there was open war, no more playful pushing and pulling and licking and nibbling. Now Brendan's hands stopped cradling that beautiful face to grab Kinosuke's ass and pull them together without any finesse, their hips moving of their own accord to grind and hump and do anything to alleviate the suddenly urgent ache in their cocks. Their tongues abandoned their little tug-of-war in favor of a messy kiss, openmouthed and wet, while Kinosuke's hands yanked Brendan's twill jacket open and shoved it harshly down his arms, making his nipples harden at the sudden exposure.

Brendan moaned into the kiss, his hands squeezing Kinosuke's tight ass, begging without words for his sensei to do something, anything, to feed this hunger he hadn't felt for so long that it was like going back to a part of him he hadn't realized he'd been carrying around like a dead weight, not even mourning for its loss because he'd forgotten it could be like this—*he* could be like this—sharply alive in the intense pain and pleasure and fear and need of wanting and being wanted in return, and eagerly so, without concession to time, place, or judgment from others.

And this man who looked too young to be anybody's sensei, this proud creature who looked too wild to share his territory, this beautiful, sexy foreigner with a complicated past, seemed to know exactly what Brendan needed and why. Those swollen lips left his for a second, dark eyes grave as they searched his, everything frozen in that moment of suspended time when all could be stopped with barely the pain of removing a Band-Aid, a quick sting that would leave no permanent scars.

Brendan looked into those eyes, offering without lies, begging without words, standing tall in the notion that he was what he'd made of himself, probably no more, but definitely no less.

CHAPTER 15

"*MENDŌ KUSAI na—*"

Brendan had heard his sensei use those words before, always with that exasperated ring to them, but only now he felt the reluctant affection behind the words, the kind of feeling troublesome children inspired, making you want both to hug and strangle them in the same movement.

He smiled involuntarily, and Kinosuke mirrored him with a smile of his own, slow and sexy and full of a promise he didn't have to wait long to see realized, because now the break was over and there was no going back, no safe cover in the vast expanse of the empty dojo.

They went at each other without warning, their teeth clicking as their mouths clashed. Kinosuke's hands linked behind Brendan's neck as he suddenly hopped to wrap both his legs around Brendan's hips. Kinosuke didn't weight too much, but Brendan wasn't exactly focusing on his balance right now, so he had to step backward to keep from falling or dropping his precious load. He kept moving until his back hit the wall with a thud, his hands glued to that sweet ass, his mouth desperate to cover as much territory as it could, closing on Kinosuke's jaw, sucking on his pulse point, biting hard on the muscle at the base of his neck.

His young sensei let out a strangled cry and bucked in his arms, the movement sending sparks up his sensitized cock as their hips ground together. The rub of harsh fabric was driving him crazy, as it was both too much and too little, the twill rough enough on sensitive skin to give them something akin to rug burn, and yet the lack of skin-to-skin contact making the friction seem far from satisfying.

Brendan groaned in frustration and pushed himself off the wall, turning around until it was Kinosuke's back that hit the plaster noisily. His sensei's eyes gave him a fierce glare and before he knew it, two rows of white teeth closed on one of his exposed nipples.

"Fuck!"

He jerked helplessly until that tongue he'd held in his own mouth came out to lick at the sore flesh, this time making him shudder from head to toe, Kinosuke watching him as closely as if he were performing a sensitivity test.

"Need skin," Brendan mumbled before surging forward to capture the sexy mouth in front of him. He desperately wanted to touch, but he was afraid to let go and drop Kinosuke.

Kinosuke made a sound that Brendan imagined was a question, and he remembered Kinosuke's English might be good, but it was still his second language, and he was bound to get confused when his brain wasn't exactly in translation mode.

"Get rid of the uniform," Brendan managed to explain when they broke the kiss for air, and he saw with relief that Kinosuke was nodding before he captured his lips again in another desperate kiss.

But just when he expected Kinosuke to undress, Brendan got sure hands pulling at *his* uniform, deft fingers yanking at the strings of his hakama pants and getting them loose in record time. Of course being Japanese Kinosuke must have a lot of experience with complicated garments, because it always took much more effort for Brendan to get rid of the pleated monstrosities. Now only Kinosuke's legs kept the hakama perched on Brendan's hips, and his sensei moved gracefully to solve the problem, pushing against the wall at his back to lift his legs a little, high enough for the hakama to slide down and pool at Brendan's feet so that he stood almost naked in the center of the black heap of fabric, probably looking like the strangest creature being born out of the mud of the earth.

Kinosuke looked down and frowned, his own hakama covering Brendan as the bulky pleats dangled from his raised legs. Brendan growled a little, his jacket still constricting his arms where it bunched around them, Kinosuke still completely wrapped up in layer after layer of cloth. Geez. Why couldn't the Japanese forget about tradition for once and go for practicality? Just because a bunch of samurais had liked fighting in their hoopskirts didn't mean they had to keep the damn things in modern martial-arts uniforms.

Kinosuke let his legs slide down to the floor and pulled at Brendan's jacket, and Brendan growled louder as the movement forced his hands to let go of Kinosuke's ass. As soon as the jacket hit the floor, though, his hands went straight for Kinosuke, but his sensei kept him at arm's length, watching him with a wide-eyed expression.

"*Etchi da na—*"

If Brendan growled any louder, someone was going to call the animal control guys, so he barked the question instead. "What?"

"You're not wearing a *zubon*."

And that answered the question of what to wear under hakama pants—if he had the faintest idea what a *zubon* was or any intention to ask right now. "Got a problem with going commando?"

"It's fine," Kinosuke said a little distractedly, his eyes never leaving Brendan's groin.

Brendan felt a smug smile spreading his lips at his sensei's rapt attention. He knew he kept his body in good shape, and his cock was more than a decent size, but it was still a boost to his ego to be admired by a younger, sexy man like Kinosuke.

"Let me see you," Brendan said, trying to get his sensei naked.

Kinosuke looked up, frowning. "Huh?"

He gestured impatiently. "Your uniform. Get rid of it."

Of course Kinosuke wouldn't obey a single order coming out of his lips. Instead of complying, he grabbed Brendan's wrist and lifted it to take a look at his watch.

"Too little time," the bastard said, kiss-swollen lips twitching slightly.

Now Brendan *did* growl, loud and clear, his hands going to their favorite place on Kinosuke's anatomy and pulling hard, his mouth attacking the long bare neck with a vengeance.

His sensei cried out when Brendan's teeth sank into his flesh, his fully clothed body rubbing deliciously against Brendan's sensitized skin. It was somehow erotic, that contrast—the sensei in his imposing uniform and the student completely naked—and as much as he wanted to see his young lover, Brendan enjoyed the kinky thrill of his vulnerability, the tantalizing pressure of Kinosuke's hidden cock against his exposed one, the hungry gaze of his sensei as those clever fingers mapped his bare skin.

Once he was satisfied with the mark he'd planted on Kinosuke's neck, he went for that mouth again, his sensei pouring noises into the kiss as they rubbed in earnest against each other, nails raking down Brendan's spine and making him shudder, his cock leaking freely onto the raspy twill of Kinosuke's pants.

The thought that he was going to make a mess on those pants crossed his mind, but he was too far gone, too attached to those sweet lips to do anything about it. So it took him by surprise when strong fingers sunk into his hips and forced him to turn until he found his backside suddenly plastered to Kinosuke's front, a hard cock pushing layers of fabric into his cleft and pressing against his hole, wiry arms firmly wrapped around him, one hand going to pinch his nipple while the other tugged at his aching cock.

Brendan let out a noise sounding very close to a whimper, his ass pressing shamelessly back, wanting more, craving the impossibility of being taken through the barrier of cloth, enjoying the strength of the man who had him pinned against his body, easily surrendering his own strength because this game had been won in all fairness—they both had gone off the start line in the same condition, with no previous advantage to mar the game and turn it into an exchange of favors, currency to be levered against future needs.

His hands searched blindly for Kinosuke, but his sensei let out what sounded like a curse and grabbed them, pulling Brendan's fingers forward and placing them where his own hands had been, one on Brendan's left nipple, and the other around his cock. Kinosuke kept his hands on top of Brendan's, forcing them to move when and as fast as he wanted, completely controlling the game as he thrust against Brendan's cleft.

Brendan abandoned himself to those masterful fingers, moaning wantonly, moving in counter rhythm to Kinosuke's shoves, his entire back burning from the friction, his hole clenching and unclenching, desperate for more sensation even though the skin around his opening was being rubbed raw.

"I'm close," Brendan said, panting, and heard Kinosuke whisper something in Japanese, something that sounded intimate and sexy, something that came right before a finger entered him roughly and hit his gland, pleasure bursting out of him with the shocking intensity of unexploded ordnance, making all the orgasms he'd had for a while simple duds when compared to this amazing improvised explosive device.

He sagged against Kinosuke, so boneless that even his brain was a relaxed, blank slate, until he noticed his sensei's erection against his hole, and then all he could think about was how well their bodies fit and how much better it would be when they could fit completely, a goofy smile stretching his lips as he got a clear visual of Kinosuke, him, a bed, and no curtains wrapped around their legs, thank you very much.

"Be with you in a second," he mumbled, knowing the smile showed in his voice.

"You're a wimp," his sensei said without much heat, his hands still wandering over Brendan's skin as if he wanted to make sure he hadn't disintegrated in the blast.

"Hmm, you're a hard sensei."

"As hard as they come," Kinosuke said, grinding his hips so Brendan could feel what he was talking about.

Brendan snorted. "That was bad, Kinosuke."

He smiled when he felt his sensei tense a little against him. Damn Japanese pride. He didn't want to spoil the mood, though, so he hurried to add, "But since you were so fucking amazing, not only will I ignore any bad jokes you choose to throw my way, but I will also do my best to make you actually come."

"When?"

He laughed. "I thought you Japanese were the epitome of patience."

"The what?"

Not the best moment to use complicated words, then. "Never mind."

He forced himself to turn around and face Kinosuke, the sight greeting him making his spent cock twitch. Those dark eyes looked completely black now, huge pupils eating away at any hint of color around them, the smooth skin flushed, long strands of silky hair falling about wildly, full lips parted and wet, asking to be kissed. But Brendan didn't stop to kiss them, because he knew if he started now he'd never stop, and he couldn't leave Kinosuke wanting.

His body made the decision for him, his knees hitting the wooden floor with a thud, his mouth nuzzling the hot bulge under the thick cotton of his sensei's hakama.

Kinosuke hissed, his hands hovering over Brendan's head, not knowing what to do. Brendan couldn't help smiling as he guided those hands to the elaborate bow on top of Kinosuke's pants.

"Lose the skirt," he said, lifting the black hems and putting both his hands under the fabric to stroke his sensei's legs.

It was a measure of how desperate Kinosuke was that the word *skirt* didn't even register, his fingers making quick work of all the strings and straps and belts and whatnot that kept the whole drapery together. And then, when the hakama slid down to bunch around Kinosuke's ankles, there was still another pair of pants under them, these ones white and simple—thank God for small favors—held only by a drawstring that his sensei pulled swiftly to add them to the cotton pile on the floor.

Brendan would have groaned when he saw that Kinosuke's jacket effectively covered him to midthigh, but he was too busy keeping his mouth from hanging open at the sight of the intricate swirls of ink reaching down to the slender knees.

Why hadn't he expected it? He knew yakuza usually had tattoos—he'd seen Matsunaga's and even Harris's through Big B's camera—but somehow, he hadn't imagined Kinosuke with one of those full-body frescoes. Maybe it was because the kid Kotarō had mentioned Kinosuke sported a tattoo under his hair, and it had sounded so extreme at the time that Brendan hadn't thought there'd be more ink in any other parts of this gorgeous body.

But there it was, ink in extraordinary hues fanning out to Kinosuke's inner thighs where it ended abruptly in thick, round-tipped bands of dark blue that made a stunning background for the storm that raged over the rest of Kinosuke's skin.

There were clouds of white and blue, strokes of intense red lightning, and the masterful shading that almost allowed Brendan to feel the strength of the winds blowing everywhere in that vibrant scenery.

Kinosuke groaned and tore at the strings of his jacket, Brendan's hands helping to pull the white garment open right until the moment when he got the first glimpse of what lay underneath.

"Fuck me raw," he cursed, his eyes roaming about in an effort to capture all there was to see—the long, flushed cock that stood out proudly from a nest of black curls, the blue dragon that sprung from behind turbulent clouds, one claw hovering over Kinosuke's pubes while the other stretched upward as if to thwart the advance of a mighty red dragon descending on him from across Kinosuke's chest, a ball of red fire preceding his advance, the movement of the magnificent beasts creating the storm that raged all over Kinosuke's body.

"Brendan!"

The desperation on his sensei's voice might have been funny if Brendan had been teasing him on purpose, but as things were, it only made him feel like a five-year-old with a very deficient attention span. So he didn't stop to apologize, focusing instead on making it up to Kinosuke, his mouth opening wide to take as much of the tantalizing length in front of him as he could in one go. And it must have been a lot, if his sensei's moan was any indication, his narrow hips jerking unconsciously, making the head of his cock bump against the back of Brendan's throat.

Craig used to say that Brendan had been forced to eat so much shit in his military career that he didn't have a gag reflect, and somehow it never sounded like a compliment on Brendan's prowess but more like another weakness that Craig could use to his advantage. And use it he did, grabbing Brendan's head to keep it in place with the same iron grip he applied to everything he wanted to fuck the life out of.

Brendan tilted his head back a little, watching Kinosuke, instinctively comparing the refined lawyer and the uncouth yakuza in their reactions to being given pleasure. He couldn't help but notice that whereas Craig had taken everything as his due, fucking Brendan's mouth with the same ruthlessness he used to smash his opponents in court, Kinosuke stood there biting his lower lip, watching Brendan with wide hungry eyes, as if he couldn't believe his luck in having this given freely to him, his thighs trembling from the effort of keeping as still as he could so as not to hurt Brendan, his hands fisted to keep them from clutching at Brendan's hair.

Brendan felt his cock trying to rise at the view Kinosuke offered, at the admiring way Kinosuke looked down at him, and a weird sensation lodged in the pit of his stomach as he felt for the first time that this was really a gift he was giving out and not some retainer fee he was advancing.

Kinosuke made a helpless sound, probably trying to warn Brendan that he was close, and Brendan grabbed those narrow hips and sucked for all he was worth, wanting this to be the best Kinosuke had ever had, wanting to get his sensei hooked on this, on him, wanting the taste of this gorgeous man in his mouth, in his gut, wanting to seal a connection between them that nothing short of a depth charge would sever.

A pull of those hips, encouraging his sensei to move, was all it took for Kinosuke to thrust once and cry out, spurts of bittersweet come gushing down Brendan's throat as he swallowed fast to try to keep it all in, his eyes fixed on the sexy abandon of his young lover's pleasure, nothing controlled or hidden in that beautiful face, dark eyes looking down at Brendan with an intensity that he would have found scary if he hadn't been used to fighting for what he knew was worth it. And this here, this man with a character as taut as his gorgeous, tattooed body—this proud, irritating, wonderful man—was definitely worth fighting for.

CHAPTER 16

KOTARŌ FELT sick. The images went round and round in his head no matter what he did, always with the same result, always with him center stage, the ziplock freezer baggie sliding from his hand into another hand, rolled bank notes burning his pocket until he passed them on to his classmate, a pat on his back and the words, most of all the words, telling him that he'd passed the test, that he was a real *moke* now, that he'd become one of them.

One of them. Finally someone wanted him to be part of something and it was this shit, this bunch of bullies he'd had to join just to escape a meaner bunch of bullies, these kids playing men's dirty games, trying to believe there was no one bigger than them because they did stupid stuff, dangerous stuff, and did it where everybody was watching, right down in a public place, risking their futures by pushing ice in a shopping mall and bragging about it with all the skinny mainland chicks that followed the trail of easy money they left behind.

And now he was part of it. When all he'd really wanted in his life was to grow up and become a soldier under the boss's command, turn into someone respected, a yakuza, a man who didn't fear danger but didn't mock it either, didn't play with his life or the lives of his brothers just for kicks.

But no. This was Kotarō the fuckup. The stupid kid who left home to join the army and joined a circus instead. As a clown.

His vision blurred. Why did he have to be late for everything that mattered? He could have been the beloved son of a small family, but he'd been born so late in his parents' life that by then no one expected him, his brother already a man who didn't want to share his inheritance, his parents already too old to bother with a squealing bundle of diapers. And then the boss had given him another family, had apprenticed him, taught him all he knew about being a man of honor, and just when Kotarō was about to reach the age to join the Shinagawa, the boss had left the yakuza for good.

He paddled forward with his arms, not really seeing where he was going and not caring too much. This was a beginner's spot, and the waves here were as wild as the ones children made by jumping into a pool.

It wasn't fair. Why did he have to learn everything from scratch, over and over again, and never get to be really good at anything? He'd started training with a bokken when he was already too old, and now he only had passable skills with either the bokken or the shinai—here, where nobody but rich Japanese-Americans cared too much about kendo. And now he had to learn how to surf when he was too old to get any good at it.

He should give up and join those firefighter dudes who'd be teaching a bunch of tourists in about an hour. He'd probably learn something more with them than just hitting the water head first like he'd been doing for some time now.

Not that he was usually this bad, but he couldn't stop thinking about the mall, and the cameras there, and the security guards, and the face the boss would make if he ever learned what Kotarō had done.

Kenshin-san had already looked at him in a strange way when Kotarō had lied to him by saying he was spending the weekend at some friend's place. Those weird eyes had studied Kotarō for a moment and then just looked really sad, as if Kenshin-san knew he was bullshitting him.

He'd felt ashamed at the time, lying to the man who'd always been so good to him, and now it felt even worse when he realized that Kenshin-san hadn't asked him for his friend's phone number, or his address, or even his name as he usually did. He guessed Kenshin-san was done worrying about him.

The salty water on his cheeks felt too warm to be seawater, and he was glad this place was empty so early, no one there to see him floating about crying on what was supposed to be a surfboard and not some inflatable pool lounger for kids.

What had he expected to achieve, anyway? Was spending the night in the sand like some beach bum going to make him a local? Or turn him into a good surfer? Or make his new *friends* forget he existed?

He stopped paddling to wipe his eyes with the back of his hand—his saltwater drenched hand.

"Shit!"

It stung like a mofo, making him tear away even more if possible, everything around him blurring so badly that he pulled himself up to straddle the board so that he could get as far as he could from the frigging water of the frigging ocean.

"Fuck!" he yelled at the top of his lungs, savoring the taste of the forbidden word, letting all his frustration push out in the four-lettered exhale, his body sagging as if all his energy had flown away with the ugly sound.

And then he just felt tired. Using all those dirty words had been fun in the beginning, when saying them in another language made them somehow more exciting, but being around his classmates and listening to them talk had turned curses into something tame, something you used between every two words just to make sure the rest of the world knew how tough you were. Now he'd rather listen to Kenshin-san, because his sentences were full of words, different words, and words that meant something, too, his curses fun to hear because they came at the right time, had a lot of feeling behind them—anger, surprise, irritation, whatever—and more often than not, had a personal angle to them, Kenshin-san adding his own touch to what had been common expressions before he altered them with his weird sense of humor.

A fat tear rolled down his cheek, and Kotarō didn't even move to wipe it off his face. It had been happening on every front. He'd been trying to jump into the outside world because it looked shiny and cool, and he'd wanted as much distance as he could have from the guys who represented his old, embarrassing past.

And then, when he'd taken a long hard look at this new, exciting world, he'd found there wasn't very much to admire under the glittering surface, and the more he dug, the more he missed the way things had been around him before he decided he didn't want them anymore. Now, all he wanted to do was run back to his family crying for help, now that it was too late, now that he'd done the unforgivable and betrayed them to join some guys who didn't even care about him.

He shuddered. The water had turned cold, or he had—too much time floating about like the dimwit he was.

He leaned forward a little and steered the surfboard until the nose was facing the beach, ready to start the swim back. He took a look, just to see if there were people out there already and decide which way to take to avoid being seen.

Blood froze in his veins. The beach was so far away it looked like one of those Google maps right after you zoomed out. And the worst part was noticing that the board kept moving on its own, some current dragging it deeper into the ocean.

"*Kuso*," he cursed in Japanese, English forgotten with everything else except that white line of sand in the distance, where he now wished he could see a crowd of firefighters who would look out for him, or even tourists who could call someone for help.

He closed his eyes and told himself not to panic. All he had to do was paddle back. It would take him a lot of time, but the beach was right there, he wasn't lost in the middle of the ocean with a bunch of sharks waiting to take the first bite.

"*Kuso, kuso, kuso*," he repeated for good measure as he lay flat on the board and started paddling for all he was worth.

The current was strong—or he was weak after spending so many hours fooling around—and he found moving forward rather difficult, as if he was in the middle of one of those nightmares where no matter how much you ran you were always in the same frigging spot. And, just like in a nightmare, there was nobody there to call for help even if he'd been close enough to be heard.

The water felt very cold now, his rash guard too flimsy a protection against all those tons of water trying to suck him in. He kept hoping the next wave would push him in the right direction, and each time he was lifted on a crest it did look like he was progressing, but the depression following each crest seemed to pull him back with equal force until he felt like a spider dangling from its thread, all eight legs flailing wildly without carrying it anywhere.

He was panting, his strokes losing strength by the second, and all he could think about was how lame it would be, drowning in sight of the beach, and a beginners' beach to boot—no danger there except for children, weak swimmers, and stupid Japanese hicks.

His chest constricted, and it wasn't because of the cold or the exhaustion; he was thinking the boss would have pulled him out of the water in the blink of an eye. Aniki would have too. Or Kenshin-san, or Shinya. Even Tachibana.

The whole lot of them would have jumped into the ocean without a moment's doubt, even if the beach had been full of lifeguards, or the waters had been bubbling with frigging jellyfish, or even if all they could see were the fins of those humongous sharks that only live in movie oceans.

Those guys would have done anything for him; even if they knew Kotarō had betrayed them, they would still have risked their lives for him, for the piece of shit that he was.

He sniffed. Maybe it would be better this way. If he drowned now, nobody would know. They would be angry with him for being so stupidly careless, but they would mourn him as family, and that was the best Kotarō could aspire to right now.

The next wave lifted him and he saw the beach as far as it had been before, or so it seemed through his tears, and he felt so exhausted, so hopeless, that when the crest of the wave passed and he was brought back down, he lost his balance on the board and sank into the cold water.

As silence enveloped him, he had time to wonder how he could be so frigging lame as to fall off a surfboard when lying belly down on it as he rode the tamest waves on earth. His arms moved on their own, survival instinct kicking in and trying to push him back up where he could breathe, but no matter how tame the waves were, the undercurrent was too strong for him, or he was too weak a swimmer, because swimming, like everything else, he had learned when he was already too old to be any good at it.

And suddenly panic was there, when all thought was swept away by the urgent need to get air into his lungs, fear so primal and overwhelming that he couldn't control the wild movements of his limbs, the manic strength that pushed him blindly upward, his chest about to explode and the words *I don't want to die* repeating in the endless loop that had taken the place of his mind.

The edges of his vision started to blur, and he moved his hands frantically, trying to reach the surface as if it was something solid he could grab. But when one of his hands did hit something solid, the pain was so big, so sudden that he opened his mouth in shock, and the ocean poured into him, his last reservoir of oxygen pushed out in coughed bubbles that he saw flying away as he sank, a beautiful cloud of red floating about them, a big black shadow looming above everything as his wide-open eyes stopped seeing.

CHAPTER 17

KINOSUKE WIPED motor oil from his hands. Tampering with his bike was what he did when he had something he didn't know how to go about—something he very much wanted to avoid if he could get away with it.

Not that it would work this time, though. Kenshin-san was not like the boss. He wouldn't simply get mad at Kinosuke and give him the silent treatment until he apologized properly. No, Kenshin-san was far more complicated than that.

"Fucking gaijin," he muttered under his breath.

Americans were all about guilt. You offended them and they didn't simply think you'd dishonored your friendship with them. They had to analyze every single word you'd said to find out the ultimate reason why you would blurt such things out, and since they believed they were the center of their little universes, they always discovered that they, of course, were to blame.

He growled and sent the soiled cloth flying with all his strength, only to see it flop limply onto the floor without hitting the wall. Not very satisfying, but being unfair to Kenshin-san wasn't satisfying either.

The man was not really as self-centered as Kinosuke wanted to believe. That was the problem. Their gaijin cared too much, not only about the boss but about the whole scruffy lot of them, and that was why Kinosuke's words must have hurt like hell.

Shit, but he was some ungrateful bastard. Kenshin-san had never asked him to leave Japan, and yet he'd done everything he could to allow Kinosuke to have a good life here, where Kinosuke couldn't quite fend for himself.

And what had Kinosuke done to repay the favor? Vented his personal frustrations in a string of petty insults that he hadn't even dared to say to the man's face.

Kinosuke was the self-centered prick if anyone was. He was bitching constantly without helping solve any problem, shirking his responsibilities with Kotarō because the kid irritated him, ignoring everyone's advice and setting up a class at an hour when nobody would come, and then pushing to keep that class going with just the one student because he wanted to fuck that student.

Shit. He covered his face with his hands. He'd actually made out with one of his students. In the dojo. What the fuck had he been thinking?

He almost laughed at the lame, unintended pun, but he didn't think it was that funny after all. In fact, it was one of the worst blunders in his whole fucking life.

If Brendan had been a stranger he'd met in a bar, now he would have been comparing casual sex with women and with men—maybe even wondering why it had taken him so long to try it with guys. But no. Brendan was a fucking student, and Kinosuke should have acted like the true sensei he pretended to be and kept a clear distance from his only student worth the name.

The problem was, even knowing it had been one of his worst blunders ever, he still couldn't stop replaying it in his mind and wanting to make far worse mistakes of the same kind as soon as humanly possible.

"Kuso gaijin," he repeated, thinking about the two Americans and the way each of them went about making Kinosuke's life miserable.

Kenshin-san was avoiding him, or rather, he was avoiding everyone, hiding behind his desk all day and most of the night, his woolgathering so pronounced now that he sometimes looked like one of those living-statue dudes who would only move if you deposited some coins at their feet. And that wasn't exactly improving the boss's cranky mood.

As for the other gaijin, Kinosuke wished Brendan did avoid him. But no. The irritating redhead had showed up the next class, right on the same day one of the usual slackers had decided to make an appearance, forcing Kinosuke's control to its limits. Not that his control was that good on a normal day, anyway, but having both to rein in his temper at the constant mistakes of one student and to rein in his lust at the constant sex reminder the other student represented had kept him so strung-up that he'd stormed out of the dojo five minutes before his time to avoid breaking his bokken on some redhead's skull.

And to top things off, when he'd gone back to retrieve his sandals, he'd found a carefully folded piece of paper in one of them, with a telephone number and a "call me" written in big block letters as if Kinosuke had some kind of learning disability.

His first reaction had been to crumple the paper and fling it as far away from him as he could manage, but then he saw in his mind's eye the exact moment when Brendan's hakama slipped down those toned legs and exposed an incredible view, perfect abs leading the eye to a shockingly red bush of curly hair nestling a hard, flushed, thick cock. And then he'd forgotten all about his sandals—again—and hurried home to deal with the problem under his own hakama.

Shit. It had only taken a few strokes for him to shoot all over the place, his nerve endings still remembering what it felt like to hold that muscled body against his own, to guide Brendan's hands and make him touch himself, to see how the man surrendered to him, moaning for him, moving with him, coming like a ton of bricks with Kinosuke's cock pressing against his hole. And Brendan's mouth. *Fuck*. That had been even more incredible, the way that strong, competitive, smug bastard had sunk to his knees and blown Kinosuke as if he'd been starved, deep-throating him as no one else ever had, swallowing Kinosuke's come as if it were the yummiest treat.

So now he had the phone number saved in his cell memory, and every other minute he thought about calling Brendan. It had almost become an itch—he desperately needed to scratch it, and he only refrained because the irritation might get even worse if he actually heard that suggestive voice on the other side of the line.

He paced all the length of his living room, pretending not to look at the phone sitting on the low coffee table. He should grow a pair and go talk to Kenshin-san, apologize to him and then to the boss, and maybe even own up to his failure with the afternoon class.

Yeah, he should do a lot of things, but he must have left the responsible side of his brain back in Japan.

"O'Farrihy."

Shit. Even answering the phone the man sounded smug. Sexy like hell, but smug all the same.

"You said to call you," Kinosuke barked, sounding peevish even to his own ears. And of course, there was fucking laughter coming from Brendan's side.

"Technically, I *wrote* it, but I'm glad you called anyway."

Technically. If Brendan got any more irritating he'd be contagious.

"Kinosuke? You still there?"

He rolled his eyes. "Yeah. What did you want?"

"Hmm. Where to begin—"

Kinosuke huffed his impatience, but it didn't even occur to him that he could end the call with just the press of a button. "I should cancel that class," he mumbled, his brain somehow making the connection between Brendan and the mess his life had suddenly become.

"Don't cancel it." Brendan sounded dead serious and too much fucking imperative for Kinosuke's taste, like the soldier he'd always suspected the man was or had been some time in the past.

"Why not? You think JAL pays us to spread Japanese culture or something?"

Brendan chuckled. "Don't get mad at me, Sensei. I can see why keeping a class with such low attendance may not be wise—"

"Wise?" Kinosuke snorted. "It's financial suicide, and Kenshin-san does too much for us already, I can't—" He shut his mouth abruptly. Why was he giving Brendan so much information? For all he knew, the man could be a serial killer, or an undercover cop, or—worse still—a journalist after the story that would make his career.

"Okay, I understand," Brendan said. "I just wanted you to know that I'm ready to pay more if it means you'll go on teaching me. I really like your classes." There was a pause, and then Brendan added as an afterthought, "And not because of... or not *just* because of... I mean—"

"Oh, for fuck's sake," Kinosuke cut in, "stop mumbling and call things by their name. We made out like two horny dogs; that's it, and that's all. It was a big mistake and won't happen again, so if what you're saying is that you're willing to pay more to get that extra bit of entertainment on the side, just go to a fucking host club and leave the dojo alone."

Silence followed his tirade, and Kinosuke started thinking he'd gone overboard, as he always did. What happened had been as much his own fault as Brendan's, and it wasn't very fair to dump all the responsibility on the guy. Kinosuke was the sensei, after all.

"It wasn't a mistake," Brendan said, so softly that Kinosuke almost didn't hear him.

He shifted from foot to foot. What on earth was he supposed to say to that?

"Maybe it wasn't the right place," Brendan went on, more forcefully now, "but you looked so down that I couldn't help myself. And I won't apologize for something I don't regret at all."

Of course he wouldn't. Smug bastard. "It won't happen again," Kinosuke said, trying to sound as authoritative as a true sensei should.

"No, it won't," Brendan agreed, and Kinosuke couldn't help feeling a little disappointed at his quick acceptance. Damn the man. He didn't regret it, but he wasn't ready to fight for it. "Not in the dojo, at least."

Kinosuke opened his mouth and closed it again. That was exactly the answer he wanted, but why the fuck did it irritate him so much?

"Can't we do this face-to-face?" Brendan had the cheek to add. "I'm dying to feel that long cock of yours filling me, and I don't want any cloth between us this time."

Shit. Americans were so shameless. How could Brendan say those things on the phone, just as if he were talking about grocery shopping? Except grocery shopping wouldn't send Kinosuke's blood rushing south like a furious mountain river after a storm.

Usually Kinosuke would have glared, but since the effect would be wasted right now, he opted for barking into the phone. "And what the fuck makes you think I'd want to put my... I'd want to... fucking do that?"

He cursed under his breath. He couldn't even repeat the words. And the little shit wasn't saying anything, but damn if Kinosuke couldn't hear him smirk.

He was about to express his opinion about rude Americans in no uncertain terms when the door to the backyard slid open with a crash and a flustered Tachibana popped his head into his living room.

"*Kuso!*" He almost jumped out of his skin, his heart slamming against his chest like a spooked horse. "Why the fuck don't you knock?"

Tachibana looked at him as if he'd gone crazy. "I heard you talk, so I figured you were with someone."

And the man probably thought that made perfect sense. Kinosuke hoped he hadn't exactly heard his words, but he couldn't control the heat spreading all over his face anyway. *Shit.* He hated feeling ashamed. And when he felt ashamed, he couldn't control the anger at his own stupidity. "I'm on the phone, you blockhead."

Tachibana didn't even blink at either his yell or his insult. He just asked, "You seen Kotarō?"

"I haven't seen Kotarō, and what the fuck has it got to do with—" The door closed with another crash before he had even finished speaking, and Kinosuke needed to take two or seven deep breaths to stop from doing something rash.

"Hmm. You sound so sexy when you're mad" came the voice through the phone still plastered to his ear.

Now he was going to have to kill someone, or fuck someone through the mattress—he really didn't care which. "How do I get to your place?" he growled.

CHAPTER 18

IT BURNED. He was coughing and something was coming out of his mouth, burning all the way up from his lungs like boiling acid and pouring out as this pinkish stuff that looked like the froth on top of a strawberry milkshake.

"It's okay. You're going to be fine."

Someone was there. The words didn't quite register, but knowing someone was close calmed him, even though he felt cold and dizzy and couldn't get enough air no matter how much he gasped for breath.

"That's it, keep breathing. The ambulance will be here any minute."

He coughed some more and blinked at some shiny object coming close to him and then moving away. He heard a ripping sound, but the voice kept talking over it and he felt safe, something warm enveloping him, hands moving up and down his back, the cold so deep in his bones that it was mostly the contact that comforted him.

"See? You're already breathing better. You're doing good."

He now saw the sand under the skin of his arm, the arm his head was resting on as if he'd just been taking a nap on the beach. The problem was that at the end of his arm was his hand, and it looked like the hand of one of those zombie dudes that gave you the creeps in the movies, all bluish and with a gaping wound in the middle that didn't bleed in spite of looking red and angry. He must be dead, then, if he wasn't bleeding.

"I guess you cut yourself with the board and freaked out. Those fins can be a bitch, they're so sharp."

He'd never been bright to begin with, but now it seemed his brain couldn't do more than one thing at a time, so he heard the voice but didn't quite get what it said, and then each time it stopped talking he kind of understood one word or two, but then he got distracted by his eyes showing him images he had to understand too. It could have been annoying if he had felt something apart from the cold and the burn in his chest and throat.

"It's a good thing the water has kept you this cold or you'd be bleeding buckets. And I bet it doesn't even hurt. Jesus. Those firefighters are taking their sweet time. Where the hell are they?"

Now the voice was talking again, and he didn't get much of what it said because he was looking at all that tanned skin and then at the face that didn't look like anyone he knew and yet was looking down at him as if they were old buddies. But his brain must be playing tricks, because one moment the man looked warmly at him, and then he looked away with something like a glare, as if the guy was very angry at someone who wasn't even there.

"*Mierda de bomberos.* It's always the same shit. You risk your life, and there's nobody there for you when you get hurt. They just wait till all they need to do is send the guy with the body bags."

The man sounded so angry, and yet the hands were back on him, trying to warm him, to sooth him, so gentle and caring that they seemed to belong to a different person. Maybe there were more people there, though all he could see as he lay on his side coughing now and then was this tanned, black-haired guy and the empty beach behind him.

"You don't worry about anything. If those show-offs don't make it here in less than a minute, I'll carry you to the ER myself."

They were probably the biggest eyes he'd ever seen—the man's eyes—brown and warm in a face that somehow looked too thin to contain huge eyes like those. The rest of his body was thin too, muscles and tendons showing easily, as if someone had peeled off some layers of him and stopped inches away from the bone. Maybe the guy was dead, too, beach zombies the two of them—just your regular surfer dead.

"Hey, hey. No choking on me now," the man said as Kotarō tried to laugh and breathe at the same time. Knowing hands lifted his head this way, turned it slightly the other way, and he breathed easily again. He wanted to say thank you, but the man kept talking as he rubbed Kotarō's back. "That's it. No need to panic. You have nothing broken, and you weren't under for long, so I guess there's not much water left inside you. They'll have to check anyway, but you'll see, it doesn't take long—you'll be in and out of the ER in a flash."

He heard something behind him, and the muscles on the man's arm tensed visibly.

"About time you showed up. The kid is freezing." There it was again, the anger, and now the people the man was angry at were really there, kneeling around him, taking away the warm cloth he was wrapped in, touching him and moving him as if he was something the waves had thrown on the beach. And he was suddenly afraid, his brain trying to tell him there was some reason why he should fear the strangers, though he only had the man's anger to go by.

"Step aside, sir."

The man moved as if to stand and Kotarō freaked out, his zombie hand grabbing that thin, tanned wrist, his throat making a strange sound like a mauled cat.

"You know the boy?"

Those huge eyes were looking at him now, and he saw something fierce in them, something that should have been frightening but wasn't, something that rang some kind of bell in his addled brain and told him he'd be safe as long as the man stayed there.

"Yeah. Seen him around my neighborhood."

"Do you know any relative, anyone we can call?"

Now someone placed on him one of those masks he'd worn on his mouth and nose when he had a cold, but this one didn't make everything feel clammy; it felt rather dry and cool, and his only fear was that he couldn't tell the man to stay. Not that he'd been able to say much of anything before he had the mask on, but still.

"No, I just moved in. I don't know anyone here. But I'll go with him, stay until he can speak for himself."

"He might be confused for some time. There's no need for you to come. I was just asking in case you knew his family."

Kotarō wasn't getting much of the conversation, as if they were speaking in another language, but he got the tension in the man's body, muscles straining under his own zombie fingers where they grabbed the man's wrist. *Please, please, please, don't leave me with these strangers.*

Sure, the man was a stranger too, or Kotarō would have remembered that face with the big brown eyes, but considering how muddled he felt right now, he only had his instincts to trust, and somehow they told him the man would look out for him.

"I'll go with him. Nobody should be alone after something like that."

After something like that. He heard the words and felt kind of dirty. Something bad had happened. Well, he was lying on the beach with an oxygen mask and a couple of dudes lifting him onto a gurney, so of course something must have gone awfully wrong, but somehow he sensed nearly drowning wasn't the whole shit. And weirdly enough, the man spoke as if he knew it too.

Now the man was walking beside the gurney and gently prying Kotarō's fingers open from around his wrist. "It's okay. I won't leave you alone, but they're gonna have to take a look at that wound."

The wound. Right. Now it even hurt a little, but he didn't want to let go. He didn't even know the man's name, so how was he to call him if he needed him?

The man was so strong Kotarō couldn't fight him—his cold fingers removed one by one from the warm, bony wrist, but then the world tilted a little, and he was pushed inside the belly of an ambulance and another stranger was holding his wounded hand away from him.

Right when he started to freak out, the man caught his other hand and squeezed it.

"Shhh. It's okay. I'm here."

Then the ambulance started moving, and he felt tired all of a sudden. He'd been in an ambulance before, and it'd felt awful then, too, because something bad had happened, but there'd been someone beside him that time, too, and it hadn't turned out so bad in the end. So maybe it'd be all right if he slept a little.

He squeezed the man's hand to make sure it was still there, and the man whispered something he didn't understand, something that made him feel safe all the same as he closed his eyes and drifted to sleep.

"*Duerme tranquilo*, Kotarō."

CHAPTER 19

BRENDAN HAD never done anything this stupid without being drunk—or under orders. One word from Kinosuke and information had poured out of him as if he had no wetware between the bone in his skull and the muscles in his mouth. Nothing there at all, it seemed, just empty space to conduct his master's voice and produce the appropriate Pavlovian reflex.

Shit. What was wrong with him? Sure this job was a bummer, but it wasn't that different from everything they'd dumped on him since his discharge, except for the piddling little fact that he had a crush on one of the targets. The problem was—apart from the obvious breach of professional etiquette—he'd never had a crush in his whole Irish life, not even when he was a drooling teenager, so he really had no clue about the whole business of getting things working when his dick was in charge of all the thinking.

"Focus, O'Farrihy," he said to the silent house.

He checked his watch. With that powerful Honda bike, Kinosuke would cover the distance between the dojo in Upper Manoa and Big B's single-family house near Harding Avenue in less than ten minutes, fifteen if traffic on the H-1 freeway was running slow. And then he'd be knocking on his door, the door to the place from where the surveillance on the dojo's inhabitants was being conducted.

The best strategy would be to take Kinosuke out of there as soon as he arrived, but that was completely out of the question—his cock would start salivating precome as soon as those black eyes glared at him, and then there'd be no blood left for his brain to improvise.

He checked his watch again. With no time to come up with a plan B, he had to go straight to damage control.

His legs took him to the den at a run, and he looked around critically. If it had resembled a war room before Bobcat's arrival, now it only lacked a sand table with a scale model of the target area to be completely operative.

His man had taken to the job with the efficiency of an intelligence specialist, adding to the previous equipment with his own upgraded laptop, two flip charts, assorted high-tech video and audio equipment, Japanese dictionaries, and a superzoom digital camera that had the old corkboard overflowing with new and ultradetailed pictures of Matsunaga and company.

Brendan groaned. It would take him hours to put everything away, not to mention the tantrum Bobcat might throw if he so much as displaced a pen from its current position. As far as his reactions were concerned, the Cuban was still in the war zone, and when you were under fire, you had to have all your gear in its right place to get to it before they blew you to high heaven.

"Okay," he mumbled under his breath. "If you can't patch the crack in the hull, seal off the damaged compartment."

The door to the den had no lock, so he had to find a way to keep it closed from the inside. He eyed the heavy rustic chairs as he patted his pants pockets for the house keys—it wouldn't do to lock himself out of the place, though he usually left the kitchen door open during the day.

He was moving a chair against the door when he heard the distinctive rumble of a bike outside.

"Shit. That was fast."

He wedged the back of the chair between the doorknob and the wood panel, sat on the windowsill and flung his legs outside as the purr of the engine came to a halt. Considering the length of Kinosuke's strides, Brendan had about ten seconds before his sensei was pounding on the door—fifteen if the yakuza was feeling less brazen than usual and had worn a helmet.

He stood on the backyard, stripping as fast as he could, and threw the discarded clothes and boots through the window he'd come out of, grimacing when he heard the jangle of his keys as they hit the floor of the den.

"Fucking brilliant, sailor," he muttered. "Just pray the back door's not locked."

He ran buck naked to the kitchen door, breathing his relief as it swung open at his push. He strode to the sink and put his head under the tap to get his hair dripping and shook himself like a wet dog, splashing water all over himself and the checkered black-and-white linoleum.

The knocks came right then, so he simply grabbed a towel from the laundry hamper and wrapped it around his waist, hoping the terry cloth didn't have any suspicious stains or smelled too musty.

"Hi, Sensei," he said as he leaned against the front door, trying to look nonchalant. It worked for about half a second, and then he had to swallow hard and fight to keep his cool.

Sweet Jesus. If Kinosuke looked fine in his fighting uniform, in street clothes he was a walking wet dream. Somehow Brendan had expected the classic biker outfit, but Kinosuke seemed to be past that stage and into something simpler, probably intended to look a little bit more sensei-respectable—with a dress shirt instead of a T-shirt, slim jeans instead of the painted-on, skinny variety—but in fact managing to appear cocksure and in-your-face hustler sexy. Must be the way he left too many buttons undone for that black shirt to be respectable, or the way those lean hips pushed forward to give a perfect view of a rather tacky dragon belt buckle, but the overall effect was mouthwatering in spite of—or because of—the trashiness.

Kinosuke's eyes burned a path from Brendan's toes up to his suddenly dry lips and stopped there, as if his sensei wouldn't meet his eyes. The man was going to drive Brendan crazy with his weird mixture of cockiness and shame, especially since he could never anticipate what would embarrass the yakuza the next time.

"Why don't you come in," Brendan said, trying to sound flippant. "I don't want to give the neighbors a show."

Those black eyes did glare at him now. "Then don't open the door naked."

So there it was. An alleged gangster worried about the neighbors' opinion. Geez. That was… cute.

He turned to let Kinosuke in—and to hide the grin he was sure his sensei wouldn't appreciate. He couldn't help it, though. These days Brendan was smiling so much that the muscles around his mouth were getting sore.

The door closed behind him, and he leaned back a little to appreciate the view in front of him. Kinosuke stood there, watching the living room with his hands in his pockets, the gesture both making his shoulders hunch and his jeans pull at that tight little ass, once again giving the contradictory impression of a bashful yet streetwise kid. Or maybe it wasn't that contradictory, Brendan thought; maybe only joining the yakuza had given Kinosuke something to brag about, something to make him walk proud when he was only the son of the son of a blue-collar worker or someone even lower on the social scale.

Either way, Kinosuke looked too foreign in that all-American living room with its overstuffed couch, big TV screen, auxiliary tables cluttered with all kinds of junk, and gaudy curtains on the sunny windows. He looked out of place, his lean figure appearing small and vulnerable all of a sudden, and Brendan's chest constricted with an ache he wasn't used to.

He reached out to touch Kinosuke's arm, feeling the muscles tense in his grip and then loosen as Brendan stepped forward and pulled the slender body against him.

"Hey," he whispered softly into a delicate ear, smiling as that simple contact made Kinosuke shiver.

"Shut up," Kinosuke said, swatting his arm without much intent.

Now that made him chuckle, the urge to ruffle Kinosuke's hair so strong that he squeezed the body in his arms really hard to stop his fingers from reaching his sensei's black mane.

Kinosuke groaned, but it didn't sound like a complaint, especially when those lean hips rolled back a little as if to remind Brendan's cock what was what. And his cock took due notice, trying to get to that sweet ass in spite of the layers of fabric between them.

"Want the fifty-cent tour?" Brendan said, his voice so husky already that no way the question could be mistaken for an actual invitation to see the house.

Kinosuke's head bobbed up and down just as he said, "No." It was hilarious—and extremely cute—how the man struggled to put up a proper sensei front when his natural exuberance always got the best of him.

"Okay," Brendan said, trying to hide his smile, "let's go straight to the bedroom. Unless you want to make out on the couch first?"

There it was again, his sex-induced stupidity. Why did he even suggest it, when Bobcat could return any minute? At least a closed bedroom door would give him time to run interference until he found a safe way to extricate Kinosuke from the house.

He nuzzled Kinosuke's inviting neck and tried to cover his faux pas. "Or we could make out in the bedroom, be already there when we need to get rid of some clothes."

"You already got rid of your clothes, Brendan."

For a moment he had the wild notion that Kinosuke somehow knew what he'd been doing, and he let out a chuckle that sounded false even to his own ears. He had to calm down and stop being paranoid; all he needed was to use Kinosuke's sense of shame to take him behind a locked door, and then everything would be all right.

CHAPTER 20

BRENDAN LET out a weird laugh, his body tensing where it touched Kinosuke's. What now? Was the man regretting inviting him over? Did it annoy him that Kinosuke had mentioned his nudity? Well, duh, he shouldn't wear a towel if it bugged him so much when people noticed—and with a body like that, all pale and ripped, people were bound to notice.

"Yeah, I wanted to get rid of the grime before you arrived, but I was counting on putting some fresh clothes back on. Guess your bike's faster than me."

Shit. He knew he should have taken his time, dragged out the ride so as not to appear eager.

"Come on, let's go to my bedroom," Brendan said, stroking his arms. "I don't want my roommate coming back and getting an eyeful."

"Roommate?" He knew it came out as a squawk, but Kinosuke couldn't help it. And the worst of it was not knowing what bothered him the most: the risk of being found in a compromising position with a male student of his, or the fact that Brendan lived with someone.

The American must have felt his muscles going all tight, because he started stroking Kinosuke's belly as if he were a dog in need of petting.

"Rents here are impossible if you don't share," Brendan explained. "But don't worry. Bobcat keeps mostly to himself; he won't bother us even if he shows up, which I'm not sure he will."

Bobcat? What kind of name was that? He started moving forward, not even knowing where he was headed but wanting to put some distance between them and the absent Catman. At least it was satisfying to notice that Brendan was in a hurry too, judging by the way he took Kinosuke's hand and pulled in the direction of a closed door to their left.

Kinosuke almost laughed hysterically when it occurred to him that it was the first time in his life that someone had held his hand like that. When he'd messed around with girls, it'd been too uncool for his ilk to be caught holding hands like the lovebirds in *shōjo* manga, and now it was more than a little strange to feel callused fingers wrapping around his. Not bad strange, though. He'd never noticed Brendan's hands were this big, but it felt nice that they were, that the one holding Kinosuke's engulfed it in a warm, strong embrace.

They passed the closed door and went down a small hallway with two more doors, and Kinosuke stopped suddenly when he saw the elaborate kanji decorating every stretch of wall between the doors.

Brendan laughed nervously again. "Bobcat loves Japanese calligraphy, but he has no idea what the words mean. I just hope we don't have grocery lists on our walls."

Kinosuke could tell it was something about a mountain and a sword, but the rest was this convoluted gibberish he couldn't read for shit. He wasn't going to admit that in front of Brendan, though. "Looks like something from the *Gorin no Sho*," he said, making Brendan wait for the translation. "You know, Musashi's *Book of Five Rings*."

"Uh-huh."

He fought the smirk that tried to reach his lips. The smug bastard couldn't admit he had no idea who Musashi was. Funny, though, that the two Americans sharing the house would be so fond of Japanese things.

Kinosuke frowned. Brendan hadn't mentioned the Catman was white too. What if he liked Japanese calligraphy because he was of Japanese descent? His hand tightened instinctively around Brendan's. He didn't want to be the other Japanese in Brendan's life, especially not if the roommate was more of a bedroom-mate than someone he shared living costs with. Brendan hadn't said anything in that sense either, but he did use a pet name for the other man; wasn't that some sort of clue?

"What are you pouting about?" Brendan said, pulling at his hand.

"I'm not—" The rest of his angry words were swallowed by Brendan's mouth, the kiss so sudden and rough that Kinosuke felt like he was drowning. Brendan must have sensed it, because he let go for a moment, green eyes searching Kinosuke's before he pulled harder and brought Kinosuke's body to press against Brendan's pale skin.

Kinosuke couldn't stop the sound coming out of his throat when Brendan's hardness bumped the crease between his thigh and abdomen, and that sound made Brendan look at him as if there was no one else in the entire world. So maybe he was being stupidly jealous and no other Japanese was in this gorgeous man's life.

He was glad when Brendan kissed him again, because he didn't want to dwell on either the fact that he was jealous or the other, even more troubling notion, that he'd considered the redheaded, freckled man gorgeous.

"Bedroom," Brendan muttered against his mouth, and Kinosuke tried to nod and reach for those kiss-swollen lips in the same movement, their foreheads butting together with a loud whack.

They both groaned, and the crazy bastard started giggling. "Did anyone ever tell you how hardheaded you are?"

Kinosuke rolled his eyes. "Dork."

Oh shit. That set Brendan to laughing, deep belly laughs shaking his whole frame and making Kinosuke's lips twitch. "What? You didn't think I'd know enough English to insult you?"

Brendan looked at him, his laughter sobering into a smile, and Kinosuke saw something in those eyes that wasn't hunger anymore, something so close to affection that it made Kinosuke nervous.

"Do you know where your bedroom is, or do you have to read the kanji on the wall to guide you?" he asked, hoping to go back to the simple mood of wanting and being wanted, or at least to that other place where they were always snapping at each other.

The smile went from tender to wicked in a second. "Yeah, Sensei. I know where my own bedroom is. I'm just considering if I should let a foulmouthed Japanese into my private quarters."

"I'm an American citizen," he didn't mention he wasn't even a resident yet, but he was trying, wasn't he? "And my mouth is not foul."

He guessed that didn't come out right, because the bastard was laughing again, but then he looked at Kinosuke's mouth and those eyes went impossibly dark, pupils dilating as if the man was high on something. "No, it's not foul at all."

The tip of a pink tongue came out to wet those lips, and Kinosuke found himself mesmerized by the small movement, so much so that his fingers followed his eyes to trace Brendan's lower lip. Kinosuke made a sound close to a whimper when his fingers disappeared inside that mouth, the suction traveling straight from his hand to his trapped cock and making it jerk against the zipper.

"*Kuso*," he spat, and Brendan hummed around his fingers, the vibrations turning into a shiver that shook his body from where it was attached to Brendan down to his shoe-covered toes.

Shit. He hadn't even taken his shoes off. Brendan was going to think he was a country bumpkin. Or maybe not, the way those strong hands grabbed two of his belt loops and pulled him forward just as Brendan walked back, the lean body slamming against a door and pushing it open. The suction on Kinosuke's fingers didn't stop even as they stepped inside what must be a bedroom—Kinosuke couldn't for the life of him take his eyes off those sexy lips to check the room out—and hungry leaf-colored irises met his every time he followed the pattern of freckles up Brendan's straight nose and back down to the reddened lips that were driving him crazy.

He heard the lock clicking shut and couldn't take it anymore. He pulled his fingers out of that luscious mouth with a loud pop that made him moan before his mouth crashed against Brendan's.

The man tasted like no one he'd kissed before, maybe even like nothing he'd tasted before. Must be the mainland factor, what with all the weird foodstuff Americans fed on. Or maybe it was something more Brendan-specific. Redhead flavor—he bet one of those shave ice places had already come up with the idea.

"What's so funny?" Brendan asked, a smile in his voice.

"Your taste." Kinosuke watched in amusement as one red brow went up, round eyes narrowing into slits.

"What about it?"

He tried not to laugh, letting his tongue lap along the seam of Brendan's lips. "Hmm. It's different."

"Different how?" Brendan was trying to sound nonchalant, but he didn't fool Kinosuke. The man needed to come out on top in everything he did, so he must be worried his breath stank or something.

"I'm not sure. Have to taste some mor—"

That mouth closed on his before he finished the sentence, Brendan's tongue pushing past his lips and exploring his mouth thoroughly, stroking here, prodding there, swirling around Kinosuke's tongue and pulling at it, one hand holding the back of his head as if for the leverage required in deep drilling.

Competitive bastard. Not that Kinosuke was complaining; he wasn't much for the sweet and slow himself, but being around Brendan was like living in a permanent typhoon season without a weather forecast to rely on—it could get scary sometimes. And Kinosuke had loved scary since his mother told him not to stick his chubby fingers in the power sockets.

He reached out for the towel around Brendan's waist and yanked. Brendan groaned into his mouth, the press of that hard body against Kinosuke's actually keeping the towel standing between the two of them like some kind of international border.

Now it was Kinosuke's turn to groan. He wanted the towel gone but his hands had found Brendan's perfect bubble butt and wouldn't let go for anything; his mouth was too dependent on those sharp kisses to unlock their lips; and his cock felt too fine rubbing against Brendan's through the layers of fabric to be tempted into moving away, so he opted for a small wiggle of his hips that had the terry cloth sliding inch after painstaking inch down Brendan's muscled thighs.

Finally all that naked skin was exposed, and Kinosuke dug his fingers deeper into Brendan's ass to pull the American flush against him, a strangled, sexy noise leaving the man's throat as Kinosuke's jeans rasped his sensitive cock.

Fuck. Now Kinosuke needed to see, no two ways about it. He took a cursory look over Brendan's shoulder to find the bed and pressed forward, his hands only leaving their grip on Brendan's ass to shove the American down onto the mattress.

Brendan gasped in surprise, but Kinosuke was again reminded that the American must have had some serious training, because his body reacted instinctively as soon as it hit the bed, muscles bunching up to help him bounce back and move away the compromised position. If Kinosuke had been an attacker, he was sure those hands would have been at his throat in the blink of an eye. As things were, Brendan was again standing in front of him, studying his face with something close to concern.

It was an awkward moment, and Kinosuke felt guilty, as if he had uncovered something he wasn't supposed to know. "*Sumimasen.*" He shook his head in frustration— he always reverted to Japanese when he felt bad. "Sorry. I just wanted to see."

Brendan frowned. "See what?"

He made an exasperated gesture. "What do you think I wanted to see? The view from your window?"

Brendan blinked. Americans seemed to be on the slow side sometimes. "Oh. Right."

He rolled his eyes, and Brendan—of course—started laughing.

"Okay, look your fill," said the crazy bastard before he spread his arms and took a back dive onto the bed without even glancing first to see where he'd be landing.

Kinosuke felt his stomach lurch, his hands automatically reaching out as if to protect a child from a bad fall. When Brendan bounced harmlessly on the bed, Kinosuke felt completely stupid, anger making his arousal deflate faster than a doggie downer.

Then, as usual, he felt stupid for getting angry and tried to cover it with a click of his tongue and a long-suffering "*Mendō kusai na—*"

Brendan smiled at him with a wide, eye-crinkling grin that made Kinosuke's insides feel weird, and his strong arms beckoned Kinosuke to join Brendan in his bed. "C'mere and explain to me what that means."

He crossed his arms in front of his chest, trying not to pay too much attention to Brendan's incredibly rosy nipples, or the patterns of light ginger fuzz that created two inverted triangles on his chest and belly, or the flexing of muscle as his legs spread in invitation, or the thick vein running the full length of his shaft.

"Please, Sensei." Brendan was still smiling, but the real pleading in his voice could not be mistaken, his arms held patiently open for Kinosuke to take.

He swallowed, his cock perking right up. The way Brendan obviously wanted him, begged for him, made Kinosuke feel powerful, easy in his skin for the first time in months. This was no weak American getting a kick out of Kinosuke's badass yakuza image; this was a strong man who believed Kinosuke could teach him something, a man whose respect was even more valuable because, even if he'd known about them, Brendan wouldn't have given a shit about clan badges or ranks.

He toed off his shoes and pulled his shirt over his head, enjoying Brendan's undivided attention as those green eyes followed his every move. When his fingers fumbled with his pants button and zipper, Brendan finally lowered his arms, and Kinosuke felt a jolt of arousal as he saw those hands move to fondle Brendan's cock and balls almost distractedly, the man's eyes fixed on Kinosuke, expectant and hungry, waiting for him to take the lead as no one ever had in a long, long time.

CHAPTER 21

BRENDAN WATCHED in fascination as Kinosuke's clothes gave way to smooth, tanned skin, tattooed dragons coming to life in the inky storm raging all over the lean body.

His sensei had gone from pouting mightily to stripping as if his life depended on it in mere seconds, and Brendan couldn't say he understood what went through that complicated mind to provoke either reaction, but he certainly approved of the progression.

When Kinosuke started working on his pants to undo them, Brendan couldn't help touching his cock to sooth the ache, precome already lubricating the glide of his fingers. Geez. He hadn't been this ready to explode since—well, since the day he'd dared to touch his sensei for the first time. Before that, he couldn't exactly remember, because nothing seemed this real, this intense without Kinosuke in his line of sight.

It was like finally acknowledging an addiction when you'd thought you were just fooling around with the stuff, just trying out some novelty that would wear off as fast as any other of the stupid things you'd tried just to feel blood rushing through your veins. Now Brendan knew he'd reached the point where he couldn't choose, where he couldn't say no if he was offered another dose. And pretty soon he wouldn't be able to wait for it to be offered.

Kinosuke pushed his pants and underwear down and stepped out of them with the pushy bravado Brendan had seen in many a locker room, hips thrust forward in some kind of challenge, shoulders squared, chin held high as if silently asking, "What the hell are you looking at?"

It should have been funny, especially when Kinosuke fixed him with a beady stare and said, "Got stuff?" almost like some gangbanger asking around for dope. But it wasn't funny at all.

Kinosuke was standing right there in front of him, the glorious tattoo making his nakedness even more sexy, as if he were dressed in a provocatively transparent outfit, his eagerness clear in his dark eyes, his cock flushed, jutting out of a raspy cushion of thick black hair, his posturing only a defensive gesture that made Brendan's heart press against his ribs, because he understood the fear, the insecurity that plagued you when you wanted something you shouldn't want, when you wanted it so badly your whole body ached with it.

Brendan squeezed the base of his shaft to the point of pain, the urge to come receding enough for him to answer with a more or less steady voice.

"Sure. It's in here," he said, turning to reach the nightstand drawer and belatedly remembering he kept his gun right there. It seemed to be chronic, his Kinosuke-induced fogginess.

The groan he heard might have been his own, because now he was all stretched and pulling at the drawer and couldn't pretend the condoms were somewhere else.

Fortunately it was Kinosuke groaning, and as he looked over his shoulder, he saw those black eyes glued to his ass.

Christ. That look made him feel like a stud, almost made him forget he didn't really know Kinosuke, didn't know how a temperamental yakuza would react if he caught a glimpse of Brendan's semiautomatic, the flashy fourth-generation Glock 22 RTF that Craig had given to him in a show of considerate present-choosing. Yeah, it must have taken him two minutes of his busy time to make the connection between ex-military and gun lover—pity Brendan wasn't really into changing his tried-and-true gun every time the manufacturer came up with a new model, design improvements or no, and even more of a pity Brendan was so stupidly considerate as to actually use the new gun just because he'd been taught to show appreciation.

He pushed down his anger, forcing his breath to go deeper, making his jaw unclench. Nobody had forced him to stay with Craig, and nobody was forcing him to risk his job, his reputation, and maybe even his life just to see what it was like to be fucked by a yakuza.

As if someone had been watching over him, the landline started ringing right then. It could give Brendan the perfect excuse to ask for a rain check and save him from the worst mistake of his life, especially since it probably was Bobcat calling—the man was so paranoid that he used the landline because he could check it every day for bugs.

When Brendan didn't pick up on the second ring, Kinosuke's cell suddenly chirped from his discarded pants on the floor, a distorted folksy melody harmonizing as best it could with the other more traditional ring from Brendan's phone.

The universe seemed to be conspiring to give them both a final chance, and when Kinosuke's eyes met his for a moment, Brendan fought the urge to close them. He didn't want to see the mixture of strength and insecurity in those eyes, didn't want to see the hunger and the shame, didn't want to be offered another proof that this young man with all his secrets was more of an open book when it came to his feelings than Craig with his out-front rules of engagement.

He held Kinosuke's eyes and allowed all the messages they were sending to sink in, the warning tingle in the back of his head growing into a full bell-ringing alarm as loud as the phone chorus itself. That, he understood; controlled fear, a warrior's best friend.

This stupid, bird-dogging job had been dulling his senses to the point of recklessness, but that was about to change right now, because now Brendan was afraid, and his fear had nothing to do with losing everything he'd thought he valued—his new career, his reputation as a solid professional, the esteem of the men he'd served with. Now was the time to make a decision, once and for all choose between what was expected of him and what he really wanted.

Both phones were still ringing when he turned further to his side and rose on his elbows to reach out, his hand bypassing the receiver and grabbing the night table drawer pull instead. He knew the bulk of his upper body might not be enough to obstruct Kinosuke's vision of the drawer contents unless his sensei had something else as his primary target.

He shifted a little until his belly was pressed flat against the mattress—aware of the full view of his backside the posture offered—and spread his legs wider to leave nothing out of sight. And then he didn't even need to check whether Kinosuke had his eyes fixed on the provided distraction before he opened the drawer, because he could feel that black stare on his skin like a laser illuminator, though much hotter than any infrared device and accompanied with a low, sexy moan.

The black silhouette of the Glock came into view, its distinctive polymer frame giving the piece a deceptive toylike appearance. Brendan flexed his ass ostensibly, as if he needed the extra push to reach deeper into the nightstand, his fingers grazing the rough gripping surface of the gun before they found the single-use lube packets and the string of condoms beside them.

His heart was hammering away, and yet he almost laughed out loud when he thought the texturized surface of the semi would be great for a condom instead— enhanced sensation guaranteed. But he didn't laugh. The risk he was taking was too big and, as he pushed the drawer closed, he realized it wasn't Kinosuke's unpredictable reactions that made it so, but the fact that, should Kinosuke see the gun, Brendan would have to lie to him.

His job definition had included a healthy dose of deception ever since he'd joined the military, and it wasn't any different now that he still needed to gather intelligence on demand, but somehow Kinosuke's openness made lying to him the worst form of betrayal, and Brendan didn't want to see disappointment in those black eyes.

His sensei didn't seem the trusting kind, either, and everything he did concerning Brendan carried a solid weight of reluctance, as if Kinosuke were fighting his attraction every step of the way. Brendan couldn't help respecting that even more than an easy surrender, maybe because he'd gone from being a sports buff to becoming a soldier with nothing in between to cramp his competitive drive, and didn't give much credit to the things you simply picked up like so much trash.

The Glock finally secure inside the closed drawer, Brendan turned to look at Kinosuke and check for signs that he might have glimpsed anything out of the ordinary. It took a second for his sensei to meet his eyes, and that more than anything else told Brendan his distraction had worked fine—remarkably fine, in fact, judging by the state of Kinosuke's dripping cock or the way those sexy lips were parted, a heavy-lidded stare fixing Brendan in place as it moved back down along his now exposed front.

He swallowed, the loud sound reminding him the phones had stopped ringing.

"You don't have to take that?" he asked just to be polite, his voice so husky it almost sounded like a proposition in itself.

"Huh?"

He chuckled. His sensei didn't even look up from his deep study of Brendan's groin.

"The phone. It could be important," he said, a smile in his voice as he reached out, beckoning Kinosuke closer.

Those lean muscles flexed under the tattoos, and Kinosuke climbed into his bed like a prowling cat, his words totally incongruent as he stalked Brendan. "That was Tachibana's ring tone."

"Uh-huh." Brendan nodded as if he had the faintest idea what Kinosuke was talking about, too distracted by the proximity of all that inked skin, his fingers stretching to finally trace the contours of dragons, clouds, red lines of lightning, and balls of fire. He wondered at the smoothness of it all, as if he'd expected the tattooed skin to feel coarse or at least a little raised, the way Kinosuke shuddered at his touch telling him there was no difference in sensitivity from his side either.

Then his sensei's hands were on him and he forgot everything about phones, jobs, or any other people on the surface of the Earth. He moaned loudly, his legs shifting in restless need, his own hands never stopping their eager exploration.

Kinosuke's fingers seemed fascinated by the hair on his body, and for the first time in his life Brendan was glad he hadn't taken a laser to all his red fuzz. It gave him a myriad of contrasting sensations as Kinosuke alternatively pulled, smoothed, or carded it, his nipples hardening to demand similar attentions, his cock jerking every time Kinosuke played with his pubes, his throat letting out so many sounds that he felt like a spoiled lapdog yipping and whining at his master for more.

And Kinosuke complied, his mouth engaging in sync with his hands, nibbling as fingers pulled, wetting the smoothed down hair, blowing after every pinch, a playful tongue coming out to taste the scar tissue clever hands uncovered here and there, lips sucking to leave a red trail of hickeys on every inch fingers found too naked.

"Sensei—" Brendan croaked, his instincts somehow taking over and making him use the title instead of Kinosuke's name, and the way that raven-haired head came up to search his eyes told him he was right on the money.

Brendan's hands framed Kinosuke's extraordinary face, and he allowed his eyes to show the boil of emotions inside him. "Please, Sensei. I can't wait any longer. I want you in me."

Kinosuke swallowed visibly, the black in his pupils so intense it seemed to overflow and soak everything around them, highlighting the beautiful tilt of his eyes as if he'd traced it with eyeliner. He looked so hungry it hurt to watch him, Brendan's heart fluttering with the knowledge he was offering exactly what this gorgeous man had been starving for—the power that came from trust and trust alone, without the ties of coercion, duty, or fear to bind it into an ugly knot—trust making the reins soft and pliant, just the kind of tool a good leader used to guide his men and bring out the best in them.

This was what Brendan had strived for all his life, what had been snatched off the tip of his hands when his prerogative to decide had been summarily removed in the heat of the battle. Without this power, Brendan felt worthless. His attitude toward his new job was tainted by the awareness of that loss, and the way he'd tried to give himself over to a domineering man like Craig showed he was still trying to find that power even if it was to be used on *him* now he had been deemed unfit to wield it.

And maybe because he was so attuned to the feel of it, he'd taken one look at Matsunaga's household and understood the man had it, that power, and the young Kinosuke stood in his shadow trying to both follow in his steps and find his own way, like a king's son striving to both obey and overthrow the father he admired as much as he resented.

Brendan watched the eyes fixed on him and looked past the obvious hunger to check for something that had been conspicuously absent from Craig's eyes every time they made love—or rather, whenever they engaged in a sweaty exercise of self-assurance on both sides.

It was there all right, in Kinosuke's whole expression, the kind of fear you only feel when you worry about something outside yourself, about somebody whose thoughts, emotions, and well-being take a lot of space in your waking mind. And it made Brendan's chest swell with pride because he was the one bringing that fear out and the one who had the experience to guide Kinosuke through it.

He let his hands follow the curve of Kinosuke's head and continue down his neck to his slender back, pressing slightly to encourage his sensei to sit on his haunches between Brendan's legs. Kinosuke closed his eyes as he complied, reveling in the caress like a large cat.

Christ. The young man was so sensual, so beautiful that Brendan knew he would explode as soon as that long cock touched his body. Still, it didn't matter much since he wasn't trying to show his prowess; this was about Kinosuke, and he had the right to know he could melt Brendan into mush with a single touch—probably a single heated look from those sexy eyes would do it, but Brendan still had *some* pride to keep.

He grabbed the string of condoms and tore the top one's wrapper; then his fingers worked quickly to cover Kinosuke's cock, his touch almost aseptic since any other contact would get him lost in the sensory marvel that was the vein-ridden shaft he now smudged with an unholy amount of lube. It would come in handy, all that lube, if the way Kinosuke kept biting his lower lip was any indication of the pace he would set as soon as Brendan let go of him.

Their eyes met for one moment, and Brendan understood that no matter how eager Kinosuke was, he would always wait for his permission before he moved one single muscle to get closer to Brendan.

God. His sensei looked so unbearably young as he sat there, waiting for a sign, that Brendan had to reach out and wrap his limbs, his whole body around that tender soul, needing to protect him, to offer his battle-hardened self as a buffer against the harsh reality waiting to engulf them and tear them apart.

"Please, Sensei," he begged, feeling Kinosuke's body tremble with need, his young lover's mouth opening to let out a growl before he went at Brendan like a hungry whelp, devouring his mouth as if he couldn't get enough of his taste, digging his fingers into his scalp to hold his head in place, pushing at Brendan with his whole weight until they both fell back against the mattress, and then lifting Brendan's legs as if they were made of a light fabric he could drape over his shoulders with no effort.

"Sensei—" Brendan panted, feeling the tip of Kinosuke's cock press lightly against his hole. "Please, fuck me. Now. Please."

The sound Kinosuke made was lost in the middle of a low, rhythmic thrum that rose from the floor, not so different from the hammering of Brendan's heart if it wasn't for the canned regularity of its artificial beat.

Kinosuke cursed, his hands digging painfully into Brendan's thighs. Brendan was about to say something when the house phone started ringing too.

And then he just couldn't hold back his anger. This was his fucking life. He didn't have to babysit every shell-shocked veteran who came his way, didn't need to learn about the latest escapade of any senator's son, didn't want to entertain any egotistical Washington lawyer in his free time. This right here, this man in his bed, was all he really needed, all he craved with the intensity they'd wiped away from him in the long years of suppressed rage.

"Leave us the fuck alone!" he shouted as if the phone could hear him, his arm swinging as best it could to knock the phone to the floor in a cacophony of plastic and recorded bells.

Kinosuke blinked at him, the strange thrumming ringtone of his cell the only sound in the room until it suddenly stopped, those dark eyes looking at Brendan as if he was seeing him for the first time, as if that outburst had been more revealing than all the time they'd spent together in the dojo. And maybe it was, maybe deep inside Brendan was as choleric as Bobcat, but he'd kept it under so many layers of control that no shrink had been able to diagnose him correctly.

He met Kinosuke's eyes. He was scared to death to lose this young man hovering over him, but he couldn't pretend he was anything other than a roughed-up veteran, a battered old weapon that still would fire if you pulled the trigger. So he just held that dark look, waiting, watching in awe as the expression in Kinosuke's beautiful face went from surprise to something very different, some sort of deep recognition that made the desire in those eyes burn like a gasoline-doused flame, the smooth jaw clenching in a determined gesture, tension spreading all over the coltish limbs, muscles flexing under the tattooed dragons, strong hands grabbing Brendan's ankles and pulling hard, stretching Brendan's legs and lifting his buttocks off the mattress at the same time as Kinosuke thrust forward with all his weight behind him, his cock sliding into Brendan in one single movement.

They both groaned at the same time, Kinosuke's chest pressing against the back of Brendan's raised legs, his breath coming out in harsh pants as he waited for Brendan to adjust to the burn.

Brendan fought the urge to shake his head. Who'd have imagined a yakuza would be such a considerate lover? Not the right time to be considerate, though, because if it wasn't for the small pain, Brendan would have come as soon as that red-hot iron brand filled him, and now his whole body ached with the need to be turned inside out, to be not just touched, or even marked, but thoroughly taken, owned, used without concessions, without the selective sampling he'd been submitted to all his life, everyone picking the parts of him they needed and discarding the rest as ballast they wished they could throw overboard with impunity.

All his life he'd been a one-dimensional cartoon image of himself—the perfect son, the college jock, the elite soldier, the hotshot security agent, the trophy lover. Nobody had wanted the whole picture, nobody had taken the time to scrape the outer layers to check for rust underneath. But maybe he had a chance now, maybe this man who knew nothing about him would want to know it all, maybe the youthful intensity that had made Kinosuke a spitfire yakuza would pass through the walls that kept Brendan's life compartmentalized in tidy little boxes and blow away all the false cardboard identities.

He bent his knees a little, forcing Kinosuke to lower himself closer, his face bracketed by Brendan's legs, their eyes meeting for a moment until Brendan reached out to grab Kinosuke's ass and pull as if there were still any room left between them. Kinosuke closed his eyes, letting out what sounded like a whimper, his face strained with the obvious struggle to hold back.

Brendan felt a smug smile reaching his lips when he saw the effect he was having on his young lover, but as he let the smile show, he wasn't surprised to feel it turn into something uncharacteristically maudlin.

"You can move, Sensei," he said, his voice filled with a compounded mix of emotions he wasn't in the mood to disentangle. "I'm not going to break."

Kinosuke nodded in what Brendan was learning to be a very Japanese way of making agreement a visible, physical thing, and then he felt the lean muscles under his hands flex as Kinosuke pulled out of him, the sudden emptiness making Brendan groan and strain to keep his fingers relaxed on Kinosuke's hips, letting his sensei control his thrust. And thrust he did. Boy, did he.

Brendan's back almost left the mattress, his cry ringing out in the empty house as Kinosuke nailed his gland in the first of a series of deep, hard thrusts that kept Brendan shuddering uncontrollably, noises torn out of him in quick succession, his cock leaving a growing pool of precome on his belly, his muscle control so completely gone that his legs would have dropped against his chest if Kinosuke hadn't held them up with a firm grip on his ankles.

And all the time, his sensei kept watching him, gauging his reactions, changing the rhythm of his thrusts if he felt the level of sensation dwindle, if Brendan so much as stopped writhing for more than a second.

Everything else disappeared from Brendan's mind, everything but this gorgeous man taking him like no one else had, with Brendan in the center of a bad case of tunnel vision, nothing but Brendan's pleasure driving every single, determined movement of the lean body dominating him in the strangest way, in the way that meant everything was given back in return for Brendan's surrender.

He'd thought he would make it good for Kinosuke, thought this time would be all for him, but his sensei had turned the tables and taught him the first lesson of teamwork all over again: nothing one-sided worked in a team, even if it was the most selfless of acts.

Kinosuke was no doubt making it good for Brendan, but as Brendan looked up and watched his sensei's rapt expression, he knew Kinosuke was flying with him, the effort to give him pleasure pushing his arousal so close to the point of no return that Brendan was sure anything he did now would make his sensei come—calling his name, changing his grip on the thin hips, contracting the muscles of his passage.

Anything would do, but he was still the same competitive bastard, and he wanted to give his lover the best he had, so he dropped his hands to the mattress for support and pushed his hips carefully up until he reached a shoulder stand, the back of his legs pressing against Kinosuke's front so his sensei was free to use his hands now.

Kinosuke let out a strangled cry, his rhythm shattering, his hands grabbing handfuls of Brendan's ass in the need to hold on to something, his breath coming out in harsh pants.

"Come inside me, Sensei," Brendan urged in a voice he had trouble recognizing as his own, so thick with desire.

"Brendan-san," Kinosuke whispered and, to his surprise, Brendan found that hearing what he knew was an honorific attached to his name in a moment like this—when there was no conscious intention to be polite or respectful—was the sexiest thing he'd ever heard, his climax exploding out of him without a single touch to his cock, his whole body shuddering violently as he felt Kinosuke grind deep into him and then stop, his spasms rocking Brendan further until he thought the whole island was shaking with them in a glorious earthquake.

CHAPTER 22

IT WAS the most powerful orgasm Brendan had ever experienced, and it left him so drained of energy that he was unable to keep his legs up and stretched, his knees bending toward his chest and bringing Kinosuke down with them.

"Hmm, hey there, Sensei," he said with what he knew was a goofy smile on his lips, his hands reaching out to touch the sensual mouth that was now, finally, close enough.

Kinosuke looked down at him, his head framed by Brendan's upturned shins, his black hair tousled, his eyes brilliant and heavy-lidded, his skin flushed, his expression so relaxed he seemed about to fall sleep on the cushion of Brendan's folded legs.

Brendan chuckled. "Nap time?"

Kinosuke gave him a soft smile and nodded. "Can I stay?"

Brendan's fingers couldn't stop touching, drawing lines on that clear forehead, pushing strands of hair back, following the arch of a brow. "You mean in my place or in me?"

The giggle Kinosuke let out made him smile even wider, their bodies shaking with his sensei's boyish mirth. Geez. If this went on, his mouth was going to be sore tomorrow—he wasn't sure he'd *ever* smiled so much.

"You're welcome to stay in my place—and in me—for as long as you want, my beautiful sensei," he said, holding Kinosuke's face with both his hands, letting all the emotions constricting his chest show in his eyes and watching in renewed awe as those black eyes changed again from half-asleep to glowing with desire in no time, Kinosuke's hands reaching for Brendan's head and lifting it so he could take his mouth and kiss him with a hunger that had Brendan's cock trying to fill, Kinosuke's shaft definitely going for a second round inside Brendan's stretched passage.

And just then the ominous thrumming ringtone from Kinosuke's cell started playing again, the grave noise somehow more disturbing than any shrill alarm tone.

Kinosuke said something in Japanese that couldn't be anything but a curse and closed his eyes as if trying to contain his anger. Yeah, he could totally relate.

"Is that—" Brendan caught himself before saying Matsunaga's name. He wasn't supposed to be that familiar with a man he had only seen once or twice in the dojo. "—important?"

Kinosuke nodded. "It's Shinya," he waved his hand in a gesture that seemed to mean explaining who Shinya was would take a long time. If only he knew. "He doesn't like phones."

"So he wouldn't call just to chat you up," Brendan translated, his hands unconsciously petting Kinosuke's head as if he were trying to sooth an upset child. And his sensei seemed to relax into his touch, anger giving way to resignation as his hands moved to mimic Brendan's movements and stroke Brendan's short hair.

"I have to go," Kinosuke murmured, his lean body not moving a single inch from where it lay on Brendan.

Brendan smiled and lifted his head to kiss his sensei's brow. "Okay, babe."

Kinosuke blinked at the endearment, but Brendan was sure he could see Brendan's own surprise at what his addled brain had not filtered, because both of them chuckled at the same time and neither tried to put words to the private joke. Geez. What a pair of saccharin-allergic toughies.

"Have time for a shower?" Brendan asked, knowing full well he only wanted to keep the young man in his place for a moment longer.

"He's phoned twice," Kinosuke answered in his usual way of avoiding a direct negative. Damn Japanese politeness—Brendan tried not to laugh at the thought that the best way to tell Kinosuke had been a street punk was he could utter one or two negations per month.

"Okay. Let's get this show rolling."

Brendan took a deep breath and literally rolled his body, pushing with his legs until he lifted Kinosuke back onto his knees. And there it was again, the giggle that made Kinosuke sound like the playful puppy he actually was when he stopped glowering like a movie samurai.

The giggle turned into a groan when Kinosuke pulled out of him, and Brendan could feel both of them sobering fast as he helped his sensei discard the condom and used the sheets to wipe the smooth skin clean of lube, sweat, and come. It gave him a strangely possessive notion, this way of touching that shouldn't have been more intimate than sex but somehow was, sharing the most personal task of grooming, smelling the unique scent of their mingled essences on his lover's skin.

They kissed softly once, kneeling in front of one another, both serious and contained like priests in some secret cult, making an offering, sealing a covenant. And then they both rose from the bed and moved in opposite directions, Brendan retrieving some clothes from the closet while Kinosuke put on his, both unable to tear their eyes from the other's body, from the contrasting skins that quickly disappeared under layers of fabric.

When they walked out of the room, Brendan felt tension coming back with a vengeance. Everything around them—Bobcat's carefully traced kanji, the legal pad and pen beside the phone on the living room table, the only closed door in the whole house— reminded him the place was being used for a stakeout whose targets were none other than the man he'd taken to his bed and his companions.

For the first time in his life, Brendan knew he was betraying everybody's trust of his own accord, and it wasn't a nice feeling, especially not if you were a stickler for duty like he'd been right until the day he'd met a fucking Japanese gangster. Yeah, the man had a body to die for, and the sex had been amazing, but was it really worth destroying everything that kept his self-image intact?

Kinosuke turned to look at him as they reached the front door, a question in his eyes Brendan knew he was too proud to ask, looking so young and vulnerable and stunning Brendan had to accept the indisputable reality that the answer to both his and Kinosuke's questions was a big, capital *Yes*.

He smiled and touched Kinosuke's cheek, nodding softly as if the gesture could convey all the words neither of them was going to say, and then he simply opened the door for his sensei and walked beside him to his bike.

When they reached the deep red Honda cruiser Brendan noticed a familiar prickling in the back of his neck—the war-honed instinct that told him danger was near—and barely a second later, a car came down the street.

Brendan instinctively placed the bulk of his body in front of Kinosuke, obstructing the view from any driver passing by. The car didn't pass them by, though. It maneuvered into a parking space, and when the sounds of a door opening and closing and light steps on the pavement reached them, Brendan understood he could hear all these only because the driver wanted him to—whoever the driver was, he was clearly announcing his presence.

The footsteps stopped behind Brendan when Kinosuke had just donned his helmet and was looking at him through the visor, his sharp black eyes momentarily drifting to watch over Brendan's shoulder before returning to hold Brendan's eye for a scorching second.

And then his sensei was gone in the rumble of a powerful engine, and Bobcat's voice said behind him, "Who was that Chink?"

Brendan forced himself to stay calm, to stop his hands from clenching into fists, his shoulders from tensing. He knew his shooter only used racial slurs when he was fishing for information, seeking to get a reaction, and knowing that Bobcat's paranoia had a real basis for once made Brendan open his mouth and lie without hesitation.

"Some cousin of Big B's wife." He stopped there—too much explaining always sounded guilty.

"What did he want?"

Brendan turned to look at Bobcat and almost winced. It was still difficult to recognize a former member of the teams in this tweaker-looking guy, even though the sun he'd been catching lately had at least given him a healthier skin tone.

"Said he didn't know his cousin had rented the place and was checking just in case." Brendan shrugged. "Apparently he lives nearby, and I bet he was as concerned about the family business as he was dying to get some fuel for neighborhood gossip."

Bobcat eyed him warily, but no more than he usually did, so Brendan thought he was safe until he remembered the chair blocking the door to the den and his clothes littering the floor.

"Oh shit," he said, not having to fake his chagrin, "I forgot about the favor Big B asked."

"Favor?"

He paced up and down the curb, his brain working so fast he expected smoke to come out of his hair. He needed to keep Bobcat out of the house for long enough to reach the backyard and get into the den through the window. But what on earth could he tell the man that didn't sound too suspicious?

"What favor?" Bobcat insisted.

Brendan stopped, and the words backyard and earth crossed his mind like heat-seeking surface-to-air missiles. "His wife wants a garden in the backyard, and Big B has hired some landscapers to do it, but you know how things get done here; he's recruited some relatives of some relatives, and he doesn't trust them to do it right."

Bobcat looked at him as if he were stupid. "If he doesn't expect them to get it right, why doesn't he hire someone else?"

"Because if he did, he'd be losing face in front of his relatives."

He watched Bobcat as he stepped right into his trap. "But then it'll be his relatives who'll lose face for a bad job."

Brendan raised both hands in a helpless gesture. "That's what I was supposed to be here for, to direct the whole operation like a fucking admiral and make sure no one loses face on any side of the blood lines."

"Then I don't get what the problem is—apart from the fact that you don't know shit about gardening," Bobcat said, frowning. "You're here, and the dudes haven't showed up yet, so why the fuss?"

Brendan rolled his eyes. "Big B gave me this speech about this being a sandy soil and lacking all kinds of the good organic stuff, so he ordered compost and fertilizer and cinder and whatnot from the nursery two blocks away, and *I* was supposed to collect it to have it ready before the landscapers came."

"Well, now that I'm here, you can go pick it up, and I'll take the guys to the backyard and keep an eye on them until you come back," Bobcat said reasonably.

"That would do if this was going to be a normal garden," Brendan snorted, "but Big B wants the whole endemic Hawaiian rigmarole. He made me learn all the fucking botanical shit—the difference between maupaka kahaka and pohuehe, how they are coastal shrubs that need lots of sunshine, how mountain species like papalai and maile only grow well in the shade, blah, blah. No offense intended, buddy, but I doubt you could tell the guys where to plant a pua pilo or what fertilizer to use with wiliwili."

Brendan kept his tone mocking and his fingers crossed in his mind, hoping the hours he'd spent trailing Ken Harris through Foster Botanical Garden would finally prove useful; that, and Bobcat's Cuban upbringing—with the neighborly helpfulness that his family had instilled in him before contact with the more selfish WASPs could spoil him.

The seconds ticked away as they stood on the curb, Bobcat searching his eyes suspiciously, Brendan squirming a little under that unblinking stare, mostly to stay in character and show the man he felt a little awkward at having to ask for a favor he wasn't even going to mention. Because, yeah, Bobcat knew he was a proud Irish bastard, or at least had been when they both were in their right minds, so many ages ago.

"I guess what you really want," Bobcat finally said, and Brendan stopped breathing until he went on, "is for me to do the dirty job and go pick up the piles of manure while you stay here fresh and clean ordering the troops around. Is that about right, *jefe*?"

Brendan's smile split his face, relief almost making his knees weak. "You know me too well, *asere*."

Bobcat shook his head. "Yeah, right. So I'll go do this shit for you, but do me a favor and put the house phone on the windowsill or something while you're in the backyard. I've tried to reach you twice."

"Oh, have you?" Brendan asked as nonchalantly as he could. "Must have been out here talking to that guy. Something important?"

Bobcat hesitated. "Could have been. Had to make an executive decision I'm not sure you'll like."

"Bullshit. We'll talk about it later, but I've no doubt whatever you did was the right thing to do."

His assurances sounded a little hollow to Brendan, but Bobcat seemed relieved enough to joke as he walked back to his car. "You don't have to suck up to me—I'm hauling your manure anyway."

Brendan laughed. "You know where the nursery is, right?" he asked.

Bobcat waved him away, and Brendan stood there smiling until the car door slammed shut. Then he forced himself to walk slowly back to the house and only start running when he heard the rental turn the corner.

All he had to do now was find the nursery's number, pray that they had all the stuff he'd told Bobcat about ready to deliver, make up some story to justify why they shouldn't mention he'd just called to order everything and, more importantly, why they should believe Brendan was going to pay for it through their website as soon as he hung up. All of that in the time it would take Bobcat to reach the nursery; then, before the man could put everything in his trunk and head back, Brendan still needed to find some landscaping service that employed mostly native Hawaiian and could send some of them right away, and finally—or at the same time if possible—he had to climb the den window to recover his clothes, dislodge the chair from under the doorknob, put it back in its place, and leave the door and the window closed, because that was what Bobcat would expect him to do if a bunch of strangers were to be roaming around the house.

All that to make sure the man he had trained and fought with, the man who'd been his swim buddy and trusted companion, his brother-in-arms, his friend, didn't find out Brendan had betrayed his trust by sleeping with the enemy *and* lying to him about it.

The problem was Brendan wasn't even sure what his friend would deem less unforgivable if he found out: the breach of professional conduct, or the lie it uncovered—and not exactly the white lie about Kinosuke's identity, but the biggest, life-altering lie about Brendan's sexual preferences. Deep inside, he feared the reality behind the lie would weigh more than the fact that he'd been hiding such an essential part of himself from the men who would have given their lives for him, the same men who might not have moved a finger for him if they'd known.

CHAPTER 23

KOTARŌ STOOD there until the car disappeared around a corner. He wished Berto had stayed with him, even if he knew he had to do this alone.

Berto. What a name. It was supposed to be a Spanish nickname for Robert, but it sounded like some kind of daikon to him, something you could add to a salad with a lot of wafu dressing. He giggled at the image and then caught himself when he remembered he hadn't even asked the man where he was from.

Typical Kotarō the Hick. He'd told Berto his whole life story and never had the tact to let the guy put in one word or two about himself. He just hoped brain damage from near drowning was excuse enough for his rudeness.

He took a deep breath and turned around to face the dojo. He'd promised Berto he'd tell the boss, and he was going to do it—sometime today.

Shit. Why was it so difficult now? He'd been so freaked out at the ER, so confused, and Berto somehow had known how to guide him through it all, how to ask the right questions to get him to remember what had happened, step by shameful step.

Must be Berto's eyes that did the trick. He looked too skinny, and maybe a little freaked out himself, but when he'd fixed those huge brown eyes on Kotarō, he'd known he couldn't possibly have hidden anything from them even if he'd tried. He hadn't wanted to try, though, not with Berto, because there was something familiar in those eyes, something the men in the dojo had too, something that Kotarō couldn't describe very well except by the way it seemed old and weathered but so sharp you could cut yourself on that look if you weren't careful.

"Oh my God, Kotarō! You're here!"

He didn't have time to brace himself before a blond tsunami tackled him and lifted him off the pavement. Shit. Kenshin-san looked like a frail artist dude, but he had the strength of a sumo wrestler.

Kotarō didn't even try to disentangle himself from the embrace, though. It felt too good to know somebody cared, really comforting after that hospital bed and all those strangers just checking on him and going on with their harried work as if they couldn't see how terrified Kotarō was. He didn't know what he would have done if Berto hadn't been there.

"You were looking for me?" he asked in a tiny voice, desperately wanting the answer to be affirmative, even if it meant the boss had just been itching to yell at him.

Kenshin-san pulled a little apart to search his eyes. "What kind of question is that? Of course we were looking for you! Tachibana has been checking all the haunts of the kids your age. Shinya has been to every beach on this island. Shigure and I split the hospitals between us, and we were about to decide if we waited for Kinosuke or left for the morgue right now."

Kotarō's eyes went wide. The morgue. Shit. He knew he should be ashamed—and he was, he really was—but he couldn't help feeling a little happy about them seriously looking for him and not just doing some half-assed checking around the dojo.

"But—" He hesitated. It was difficult to confess to having lied, but he wanted to know what had tipped them. "But I told you—"

"Yeah, I know what you told me." Kenshin-san's look was stern, and Kotarō blushed for all he was worth, especially when Kenshin-san's expression turned from angry to sad. "It was my fault too, for not paying attention. I should've asked you for a contact phone or an address."

"You usually do," Kotarō said sheepishly. "I thought you were fed up with me."

"Kotarō—" Those strong arms tightened around him, and he hid his face in Kenshin-san's shoulder. Kotarō loved the way he smelled, the way he didn't mind being all touchy-feely even though they were in the middle of the street.

They stood like that for a moment, and then Kenshin-san went on talking. "I was distracted, you know? And when I realized I had no idea where you were, I started calling the numbers I had from other times."

Oh shit. He could just imagine how that went.

"I didn't start worrying until one of your friends told me you'd be hitchhiking to the North Shore to catch some waves."

He wondered which one of the bullies had come up with that piece. "They're not my frigging friends. They just want another Japanese *malihini* to—"

Kotarō knew he'd said too much when there was an awkward pause. He kept his face hidden, hoping that Kenshin-san didn't ask him the obvious question—why the hell was he hanging out with them if they weren't his friends—but, as always, it seemed he had underestimated the gaijin.

"You were hiding from them, weren't you?"

He felt a lump in his throat, and his hands balled into fists in Kenshin-san's T-shirt. It was like being a lost kid all over again and suddenly finding a grown-up who knew everything, all his little secrets, all his faults and misdeeds, all his troubles, all his fears; someone who knew and yet wanted him close enough to help and protect him without expecting anything in return. Someone like the boss, or Aniki, or Kenshin-san.

He sniffed, and those fingers he'd seen draw monsters stroked his back in a soothing motion.

"Shhh. You're safe now, Kotarō."

Maybe it was because he really needed to hear those words, or maybe it was the way Kenshin-san said his name, as if it was something still new and special after all this time, but Kotarō started bawling like a three-year-old.

Shit. He was so frigging lame.

KINOSUKE LEFT his helmet on the bike seat and toed off his shoes. Now that he was home, dread started to replace the anger he'd felt all the way here, right from the moment his eyes had met those of Brendan's roomie.

Fucking Catman. Had the eyes of a cat too, and not of the friendly kitty kind. No. Those were the mean eyes of an alley cat—wide open, unblinking, with the big, round, high-on-*shabu* pupils that stared at you as if you were an overgrown mouse.

And Brendan lived with that man—24-7. And that made Kinosuke so angry he was surprised he hadn't been ticketed for some traffic violation.

All the ride home he'd been too mad to even think, but here, in the silence of his place, his brain was trying to make some sense out of the mess without much luck, especially because Kinosuke wouldn't let it reach the obvious conclusion that the cause of his anger was jealousy. As soon as his mind tried to go there, Kinosuke would divert its attention to the lost calls and start fearing something grave might have happened for Shinya to call twice. Dreadful as it was, that thought was easier to handle than the other one.

He slid the door to the garden open, feeling like a piece of shit. He didn't want anything bad to happen to his people, but he hadn't even returned the calls to check. Because he'd been too busy fuming about a stranger he'd just fucked. And yet it felt even lousier to be ashamed of his possessive feelings for a man who had given himself to a near stranger like Kinosuke in such a beautiful way.

Yeah. He might bristle at it, but beautiful was the right word for what Brendan had done, letting Kinosuke lead even though he was younger and obviously less experienced, trusting him as if he'd done something to deserve it, looking up to him as if he was still Brendan's sensei even in his bed, so aroused by Kinosuke, so in tune with him that he had come all over the two of them without Kinosuke even touching that thick, dark red cock.

The black slabs under his feet were so hot that he leaped from one to the next in an improvised hopscotch game until he reached the shade of the tree in Kenshin-san's studio. He peered through the glass to check that the gaijin wasn't there, then hesitated for a second.

How should he go about this? Should he pretend nonchalance and go into the dojo to see who was there, and then fake surprise when they told him they'd been calling him? Or should he grow a pair and go straight to the boss to ask what was wrong? And apologize for not taking the two calls—or probably three, since Tachibana might have been calling about the same thing?

He gasped in the silent backyard. He remembered Tachibana popping in to ask about Kotarō. Could something have happened to the kid?

He cursed under his breath and ran all the way to the boss and Kenshin-san's place, leaving behind all pretense of indifference. He wouldn't be able to forgive himself if Kotarō was hurt or in trouble—especially not after all the shit he'd given him. Of course Kotarō had been acting as if he didn't realize how precarious their situation was, but then again he was just a teenager, and Kinosuke should have known how knuckleheaded teenagers could get. He should have known.

"Boss? I'm coming in," he said as he slid the door open and stepped into the living room without waiting for an answer.

Fuck. Everybody and their mother was inside, but at least Kinosuke felt relief flooding him when he saw Kotarō there too—apparently unharmed, though the way he knelt in front of the others was a clear enough sign that he'd been up to no good.

The boss glared at Kinosuke but didn't say a word, and it was much worse than if he'd said something sarcastic about bad phone reception in downtown Honolulu. Sitting beside the boss, Kenshin-san didn't even look up to acknowledge Kinosuke's presence, and neither did Shinya, who seemed too busy studying Kotarō's bowed head as if he could ever get to see through that thick skull and understand how in hell the kid's brain worked—or why it didn't work at all.

Only Tachibana deigned to give him a half-amused nod. "You've missed out on the fun," he said. "Where were you? Riding that damned bike?"

He would have kissed the guy for giving him an excuse that wasn't an outright lie, and he tried not to be too obvious in his eagerness. "Yeah. I only saw you'd called me when I got back home and checked the phone." Now a polite pause—not long enough for anyone to say anything—and then he asked, "What happened?"

Tachibana made a face. "Well, I don't really know where to start." It was obvious that he did, and that he was enjoying himself more than the situation warranted, so Kinosuke was rather glad Shinya cut in with his usual laconic style.

"Kotarō sold some *shabu* in a crowded mall, lied to Kenshin-san about a sleepover at a friend's place, spent the night on the beach, and almost drowned."

Kinosuke shot a bewildered look in Kotarō's direction, somehow trying to find any revealing sign of that chain of incredibly birdbrained acts, but Kotarō looked the same as he always did—a little more ashamed and quieter than usual, but just the same. And now Kinosuke didn't know what to ask first.

"Almost drowned? What the fuck was he trying to do, ride the wave of the century?" He started pacing, getting angrier by the second. "And dealing. He was dealing? In a mall? In front of the security cameras?" He stopped short. "Did you have to bail him out? No, I guess you didn't if he managed to nearly drown after that." He resumed his pacing, grabbing handfuls of his own hair and pulling at it, as if that could get him an instant haircut. "*Kuso gaki.* Do you think someone saw him? Well, of course dozens of people saw him if he went about it in a mall, at regular shopping hours, but are we in danger of someone recognizing him and making our lives hell? Should we have our passports at the ready? Though I suppose getting out of the country will be easier than getting in. I bet they'll let us leave even if we forget the fucking passports—less rabble for them to deal with."

He was about to go on with his tirade when the boss said, "That's enough, Kinosuke."

Oh, that shut him up all right, but his anger ratcheted up so fast that he felt queasy and had to sit down in the nearest cushioned surface. And the boss probably took it for obedience, because he went about his business of being the fucking king of the jungle as if Kinosuke hadn't interrupted him.

"Do you have Berto's number, Kotarō?" Matsunaga said.

When Kotarō shook his head, Kinosuke asked, "Is this the one he got the drugs from?"

But he only received a royal glare in return, the boss going on with his questions. "Do you know his last name?"

Obviously too ashamed to shake his head again, Kotarō just apologized. "*Sumimasen*, Boss. I forgot to ask."

Kinosuke tried hard not to yell, but he couldn't help raising his voice a little. "Can anyone tell me who's this Berto and why the fuck we need to locate him?"

Now the boss turned his full attention to Kinosuke. "You'd know if you'd been here when you should, instead of running around on your bike."

"So my duty is to be here all the time like a fucking temple dog, is that it?" Kinosuke said, almost relishing the view of Matsunaga's neck muscles clenching.

"Your duty is to act like Kotarō's senior, not like another kid who abandons his responsibilities whenever a new toy catches his attention," the boss countered, his voice lowering into that frozen register he had mastered during his years as *wakagashira*. It was supposed to inspire fear and compliance, and it usually did, but the word *toy* felt like a punch to Kinosuke's solar plexus, because he understood the boss wasn't talking about his cruiser, and the way he said it carried the sickening suggestion that what he had with Brendan was the worst kind of entertainment, the kind that made you shirk your duties to go whoring.

He stood, rage propelling him forward until he was inches away from Matsunaga, staring down at him, not really caring about the offense implied in his posture, never mind the words he was about to spit at his former boss. "And why the fuck should I babysit a kid *you* brought all the way from Japan? Do you think a few minutes of my watching him would be of any good after the hours he spends in that school *you* put him in, a place full of gangbangers with easy access to drugs and weapons like everybody else in this shithole of a country? And why in all hell should I care about what *you* think my duties are anyway?"

Matsunaga stood very slowly, each muscle moving purposefully, in perfect control of the strength coiled in tightly bound skeins of anger. His eyes met Kinosuke's, and Kinosuke had to fight to hold that solid stare, to stand tall even though his inner self was cringing at what he saw in those narrowed eyes, or rather, at what he didn't see—the mentor, the leader, the friend Matsunaga had been, now patently absent from the cold, penetrating gaze.

"You are right. You needn't pay any mind to what I may consider to be your duties since we're not family and you don't even work for me. And of course you shouldn't worry about Kotarō because he's not your blood. So if you'd be so kind as to leave my house right now, I give you my word that you will never again be disturbed about matters that don't concern you." Kinosuke forced himself to stand still as Matsunaga delivered the final blow.

"From now on, should you have any complaints about your working conditions or ever want to return to Japan, please contact your employer, and I'm sure he will be glad to negotiate the termination of your contract in satisfactory terms."

Kinosuke blinked, surprised he couldn't hear the deafening sound of the world shattering in a thousand pieces all around and under him. It should have been loud, the noise, especially because the six people in the room were suddenly so silent Kinosuke could hear his own ragged breath and some tiny little sniffing that seemed to come from Kotarō's direction.

But even the kid was silent apart from that, no *aniki* or *sempai* or even one of those pleading puppy looks he was so skilled at. Nothing. Just his mussed, raven-haired head bowed down, looking even more unkempt than usual—Kinosuke noticed now—probably because you don't have time to rinse the salty water off your hair when you've just nearly drowned in that same water.

Nearly drowned. Almost died. And all Kinosuke had done was pass around the blame like a hot potato. And talk about Kotarō as if he was some neighbor's untrained mutt that kept pissing in his flower beds. Small wonder the kid wasn't even looking at him.

Neither was Kenshin-san. And Kinosuke was almost glad Kenshin-san wasn't looking up from his deep study of the tatami floor, because if there was something he couldn't deal with right now was the hurt he was sure was deeply lodged in those strange gaijin eyes.

Yeah. That was something he excelled at—hurting the gaijin. Matsunaga, he just plain insulted or enraged him, but with Kenshin-san it was always a game of finding the most painful way to hurt either his flesh or his feelings, didn't matter which as long as he made the gaijin suffer. And he was so good at it, he did it without thinking.

Kinosuke didn't know he'd been looking around the room, but he now found himself meeting Shinya's eyes. Funny how an expressionless, scarred face could appear so hostile when you'd lost all your rights to be considered a friend.

Only Tachibana gave him what was at best a neutral look, but as he stood to gently guide Kinosuke out of the place and into the garden, his nonchalance had a touch of warning about it, a well-balanced mixture of sympathy and dismissal that made Kinosuke's stomach turn.

Now more than ever did Kinosuke miss the noise Western doors made when they slammed closed, the soft click of the shoji door sounding too polite, too definitive, terminal in a way violent emotions never were.

As he stood frozen on a warm black slab of stone in the wonderful garden he'd taken for granted, facing a building very much like the one he lived in but filled with the people who had been his world up until that very moment, Kinosuke finally understood— since the day they'd set foot in this country, he'd been acting exactly like Kotarō.

They'd both tried to make a place for themselves in this crazy new universe, each in his own way, but mostly distancing themselves from their immediate past and the people who represented it, because those people, those old rules, felt like simple hurdles they had to jump over to move forward.

The difference between Kotarō and him, though, was that Kotarō had gone at it headfirst, bravely embracing everything new this country had to offer, while Kinosuke played both sides of the fence like a coward, picking out what he found pleasant of the new environment and hiding from the rest behind the wide backs of his friends.

Kotarō might have made some big mistakes, but when they threatened to hurt his family, he'd come running to ask for their forgiveness and help. Kinosuke? Well, even now that he'd lost them, he was too proud to even try to knock on the door they'd closed in his face.

So what did he have left that was his own, that the men he'd just pushed away with his insults hadn't given to him? What he had was a big noisy motorcycle he couldn't keep without the dojo salary and a redheaded American who might or might not want to see Kinosuke's face ever again.

CHAPTER 24

THE WAITRESS finally brought their plate lunches to their table. She was a pretty one, all fine bones and delicate Asian features, but Brendan had met Navy SEALs with less flinty expressions on their faces—their combat faces.

"Mahalo, sistah," Big B thanked her with a smile the size of the Big Island, mostly directed at the girl's back, since she didn't even wait for him to finish the sentence before turning and scurrying away.

Brendan couldn't blame her. As Big B had explained, Hawaii was one place where Asian-Americans were a privileged group, but only if you happened to be the *right* Asian-American—namely Chinese- or Japanese-American. The rest, well, they had the usual shitty jobs and the frustration that came with them like grease with hamburgers.

He checked the hamburger patties on his plate and nodded to himself at the sight of the gravy nicely dripping into the rice under them. Rice. A clear sign that this was Hawaii, where instead of bread they served rice with everything, in a very Asian way. The excess protein was clearly American, though, and Brendan's plate—called *loco moco* for whatever reason—carried two hamburger patties and two over easy eggs on top of the white rice, all of it soaked in brown gravy.

"You should try this, Bobcat. It's tasty," he said, eyeing the no doubt healthier salmon salad the Cuban had ordered. Brendan didn't mention it, but Bobcat was still too far from his fighting weight to look healthy.

"No way I'm eating something called loco moco," Bobcat countered.

Brendan snorted. "Well, sorry to burst your bubble, but lomilomi salad doesn't sound much better."

Bobcat looked at him as if he thought Brendan was crazy. "You know what loco moco means, right?"

"Should I?" Brendan asked. "The only Hawaiian words I know are aloha and hula."

"That's not Hawaiian, man. That's plain Spanish, and I won't tell my mother I've been eating something called *crazy snot*."

"Ew."

Big B had been looking at them with a grin plastered to his face, but now he burst out laughing, the bastard. Bobcat pointed a finger at his wide chest. "And you shouldn't be laughing your ass off when you're the one having *pipí* for lunch."

Brendan made a face, but Big B laughed even harder, his rumbling, highly contagious laughter making other patrons turn to look at them with indulgent smiles.

"This, you disgusting jerk, is pipi kaula," the big man finally managed to say. "And *pipi* has nothing to do with piss because it's the Hawaiian word for beef. Hawaiian, you hear me? Not fucking Spanish."

Now it was Brendan's turn to laugh. He'd really missed this kind of light banter between friends. In the District, everything—even jokes or sex—was about politics, and people used a sort of Pantone formula guide for mirth that covered every grade in the scale, from uncompromising grins to bootlicker guffaws, each one with its strict rules of application—like, never use the homophobic smirk around a Democrat.

This was very different, relaxed and open, even if they were just enjoying their meal in silence. Here, with these men, Brendan was sure whatever he said would be taken at face value because it came from him, and his former boat crew knew he never lied. Well, except for the little fact that he'd always kept his sexual preferences hidden, though that wasn't exactly lying but being private about private things. Nothing to be bothered about.

Lying was what he'd done to cover Kinosuke's visit, first to Bobcat and then to Big B—he'd had to tell him something about the garden that had sprouted overnight in the man's backyard. And that was definitely bothering him.

Maybe if it'd only been Bobcat he wouldn't feel this bad, since his paranoid behavior sort of deserved some reprisal, but using Bobcat's mental health as an excuse to get away with his own unprofessional behavior was making Brendan feel like a traitor. He'd told Big B that he'd hired a landscaping service because Bobcat kept complaining that the empty backyard offered too clear a view of the house for anyone to spy on them. And of course Big B had believed Brendan.

He wiped gravy from his lips. This was beginning to feel like a last meal, probably because his conscience felt as heavy as that of a death-row inmate. And it sort of made him angry, too, that he would feel so conflicted over such an inconsequential white lie. Hadn't he learned anything from Craig? Lawyers had developed the lying muscle to such degree that they even believed their own lies, making for long, restful nights of dreamless sleep.

"So, what now, boss?"

And wasn't that the million dollar question? He looked up to meet Big B's eyes.

"The job is pretty much done," he said. "We aren't going to come up with any significant piece of new intel if we keep at it any longer."

Big B nodded and turned to Bobcat. "Nothing juicy in those translations of yours?"

"No," Bobcat answered, but he wouldn't look at the big Hawaiian and Brendan knew exactly why. The transcripts from Harris and Matsunaga's bedroom had uncovered some very juicy conversations—or equally meaningful absences of them.

Brendan tried to laugh at Bobcat's discomfiture, but his embarrassment hit too close to home to be funny. What if it had been Kinosuke and Brendan on the other end of a microphone? Or, worse still, Craig and him? Yeah, surprisingly enough, he'd feel angrier than anything else in the first case scenario, while humiliation would have rated much higher as the major emotion for the second one. That was pretty meaningful in itself.

"I've no doubt that Matsunaga was a force to be reckoned with in yakuza circles back in Japan," Brendan said, "but I've also no doubt that when he left the Shinagawa gang, he left it for good. Now it's obvious he and his men are living on the income generated by the dojo, with no other activity—legal or not—on the side."

Big B shook his head in disbelief. "So, if what the Fuwa kid told Bobcat is true, these hard-boiled yakuza criminals left their profitable careers in Japan out of loyalty to an American who someone working for them kidnapped and tortured?"

Put like that, it sounded almost incredible, almost like the senator had believed it was. "Yeah, but don't forget that the kidnapper acted on his own, without Matsunaga's or his men's knowledge," Brendan tried to explain, "and you know how the Japanese react to blunders; they probably felt killing the man wouldn't be enough payback, that they ought to further compensate Harris."

"That makes sense," Big B said. "If *yonsei*—that's fourth generation Japanese-Americans—still go to great lengths to avoid losing face, I can't begin to imagine what a Japan-Japanese—and a yakuza to boot—would feel he had to do to repay that kind of debt."

"And don't forget that Matsunaga and Harris were...." Bobcat searched for the right word, and obviously couldn't find anything suitable because he just added, "together."

Geez. It sounded like they belonged to the same bowling club or something. Brendan had to work hard to keep the anger from his voice. "If Kotarō is to be believed, they were lovers before anything happened, so at least Matsunaga had a good reason to follow Harris here, and his men might have followed him out of loyalty to their former boss."

"Not that I know shit about Japan, but aren't yakuza these ultranationalist, supermacho gangbangers?" Big B asked now.

Brendan knew what was coming next, but he still made the question. "Yeah. So what's your point?"

"My point is, supposing we believe the kid about Matsunaga and Harris being an item—"

"No need to suppose there, B," Bobcat interrupted. "I don't know if they're an item or the full warehouse, but they sure go at it like rabbits. Every fucking night. And they can't fucking shut up while they're doing it, man. It's driving me nuts in two languages."

Great. Now Big B was laughing his head off. "Every *fucking* night?" he wheezed. "And what do they do the rest of the nights? Hold hands?"

"Very funny," Bobcat said. "Next time I'll make sure it's you getting an earful, not me."

And Brendan had to say it, had to. "Yeah, I bet they've scarred you for life."

"You know what would scar me?" Big B asked over Brendan's sarcasm, actually trying to be serious, but not managing to contain his chuckles very well. "If you said Matsunaga was the bottom. Now *that* would scar me for life."

Brendan hoped his laughter didn't sound too false among the other two. He felt so stupid. Not for pretending that he found Harris and Matsunaga's relationship laughable. No. That was necessary, had been from the very moment he'd joined the Navy's ultimate reserve of testosterone.

He felt stupid for having a bad conscience about lying to his men, for even thinking they were still his men, that they would ever be his friends. You could be an Islander if you were Black, or Hispanic, or native Hawaiian, because you could be a man's man no matter the color of your skin. Queers? They weren't exactly men, were they now.

"So, seriously, boss," Big B said, "if Matsunaga is this big macho yakuza, do you think he would go to his godfather—or whatever they call the top bosses over there—and tell him he was quitting the yakuza to go live with the love of his life—the man-love of his life?"

"Are you trying to say that he's still a yakuza? That he's so fucking careful he doesn't bring any yakuza-related business home for us to catch on tape?" Brendan asked, impatience clearly showing in his voice. This was getting ridiculous.

"No," Big B shook his head vigorously. "No, boss. I think you were right on the money from the beginning."

Thank God for small favors.

"Yeah," Big B went on. "I think Matsunaga left the yakuza because Harris offered him a substantial deal for him and his men to be his personal army in paradise. That, plus a good dose of this crazy Japanese sense of obligation, and you can explain everything that's going on in that dojo."

Brendan was so tired of all the bullshit. Of course there had to be money or duty involved for a man to care about another. And yet, he'd heard the conversations the mics picked up, and even before he could read Bobcat's translations, he'd known the men in the dojo were more than a rich kid and his bodyguards having a nonstop party. There was true loyalty there, and, yes, true affection, and not only between Matsunaga and Harris—between those two, that was fucking love, whatever his enlightened mates chose to believe.

"So you agree those men are no longer yakuza and mean no danger to Harris at all?" Brendan asked, letting his irritation show as if he was simply tired of a long, boring job. "Because that's what my report is going to say."

"Yeah. I don't think Daddy Harris has anything to fear," Big B said.

Bobcat nodded. "The way Harris Junior behaves—and dresses, for Christ's sake— it's probably him who has something to fear. Hell, going by what Kotarō said, it wouldn't surprise me if he'd hired the whole gang to protect him from his father's meddling."

"Yep. Election time coming," Big B added. "The senator is gonna want this mess of a son put very down on the down-low scale."

"Okay. So I send a friendly report with beautiful pictures. Son doing well. No yakuza but private security. No danger *or* scandal in sight. Yours truly. And what about Kotarō's little screwup? Should I include that?"

Bobcat gave him one of his intense stares, made more intense by the fact that these days he was all bones and eyes. "He's a good kid, boss. He shouldn't have to pay for one mistake. And Matsunaga will keep him on the straight and narrow—you heard how he reacted on hearing the kid's confession."

Yeah. He'd heard that harsh, clipped downpour of Japanese followed by what could only have been Kotarō's repeated apologies. He'd also heard what sounded like Kinosuke defending the kid and then leaving the room after a chilling confrontation with Matsunaga.

But then Bobcat had finished the written translation, and Brendan had needed to sit down and try hard not to ask his man if he'd understood right. God. He'd had no clue the power struggle going on between Matsunaga and Kinosuke could have gone that far, even though it had been right there in everything Kinosuke did and said, from his insistence on keeping up a clearly disastrous class at the dojo to his lashing out every time someone tried to make him responsible for Kotarō.

Brendan should have seen it. Once he'd left the yakuza behind, Kinosuke had nothing to be proud of; he wasn't a respected sword master like Matsunaga, wasn't an artist like Harris, had no professional experience he could put down on a CV, probably had no education, and sure as hell didn't want to be in charge of babysitting any kid who wasn't some kind of apprentice to whatever skills he'd pass on to him as his senior.

Brendan should have seen it, because he could relate. Leaving the teams had been like cutting a golden thread that kept his head high and his back straight. Without that, Brendan could give himself high-sounding names like security consultant, but all people saw was a more or less well-behaved thug.

"Boss?"

He looked up to see both his men staring at him. "Huh?"

"So, you're going to, um, include Kotarō in your report?"

Bobcat was trying to be casual, but Brendan could tell he cared about the kid. And in spite of how much Brendan wanted to chastise both him and Big B for being so narrow-minded, it was good to see Bobcat actually interested in something he wasn't suspicious about.

"I cannot leave him out of my report." He saw Bobcat's jaw clench and decided to cut the fun short. "He lives in the dojo too."

Big B smiled. "I told you the boss was a softie at heart."

"You mean…?" Bobcat said, still doubting his intentions.

"Yeah," Brendan answered, rolling his eyes. "I'm not gonna send that security camera footage you retrieved with such difficulty. Okay?"

And sure enough, there it came, the smile he hadn't seen on Bobcat's face for a long, long time. So yeah, Brendan was probably a softie, because he couldn't help caring about these lads, no matter how hardheaded, paranoid, or gay-allergic they were. It was like having teenage sons who turned out to be skinheads, skate punks, or hot-rodders; you had to love them anyway.

CHAPTER 25

KINOSUKE STOOD on the lanai, facing the garden of what Brendan had called a 'vacation retreat,' a surprisingly secluded hotel a few miles southwest of Hilo.

The rain had stopped a long time before, but it still looked damp and shady around the cottage. Every detail that Kinosuke could see had been taken good care of, from the heavily landscaped tropical garden to the way each cottage gave off a sense of isolation in spite of being relatively close to the next little house.

It was beautiful, but sort of gloomy, like everything else they'd seen so far on the Big Island. Maybe it was because of the light here. In Oahu, you had this crisp sunlight making things look sharp, but here the sun always seemed to be traveling through thick forest leaves before it reached you, and even where no tree was in sight, there came the mist, or the rain, or those volcano miso-soup vapors they called *vog*.

Whatever it was, the Big Island seemed dark to Kinosuke, green and black all over, while Oahu had been as multicolor and bright as an aloha shirt. Or maybe it was his own mood, sort of coloring everything.

"Hey."

He almost jumped out of his skin when the soft word was whispered in his ear, strong arms wrapping around him and pulling him back against a warm wall of solid muscle.

"*Kuso*," he spat. "What kind of sailor were you again?"

His body shook with Brendan's laughter, and Kinosuke was glad the smug redhead couldn't see how that musical, belly laughter made him smile.

"SEAL, Navy SEAL," Brendan repeated patiently. "We are a little more expertly trained than your normal Black Shoe."

Here they went again. He had no idea what Brendan was talking about, and even though he was curious, he couldn't tone down the fear of appearing like an ignorant hick and so, whenever he wasn't sure it'd be something every American toddler knew from the cradle, he just kept his big mouth shut and seethed with the frustration of being left in the dark.

Brendan didn't need to tell him that he was some sort of private eye for Kinosuke to know the man was sharp, though. The more time they spent together, the faster Brendan was able to read Kinosuke's silences, and it was getting to be a very irritating habit—because it irked Kinosuke to be so transparent—and a very comforting one at the same time—because Brendan was finding more and more ways to explain things without making Kinosuke feel stupid. The man would have been a good sensei.

"Before Bin Laden's death," Brendan explained now, "everybody thought a SEAL was this dumpy beach dog with whiskers. Now I've met cabbies who could not only tell you what a special ops team does, but even that SEAL stands for Sea, Air, Land."

Shit. Small wonder the man was all controlled movement and stealth. "Air? You can fly planes?"

"Nope. I jump from them."

Right. As if that sounded much easier than being the fucking pilot. Now Kinosuke felt doubly like an ignorant hick *and* a good-for-nothing ex-yakuza. And of course he must have tensed in Brendan's arms, because those strong hands started moving over his tattoos, petting the fire dragons as if that would calm Kinosuke's spirit.

"Those things I learned?" Brendan said softly. "I don't do most of them anymore. My job now is pretty much lots of boring surveillance and strutting around people to make the bad guys know I'm right there between them and my client of the moment."

There was some bitterness to Brendan's tone that Kinosuke hadn't heard before, so maybe leaving the Navy stint hadn't been a good move. Maybe Kinosuke wasn't the only one making bad decisions every step of the way. "That's something you do very well."

"Hmm?" Brendan asked, his hands still doing their best to distract Kinosuke.

"The strutting part."

Brendan laughed and smacked Kinosuke's head playfully. "I don't strut that much."

"Uh-huh."

"I don't, Mr. I'm-so-samurai-there're-no-bulky-pants-bulky-enough-to-contain-me."

Now it was Kinosuke's turn to laugh—he might even have giggled. "I don't wear hakama pants to—" He waved his hand helplessly, unable to find the right words.

"Make a statement?" Brendan finished for him. "No, for that you use the big wooden stick."

"Shut up," Kinosuke said, making a very undignified noise as he tried not to laugh.

Brendan chuckled. "Now that's rude, Sensei—telling your student to shut up when he's singing your praises."

"They also taught you how to sing in that sea-air landing course?"

Shit. If Brendan laughed any harder, he was going to bust some vein. And Kinosuke couldn't help smiling at the way the man laughed, even if the joke was mostly on him. He turned to better watch Brendan bending and holding his flat belly as if it hurt, fascinated by the ripples in those hard muscles, by the way the skin around those eyes crinkled, the green in them turning into the dark shade of a tropical forest.

Funny how that plain face could change, as if Brendan usually did his best to hide the mischievous devil that he really was behind a seriously professional appearance. It made sense, if he'd been in the military, for him to appear deadly serious, and all that special operations shit explained a lot of the man's irritating smugness—though Kinosuke would bet he'd been born with a healthy dose to begin with.

Brendan had finally stopped laughing and was looking at him with an odd smile, something bright and shiny but sort of wistful too, as if for some reason he thought he couldn't reach Kinosuke in spite of them being so close. It freaked Kinosuke a little, the idea of being separated by an invisible wall, and his fingers all but shot out to make sure there was nothing solid between them.

"Hmm. Love your hands, Sensei," Brendan said, his smile turning both dreamy and hungry as Kinosuke's fingers traced the outline of his face.

He fought the shudder that threatened to travel from his head to the tip of his toes. When the man said *sensei* that way, Kinosuke's knees went weak. He couldn't help it, couldn't help feeling like someone important when Brendan looked at him the way some men looked at the pretty bottles of expensive *daiginjō*, with a mixture of need and admiration that made Kinosuke's toes curl.

"Want you," Brendan said now, his voice turning into a sexy growl.

"No shit," Kinosuke answered, and yes, there it was, that laughter he so loved to hear. If any other man had laughed at him while they were getting in the mood, Kinosuke would have kicked his ass, but with Brendan, he liked teasing a good laugh out of him, even when they were about to go up in flames, or maybe because they were, because if they didn't laugh, this crazy thing between them would look a little too scarily hot.

"C'mere, Sensei," Brendan said, his fingers curling around Kinosuke's hips, right under the waistband of his shorts, pulling only enough so it was an invitation instead of a command.

It bugged him every time, the way Brendan had of being careful around him, as if Kinosuke would bolt for the door if he was a little rough, or demanding, or whatever it was he thought would freak Kinosuke out. And it wouldn't bug him so much if it wasn't such a turn on, having this man who might have spent years dishing out orders suddenly turn all respectful and polite on him, as if he either thought Kinosuke had a short fuse— which he didn't, not him—or he believed it was somehow Kinosuke's due, all this consideration that Kinosuke had never received in his whole fucking life.

So, yes, every time Brendan said *jump*, Kinosuke would jump like a monkey, just like he was doing now, all but crashing against that solid chest because Brendan had asked him to.

"Much better." The growl was back in Brendan's voice, and his roaming hands now pushed right under Kinosuke's waistband. "Don't know why you bother with the shorts. There's nobody else in here but me."

Kinosuke went on tiptoe when those fingers found his ass and squeezed, hoping they were too close for Brendan to notice the flush of his skin and trying to dodge the question with one of his own. "Why are *you* wearing them, smarty-pants?"

Oh, listen to the man laugh. It felt almost as good as the pressure of Brendan's erection against his. Almost.

"Smarty-pants?" Brendan shook his head, smiling. "Geez. Where did you learn that one? *Sesame Street*?"

He decided to ignore the taunt and simply tried to push Brendan's boxer briefs down. The pair he was wearing now looked exactly like every other pair in Brendan's drawer, all black or dark gray with just the smallest white lines or letters for contrast.

It might be a military thing, going for drab colors, or maybe Brendan thought the black looked good on his pale skin—which it sort of did, but it also looked as if he was about to start one of those Ironman races any moment.

"Want to go inside?" Brendan asked, and Kinosuke realized just as he said it that he'd been trying to move in that direction all the time. Shit. How weird was that? He couldn't keep anything from Brendan, not even the things he'd somehow managed to keep from himself.

A strong hand landed on his brow, moving gently from side to side as if trying to smooth Kinosuke's skin. "Shhh, Sensei. Don't frown at me. I know you're not very fond of PDA. It's okay."

He rolled his eyes. Another hint—besides the drab underwear—that Brendan had been in the military, was his using abbreviations every two words. And even if Kenshin-san was always telling him how fast he'd learned to speak English like an American, Kinosuke didn't know shit about abbreviations—and anyway Kenshin-san was too nice for his own good.

Kenshin-san. If Kinosuke hadn't been so unforgivably awful to the gaijin, he was sure Kenshin-san would have helped him cope with all the weirdness. Not the Brendan-weirdness—habit was taking care of that one—but the gay weirdness.

"What's wrong, babe?" Brendan asked, pulling Kinosuke even closer, the full contact surprisingly comforting when it should have been simply sexy. But of course Brendan was that kind of lover, anticipating his needs every time and going about it in the most simple yet delicate way, never making Kinosuke feel he was acting like a prudish virgin.

"It's this place," he finally said, though he knew he wouldn't be able to explain it. "It's kinda…."

Brendan waited an eternity for him to go on, but even if he'd been using Japanese, he wouldn't have made any sense. The place was nice enough—more than, really; it was high-standing, ultraexpensive nice enough—but Kinosuke had read the sign saying it was gay friendly and it had boggled his mind, because from that moment on, every time he saw two men together, he *knew* they were *together* together, and somehow he couldn't get used to the knowing it part.

It made things too crude, like, if he went around naked—which Kinosuke didn't give a rat's ass about—here it would only mean he was looking to get some action, and even if it was true half the time—more like three quarters, really, the way he and Brendan couldn't keep their hands to themselves—Kinosuke still didn't want to advertise it. Not that he was ashamed, but if he wanted people to know he was doing it with a man, he'd go to a love hotel, not this perfect little house for lovebirds and newlyweds.

"Obvious?" Brendan asked.

"Huh?" The way Brendan pushed him gently to get inside the front room, managing to close the door behind them without breaking eye—or body—contact got Kinosuke distracted.

"This place," Brendan repeated. "Is it too obviously gay for you?"

Shit. Maybe Brendan had received psychic training too.

Kinosuke searched those green eyes, trying to see if the man was mad at him, but they sure had taught Brendan how to keep his face blank when he wanted to, so no help there. "I'm just not, um, used to it. That's all."

"You're not used to seeing it?" Brendan said, taking a step back and, when it seemed he would let go of Kinosuke's hips, grabbing a handful of cloth and bringing Kinosuke's gaudy, lucky-number-seven shorts forcefully down in one efficient move. "Not used to doing it? Or not used to be seen doing it?"

Uh-oh. Not blank anymore, Brendan's face. More like angry, or horny, or horny-in-spite-of-angry, but definitely not blank. And Kinosuke's traitorous cock chose that moment to twitch in excitement, when there was no way to hide how Brendan's aggressive drive turned him on.

"Not used to doing it with a smug, jumping-off-planes, can't-swing-a-bokken-for-shit, American supersoldier." He could do aggressive too. But he couldn't shove down Brendan's underwear in retaliation because the man's hands shot out to grab Kinosuke's wrists when he went for it, and now he was holding Kinosuke there, exposed and helpless, those green eyes lit with an evil spark as they travelled up and down Kinosuke's body.

"But you get a kick out of it, huh? Screwing the American?" There was something slightly wrong with Brendan's voice, his wry smile just this side of being derisive, his fingers squeezing Kinosuke's wrists a tad too hard. "What you don't dig so much is other people guessing. Because you fear they might start wondering who tops. That's what got your panties in a knot, isn't it? That they might think the tough yakuza takes it up the ass?"

Kinosuke froze, all the blood leaving his cock and making his heart pump so furiously that he wouldn't have heard a volcano going off if it had happened right next door.

Yakuza. Brendan had said yakuza. Not Japanese, or sensei, or even fucking immigrant. But yakuza.

"Let go," he said, letting the cold he felt seep into his words.

"Kinosuke—"

Of course he wasn't *sensei* anymore, now that Brendan had given away his game.

"Let go or I swear I'll—"

The theme from *Naruto* exploded in the room with its loud opening bangs, and they both moved instinctively to crouch low and search for cover. Yes. That was what people trained to fight would do when something seemed to be exploding in front of them. People like a Washington security consultant and a former yakuza.

CHAPTER 26

KOTARŌ'S FINGER hovered over the call button. Aniki was away on a trip, and even if he wasn't, Kotarō wasn't sure he'd take his call. He'd hear that frigging song from Naruto and just let it go into voice mail.

He sighed. That had been a good day, when he'd convinced Aniki to get a different ringtone for each of the names in his contacts list. Kotarō had rolled around laughing when Kinosuke-sempai had chosen the Imperial March—the music that sounded every time Darth Vader showed his scary mug—for the boss. And then they'd fought over Kotarō's ringtone.

Aniki had suggested something totally uncool like the song from *The Prince of Tennis*. Ew. And then he'd gone over a list of the silliest shōjo anime on earth while Kotarō tried to make him choose the music from *Bleach*, *Samurai Champloo*, or even *Yū Yū Hakusho* instead. Dude, that had been fun.

They'd settled for *Naruto* because Aniki could shout his head off as much as he wanted, but Kotarō knew he was a softie deep down, and *Naruto* at least had these cool characters like Kakashi, and it wasn't girly even though it had ninja girls and this guy who was always saying *what a bore* in the same tone Aniki said his own *mendō kusai* with exactly the same expression and—

"*Moshi moshi.*"

There. He couldn't help it. Aniki had said some ugly things, but Kotarō knew he always did when he was mad, that he couldn't keep the hurtful shit to himself like the boss knew how, because Kinosuke-sempai was like rice you put to boiling and it made froth spill all over the rim of the cooker, but the rice was still there at the end of the fuckup for you to eat. So he'd made the call.

"Aniki?" He was a nitwit. Who else could be saying *moshi moshi* into Aniki's cell? His evil Menehune twin?

"It's me. You all right?"

Wow. Aniki sounded like... well, like Aniki—all rough and shit but still concerned. Because he cared, no matter what he said.

"I'm all right," Kotarō said, his voice cracking like a ten-year-old's. "I just... I don't know what to do, Aniki."

"About what? What's happened?"

He sniffed. Aniki hadn't asked *what have you done?* even after the... big fuckup. "I'm not sure. Tachibana-san says to give it time, that things will go back to normal, but I don't think he's right and it's scaring me."

"They're giving you hell? Is that it?"

Now Aniki sounded angry, and if Kotarō wasn't wrong, he was muttering all kinds of ugly things with the phone an almost safe distance away from his mouth. It shouldn't make Kotarō happy, but it did.

"I fu—did all kinds of stupid stuff, but they were just a bit serious at the start—made me do some extra chores, kept me grounded, that kind of sh—stuff."

Silence came from the other end, and Kotarō felt his stomach try to become three sizes smaller. He was about to blab any dumb thing when he heard Aniki's voice come back, all low and hesitant.

"I, um, I guess I've been the only one to give you hell, all this time."

"No, no, Aniki, you never—well, sometimes you sort of did, but I know you were just mad at me because you knew I was about to act like a numbskull and get into trouble."

"Well, you sort of did get into trouble, not to mention you almost managed to kill yourself, you *boke*," Aniki said a little testily and then stopped as if counting to ten. And then dropped the big bomb. "I'm sorry anyway, Kotarō."

Another silence followed, but this one didn't freak Kotarō out because he was just in frigging awe. Dude, this might really be Aniki's Menehune twin, because you could count with the fingers of one hand the times Kinosuke-sempai had ever apologized.

"So, what's wrong?" Aniki finally said, and Kotarō had to fight back a giggle at the way he could tell, even through the phone, that saying *sorry* had thrown Aniki's mind for a loop and he needed to change the subject fast.

But Kotarō still had to tell him what was wrong, so he swallowed and got to it. "It's Kenshin-san, Aniki."

"Is he acting weird? I mean, weirder than his usual gaijin weird?"

Kotarō took a deep breath and forced himself to say the words. "He... he's gone."

"What! Gone where? How? For how long?" Aniki's voice got so loud that Kotarō could still hear him with the phone at the end of his outstretched arm.

"I don't know," Kotarō answered when the string of questions stopped. "He just wasn't here one morning, and when I asked the boss, he said nothing—like he does when he doesn't think you should learn about some stuff—and so I thought maybe the boss was mad because Kenshin-san had gone out to draw some shit early in the morning and had forgotten to tell him where he was going, because you know how mad the boss gets when he can't be around to keep an eye on him after what happened, but when I came back from school, he still wasn't there, and Shinya-san told me he hadn't been there for lunch either, and when he didn't show for dinner, I was worried, but the boss just gave me this look, and I didn't dare ask, and then Tachibana said they'd probably had a tiff and I should let them figure it out, but I—"

"Wait, Kotarō, wait a second. When did this happen?"

"Last Thursday."

There was a pause as if Aniki was calculating how many days had gone by—which was silly because today was Thursday again, and even Kotarō knew without much thinking it was eight days if you counted—

The loud *plonk* startled him, and he strained to hear what was going on at the other end of the line. Had Aniki dropped the phone? He heard more loud noises, some sort of thumping and then some scraping, and Kotarō started to worry because it sounded as if something was attacking Aniki. Were there wolves in Hawaii? But then he could hear Kinosuke-sempai shouting his head off in English, so maybe he'd surprised a burglar entering whatever place he was at.

"You son of a bitch! What have you done to Kenshin-san?"

Huh? Did the burglar know Kenshin-san? Kotarō heard a different voice now, clearly American, shouting almost as loud as Aniki.

"What the fuck was that for? And who the hell is Kensheensun?"

"Don't play games with me, you lousy motherfucker!"

Oh wow. Aniki was seriously mad. There came more sounds, more furniture scraping and some scuffling, and Kotarō wondered if they could somehow trace Aniki's cell signal like they did in the movies to go help him.

"Kotarō?"

His legs banged against the bed, and he sat hard, bouncing on the mattress for a moment. Shit. Aniki had surprised him, suddenly calling his name into the receiver like that.

"*Hai*! Aniki, are you all right?"

"Yes." He sounded out of breath and mad as hell. "I'll be there in… a while."

And then the call ended, and Kotarō looked at his phone as if it had sprouted one of those weird hats the Menehune were often seen wearing.

CHAPTER 27

ANY OTHER day, there wouldn't be a parking space right in front of the dojo, but today seemed to be Brendan's lucky day, since that stupid phone call had changed the position of all the planets in his horoscope.

Now, six hours and 209 miles later, he'd lost his favorite rotary shaver, his dark gray windbreaker, eight Bikkembergs boxer briefs, a prepaid five-day vacation in a luxury resort, and… Kinosuke.

His sensei sat close—right there beside him in the passenger seat—but Kinosuke had stopped being his sensei, his lover, and even his friend, as the darkening bruise on Brendan's jaw showed.

Geez. All those combat-trained reflexes and it only took a nanosecond of hesitation for a street punk to almost knock him out—never mind that the street punk was his lover, or that Brendan had been feeling guilty and stupid for letting one single word said in anger betray him.

He'd been so mad. He'd left the Navy two years ago, and he still had to hear those same obtuse jokes about pillow-biters and fudgepackers, over and over again, and he still had to keep his mouth shut for fear of losing his next contract, his old reputation, his new friends—and the old ones.

Somehow with Craig it hadn't mattered that much, keeping it quiet, maybe because Brendan didn't particularly enjoy the image it projected of himself—his being with that successful, sophisticated snake of a man. But with Kinosuke, he'd done a one-eighty and actually wanted to be seen with him, even if the beautiful, cocky bastard was a nobody in Washington's scale of things.

That was why he'd been so glad when Kinosuke had called him after the argument with Matsunaga. Brendan had listened to him rant, had offered his advice, his place, the comfort of his arms. And Kinosuke had taken it all, greedily, almost as if he feared he might lose Brendan too if he didn't hold on to him so tight that Brendan wore the marks of those long fingers on his back for days.

Then Kinosuke had barely hesitated when Brendan suggested a trip to the Big Island, and then only because they needed to negotiate what each of them would be paying to keep that damned Japanese pride intact.

The trip had been great, too, with Kinosuke becoming more relaxed and open the farther they got from Matsunaga's territory and Brendan managing to forget the reason why they'd met, Kinosuke and him, the report he'd sent the senator, the way Bobcat had looked in that airport full of tourists before he caught his flight home.

It had been great, getting to know Kinosuke better, to see that playful, boyish nature he never showed when he was trying too hard to be a proper sensei. But it had also been great—or especially so—to realize that Kinosuke trusted Brendan enough to show him how much the events following Kotarō's mishap had affected him.

The sex between them had been incredible too, flowing with Kinosuke's moods, sometimes passionate and wild, sometimes all about the comfort of two bodies touching, sometimes tender and affectionate like a new, delicate being growing from the best in them both.

Yeah. Everything had been hunky-dory until they'd reached that posh resort and Kinosuke had noticed it catered mostly to gay men. Because, well, Kinosuke didn't have anything against gays, but he didn't want to be confused with one. And after days of trying to respect his fears of being seen together in public as just a question of Japanese primness, Brendan had simply lost it. Because it damned hurt to be treated as a mongrel his owner couldn't bear to be seen petting.

He supposed he could have tried to talk about it, since it was obvious Kinosuke was new to gay relationships, but Brendan was not exactly relationship material himself, and he hadn't been able to keep his anger down for a second longer—the anger he'd been storing for so many years under so many layers of pressure that when a single crack had opened in his control, it had poured out like molten lava, scorching away any filter his brain might still have tried to place between his thoughts and his actual words.

It was a moot point now, anyway. Maybe if Kotarō hadn't called, Brendan could have made up a story and pretended to be an undercover federal agent investigating possible yakuza ramifications in Hawaii, but once Kenneth Harris popped up into the equation, Kinosuke wouldn't have bought anything but the truth. And the truth had brought them here, back to where it all started, except this time they had no hope for a future uncontaminated by both their pasts.

"Kinosuke…," he said tentatively, not knowing exactly what he would say but needing to break the tense silent between them.

"Out!" Kinosuke barked without even looking at him. "Get out now."

The door of the rental slammed shut, and Brendan took a deep breath before getting out and clicking on his key fob to leave everything locked. In truth, he wouldn't have minded if someone had stolen the rental—it might have even been fun compared with what he had to face now.

They entered the dojo to be greeted effusively by a plump Filipina Brendan recognized as Tachibana's wife.

"Kinosuke cuz! You no went stay on vacation? Who dat malihini?" she said without pause as she hugged a very rigid Kinosuke. If the situation had been different, it would have been amusing to observe the culture clash, but Brendan—and obviously Kinosuke—had other things to worry about.

"I need to see the boss, Alma-obasan. Is he in?"

The woman's expressive features went from happy to dark in a second. "He stays with da little *keiki*," she said, pointing in the direction of the dojo hall. Then she added in what she probably thought was a whisper, "I no like fo' talk stink, but he stays all piss off since his man went leave. I no kid you, you bettah stay away from da boss, yeah?"

Brendan didn't know if Kinosuke understood or even paid any attention to what she said after the obvious indication that Matsunaga was teaching a class, but he looked at the grandfather clock in the corner, bowed to Tachibana's wife, and strode out of the reception area without so much as a backward glance.

Geez. This was getting ridiculous. If it wasn't for Brendan's pride—and, yeah, a nagging sense of guilt—he would have turned around and left the damned dojo for good. Instead, he forced himself to smile at the woman regarding him with more than a little suspicion, and went after the fucking stubborn yakuza. The hotheaded punk was right there in the middle of the garden, glowering at him—or at the place he was supposed to be—probably about to go pick a katana from wherever it was they kept them and go after Brendan with it.

"Move it," Kinosuke spat and turned on his heels before he could see Brendan's eye roll.

He kept his distance from Kinosuke constant just to piss the man off, and sure enough, his former sensei had a scowl ready for him as soon as Brendan reached him by the sliding doors to Matsunaga's place.

"Take off your shoes," Kinosuke ordered as he toed his own off.

Brendan looked down at the thin strip of concrete they were standing on. "I'll wait until we're inside for that, if you don't mind."

Obviously, it was the wrong thing to say. Kinosuke took two steps toward him and pointed a threatening finger at his chest. "Take. Your. Shoes. Off." And Brendan was sure he didn't accompany each word with a jab of that finger just because he was Japanese and still avoided direct contact even when he was about to punch someone's lights out.

"Okay, Sensei," he said angrily. "This is your fucking place, and we'll go by your fucking stupid rules."

He tugged at the strings of his hiking boots and got rid of them in a few jerky movements.

"There you go. Happy now?"

Kinosuke just glared at him. "Kneel."

"What?"

"The next of my fucking stupid rules is that you kneel and sit back on your heels," Kinosuke shouted in his face. "Can you do that, or is it too difficult to get it through your thick skull?"

Brendan snorted without much humor. "I understand pretty well what you're trying to do, you little shit, but I've never knelt before anyone in my whole fucking life, and I'm not going to start now."

"Take it outside, you two. I won't have you brawling in my house."

Great. The alpha dog of the pack had managed to sneak up on them. If any of Brendan's old instructors had watched him for the last few hours, they would have pegged him for a staff weenie, not an ex-SEAL. Fucking yakuza.

CHAPTER 28

IN THE perfect silence of the room, Kinosuke could almost hear the crackling of Brendan's temper. Fucking asshole. He should be grateful that the boss had agreed to receive them, should be grateful that, as soon as Kinosuke had revealed a few details, the boss had called the other men in to *listen* to him.

But no. The smug bastard thought that having been a soldier once had turned him into an invincible one-man army—even if he was outnumbered by four yakuza and a half—and he probably believed that being American gave him the right to be taken at face value every time he opened his mouth. Like he was about to do now, instead of waiting for the boss to speak. Didn't he have eyes on his face? Couldn't he see how the other men hadn't jumped from their seiza to beat the shit out of him after what he'd revealed? Couldn't he see that even a kid like Kotarō had the sense to wait for the head of the house to make the first move?

"Listen, Mr. Matsunaga, you all," Brendan said in his typically condescending style. "I understand it's not very nice to discover you've been under surveillance, but all things considered, I believe it's a small price to pay. The report I sent Senator Harris was an objective one, and it will prove that Kenneth has nothing to fear from you. Besides, you must at least concede that a father has a right to worry about his son, especially after what happened to him."

Tachibana and Kinosuke snorted at the same time, but it was the boss who answered Brendan in the measured tone he only used when he was well past the limits of his patience. It never helped to call him *Mr.* Matsunaga.

"Well, Mr. O'Farrihy, you seem a very conscientious investigator. I take it you did a good search on the senator's background to check who you were working for—objectively speaking, I mean."

Brendan had nothing to say to that, of course. Why would he doubt the word of an American senator when the ones calling his bluff were just a gaggle of foreign criminals?

"So I assume you know Senator Harris refused to pay any ransom for his son," the boss went on in the same cool voice, "even when it became obvious that Ken was being tortured."

Kinosuke studied Brendan's face. To anyone else, his expression might have looked completely blank, but Kinosuke had spent too much time observing those foreign features not to notice the little flicker of something that crossed the green eyes.

The bastard knew, probably had known all the time, and yet had taken the job to spy on Kenshin-san. It made Kinosuke clench his fists, made him want to scoot farther away from the treacherous bastard and break the line that connected them both as they sat facing the group Kinosuke had once been part of, the family he had abandoned just to end up with a lying son of a bitch.

"And I suppose you know," the boss prodded on, "that Ken's father sent a pair of marines from your embassy to transfer Ken to another hospital while he was unconscious and therefore unable to give his consent. That hospital, of course, wouldn't have allowed any of us *yakuza* to visit him.'"

Brendan blinked twice. So that little piece of information had escaped him.

"And I'm certain that you are aware of the fact that, as soon as Ken was diagnosed with PTSD, his father tried to have him incapacitated on mental grounds so that he could be appointed as his son's guardian."

The silence in the room had a different quality now. From where the boss sat with his men on the tatami mats—Shinya and Tachibana to either side of him and Kotarō near and slightly behind Shinya—the wave of hostility had taken on the solidity of a newly forged metal, and Kinosuke understood that whatever Brendan might say now had little chance of making a dent in their judgment. Brendan, from where he sat cross-legged like a cheap Buddha statuette in front of Matsunaga-san, had lost a little of his smugness, something very close to confusion showing in his eyes, as if he were thinking too fast in too many directions at once.

When Brendan finally spoke, his face was set in what Kinosuke had come to recognize as his I-did-it-my-way expression, which meant that even if he apologized, he'd still think he'd been right, in what seemed to be the well-respected American tradition of *I'm sorry if life sucks.*

"I must admit," Brendan said, "that I had my doubts about some parts of the story the senator told me, especially when I confirmed the friendly relation Kenneth has with all of you, but I never question my clients' motives unless they interfere with my professional ethics."

Nice fucking speech. And he wasn't even done.

"Whether you believe it or not, I'm really sorry my investigation has breached your privacy." There was the apology, and now he would pull the carpet from under their feet. "But I can assure you what I transmitted to the senator was the minimum of information required to confirm that his son is safe here with you—safer, in fact, than he would be on his own or under the protection of hired professionals. So, however unsettling my interference has been for you, it will only bring what I assume you'll consider a blessing, since you'll no longer be an object of interest for Senator Harris."

"What about Kenshin-san? Where has he gone?" Kotarō blurted before he realized he had even spoken and then added sheepishly, "*Sumimasen*, boss."

Kinosuke almost smiled. Kotarō might be irritating, but he was loyal to the death—and he had the excuse of his teenage years. Others didn't have that excuse.

"Sorry, kid," Brendan had the guts to say, "but I don't know anything about that. My investigation was well finished before Kenneth left, and neither I nor the senator have anything to do with his leaving. I am sure Mr. Matsunaga here will be able to say more on the matter than I can."

Kinosuke felt so ashamed that he bowed his head to avoid seeing what he knew had to be in the boss's eyes. Shit. How could he ever have found a bastard like that attractive? How low had he fallen?

All he wanted to do right now was die—or kill Brendan, that would be equally comforting—and since he had his head down, the subtle movement of Matsunaga-san's hand in Shinya's direction didn't escape him. He wasn't the only one wishing the bastard dead, then, and the fucker would never understand that the boss had just saved his life without making a fuss about it, because Brendan would never understand what honor was about and would never imagine that all his stupid military training would be nothing against a man like Shinya who went about fighting with the inhuman determination of a killer dog breed.

"Mr. O'Farrihy," the boss said now, and not for the first time, Kinosuke wished he had the kind of control, elegance, cool dignified composure and sharp intelligence that made the boss the boss and Kinosuke just a shabby alley cat with all his ineffectual hissing and scratching. "I would very much appreciate it if you would stop giving me orders when you are a guest in my house."

At least now Brendan had the good sense to keep his mouth shut, because the boss hadn't even started.

"As for the personal insights you've been kind enough to enlighten us with, I must admit I never believed the stereotype of the naïve American until now. I should have thought a man with military training like yourself would have hesitated before believing everything he was told—especially if it came from a politician—but maybe it's my mistake and politicians in this country are renowned for their transparent motivations.

"Anyway, I don't care if it is Santa Claus you choose to believe in, but I'd rather you didn't insult our intelligence by telling us you sent an *objective* report with *minimum* information on us. Raw information might be objective, but once it leaves the source, it stops being so—no matter what your intentions are, you *always* have intentions about it. And the consequence is that however little information you give an enemy is always too much.

"If none of your instructors passed these basic notions on to you, Mr. O'Farrihy, I'm not surprised your Army is having so much trouble fighting a bunch of turbaned civilians with faulty AK-47s.

"As for the blessing we are supposed to thank you for, there's the little problem of your initial failure to understand the senator's motives. If he'd just been a father worried about his son's safety, I'm sure your report would have eased his mind enough to leave us alone, but since that's not remotely the case, I'm afraid we can only wait and see what his next move will be—because there *will* be a next move. Never think for a moment that your pretty little report will gather dust in a drawer.

"And before you interrupt me, as you're wont to do, let me remind you that I'm only an ignorant ex-yakuza who's just learned your language, so when you speak about your 'professional ethics,' I must admit I'm a little confused. The professional ethics of a PI in America allows him to go on vacation with one of his targets?"

Shit. Kinosuke didn't know about Brendan, but he was in awe of the boss. When had he found the time to polish his English until the man sounded like a college professor with an accent? And how the hell could he swing words like he did a bokken? How did he manage to say "*go on vacation*" and make it sound dirtier than if he'd actually said *fuck*?

Now more than ever Kinosuke understood how stupid he'd been to let the world outside the dojo make him lose sight of where he stood. This wasn't about being a yakuza, or even about Brendan; this was about reverting to those sick years when Kinosuke had tried everything because nothing seemed to matter.

Matsunaga-san had pulled him out of that aimless life—yakuza or no, the man always knew where true north lay, and now Kinosuke would sweep the streets of Honolulu with his tongue if that was what it took for the boss to take him back.

CHAPTER 29

KOTARŌ HOPED nobody noticed he was shaking. He couldn't help it. When he'd sat facing the boss like Aniki sat now, he'd thought Matsunaga-wakagashira had been hard on him, but that had been nothing compared to the beating Kinosuke-sempai was taking right now.

He didn't understand half the words the boss was using. Kotarō knew those words were directed at that awful redheaded man, but Aniki had somehow taken sides with the redhead and now had to face the music—much like Kotarō had done when he'd sided with those new *friends* of his.

Aniki had looked ashamed all the while, but now that the boss had finished speaking, he looked sad, as if he thought Matsunaga-san would never forgive him.

The shitty redhead didn't look ashamed at all. Kotarō wasn't very sure, but maybe he looked a tiny bit sad too, but mostly what he looked was angry enough that his skin was turning the same color as his hair.

"I may have underestimated you, Mr. Matsunaga"—the redhead was almost shouting now—"but I sure as hell don't underestimate any Washington politician, however sincere his intentions might appear, and I sure as hell know the power information has in the wrong hands. That's why my report only expanded on data I'm sure the senator already has—like the names and appearances of you and your men, your present, most obvious activities, and your outward relationship with Kenneth.

"What this means, Mr. Matsunaga, is that I left out some occasional side activities of your men that would give the senator the wrong impression...." The redhead made a pause here that was supposed to mean something, looking at Kotarō like one of those dudes in *Nō* theatre who look at you and make faces and you still don't get what they're trying to tell you. "And I also left out the fact that you and Kenneth share a bed, something that I don't think would sit very well with a Republican senator."

Now *that* Kotarō understood. He felt himself blush on top of everything, and it made him really angry. He might have been younger and more innocent when they had lived in Japan, but he'd never stopped to think what it meant that the boss and Kenshin-san lived together; here, it seemed everybody was thinking about it all the time and giving it names that made it look ugly and dirty, and Kotarō felt like a traitor even thinking about what people thought.

"That's why I told you the senator would leave you alone from now on," the stupid redhead said, "because even if for the first time in my whole fucking life my professional ethics hasn't been up to standard, I do know my fucking job, and even though my report contained a real minimum of new information, it was delivered in the redundant, excessive way Washington bureaucrats mistake for accuracy, and that's why I'm sure it will gather dust in a drawer, contrary to your no doubt informed opinion."

The man paused as if to consider his next words.

"The only thing I regret about my behavior is that Kinosuke might think that I was only using him to get information. I suppose it can't be helped now, but before I leave your house for good, I want to make two things clear: First, Kinosuke had no idea whatsoever of what I was doing and for whom. And second, I e-mailed my report late on Sunday night. Considering the time difference, the senator would have read it on Monday morning. If Kenneth left on Wednesday or Thursday, do you really believe the senator had time to do something about it from almost five thousand miles away? Unless he mobilized SEAL Delivery Vehicle Team One stationed here in Pearl Harbor, I'm afraid he hasn't yet made that move you're expecting him to make."

Kotarō wanted to slap the redhead. Shit. How could he be so rude? The man wasn't even sitting in seiza, and that somehow made his smart-assed tone even more smart-assed. He was staring too, in a way that not even the oyabun—the boss of the boss—had ever stared, and the boss seemed to be deciding whether to take it as a challenge or to think the American didn't know shit about manners and would stare the same way at the servers in one of those Teddy's Bigger Burgers places.

Aniki was so ashamed he didn't look up even when the redhead mentioned him, but Tachibana looked from the boss to Shinya and then did that thing he did when there was danger, letting his whole body go slack as if he didn't give a shit about the whole frigging thing, while Shinya seemed to be doing the opposite, all his muscles tensing in a way that made him look even taller and scarier.

Kotarō swallowed. Things could turn very ugly if Shinya thought the boss had been insulted. And the shitty redhead had no frigging clue. The boss, though, knew everything about it.

"Mr. O'Farrihy, I believe now would be a good time to leave my house for good."

Someday Kotarō wanted to learn this—the way to slap someone in his stupid face with just a few words that weren't even swearwords. For now, he had his hands full with trying to control the muscles in his own face to keep them from making a smirk.

The redhead managed to stand quickly without looking awkward but mean. He nodded at the boss and looked for a moment at Aniki, but Aniki didn't look up, so the redhead turned and stomped out of the house.

Everybody was silent for a long time, even though Kotarō clearly heard that the American hadn't stopped to put on his shoes on his way out—he must have picked them up as he went—but it probably was good to be careful around a bastard who had been spying on them without them knowing.

"Matsunaga-sama," Aniki said before he placed his hands in front of his knees and bent forward until his forehead touched the tatami. He was going to apologize formally, and Kotarō felt his throat close in sympathy. "*Mōshiwake gozaimasen deshita.*"

Then Aniki rose a little from his *dogeza* position and turned so he was facing Shinya. "*Nakatani-san, mōshiwake arimasen deshita,*" he said as he bowed to the floor again. He did the same with Tachibana, and Kotarō felt sick. He hated seeing Aniki like that, because Aniki was very proud, and doing this had to be killing him.

"*Fuwa-san, mōshiwake arimasen deshita.*"

Oh shit. Aniki was apologizing to him. To him! It was probably the worst frigging moment of Kotarō's life—drowning didn't hurt nearly as much as hearing Aniki call him *Fuwa-san*, as if Kotarō were some employer Kinosuke-sempai had to answer to—and it took all his strength to stop from jumping to make Aniki rise from his bow. The tears, though, he couldn't have stopped even if the Emperor himself had told him not to cry.

The silence went on and on, and Aniki was still there, with his forehead on the floor.

"You may rise now, Kinosuke," the boss finally said, and Aniki sat back in seiza with his head carefully bowed. "There have been some harsh words between us, but I am sure you didn't know anything about that... man's activities."

Of course they all knew that, but it was good to hear the boss say it aloud.

"I also know Kenshin's father had nothing to do with his leaving."

Now even Aniki looked up to stare at the boss like everyone else in the room. It took a moment for the boss to continue, and it seemed every word he said was an effort, because if Aniki was proud, the boss was proud with a capital P.

"Kenshin left because I failed to make him see this is our place now, and we have to face whatever happens here in this present moment. The past doesn't exist anymore; it's not important what we were or could have been."

"Uh-huh," Tachibana said. "So you had one of those arguments in which the gaijin shouted his head off and all you said was that he didn't understand." The boss was starting to frown dangerously, so Tachibana raised his hands. "Hey, I'm just repeating here what my wife says we all *Japanee* do—I mean that's what I used to do too, so I'm not the one to judge you, but I guess that's why Kenshin-san picked up his things and left, because that one is as stubborn a gaijin as they come."

"He didn't take any of his painting things. That's weird," Shinya said, and they all looked at him as if he'd sprouted a third eye.

The boss nodded, though. "That's why I thought he'd be back in a few days, but he's so bullheaded he must have bought what he needed all over again before having to show his face around here."

Kotarō hated to break the silence that followed, because everybody seemed to be thinking hard, but he knew he was going to explode if he didn't ask it. "But why did he leave, boss? Was he angry at me too? Was it because of what I did?"

That extra second it took the boss to answer was a dead giveaway, even if he tried to soften it afterward. "It was because of our situation here, Kotarō, not just about what happened to you. Kenshin thinks leaving the yakuza made us come down in the world, and that's making us so"—here the boss rolled his eyes—"*unhappy*, that we'll get into all kinds of trouble if we go on like this."

"He blames himself," Aniki said so softly Kotarō almost didn't hear, and he wished he hadn't, because if he started crying again they'd all notice for sure now.

"He knows we left Japan for him," the boss said, "so he assumes whatever happens to us here is his responsibility. And you must admit these last few weeks haven't been exactly peaceful, what with Kotarō almost dying and you saying the things you said."

Aniki couldn't control himself. "That silly gaijin! Doesn't he know I'll be the same brainless *chinpira* anywhere you set me loose?"

"Nah, that silly gaijin thinks we're all men of worth," Tachibana said, and added with a shrug, "Go figure."

The boss looked at Tachibana and then at Aniki, and Kotarō could see his lips were twitching before the three of them started laughing like loonies. And Kotarō had to swipe angrily at the tears that embarrassed him when he laughed while still wanting to cry, and then Shinya went and said something that got them going again.

"Where do we start looking for that silly gaijin?"

CHAPTER 30

BRENDAN LIFTED the glass to his lips and forced himself to drink at least a little of the lager Big B had offered him. It had one of those names supposedly infused with local flavor, but right now Brendan couldn't remember if it was Rainbow, or Pipeline, or Longboard, or Aloha. Whatever. Not much else that he could remember now apart from the samurai flick he had playing in his head in an endless loop.

That bastard Matsunaga sure knew how to stage a court martial. And the big SOB must have been attending night classes to speak like a Marine Corps judge advocate with a sarcastic twist. Yeah, well, Kenneth Harris must have seen to that—private night classes with a lot of tongue involved.

The other thugs had filed into the room in perfect formation, stationing themselves according to rank in that stilted half-kneeling, half-sitting posture the Japanese were so fond of. Geez. They must have rehearsed the whole shebang for even the kid to sit exactly ten inches back from the others, like the only grunt in a room full of officers.

Of course the defendant's seat had been reserved for Brendan and Kinosuke. He supposed he was expected to kneel like the others, but just to be contrary, Brendan had sat tailor-fashion—he would have put his feet on the table if there had been a table in the whole tatami-matted, empty room.

Funny how after this exhilarating experience, he was beginning to understand the utility of Japanese minimalist decoration; he knew now that the stage setting only took the attention away from the actors. And everyone in that room had been perfectly cast in their roles. Even Kinosuke looked the part of the chastised dog, not daring to look up even when others talked about him.

Kinosuke. That proud, aggravating, beautiful schmuck.

Brendan closed his eyes. How did you go about missing something you hadn't even known you needed? Landing on another planet must feel like this, suddenly realizing how badly your lungs depended on another dose of oxygen. But what if you had to live the rest of your life in an artificial atmosphere? How did you manage to forget when every breath you took went rasping down your throat? How did you live with twice the gravity of Earth pressing against your chest?

You adapted, you moved on, you survived. Here or on Jupiter. And the scars you carried made for the perfect body armor, because scar tissue was like Kevlar; it didn't stretch.

Brendan should know. He'd been a SEAL, been flying on high levels of adrenaline only to land back in the dirt with a loud smack; he'd had the kind of deep friendship that grows in life-threatening situations, only to lose it to either death or career changes; he'd been a leader of men who could change the course of history, only to become the lickspittle of men who meddled with history to change the course of the present; he'd had a lot of lovers and sex buddies, only to discover there really was someone right for him that he couldn't have.

So he should know how to jump from one environment to another. Sea, air, land, wasn't it? He only had to look around, gather enough intelligence, plan a strategy, and act on it. He missed one Japanese dude? Right here in Big B's garden were plenty of ethnic beauties to choose from.

Brendan studied the crowd filling B's backyard. This was what a Hawaiian luau looked like—very much like a BBQ party with more aloha shirts than usual, different spices, and a bunch of guitars a mad scientist had been experimenting with, shrinking some and altering the tuning in others. People looked better here too, less pasty, more laid-back, high-pitched laughter and high-octane tans more authentic all over. And the racial mix produced some very fine specimens.

Before he actually came to the islands, Brendan had thought most local people would look like Big B—dark-haired, brown-eyed, big-boned, with a wide nose and full lips—but he'd never considered even B had Portuguese ancestry, and looking at his relatives now was like peeking into the cafeteria at a UN building; you really couldn't tell where anyone came from or even who they were related to. If you threw B's wife's relatives into the mixture, plus some neighbors and a lot of friends, you actually had the proverbial melting pot right in front of your eyes.

So what was there to be depressed about? His life sucked right now? Tough shit. People led worse lives all over the world, and they didn't get the luxury of moping around.

"You no like ohana partay, brah?"

Besides, nobody could stay down looking at Big B's big aloha grin. He had da kine smile down to a T.

"Don't mess with my head, B. Didn't you say this was a luau?"

B's grin turned mischievous. "Nah, this is just a family potluck. We'll do the real thing for my girl's birthday next week, with kalua pig, hula dancers…. Oops. I forgot you won't be here next week."

Brendan chuckled. "You bitch."

"Yep, that's me. Bitch Petty Officer Nahele Fernandes at your service, sir."

A booming voice came from the other side of the garden. "Cuz, you need fo' turn da grinds!"

Big B rolled his eyes. "Jesus. You'd think a barbecue had as many controls as a nuclear sub the way those guys avoid touching it."

"It's only logical for them to trust your expertise, you being an engineman and all. But if you don't want to bust your chops—"

"With all due respect," B said, "you're a chowderhead. Sir."

Brendan laughed as Big B crossed the backyard toward his spicy chops. The smell was delicious, and his stomach gave him a loud reminder of all the meals he'd skipped for lack of appetite. Maybe now would be a good time to start leaving behind all that he couldn't fix.

"Brennan's tummy grrrowls."

He looked down to find a little Chinese doll pointing an accusatory finger at Brendan's midsection. There she was, the soon-to-be birthday girl, nattily dressed in one of those flowery muumuus and giving him a miniature version of B's most mischievous glance.

"That's because Brennan's hungry," he said, trying to avoid the silly voice grown-ups reserved for children.

The girl nodded three times for good measure and then asked, "Wanna play?" as if it was the logical solution to Brendan's problem. Then again, maybe it *was* the solution to everything—considering where his usual logical solutions had led him.

"Sure," he said, and it was like giving the start signal in a race. One little hand clutched at his pant leg and pulled in the direction of the house without waiting to see whether the rest of Brendan would follow.

"What game are we playing?" he asked as he was towed into the living room.

"Counting the people in the wall," said the girl without stopping.

Well, that one was new. As they walked down a hallway, though, Brendan had a eureka moment when he saw the family pictures hanging on the walls. "You mean these people here?"

The girl stopped to look at Brendan as if he were a five-year-old—a *dumb* five-year-old—and Brendan had a hard time reining back laughter. Geez. This one was going to be a handful.

"These aren't real people," she said in teaching mode. "They're photos."

Now, now, the things you learned. "Oh, I see. So where are the real people of the wall?"

She didn't even have to roll her pretty black eyes to give him a duh look. "In the wall." He must have descended three whole rungs in the dummy scale, because she felt the need to add, "I'll show you."

And there they went again, the little princess and her trained… SEAL.

"You pull the little one, and I turn the big one," she said when they stopped in front of a closed door. Brendan looked up and saw some kind of plastic latch attached to the wood near the upper corner of the door, well out of the reach of children. Not that he had much experience on the matter, but it looked like a simple form of baby proofing, a safety catch for fridges or kitchen cupboards.

"Um, are you supposed to open this door?" he asked cautiously.

She looked him straight in the eye and said, "The little knobbie is for Palani 'cause he's a baby and he's always pinching his fingers when the door's open 'cause he don't know how to close it right, but I know 'cause I'm a big girl now."

Brendan had to bite his lip to keep a smile from showing. The whole speech sounded too well rehearsed to his ears, but he had to admit the girl's poker face was brilliant. Besides, if her daddy really wanted the children out of the room and not simply protected from door-related accidents, he would have turned the key that was actually in the lock and taken it with him.

"Okeydokey," he said. "I'll deal with the baby knobbie while you open the big one for me."

Look at that smile. No wonder daddies had to carry bibs around, and not exactly for their babies' drool.

Brendan had to hurry to unlatch the childproofing device, because the little manipulator didn't have any trouble reaching up and turning the doorknob. And once the door was open, she slid in without hesitation, so it definitely had to be a room she was allowed to enter on a regular basis.

Or not. Fuck him sideways. Speaking about nuclear submarines, he was sure any sub skipper would have felt at home in this command-room-style den, with all its monitors, controls, and whatnots. Bobcat would have died happy here.

"Don't touch anything," the girl said, and Brendan had the feeling that was exactly what her daddy told her every time she entered the den.

This felt slightly worse than going to the main bedroom to take a sneak peek into the nightstand drawer, but he couldn't help being curious about the *people in the wall*, so instead of convincing the little girl to leave the place before daddy caught them snooping around, he crossed the room to stand beside her in front of a wall-mounted LCD monitor.

"Now you watch the wall," the miniature admiral instructed, "and when I say the magic words, the wall changes and you watch for the little people, and you say *one-two-three* before I say it or you lose."

"Roger that."

The girl nodded sagely and made what she must consider a stealthy move to push at a wireless mouse on the table behind her while she gestured with her other hand and uttered some Chinese-Hawaiian gallimaufry.

Brendan managed to keep a straight face as he watched the monitor wake from sleep mode and show five or six windows with simultaneous access to the same number of camera feeds.

He supposed once you trained your body to react to threats, you never stopped noticing them, so it was not surprising that B felt the need to control his surroundings to get some peace of mind. The problem was, the images filling the screen weren't views from outside B's house, or even from inside its rooms.

Brendan blinked twice, but the images were still there, showing some rooms he'd only seen once and others he'd actually been in. Then there was a flicker of motion in one of the screen windows, and one of the desktops behind him came to life with a whirring sound.

"One!" the little girl cried beside him, but Brendan didn't even react. He was too busy trying to breathe regularly, trying to make his brain work to understand why he was seeing Kinosuke's image on Big B's wall. "Two! You have to be quicker or I'm gonna win. Three!"

He heard the girl's babble as he would the sound of rainfall, his eyes fixed on the screen that showed the Japanese faces he never expected to see again, one after another, his ears ignoring everything except his racing heartbeat and the grave voice that came from the door to the den.

"How do you like being betrayed, *sir*?"

CHAPTER 31

KINOSUKE ATE his futomaki as if he hadn't had a bite the whole week. He was beat, and Kotarō was about to drop his chopsticks and doze off any moment now.

They'd been treading every beach, every mall, every garden, every art supplies store in the city, like tourists in a hurried low-budget trip, and so far they hadn't found any trace of Kenshin-san. Whenever they bumped into a group of surfers, Kotarō also asked about that guy Berto who had pulled him out of the sea, but since he didn't have a picture or even a full name, it was kind of useless anyway.

"I checked with Okamura-san," Shinya was saying, "and nobody looking like Kenshin-san has rented or bought a car from him or his family in the last weeks."

Since Shinya had always been in charge of the boss's cars—the rentals first and then the fancy SUV—he knew so many people in the car renting, selling, and fixing businesses that in a few more days he'd know for sure if Kenshin-san had left in a car, and if so, its make, model, and license plate number.

It was amazing the amount of contacts they had made in the time they had been living in Honolulu. Kinosuke thought it would be nearly impossible to trace Kenshin-san without the yakuza network, but people here built their own networks based on family ties or customer-owner relations. And they reached everywhere.

"Inariya-san's niece told me Kenshin didn't appear in any passenger list these last few days," the boss said, speaking of one of his kendo students. "And Minami-san is checking the ferries. Any luck with the hotels so far?"

Many relatives and acquaintances of Tachibana's wife cleaned or cooked in hotels all over the city—or knew people who did. "Not yet, but Kenshin-san doesn't know anyone in Oahu, so he has to have checked in somewhere."

Kinosuke stopped eating. Even he had met a lot of new people here, from the dojo students to the guys in the motorcycle shop, but it had never crossed his mind that Kenshin-san worked alone and didn't really know many more people than the five of them. And now that he thought about it, the gaijin was not even very social. He had looked like he was to Kinosuke in the beginning because all Americans seemed outgoing from a Japanese point of view, but now Kinosuke knew better.

Shit. How could he be so dense. He was still thinking Kenshin-san acted from that stupid gaijin sense of guilt, when Kenshin-san was trying to protect the only people who really mattered to him. Something Kinosuke sucked at.

"What if he's rented an apartment?" Kotarō asked, and Kinosuke turned to look at the boss. So many possibilities existed, they might be leaving out something important and missing another chance of finding Kenshin-san. And even though his life was not in danger, the gaijin was still Matsunaga-san's gaijin, and it must hurt like a mofo not having him around—if the pain Kinosuke felt every time he absently checked his phone for a word from Brendan was anything to go by.

"We'll have to look into that too," the boss answered, "but even if he has rented an apartment, it must have taken him at least a few days to find it, so he would have needed to spend some nights in a hotel anyway."

The boss sounded confident because he would never stop being the boss no matter how he tried, and he always felt the need to inspire his men, but he looked as tired as Kinosuke felt, and his loose shirts seemed looser than ever these days.

Fuck. If that asshole hadn't turned out to be a traitorous skunk, he would have had no trouble finding Kenshin-san. He was American, for one, and also a detective, or a security dude of some kind, but above all, he was one of those fucking supersoldiers who could win a war with just a knife between his teeth.

But the scumbag must be thousands of miles away by now, and Kinosuke told himself the way his stomach closed at the thought was only the consequence of not having landed enough punches on that homely freckled face.

FROM SOME corner of his brain that still kept working, Brendan could appreciate the gentleness Big B used to chide his daughter without scaring her. The rest of Brendan's brain had turned to mush, though, and even the simplest bodily functions seemed beyond his ken right now. So when the stranger he'd known what felt like ages ago as Big Brudda closed the door behind the little girl and approached him, Brendan couldn't move, couldn't even force his lips to take the shape of the urgent word filling his mind in big, red, capital letters.

"Shocked speechless, huh?" B said with a humorless chuckle. "Must be the first time in your whole fucking life someone surprises you enough to shut your trap."

He looked at the monitor behind Brendan. "Pity you had to go there and rat about the bugs. Fucking Japs made me spend a fortune in new equipment, and let me tell you, it wasn't easy to reinstall it this time."

B looked straight at him. "What? Can't find your voice yet? This must be a new Guinness record, dude."

Brendan forced himself to feel angry to be able to push the one word out. "Why?" he managed to whisper, his eyes never leaving those brown ones that had always seemed so warm.

"'Why,' the man asks," B said, scorn weighing heavily on every word. "I'll tell you why if you tell me why you gave that fucking order, Lieutenant."

Brendan frowned. "What order?"

Big B moved so fast that even if Brendan hadn't been in shock, he doubted he could have stopped B from shoving him against the nearest wall and pressing a thick forearm against his windpipe. "Don't you dare play dumb with me, you piece of shit. Keep your acting for your faggot friends."

So B knew. Brendan had been so careful, and B knew. But how? At least in the beginning there hadn't been any cameras in the dojo itself, only in the living areas, where Kinosuke and he hadn't been together. They'd only done it in—Shit. Of course B had the place he'd rented to Brendan monitored from day one.

"Do we have a deal, Lieutenant?" B asked, his eyes hard, the pressure of his arm increasing to send a clear message; Brendan had stopped being one of the friendlies since who knew when. "Are you gonna spill the beans? I want to understand your fucking motivation."

Brendan nodded, even though he had no idea what B was talking about, but he had to survive first; that was combat rule number one, and Brendan didn't delude himself into thinking this would be less deadly just because he used to know the man.

Big B let him go but didn't budge an inch from where he stood in front of Brendan. He crossed his arms over his chest to show Brendan he was waiting for an answer, and Brendan racked his brain for that answer, thinking quickly back to the time when his orders had meant anything.

"You want to know about FOB Blessing," he chanced, using the old name of a forward operating base way down that insurgent shithole that was the Pech River Valley. The FOB had been returned to Afghan forces, renamed Nangalam, and ruined by that oxymoronic entity called the Afghan National Army. It took them less than three months to strip the place of anything sellable and let Taliban training camps spread in full force, so much so that US troops had to come back to reestablish some semblance of control over the area. The problem was, the new mission had been under that damned economy of force policy, and the number of troops deployed was close to ridiculous for the expanse of territory to cover.

"Yes, Sherlock, I want to know about the fucking hill we had to take at any cost."

Strangely enough, it was a relief to finally know for sure he hadn't been alone in blaming himself for what had happened.

"There's nothing that you don't already know, B," he said, sagging a little against the wall. No words he managed to find now could lighten the loss they'd suffered, so he didn't even try to apologize. "We were issued an order and we followed it. That's what soldiers do. And that's all there is to it."

He saw the blow coming, saw the muscles contract under B's T-shirt, but he didn't move a finger to stop it, and the punch hit him square in the jaw, sending his head to the side and against the wall behind him. This had been due for two years, and neither the pain that exploded inside his skull nor the blood he tasted in his mouth were close to the price he believed he deserved to pay.

"Is that what you've been telling yourself all this time, huh?" Big B shouted in his face. "Is that the lie that lets you to sleep at night?"

Anger made his own muscles contract reflexively. He was many things, but no matter how the very nature of his job forced him to deflect questions and spread out misinformation, he'd never been a liar—much less so with the men he trusted.

"I never lied to you," he answered, almost shouting himself. "I told you it was a fucking suicide mission, but I didn't think you'd joined the SEALs to push a golf trolley. And you know what doesn't let me sleep at night? That I keep thinking against all odds maybe there had been the remote possibility that if I'd done more than object, if I'd flat out refused to go there, campaign management might have aborted the operation instead of replacing me with a more willing team leader and carrying it out anyway. That fucking infinitesimal possibility is my nightmare, and that's the weight I have to shoulder until the day I die."

Big B's jaw clenched. "They should give you an Academy Award; you had us fucking convinced you did your best to get us out of the mission. Christ. Even now that I've learned the truth you almost just managed to make me feel sorry for you, you cunning bastard."

The truth. B had uncovered something he believed was the truth, so it would be useless antagonizing him. Brendan had to change his strategy.

He smirked, trying to convey the notion that B might have caught him with his hand in the cookie jar. "Okay, big man; go ahead and enlighten me. What is it that you've learned?"

"Oh, nothing much," B said with a nasty smile. "Just the trifling little fact that you were ordered to stay put and leave those caves alone."

It took a great effort to keep his face blank when a gaping hole had just opened right under his feet. He forced himself to whistle in admiration. "Well now. Correct me if I'm wrong, but shouldn't that be classified?"

He knew for damn sure it was, the more so because the operation had been a complete FUBAR and nobody wanted it aired on CNN after the recent Chinook debacle.

B snorted. "Haven't you heard about WikiLeaks? Dude, there's always someone with access to classified information."

Brendan's knees buckled, and he had to lean heavily against the wall, the sinking feeling in the pit of his stomach strong enough to make him sick. God, how could he be so stupid? How had he overlooked something so simple? *There's always someone with access to classified information.*

"I should've figured it out," Big B was saying from what seemed like miles away, but Brendan wasn't listening, his mind racing ahead into all the implications that began unspooling in his mind. "You were always whining that targeting population-centric counterinsurgency was like taking over-the-counter cold relievers to reduce the symptoms. You wanted to attack the illness, crack down on Taliban's recruiting and training areas, cut their financial sources and their supply lines. And of course we all agreed with you; it just never crossed our minds that you would assume that task on your own. Did you think that was God's mission for you? Or was it just your bloated ego talking? Because either way you—"

"B…." There must have been something in his voice, for as soon as Brendan said B's name, he cut his tirade abruptly to look at Brendan.

"Did you never wonder," Brendan asked very slowly, "why Senator Harris had access to the classified military information he passed on to you?"

CHAPTER 32

KINOSUKE WAS starting to dread gathering in the tatami room, because lately it meant some shit had gone south, and honestly, there wasn't much that could get any worse.

Kenshin-san had fallen off the face of the earth; the boss looked like death warmed over; Shinya was getting even more tight-lipped than usual, while Tachibana talked twice as much; Kotarō was obviously having problems wresting himself from the bunch of school thugs he used to hang out with; and Kinosuke, well, he was doing fucking fine for all the three or four seconds every day his mind was Brendan-free.

And now the boss wanted to talk to them in the tatami room. Fucking fantastic.

"Kinosuke."

At least he was back to plain Kinosuke, even though the boss still wouldn't look him in the eye. That was all right—he couldn't meet his own eyes in the mirror either.

Tachibana patted the mats beside him, and it was a relief to not sit alone facing the others. Today it was the boss who would face them all, and it somehow felt like they'd be judging the man for some imaginary fault. Shit. He was so fed up with the whole self-blaming routine.

"*Osoku narimashita*," Shinya apologized from the door. Kotarō trudged right behind, babbling as he always did.

"It's my fault we're late, boss. I had to talk to the history teacher, and when I went out, some guys were waiting for me, and Shinya-san had to—"

"It's all right, Kotarō. Sit down."

Much better. If Kinosuke learned those punks were still pestering Kotarō, he might feel tempted to visit the schoolyard and play some game with them—and it wouldn't exactly be *jan ken pon*.

"Now that we're all here, there's something we have to discuss," the boss began, and Kinosuke braced himself for the bad news. "You've all been doing a great job of searching for Kenshin, and I want to thank you for your efforts, but I think it's time you stopped."

Whatever Kinosuke'd been fearing, it wasn't this. What the hell did the boss mean it was time they stopped? Was there a rule about how long you went gaijin-searching?

"I should never have let you get involved in what is only my problem, but I was weak; I thought maybe if it was you who found him, there'd be some hope of going back to the way things were."

Kinosuke was glad Tachibana interrupted, because his situation in the group was still a little shaky, and he didn't want to open his big mouth and anger everyone.

"Not to gainsay you, boss," Tachibana said, "but Kenshin-san is family; he's not *your* problem."

There it was, and by the way Shinya and Kotarō nodded, Kinosuke hadn't been alone in thinking it. The boss raised a placating hand.

"Sorry if I didn't express myself correctly. I didn't mean to imply you don't care about Kenshin; I meant it's my problem because it's my fault he left."

"What?" Kotarō asked, his eyes wide. "Didn't he leave because I put you all in danger?"

The boss sighed. "No, Kotarō. I've told you already it wasn't because of you. He wanted to protect us all, that's true, but the main reason he left was because…." It wasn't every day that Matsunaga hesitated, so whatever he was going to say must be a tough pill to swallow. "He left because he didn't want to be with me anymore."

"Bullshit," Kinosuke exploded. He didn't care if they kicked him to the curb; he had to say it. "I may be stupid, but I can still see what's right under my nose, and the way that gaijin loves you is not gonna fade just because you've had some tiff. That one can argue and shout like the best of us, but he's not gonna abandon you just because you've said something silly while you were mad, so don't go putting things in his mouth we know he'd never even think because—"

"He left me a note, Kinosuke."

"I DON'T think they're in," Tachibana's wife said for the third time, and Brendan knew he was at the end of his rope. He'd been trying to call Kinosuke on their way to the dojo, but he always got voice mail, and Kinosuke wasn't reading his texts or listening to his messages. Not surprising after what had happened, but Brendan needed to contact him or Matsunaga right away, and he fucking knew for sure they were in—Big B's handheld DVR showed their exact location at all times.

"Look, Auntie," Big B said patiently, "we don't want to intrude, but this is an emergency, and Mr. Matsunaga is going to be glad to learn what we have to tell him."

"We have information on Kenneth Harris," Brendan put in, only to see the Filipina frown.

"Kenneth?" she repeated, and she sounded sincere too. Christ. This was taking too fucking long.

"Kenshin-san," Big B said, and the woman nodded, smiling in recognition. Thank God for small favors.

"Good man, Kenshin. He's got delicadeza," she said, and there came the apologetic smile once again. "But I don't think he's in."

He would have never imagined there would be another people on earth who dreaded answering a question with a plain "no" more than the Japanese did, but it seemed he hadn't yet met any Filipino.

"We know that, Auntie," Big B said. "We just need to talk to Mr. Matsunaga for a moment. It's very important."

She nodded and smiled, but Brendan guessed what she was going to say next anyway. "I don't think he's in."

And it was the last straw. "Fuck this," Brendan muttered as he simply strode into the hallway—he knew the fucking way by heart.

"*Walang hiya*!" the woman shouted behind him, but by the time she came around the reception desk, Brendan had already slid open the door to the garden and was almost running along the black stone slabs, the sound of Big B's footsteps following right in his wake.

Maybe spending time in Hawaii had made it second nature to him, or maybe it wasn't easy to forget the last time he'd been here, but whatever the reason, he made the mistake of stopping in front of Matsunaga's place to take off his boots, only to look up into the barrel of a .38 pointing right between his eyes.

"These men gave you any trouble, Alma-chan?" Tachibana asked, his eyes never flickering from Brendan, his hold on the gun steady. Obviously the guy knew his way around weapons, so Brendan raised his hands slowly, palms up in the universal surrender sign.

"Yoshinori! Put that thing down!" Tachibana's wife said from behind them. "They're just shameless military haole, no need to start shooting."

"I'm not haole, ma'am."

It would be funny how offended Big B sounded if Brendan didn't have a gun in his face. And why on earth was it so easy to peg them as military?

"You're hapa haole at best, or you wouldn't have followed this rude man into a house you hadn't been invi—"

"*Masaka*! The bug man!"

That would be Kotarō, and of course he had recognized Big B as the man who had pretended to be a bug exterminator as an excuse to plant, well, *bugs* of his own. So, yeah, definitely "bug man" was right. And they were in deep shit.

CHAPTER 33

IF HE'D dreaded gathering in the tatami room before, now Kinosuke knew for sure he fucking hated it.

At least this time he was on the right side of the divide—the redhead and his humongous native Hawaiian sidekick sitting in front of them all, Tachibana's gun resting on the mat beside him to send an obvious message in case the boss's glare wasn't enough.

Shit. Poor Kotarō. His face was now almost as red as Brendan's hair. He had led the big Hawaiian into every room of their house, never noticing the man was scattering those devices they'd found and crushed after Brendan's confession. And even though he knew Kotarō was an easy target, Kinosuke had to admit the big man had one of those open faces it was difficult not to trust. *Fucking bastards.*

"I thought I didn't have to tell you in so many words that you're not welcome here," the boss said, and as always Brendan didn't wait for him to continue.

"That was very clear to me, sir, but there have been new developments in Kenneth Harris's case that I thought you should be warned about."

Case. Kenshin-san was a case now—probably had been from the beginning, now that Kinosuke thought about it. At least Brendan called the boss "sir," and his tone, his whole posture seemed more respectful this time. He even waited for the boss to nod his permission before he started explaining.

"This here," Brendan said, turning to the big man beside him, "is Nahele Fernandes. He used to be one of the six men in the SEAL combat element I commanded, so when Senator Harris hired me to investigate his son's situation here, I contacted my former crewman to help me with the surveillance. As Kotarō has told you, he was the one who got this placed wired."

"Sorry about that, kid," the big man said, and Kinosuke wasn't surprised to see that he looked honestly sorry. Shit. These men were dangerous, and not because their training made them great fighters, but mostly because it made them glib liars.

"As you can imagine, most of the conversations I got on tape were spoken in Japanese, and since I can't understand your language, I had to hire a translator if I didn't want Big B's effort to go to waste." Brendan paused. "Sorry. When I say Big B I mean Nahele. Everyone in the teams has got a nickname, and we called him Big Brudda— that's slang for big brother—because he's... um... well, you get the idea."

Kinosuke rolled his eyes. Stupid bastard. Which tree did he think they'd fallen from? It might just be wishful thinking, but he hoped the bluish spot on Brendan's jaw meant someone had recently popped him a good one in the kisser. He fucking deserved it.

"I didn't want anyone I couldn't trust hearing those conversations, so I hired another of my former men, Robert Catalán."

Huh. And what nickname did that one get? Robust Robert? Rob the Robber? Bob the—*Chikushō*. Kinosuke had to close his eyes.

Robert Catalán. *Bobcat*. That was the guy who'd been living with Brendan, the fucking Catman Kinosuke had been so jealous of.

"And what did your men call you, Brendan the Big Fucking Rat?"

The room went silent after Kinosuke's outburst, and the slimy redheaded bastard wouldn't even meet his eyes.

"We called him worse things behind his back," Big B said, the smile in his voice unmistakable, "but mostly he went by Freckles—for obvious reasons—or Brendan the Bold—after that crazy Irish monk who's said to have made it to America in something like a medieval Zodiac."

Brendan shook his head. "Okay. As I was saying, Bobcat translated your conversations for me, he and Big B helped me investigate your activities, and I enrolled in the dojo classes to check that they were legit. Up to here, things went as I told you; I analyzed the data we collected and sent my report to the senator, suggesting you represented no threat to his son.

"What you don't know—and neither did I until a few hours ago—is that I wasn't the only one the senator had hired to keep an eye on Kenneth."

"What?" Kotarō interrupted. "You mean another man came here to install—"

"No, no, don't worry," Brendan hurried to explain. "You didn't let anybody else in. As it turns out, it was only the one man playing two sides."

"He four-flushed me," Big B protested, and everyone started talking at the same time until the boss raised a hand.

"Are you saying," Matsunaga-san asked Brendan, "that one of your former soldiers pretended to work with you while he reported your activities to the senator?"

The muscles on Brendan's jaw twitched. "Yes, I'm saying that one of my men betrayed me. That's what I'm fucking saying."

THAT BASTARD Matsunaga. Brendan held his stare, letting the yakuza know he understood Matsunaga was aiming for the most sensitive areas. Yes. The man had also been a team leader in his own way, but his men had chosen to follow him into another country out of loyalty, while Brendan's men had conspired against him.

"And what does it have to do with Kenshin-san? We're still as threatening to him as we were before your man ratted on you."

Geez. If Kinosuke used one more rat-allusion, Brendan was going to say something he'd no doubt regret. The guy was angry because he felt betrayed? Tough luck. Brendan had gone through the real thing; he had been betrayed on purpose, with premeditation, deliberation, and obvious malice, so Kinosuke was going to have to grow up and deal with mere *feelings*.

"That's a moot point now." Brendan was beginning to sound like Craig. It must be the fucking barren room making him react as if he were on the defendant's seat. "Remember I told you I only sent the senator a minimum of information on you? Well, cross that out. He received every piece of information available, including those pieces that didn't relate to Kenneth but could be used against you."

"If this man is a traitor, why is he sitting here beside you?" Shinya asked.

So Mr. I'm-so-scary-I-don't-need-to-open-my-mouth had finally decided to speak. Of course from a yakuza point of view, Brendan should have killed B, tortured him, or at least eaten his pinkie with ketchup, but this was beyond ridiculous. Couldn't these guys see what Brendan was getting at?

"I'm not a traitor, you slant-eyed fucker."

Oh shit. Brendan didn't even have time to let out a frustrated grunt before the scarred goon rose from his kneeling position in a fluid, lightning-fast movement that allowed him to close the distance to Big B and strike with a blow that would have hit B's windpipe if B hadn't had SEAL's reflexes and pivoted out of the yakuza's reach.

Brendan was sure that if the man had been carrying a sword, Big B's head would be rolling over the tatami mats right now. Even as it was, B was finding it difficult to keep his position stable on his knees, and he was barely parrying the yakuza's powerful blows. And Brendan couldn't move to his help because Tachibana's gun was pointing at his head while the man tsked in warning.

The moment seemed to last an eternity, probably because Brendan was helpless and it looked like any second now Shinya was going to pummel B into the floor, but then Matsunaga shouted, "*Yamero!*" and the scarred goon froze with his hand in midair. "*Suware.*"

Relief flooded Brendan, and he had to admit Matsunaga had one hell of a commanding voice, though he would die before saying that aloud.

He kept his eye on Tachibana, who gave him a nasty smile as Shinya moved back to his seat, eyes still locked with B's like two cobras about to strike.

Fucking yakuza. They were far more dangerous than Brendan had given them credit for, nothing like those tacky, brainless guys in the movies—though Tachibana had the frumpy image down to a T, but look at the way he handled a .38 as if it was an all-time favorite toy.

"What piece of information has Kenshin's father used?" Matsunaga asked.

CHAPTER 34

KOTARŌ DIDN'T know where to hide. The redhead had a video of him pushing ice at the mall, and the other man had sent it straight to Kenshin-san's father.

"Why?" was all he could muster, trying hard not to cry.

"I can't begin to tell you how sorry I am, kid." Yeah. Like he could frigging believe the man who had used him to spy on his family. "But that bastard made me believe Brendan had murdered two friends of mine, and this camera footage was all I could find to get back at him."

Huh? The big man had used a video of *Kotarō* to get back at *the redhead* through *Kenshin-san's father*?

"The senator told you Brendan had killed your friends?" Aniki sounded as bumfuzzled as Kotarō felt.

The redhead rubbed a hand over his face. "I don't know if you're familiar with the Afghanistan War—" the guy started, but Aniki cut him off straight away.

"What? You think 'cause we're yakuza we don't read the papers or watch the news on TV? What kind of ignorant morons do you think we are?"

Now that made the Brendan dude mad. "I don't think you're more ignorant than the average American who never knew where the fuck Afghanistan was until some relative of his came back from there in a coffin. And correct me if I'm wrong, but you haven't been in the yakuza for quite some time now."

Funny that, but Kotarō would have sworn that the big man—what was it? Big B?—found the conversation amusing, and even though the boss kept his usual poker face, Kotarō could see that his eyes were not glaring anymore. This was some crazy shit. Why would they both find it hilarious that Aniki and Brendan kept barking at each other?

"Well, then, if you're that familiar with the Afghan War," Brendan said a little too smugly, "I'm sure you'll know that US troops are abandoning many combat outposts in remote valleys, closing them or turning them over to the Afghan police and the ANA. The rationale behind this is that locals in rural areas will stop fighting if US forces leave, and that it's more cost-effective to secure population centers instead.

"The problem is al Qaeda and the Taliban don't seem to be working along those lines, and as soon as we leave a place, their camps pop up like mushrooms after the rain. That happened at Nangalam Base—the former Camp Blessing—in the Pech River Valley.

"To cut a long story short, our troops left, the Afghan Army in charge of the place turned it from military base to pigpen, and the Taliban saw their chance to reacquaint themselves with the locals."

Kotarō tried to look as if he understood where this was going as Brendan went on with his story.

"The situation at Nangalam was so shameful that command management decided to send back troops. And since base defenses had been stripped of their early-attack warning systems, our unit was assigned to reinforce the platoon that had to patrol the surrounding area.

"I can't tell you exactly what the rules of engagement for our troops are since that's sensitive information, but these policies were established to protect civilian noncombatants and, so to speak, to *play fair*. That's great when the enemy is a fair player too; otherwise, ROE are just casualties waiting to happen.

"So there we were, walking on tiptoe while the Taliban fired at us with increasing confidence until they hit a Chinook with an RPG—that's a rocket propelled grenade.

"Nobody was killed, but the incident made international headlines, and someone back home decided we had to make some token gesture to show the world we were still in charge, especially since this was the second helo downed in the area."

Big B muttered, "Fucking politicians."

Brendan nodded and went on. "So what do you do when the situation sucks, you have few effectives, and you need the most dramatic effects by yesterday? You call in the teams. And since my unit was already in place, I was ordered to go into the mountains and make some serious noise.

"I objected until my throat was sore, but the base commander wouldn't hear any of it."

Kotarō frowned. Why wasn't he happy with that order when he'd more or less said that was what had to be done? Brendan seemed to notice he wasn't making any sense, because he explained, "Obviously I had nothing against chasing the bastards into their strongholds, but not before we had a well-planned operation in our hands. We needed more time, new intelligence; going into the mountains with three-month-old intelligence and no ready backup was suicide, and I clearly stated so."

Brendan took a deep breath, as if what he was going to say next was especially difficult. "I could have refused—I'd done it before—but I had the gut feeling there was a lot of pressure from high up, and even if I refused, someone else would lead my men to the slaughter, so I decided to obey and do my best to keep them safe, which wasn't much, as things turned out."

"It wasn't your fucking fault," Big B spat, and his words seemed to throw Brendan for a loop. He sat there looking at his friend as if he'd sprouted two heads. "Until that bastard conned me, I always thought the way you split us and put twice the usual distance between us saved us from being killed to the last man."

Brendan couldn't seem to react, and Kotarō had to be mistaken, because the man looked as if he was about to cry, and that couldn't be, because he was one of those frigging SEALs who wrestled alligators in their free time.

"So I take it two of your men died," the boss said.

Brendan shook himself out of his funk and nodded. "Our maps were wrong," he said, his voice sounding a little strange now, raspier and lower than a moment before. "We went at them from the wrong side and stepped right into a trap. My point man was blown to pieces. He and his swim buddy died instantly, another man was badly injured, and the rest of us were covered in shrapnel.

"We brought back one corpse, and the medics took the best part of an hour to recover the few remains left of the other from where they had landed all over Bobcat."

Shit. Kotarō had an image of a man with slices of human meat stuck to his uniform and he almost gagged. What if some of those slices had recognizable shapes? Could he look down at himself and tell what piece came from the brain, the guts, or the hands?

They were all silent, probably thinking about human parts, until the boss said, "So Kenshin's father tells your man here that you took on the mission in spite of having been ordered not to, and obviously he's angry enough to report your actions back to the senator. But why did he hire you in the first place if he didn't trust you? That's what I don't get."

Brendan nodded, his face grim. "It appears there's more to the senator than meets the eye."

Ha. As if the boss didn't frigging know that. The redhead wasn't completely stupid, though, because he raised a hand as if the boss had been about to say *told you so*. "I know I should have suspected something when I found some incongruities in the story the senator told me, but you have to understand that everyone lies in my line of work, especially now that my clients are mostly politicians."

Kotarō had to hide a smile when the boss lifted just the one eyebrow. Dude. Nobody could beat the boss at speaking without saying a word.

"Yeah, well, forgive me for being candid," Brendan said angrily, "but I thought even a politician would care about his son. As it happens, it seems Senator Harris only cares about his fucking career.

"He hired me because he wanted to tie up the loose ends. His son was clearly one—the possibility of a scandal always there as long as Kenneth remained with you—and my men and I were the other—witnesses to a notorious political failure."

Kotarō was lost again. What had the SEALs got to do with the senator? What had they witnessed?

"I always thought," Brendan went on, "that the pressure to strike at the insurgents after the Chinook debacle had come straight from the White House, but as soon as B told me what the senator had tried to make him believe, I knew he had taken part in that decision.

"The details of the operation are classified material—the more so since it was a perfect example of a clusterfuck. It never made the news, and the only people who knew what went on, apart from us, were the base commander and the ones back home who had instigated the action.

"I don't know what kind of leverage the senator had on the military, but he managed to force their hand into sending a SEAL combat unit after the insurgents in the Pech Valley."

Aniki frowned. "Don't you military people sign those confidentiality papers that prevent you from running your mouths off?"

Brendan didn't smile in his usual smug way, but Kotarō noticed his eyes were crinkling weirdly, as if he found what Aniki said funny—or absolutely brilliant. "Yeah. Some of us have to sign nondisclosure agreements, but it doesn't stop some guys from leaking sensitive information. Look at that Team Six dude who's written a book about the mission to get Osama bin Laden, or the guys who worked with a video-game maker and revealed too much technical information.

"We're not supposed to talk, but there's always a chance that we might— especially those of us who hold a grudge against meddling politicians."

"But what about the others?" Aniki asked. "Why does the man believe they won't talk?"

"He doesn't," Brendan said. "We suspect that's why Bobcat has been discharged on mental health grounds. Not that he isn't a walking case of PTSD, but it takes a lot for the Navy shrinks to give someone a 100 percent disability rating, and Bobcat looks pretty functional to me."

"Hell," Big B added with a smirk, "you've got to be a head case to join the frogmen in the first place."

Brendan nodded. "So we believe the senator had a hand in getting Bobcat out of the way. And once he's been declared mentally incapacitated, his credibility is close to zero, should he decide to talk.

"The other two members of the unit are still in the teams, so they're controlled, and might end up dead or incapacitated anyway. That only leaves Big B and me."

"And Kenshin's father pitted your man against you," the boss said, "hoping to get some compromising information on you."

Brendan shook his head. "No, not that. I think he was acting on the common belief that special ops people have violent natures that only military training can somehow tame, so he probably expected B to get mad and kill me. Otherwise there's nothing either in my service record or in the cases I've worked up until now to suggest that I was going to… um… act out of character and blunder my way through this assignment."

"Maybe you're right," the boss said with a face that clearly meant Brendan was wrong. "But if your man had killed you, sooner or later the police would have followed the paper trail to the senator, and someone who'd go as far as Kenshin's father has gone to avoid a scandal wouldn't be very happy to see his name come up in a murder investigation."

Brendan snorted. "So, according to you, the senator put B on my trail hoping to catch me in what? Illegal garbage disposal? Smoking in restricted areas?"

The boss kept his imperturbable face. "I believe the senator had a good reason to expect you to do something he'd be able to use against you, no matter your past record."

Another snort. Kotarō didn't know why the boss bothered to talk to the stupid redhead. Now the man smiled and asked in a mocking tone, "And what reason would the senator have to believe I would do something to damage my reputation?"

"Let me see," the boss said as if he had trouble coming up with a reason, "What about the fact that you're gay?"

CHAPTER 35

KINOSUKE FELT both angry and embarrassed—angry because that seemed like a low blow coming from the boss, and embarrassed because, well, it was the fucking truth.

He should know. He was the costar in the porn flicks the big Hawaiian was sure to have sent along with the documentary about drug-dealing juvies starring Kotarō.

Pissed off as he was, Kinosuke still had to give both Brendan and the boss credit for not doing the obvious and turn to look at him as part and parcel of the fucking *gay* thing.

"I've been gay all my life," Brendan said in a tightly controlled tone, "and it had never compromised my work before. Never."

"Yeah, nobody had a freaking clue," Big B spat, and Brendan did turn his head this time to look at the man.

"So it helped you believe I betrayed you," Brendan said, a wry smile on his lips, "knowing that I was a faggot, huh?"

Big B straightened as he turned to face Brendan, looming over him like a huge, enraged volcano. "No, you stupid son of a bitch. It was the fact that you'd kept that little detail from us. Did you think we couldn't be trusted with your dirty secret, that we'd let you die if we knew?"

"It wasn't your fucking business," Brendan said, though it almost sounded as if he were trying to convince himself.

"It wasn't your fucking business that Paul was cheating on his wife either," Big B shouted, "or that Bobcat felt guilty about his brother's death, or that my wife's family didn't want her to marry native trash, but we still told you, because you weren't simply the boss or a fight buddy—you were a friend."

Brendan fell silent and Big B took the chance to go on with his tirade. "Didn't you know us well enough to understand our faggot jokes meant nothing? Hadn't you heard our Marielito jokes, or the times we called Otter *homey*? Hell, man, you can't imagine how much easier things would've been for the Twins if they'd known, if they could have talked to someone who wouldn't just give them birdbrained straight advice on relationships."

Now Brendan's eyes went wide as some realization hit home. "The Twins are…?"

Big B snorted. "Yeah, you self-centered prick. Did you think you were the only queer in the teams? The Twins aren't just gay either, so you know; they're boyfriends, or partners, or soul mates or whatever fancy name you want to give them—'cause they're sure more than fuck buddies to still be together after three years."

Kinosuke tried hard not to gawk as Kotarō was doing, but it was really difficult. Brendan had two brothers in his team who were making out with each other? Twin brothers? And the rest of the men gave them advice on relationships?

"Three years," Brendan repeated, flabbergasted.

"Three whole years and counting. And you, smart-assed fucker that you are, hadn't the foggiest idea. I bet you even thought they lived together to share expenses," Big B said. "Jesus, man, you made us all feel like losers with all the chinks in our armors while you shone like perfect Saint Brendan of the SEALs."

Brendan blinked in surprise. "I never—"

"Mr. O'Farrihy."

Everybody looked at the boss as he called Brendan's name, and Kinosuke did a double take. Fuck. He knew that expression, knew that when the man looked almost as pale and stiff as a temple statue, they were up to their necks in shit.

"Did the senator threaten Kenshin that he would use this video of Kotarō if he didn't leave me?"

CHAPTER 36

BRENDAN TOOK a deep breath. Matsunaga was smart, no two ways about it, and now all the goons were cussing and glaring at B and him as if they were the ones who had threatened their precious *Kenshin-san*. Not that they were too far off the mark, but the fact that they'd come here to tell them had to mean something.

He grabbed the Netbook they had brought with them and opened the file with the video. If he said a word now, any word, it would take the Blue Helmets to stop the fight that would ensue, so he just turned the small screen to face Matsunaga and company, then pressed play.

"Mr. Harris?"

Brendan didn't need to watch the screen to see the four men entering Ken's studio, the way they spread to cover the exit, the way Ken almost jumped off of his stool when he heard his name called that way.

"Who are you? How did you get in here? This is private property. I'll call the police if you don't leave right now."

"Your father sent us, Mr. Harris. There's no need to involve the police in what is strictly a family matter."

The fucker in the suit spoke like a fed—dressed like a fed too. Brendan had studied the video enough times to know these men were trained professionals, ex-government agents or military, and no street toughs hired on the spot. They had stalked Harris, waited patiently until all of Matsunaga's men were out and the woman at the reception desk was distracted for some reason.

"Yeah? And what family matter has my father hired you to discuss with me? Thanksgiving dinner?"

"Senator Harris wants you to come with us so he can discuss it with you."

Of course Ken hadn't fallen for that ruse.

"You want me to believe my father has traveled all the way from New Hampshire to talk to me when he didn't even phone the Tokyo hospital I had to stay in after...?"

There was an awkward pause, and one of the suits checked his watch ostensibly.

"Just tell my father this is my home now, and I only want to live my life in peace; I won't bother him if he doesn't bother me or the people I care about."

It was obvious nobody expected Ken to go willingly, because the men had come prepared to put some pressure on him.

Brendan watched the faces of the Japanese in front of him as one of the suits showed Ken the video taken at the mall. The kid Kotarō looked about to cry, Tachibana kept fingering the gun as if he wanted to shoot the moving images, Shinya's eyes had narrowed to slits, and Matsunaga was clenching his jaw so hard Brendan could almost hear his teeth grind.

But the worst was Kinosuke, because he didn't look angry. He looked guilty, or rather ashamed, and it was Brendan who had put that look on his face.

"Okay. Where are you taking me?"

Ken had not hesitated, and Brendan admired the way he'd kept trying to wring some information out of the hired men, the way he never quite surrendered, fumbling for a way out even though the situation seemed to offer none. Harris was a fighter, and it didn't surprise Brendan anymore that a man like Matsunaga had fallen for him.

"Don't worry about that, Mr. Harris. Just follow us."

"I'll need to pack a few things."

"We'll get you anything you need on the way."

"Fine, then, but at least I'll have to leave a note."

"I'm afraid I can't allow that, Mr. Harris. Please come with me."

"Don't you fucking touch me. I'm going with you, but if I don't take anything with me or leave a note to make it look like I left of my own will, you're gonna have five angry yakuza on your trail, and I don't know if you understand how far these men are ready to go for a question of honor."

The video went on for the very short time it had taken Ken to write the note he left on the coffee table of his and Matsunaga's place. When the video finally ended, the five Japanese kept looking at the blank screen as if they expected to see where Harris had been taken if they focused with enough intensity—and intensity was something these guys had in spades.

It was Matsunaga who spoke first. "You don't have cameras covering the street." It wasn't even a question, but Big B answered anyway.

"No. I would have been too exposed if I'd tried to plant them there, so I just waited until you and your men were at the dojo or out to sneak in and set a few in your living quarters."

Matsunaga gave him a hard look that told Brendan how imposing he must have been as a yakuza boss, but Big B and he had faced far worse elements in their time, and if B seemed to be squirming a little under the unforgiving stare, it was only because he felt guilty.

Yeah. This was turning into a guilt slugfest, with all of them fighting to prove their own flubs were the worst ever. Kotarō was obviously thinking it was his fault that Harris had been forced to leave; Tachibana and Shinya seemed to be scolding themselves for letting their guards down and allowing not only B to place the cameras but also four strangers to enter their house and take Kenneth with them; Matsunaga must be cursing his pride for making himself believe whatever the note said; B was angry because he'd been conned into thinking he was doing the right thing; Kinosuke must be feeling Brendan had used him and believing that, by trusting Brendan, he had all but conjured the four men who had taken Kenneth. And Brendan, well, he just knew that, contrary to what everybody else thought, it was *him* who had caused this clusterfuck and had managed to make his friends almost hate him and the man he'd fallen for hate him all the way.

"I'm sorry," B said, "but it wasn't personal. I was just doing my job."

Brendan opened his mouth to state the obvious, but Matsunaga beat him to it. "Where I come from, revenge is a very personal affair."

B looked angry now. "My *revenge*—if you want to put it that way—wasn't against you, and in any case, I never intended to cause you any harm. I just thought my former CO was too involved in the case to be objective, and yes, it gave me a certain satisfaction to spoil his apparent plans after what I was told about him."

Matsunaga kept his impassible countenance, though Brendan was starting to understand that the more inscrutable the man's expression became, the more dangerous the situation was. He bet Matsunaga would look like one of those serene, meditating Buddha statues before he unsheathed his katana to chop some heads off.

"Excuse me if I don't care about your motivations, Mr. Fernandes," Matsunaga said in his most patronizing, I'm-the-fucking-emperor-of-Japan tone, "because the truth is you both acted in a completely unprofessional way, and while I can understand why Mr. O'Farrihy would believe an American senator over a bunch of Japanese thugs, the fact that you chose to believe a stranger over a man you considered more your friend than your leader tells me how much you value honor. So please save your apologies for someone who enjoys empty words."

Brendan couldn't hold back his anger. "Don't you give us fucking classes on the value of honor when you've betrayed your own lover. You know as well as I do that Ken is too smart to leave a meaningless note behind; he must have found a way to spell out his situation for you, but you were too damned proud to see beyond the fact that he was leaving you—*you*, the great Matsunaga—and so you chose to believe every single word of that note and abandoned the man who'd almost been killed once because of his association with you and who is still in danger for the very same reason. And don't tell me Americans have no honor, because Kenneth Harris has more honor and more courage in one of his bleached hairs than the whole lot of you pretentious yakuza."

This time both Big B and he jumped to their feet at the same time the Japanese did, but before they came to blows, Matsunaga raised a hand and shouted, "*Yamero!*" effectively stopping his men.

"Mr. O'Farrihy." Brendan turned to Matsunaga, surprised to realize he'd been ambling toward Kinosuke, as if he craved his contact so much that even a fight with him would have done. "We all have our mistakes to regret, and this is not the time to exchange accusations. I appreciate your sharing your information with us, but I hope we don't have to ever meet again."

It was a clear dismissal, and suddenly Brendan felt depleted, empty, as if he hadn't achieved a single thing by coming here. And didn't it sum up his whole career, this fumbling about with the best intentions that always ended with someone he cared about hurt?

His eyes traveled to Kinosuke of their own accord, finding only anger and pain on the young man's face, a face Brendan might never see again. He then turned back to Matsunaga and saw that, even though the man wore an imperturbable mask, there was clearly the same pain in his eyes—the same anger and shame at his failure to protect his own—and that was something Brendan understood only too well.

He knew this was his last chance to try to fix anything, so he swallowed his pride and knelt in front of Matsunaga, leaning forward until his forehead touched the floor as he'd seen Kotarō and Kinosuke do.

"Please accept my apologies," he said, every single word that he uttered in that humiliating posture hurting like hell, but maybe because of that, also managing to relieve him of some of the weight he'd been carrying on his shoulders. "I'm at your disposal for anything you might need to find Ken and bring him back home."

When Matsunaga didn't answer, Brendan raised his head and saw him nod. He stood then, and the ex-yakuza surprised him by holding out a hand for Brendan to shake. Of the few things he knew about Japanese culture, this was one of them—the certainty that they avoided physical contact as a principle—so Matsunaga's gesture was an obvious concession to him, reciprocity for the way he'd forced himself to do something so alien to his own culture.

They shook hands as Matsunaga said, "I'll let you know if there's something you can help us with."

That was what Brendan had learned was the Japanese way to say "No," but he could do nothing about it. He nodded, forcing himself to not look in Kinosuke's direction. As much as he'd wanted to build a bridge between them, this was not about the man who'd been his sensei, the man he loved; this was something Brendan needed to do for his own sake—the proof he needed that he was still man enough to own up to his mistakes. Atonement would come later, when he left the dojo for good, when he took a plane knowing that he was leaving his heart behind, that the men who'd been his friends would never look at him the same way, even though all the lies had been cleared, and that he'd wrecked the life of a man he'd come to admire through the eyes of the men who loved him.

He would fly back to a place he had never really considered his home with the heavy knowledge that, one way or another, he had failed everyone.

CHAPTER 37

KINOSUKE TRIED to focus on the words the boss was reading aloud, but the image of Brendan kneeling on the tatami kept flashing through his mind.

That must have cost him an awful lot, considering how swellheaded the man was. And yet he'd done it; he'd come to them as soon as he'd discovered what had really happened to Kenshin-san, he'd told them about his friend's betrayal even though it must have shamed him to do so, and he'd even offered to help after he apologized.

Of course the boss hadn't accepted that offer. They had no way to know if this was another, more elaborate plot to keep an eye on them and prevent them from ever getting Kenshin-san back.

The big Hawaiian had made a show of removing every single camera he'd installed, but Brendan and he wouldn't need any device if they were to team with them and be given first-hand information on their movements.

And yet, Brendan had been right. The boss had waited too long to start looking because he'd believed Kenshin-san had left him—he'd believed the note he was reading to them now, the note he had only recently admitted to having. Because he was too proud and because, no matter how he felt about Kenshin-san, the man was still a gaijin, someone who was likely to act in ways that would bring shame to those close to him. Just like Brendan.

"Why does he say 'Fujiyama'?" Kotarō asked. "Is that the American name of Fujisan?"

The boss closed his eyes. He should have known Kenshin-san knew too much about Japan to avoid that common mistake in reading the kanji for Mount Fuji. But obviously he hadn't. Because he'd been too angry to really pay attention to the words. Angry because he'd felt betrayed, abandoned. Just like Kinosuke.

"That's a hint, Kotarō," Tachibana explained without looking at the boss. "Kenshin-san is trying to tell us that the note is a lie."

"Oh, so that thing about the lake is a lie too?"

Kinosuke frowned. Lake? What was Kotarō talking about?

"That's what's different from the rest of the note," Tachibana said. "I suppose there must be some hidden meaning behind all that nonsense about the lake and Fujisan, but I don't get what he's trying to say."

Kotarō looked like a little kid who had just been given a jigsaw puzzle, completely focused and content, as if the more irregular the pieces, the more fun he'd get out of it. Kinosuke hadn't even paid attention to the words, but he bet Brendan's experience as a private detective would have helped him solve the riddle in a few seconds.

But Brendan wasn't there anymore, and he hadn't been there when the men beside him had found him and Kenshin-san the first time, when it was a question of life or death.

Kinosuke doubted the senator would hurt his son—at least not physically—and that gave them some margin to work all this mess out.

They could do it, even if this wasn't their territory, even if the rules here were different, even if they had never dealt with politicians and spooks before. For Kenshin-san, they could do this and much more.

"Can you read those words again, boss?" he asked, forcing himself to focus.

The boss nodded and started reading. *"I can only hope that this separation is temporary, that we can do like those couples who take some time off to visit an onsen beside a lake with the Fujiyama in the background."*

True, the sentence was a little offbeat. Why mention a visit to a spa in Japan? Was it only to write the word *Fujiyama* so they knew something was wrong?

"Did you ever talk about that?" Kinosuke asked the boss.

"About going to some onsen?" the boss asked, and at Kinosuke's nod, he answered, "I don't think we ever mentioned that; at least I can't remember talking about it. Kenshin must have tried to hint at something the Americans with him wouldn't know, something Japanese that isn't common knowledge here."

They kept silent for a moment, thinking about the words.

"You can see Mount Fuji from the Five Lakes," Shinya said.

There were five lakes called Fuji-Goko for the reason Shinya had mentioned, but still Kinosuke couldn't figure what that had to do with anything. It was ridiculous to think Kenshin-san would have been taken to Japan, to an onsen near a volcanic lake of all places. And just the thought of volcanic lakes brought back those days with Brendan on the Big Island, driving from volcano to volcano and fucking like rabbits on the plush bed of that expensive place that sure as hell must have a spa somewhere in all the acres it sprawled across.

"What if he's talking about some place here?" he asked. "These islands are full of volcanoes; it shouldn't be difficult to find a few with a lake close to them, and if there's a good view, these people would sure have built a resort there for tourists."

Kinosuke saw the men perk up at the possibility, and he tried not to blush at the association that had made him come up with the idea. No matter what happened later, those days had been good. He didn't remember any other time he'd felt so much at ease—and so horny—around someone before. And even if Brendan had been using him, he couldn't fake the way he seemed to want Kinosuke, how he looked at him as if he had hung the moon. The trip by itself didn't fit in the whole spying scheme either, unless Brendan had expected to grill him for information, but Kinosuke didn't remember him ever mentioning Kenshin-san or trying to steer any conversation in that direction.

Shit. How he wished he'd stop thinking about the lying bastard and his shock of red hair.

"You saw the video," the boss said. "Those men never told Kenshin where they were taking him; there was no way he'd known it before he wrote the note."

That was true. Whatever their gaijin was hinting at, it wasn't a place.

"What if he just used the Fuji trick to let us know he was in danger and there's no other clue in that piece of paper?" Tachibana said. "It's not like he had much time to think with those bastards breathing down his neck."

Kinosuke saw the boss hesitate and start to believe what Tachibana was saying. And it made him so angry, the way the man didn't know his own lover, the way he kept doubting him, that Kinosuke almost shouted his answer. "That's bullshit. Kenshin-san might be a space cadet sometimes, but he sure as hell can outsmart any hired muscle."

"I wouldn't call American special agents *hired muscle*," the boss said, his lips twitching a little, "but you're right about that. Kenshin is nothing but smart, and we know he doesn't break under pressure."

The boss sobered after those words, and well he might, because if the man didn't know it, Kinosuke did. He'd been locked in a basement with Kenshin-san for days with nothing to do but wait for the crazy fucker who'd caught them to make an appearance and choose a new way to torture the gaijin.

He knew damn well Kenshin-san didn't break under pressure because the man had fucking saved Kinosuke's neck under all the pressure in the world. Some military-trained, fucking sea-air-land blowhards could learn a thing or two from that skinny gaijin.

"You can see Fujisan from Ashi-no-ko too," Kotarō suddenly said and all of them turned to look at him as if he'd gone mad. All this time and he was still thinking about lakes with spas?

"What?" the kid asked defensively. "That lake is in the Hakone area, and Hakone is famous for its onsen."

Tachibana patted Kotarō's head. "You know your geography very well, *Kō-chan*."

They tried not to laugh at the kiddy pet name, but they lost it when Kotarō pouted mightily. He probably believed he had outgrown the men's banter by now.

The boss took pity on him and explained, "We think Kenshin is not talking about a real place, Kotarō, but giving us clues about something connected to Japan in some way only we—"

Kinosuke's eyes widened when he saw the boss jump to his feet, a curse leaving his lips as he ran out of the room. Kinosuke looked at the others in confusion, but after Shinya got up and followed the boss, they all peered into the bedroom where Matsunaga-san was in the process of tearing up the closet.

The man kept murmuring something as shirts, pants and sweaters flew every other way, and it took Kinosuke some effort to understand he was saying the words *Hakone box* like a mantra.

What the fuck?

CHAPTER 38

BRENDAN ZIPPED up his leather bag. And then unzipped it, just to have something to do.

He hadn't needed to buy an extra bag, because he wasn't taking anything with him on his way home. The T-shirts and light pants he had bought didn't take much room, the suit he'd been wearing when he arrived he would be wearing when he left, just like the broken heart.

He snorted. He'd never expected to wax poetic at the flip of a coin. Living in Washington, working in an environment where nothing but power really mattered, had numbed what was left of him after Afghanistan, and the few emotions he had buried deep inside were kept safely there by Craig, who offered him the much-needed tension relief but had never wanted to scrape his filmy surface for fear of what might lurk beneath it.

Not that Brendan was blaming Craig; he'd always been upfront with Brendan about his expectations—or rather, his lack of them—but Brendan felt let down, disappointed, because now that someone had shown him what being alive was—with all its conflict and pain but also true joy and pleasure—he couldn't bear the weight of the protective blanket he'd hidden under. And yet, he didn't know what to do with that new knowledge, where to go from there without guidance, without help, without someone who would prod, coax, and look after him until his new skin stopped being so raw.

Maybe if Matsunaga had let him help, it would have been different—at least he would have felt useful, spent some time with Kinosuke even if the young man wouldn't talk to him, found some closure by using his skills for something that was clearly on the right side of things, way past those blurred, gray boundaries he'd been sinking into.

But just because he'd apologized didn't mean the yakuza boss had any reason to trust him—Matsunaga was too clever to fall for that trick, even if it wasn't a trick at all. The man was protecting his own, something Brendan wished he had been able to do.

His own. Brendan had once believed his crewmen to be his closest friends, his family, his own. But even at the best of times, it seemed Brendan's behavior had set him too far apart and above them, as if he'd needed the distance to maintain his authority, as if he were too aloof and self-righteous to stoop to their level.

Keeping his sexual orientation from them had proven fatal, because it put his friends in the same place as the Navy—that faceless, anonymous institution that would judge Brendan for that trait only, without caring about who he was as a whole. He should have given his friends the chance to decide if they cared, but he'd feared some of them might leave the unit, might even ruin his career if they thought being a faggot made him unfit to lead. Simply put, he hadn't trusted them. And it served him right that they hadn't trusted him back.

Christ. Just to think about the Twins made him mad. How blind had he been? How worried about not giving himself away that he hadn't seen the signs in those two? It must have been so difficult, especially for Otter. Making it into the teams had taken some balls, but being a SEAL, African American, gay, and in love with a white man was really topping it all. And it wouldn't have been exactly a walk in the park for John Burka either, since being almost albino must have been enough of a bully magnet all of his life without adding being queer—and in love with a black man.

"You shouldn't leave the door unlocked. Some undesirable might sneak up on you while you're playing fetch with your rock-star luggage."

He didn't turn around to answer. "Oh, don't worry. I can take on any tattooed thug who comes through that door. I used to be a SEAL, you know."

"Yeah, well, but dinosaurs were roaming the earth at that time; you might be a little rusty now."

He reached back to flip the bird in Big B's direction and heard the man chuckle. He finally turned to meet a rather subdued version of B's signature smile.

"Why don't you stay a little longer?" B said. "You could do some sightseeing, some surfing, meet some—"

B checked himself before he said something about meeting chicks in Waikiki. Yeah. It had been too many years of pretending; it slipped easily, even though the man had seen him with Kinosuke in compromising enough positions to know what Brendan was all about. And it was Brendan's own fucking fault, so he just smiled as if he hadn't noticed a thing.

"I have to go back, B," he said. "I need to make some changes, move out of the District, start a chinchilla farm in the Rockies, that sort of thing."

He tried to make it light, but B could see right through him, and he wasn't the kind of guy to keep his thoughts to himself.

"You're good at what you do. Don't let this... mess make you go thinking about career changes. What you need is some clientele change, get your ass out of that back-stabbing politician milieu."

He wasn't smiling; no sir, he wasn't.

"What? You thought Hawaiians were too ignorant to know some fancy-assed French words?"

"*Fancy-assed* is French?" Brendan joked, the smile finally showing on his lips.

"No, but *go fuck yourself with the Eiffel tower* is."

Brendan laughed. What seemed like ages ago, it had been easy to laugh like this with his men. Now, even though B was smiling, there was a certain something in his eyes—maybe pain, maybe regret—but the simple, open bond of comradeship was broken, if there had ever been such a thing between them.

His phone message alert brought him back to reality, to this room that had no trace left of him except for his packed bag on the bed. That was him, moving from here to there with the stealth of a special operator, inserting and extracting himself without a fuss, never leaving anything to be remembered by except destruction.

He retrieved his cell to check the caller ID and his heart stopped short.

Kinosuke. Texting him. Was he so angry that he needed to at least send him a choice of written insults? Brendan didn't dare explore other possibilities, but as he clicked the message open, he couldn't help feeling a little hope, something small and flickering but still warming his chest like a timid candle flame.

Get your ass over here ASAP. Bring help.

THERE THEY were again, Big B and him, making the same trip through the streets of Honolulu to reach the dojo. And if Brendan had been concerned the first time, he was fucking vibrating with worry this time.

Knowing Kinosuke—and the man's pride—it would have taken all but a tsunami alert for him to call Brendan after what had happened, and in less than twenty-four hours too.

Had Senator Harris decided keeping his son away from the yakuza wasn't enough, that he had to erase the threat once and for all? However conveniently far from the mainland Hawaii was, it still was US territory, so the man had to be careful about who he hired and what for if he didn't want an even bigger scandal hanging over his head. And yet it was obvious the senator had contacts in the private military sector—he'd hired two ex-SEALs first and then a bunch of what looked like ex-government agents—and it was not too absurd to think he might even be able to pull some strings with Homeland Security. A new yakuza gang settling in Hawaii would no doubt capture the attention of a number of agencies, from the DEA to the ATF.

Brendan felt the reassuring pressure of the Glock against the small of his back and pictured the dojo in his mind, focusing on the best way to surprise anyone who might have made their way in.

Planning always calmed him, grounded him, maybe because it offered a semblance of control over the events that allowed him to believe he could influence the outcome. But it was difficult to keep the image of Kinosuke in danger from interfering with his thinking.

"They aren't defenseless civilians, you know," Big B said, as if reading his mind, though Brendan didn't think he was doing such a good job with his poker face.

"Yeah," he agreed. "They're not your usual clueless goons."

He remembered the way Shinya, the one with the awful scar, had been about to pound B to the ground—and it took a lot to outmaneuver a SEAL.

"And it's a good sign that Kinosuke has been able to use his phone," B insisted and Brendan almost laughed. Funny that one of his men had to reassure *him*, when he was supposed to be the one on top of things—or at least had been supposed to not that long ago.

He told himself this was the chance he'd been waiting for, a way to do something with a purpose he understood and approved of from beginning to end. Yeah. He could do this, and do it well because he had the training, the experience, and the guts to succeed.

"Did you sneak in through Matsunaga's garage to plant the cameras?" he asked B, already focused on the action ahead.

B smirked, recognizing a fellow predator on the prowl. "Nah, I tampered with Kotarō's window the first time so it could be opened from the outside."

Brendan shook his head. "You lazybones."

"Yup, dat's me, da lazy moke."

He snorted, feeling his tension recede to a point where it would only help to keep him alert, not hinder his every movement. They fell into the familiar silence of an op, made more comfortable by their shared experiences; they didn't even need to exchange hand signals to know what the other would do next.

B parked in a deserted side street, and they jogged to the dojo, using the parked cars to cover their approach. It was lunchtime on a Saturday morning and the residential area around the dojo was dead to the world, so they didn't call undue attention by playing hide and seek behind the rows of cars.

Matsunaga's garage door was closed, and Kotarō's window looked perfectly closed too but, as they pressed their backs against the outer wall of the former warehouse, Brendan could see the window didn't quite fit in place. He made a mental note to remind Matsunaga he was in America now and that window badly needed some burglar proofing.

B slowly pushed the window open as Brendan watched the street. When no movement came from inside of the building, they both pulled their guns and Brendan shoved the curtain aside with the muzzle of his Glock to take a peek. He made the clear sign to B. The big man climbed soundlessly in and Brendan quickly followed.

The sliding panels facing the yard were partially drawn to one side, so B and he stayed low until they were sure there was nobody near. Then they moved to the side door that connected the room to Matsunaga's place through the garage and slid it open without a sound.

All was quiet here too. Brendan took note of the ledge where the keys for the SUV lay, in case they needed a quick escape, yet the fact that the car was there and no noise came from the rest of the house was giving Brendan a bad feeling.

It stood to reason that the yakuza would be together in Matsunaga's place if they were discussing the new problem that had arisen, and even if they talked more or less quietly, Brendan should have been able to hear them. The overwhelming silence could only mean his worst fears about possible intruders had come true.

He looked at B and saw the same realization in his eyes. This was a hostage situation; the first few minutes—the way they crossed this threshold—would determine whether they won or lost.

They stood to either side of the door, listening for a few seconds. Nothing. At least the sliding panels had the advantage of leaving no place to hide immediately behind them, so if someone was near, they'd be either too far to react quickly or close enough for Brendan and B to see them first.

Brendan took a deep breath to steady himself and nodded to B, who yanked the door open without any finesse. Time took that strange quality that combat adrenaline always granted, instinct and training mixing to enhance each other, giving Brendan an extraordinarily acute perception of every detail around him.

He concentrated on his side of the door, his vision sweeping the room from that side to an imaginary line that started in the area B would control, the area Brendan didn't need to worry about because that was what teamwork meant, leaving yourself deliberately open for someone to get your back.

When he was sure there was no one lurking close by, Brendan rushed into the room, his posture slightly hunched to make a smaller target, his Glock held steady and moving in sync with his eyes.

They were in the middle of the room, B and him, when all hell broke loose. Brendan caught a blur of movement to his left and, as he had predicted, whoever had been out of Brendan's sight before he entered the place was now in too much of a hurry to shoot straight, and obviously too far to try to hit him—or he would have been if the guy hadn't been brandishing a fucking baseball bat.

Shit. Brendan barely had time to jerk his gun out of reach of the downstroke, but as he did, the damned bat twirled like a majorette's baton and rushed to hit the unprotected side of his neck, and in that fraction of a second before the wood connected with his flesh—in that window of time when he should have reacted and moved away—Brendan clearly saw his attacker and froze in place.

CHAPTER 39

"*KUSO* AMERICAN! Can't you fucking use the front door like a normal person?"

Kinosuke was so angry he wanted to smash the bokken on Brendan's head. And those green eyes were blinking, looking at him as if he were a three-horned *oni* with the tongue of a snake and the sharp-toothed smile of a jackal.

Shit. Any other person in the whole fucking world would have been shitting his pants, seeing that Kinosuke had been about to knock the man out cold, but the wacky redhead looked like a love-struck puppy instead.

"Sensei," Brendan whispered, and damn if it didn't turn all the anger tightening Kinosuke's chest into something even more furious and hot, but so different that Kinosuke was sure everybody else in the room could see his skin burning red from head to toe.

Fortunately Brendan shook himself out of his daze at that moment, and he turned to look for his crony. The big Hawaiian had the tip of the boss's bokken pressing under his chin, and he was holding his—empty—gun hand as if it hurt.

"Please, Mr. Matsunaga," Brendan said carefully, "we meant no harm. I just took Kinosuke's text to mean you were being held up, and we barged in this way trying to surprise your attackers."

Right. Now of course it was Kinosuke's fault. He opened his mouth to give the man a piece of his mind, but he saw the boss raise a brow, and he shut his trap.

"You thought Kenshin's father had sent an army?" Matsunaga-san asked.

No, by the way Brendan looked, he had underestimated them, had thought that even after what had happened, they'd let anybody stroll into their house and catch them unprepared. He didn't seem to understand that even Kenshin-san would have given his father's men a hard time if they hadn't threatened him with Kotarō's video.

"We came to help, okay?" Big B grumbled. "Just think that we're rude Americans who never knock and let it rest, for Christ's sake. I bet there are more pressing things we could be discussing right now." He looked at the boss pointedly. "And would you mind taking the fucking chopstick off my face?"

From where he stood pointing at Brendan with his gun, Tachibana snorted. "You tell your boss man to drop the glitzy RTF, and I'll tell mine to drop the chopstick."

Kinosuke rolled his eyes. School kids, the whole lot of them. Brendan made a show of placing his gun on the floor while the boss put the bokken away ever so slowly, the two of them barely managing to contain a smirk. *Kuso gaki.*

"If you're finished measuring your—weapons," Kinosuke said testily, "we could decide how to help Kenshin-san."

"*Hai*, Sensei," Brendan said with his thick American accent, and Kinosuke would have sworn even Shinya was trying to hide a smile. Fucking first graders. He was almost out the door to the garden before he realized what they had to show Brendan was in the room he was about to leave. Shit. If any one of them said a single word, he was gonna put the bokken to good use.

The boss cleared his throat suspiciously as the rest of the goofballs ducked their heads. Good thing Kotarō was manning the reception desk, or he would have giggled in the worst Kotarō-style. "Um, Mr. O'Farrihy, there's something we want you to take a look at," Matsunaga-san said.

"Please, call me Brendan."

Kinosuke rolled his eyes and plopped down by the coffee table unceremoniously—he wasn't playing the good host to someone who'd entered through the window. The boss offered the couch to Brendan and his man, and he sat in the matching armchair while Shinya and Tachibana took places on the floor near Kinosuke.

"The note Kenshin left," the boss said, "had a hidden message about this box."

Brendan and Big B eyed the wooden piece warily, as if it were rigged with explosives or something. When the boss waved for them to go ahead and grab it, Brendan reached out and lifted it off the table.

"The Hakone area, back in Japan, is renowned for its woodcraft," the boss explained. "They make this signature mosaic marquetry called *yosegi-zaiku* using timber with different natural colors that they cut and glue into traditional patterns. The result is shaved into very thin sheets that can be applied to boxes like this one, or trays, or pieces of furniture."

Kinosuke suppressed a chuckle at the picture Brendan and his man presented— two mean supersoldiers huddled together over a dainty little box, listening to the boss like attentive pupils and running awkward fingers over the smooth surface as if they could tell the different kinds of timber used to build the geometric pattern.

Brendan hefted the wooden cube in his hand and turned it every other way while the boss kept silent. Oh man. This had to be good. The boss was going to let them try to open it.

"You said it's a box?" Brendan asked, shaking the piece carefully. "So I take it there's something important inside?"

The boss nodded. "It's a *himitsu bako*, a box for secrets—or what you'd call a puzzle box."

"Uh-huh," Brendan said absently, already too engrossed in the task to even look at Matsunaga-san.

Kinosuke shook his head; the guy loved a challenge, no matter if it was going through the toughest military training, learning a new martial art, or—yes, maybe Kinosuke'd been a challenge for Brendan too—seducing the yakuza, making the tough Japanese dude bend to his wishes or some shit like that. Although if he was honest, he had to admit it almost looked like the other way round, as if Brendan had wanted to bend to *Kinosuke's* wishes—and literally too. It had given Kinosuke a powerful feeling to see someone as strong as Brendan willing to let Kinosuke have his way, but maybe the man was trained to find out what made the enemy tick and use it against him.

And yet, Kinosuke had only needed to call for help to have Brendan storming the fort to his rescue. Why was he even here? Was it just because he felt guilty? Was he getting anything out of it? And why the fuck had Kinosuke called him in the first place?

The information Kenshin had left behind was so murky they didn't know how to go about it, and the first thing Kinosuke had thought was that Brendan would know what it meant. He still wasn't sure the redhead could be trusted, but he was damn sure the man was good at what he did—and maybe Kinosuke couldn't trust him because the wound to his pride was bone-deep and humiliation was the worst place to judge anyone from.

Nobody in Kinosuke's life had ever made him think so much about his fucking feelings; it made him so angry he wanted everyone else in the room gone so he could shout his head off at Brendan—and maybe fuck him through the floor after that. Shit. What a mess.

"There," the big man pointed to one side of the box, "the surface looks different there."

Brendan slid a small wooden panel to the right. That was the easy first step—*good luck with the fifty-three other ones left.*

CHAPTER 40

BRENDAN WANTED to smash the damn box against the wall. Between B and him, they had already slid the delicate wooden panels back and forth, up and down, right and left about twenty times, and the thing kept tantalizingly half-closed, showing glimpses of the interior compartment but never the whole of it, or at least not enough to empty its contents through the open slot. And when Brendan shook it, the box sounded empty, which was even more maddening.

He hadn't checked his watch at the beginning, but he guessed at least fifteen minutes had already gone by. How long had the others been trying before they gave up? Hours, he supposed, considering how much it would cost the proud bastards to admit they needed help from the likes of Brendan.

Had Kinosuke texted him because they didn't know anybody else here? Or had he believed Brendan could really help, would *want* to help? And what did it mean either way? Unconsciously, Brendan's gaze lifted from the wooden patchwork in his hands to meet Kinosuke's eyes. The young man was glowering at him, but there were so many emotions boiling in those black pits that Brendan felt dizzy.

He hadn't thought his sensei would be ready to forgive him, so yeah, he'd expected the anger and the hurt that he could see right now, but somehow Kinosuke kept watching him eagerly. It surprised the hell out of Brendan that Kinosuke seemed to be waiting for his former pupil to do the right thing and going out of his mind with impatience because Brendan wasn't getting it.

Was this a test, then? But how could he succeed at a Japanese puzzle even the Japanese hadn't been able to solve? And suddenly a realization hit him.

He looked around at the faces of the other yakuza. They were watching him dispassionately, seemingly biding their time until Brendan got something done—or admitted that he couldn't. Was that it? A question of pride all over again? Would Matsunaga waste precious time when his lover was in danger to teach the stupid Americans a lesson? As far as Brendan knew, he might; and Brendan was a stupid enough American to have plunged into the challenge without asking first—God forbid he, the mighty SEAL, should admit he couldn't crack the simple mechanism of a wooden box.

Christ. He was so tired of all the bullshit. He reached out over the table and offered the damn box to Kinosuke. "Would you mind opening this for me, Sensei? I don't think I'd be able to do it before Christmas."

The surprise in Kinosuke's eyes would have been comical in any other situation, but now it mostly hurt. How had Brendan managed to give the impression that he would risk anybody's life to save his pride? Was that why his men had so easily believed he would put them in danger just to prove someone wrong?

He turned to look at Big B and saw to his chagrin that his former crewman was as stunned as Kinosuke, though he tried to hide it when he found Brendan looking at him.

It was Shinya, the scarred guy, who reacted first, taking the puzzle box from Kinosuke and placing it carefully on the table beside a closed folder that he pushed toward Brendan.

Geez. The contents of the box had been on the table the whole fucking time.

"This was in the lid's secret compartment," Shinya said, his hard eyes meeting Brendan's in a silent threat that he understood only too well. These people had no reason to trust him, and it must have taken Kinosuke a lot to convince them that they needed to call Brendan in the first place. Whatever was in the folder must never reach Senator Harris.

B was grousing under his breath, something about damn compartments and crafty Buddhaheads, but Brendan was already too focused on the single picture inside the folder to pay attention.

"Do you have the original file?" he asked without lifting his head, but the answering silence made him look up into blank faces—it seemed not all the Japanese were techno geeks after all. "This is a printout; if we could access the original image, we might be able to enlarge the details."

Matsunaga stood up and disappeared into the next room without a word. Brendan shook his head. He could understand their trust issues, but this was getting beyond ridiculous. How did they expect any help if they didn't share all the intel they had?

"Let me see," Big B said, and Brendan passed him the picture right when Matsunaga came back carrying a—magnifying glass? Fuck him sideways. A magnifying glass with a dragon carved on the jade handle.

"Kenshin doesn't have a computer," Matsunaga almost growled. "He hates them."

Yeah, well; the *wooden* box should have been a telltale. Brendan took the glass, trying to keep his composure, but when he exchanged a look with B, he had to duck his head to hide a grin.

The picture showed a group of men and women standing on the deck of a ship and wearing hard hats. They were looking with apparent interest at something the only man in uniform was pointing at, something out of the picture's frame.

"Is that an eagle on his shoulder?" B asked, and Brendan tried to use the magnifying glass to get a closer look at the insignia, but the image didn't have much resolution in that area.

"The shape seems about right. So a captain, I guess." Brendan moved the glass to the man's hat, trying to read the golden block letters on it. "Yeah. It says here 'Capt. K.' But the rest of his name is blurry. Below, it reads 'Ship…. Comm'—ship commander?"

B shook his head. "That ship looks too small for a captain to command."

"Aren't all ships… um… commanded by captains?"

It was Kinosuke asking, and Brendan looked up, trying not to smile. He was sure his sensei would mistake the encouragement for mockery, and that was the last thing Brendan needed right now. "Any officer who commands a ship is called 'captain,' but that doesn't mean it's his rank—it's more of a tradition than anything else. Captains in the Navy are like colonels in other services, so they usually command large ships— cruisers or similar."

Kinosuke nodded, but Brendan had learned the gesture just meant he was listening, not that he really understood what was said. And still it felt more than enough for Brendan, knowing that the young man could put aside his anger to talk to him and listen to his answers as if they were important. Brendan had it bad enough that even such a little nothing gave him hope.

"*Low water*?" B asked. "Why would they put that in block letters?"

Brendan looked back at the picture, at the banner on the deck railing B was reading aloud. "No. That banner is cut out of the photo; there's room for more words."

He tried to imagine what the missing words might be, but he found he needed something to write on; he always thought better when he could take notes. "Can I borrow some paper and a pen?" he asked Kinosuke.

And wasn't it cute, the way Kinosuke immediately sprang to his feet like any good-mannered Japanese boy, only to realize he didn't know where to go to find the things Brendan was asking for? Of course he blushed and then glared to hide his embarrassment, while Brendan found he was looking at the yakuza as a mother would watch the first awkward steps of her baby—with exactly the same rapture.

CHAPTER 41

"SO, WHAT we have so far is a small ship, probably a barge or a tugboat," Brendan said as he scribbled on the notebook Kinosuke had handed him, "a group of spiffy civilians in hard hats being shown around by a certain Captain K—who is ship commander or something close to that—and a banner with a slogan ending in 'low water,' which is obviously not a warning. What else?"

Kinosuke watched as the man Brendan called B put the trashy magnifying glass close to his eye and then raised the picture to study it. The jade dragon was completely hidden inside the grip of those thick fingers, so the glass looked almost normal and not like the ugly New Year's present the boss had only kept because Kenshin-san said it was kitsch. Kinosuke still couldn't work out what magnifying lenses had to do with kitchens, but it was the kind of wacky idea Kenshin-san would have. Shit. He was missing the guy something awful, especially now that Brendan was there, acting as if he cared and looking at him with a soft expression that had Kinosuke's insides in a knot. Kenshin-san would know what it all meant and wouldn't be embarrassed to put it in simple words.

"Here's part of the funnel," B said. "It's painted black with a big white M on it—I guess it's an M, though it could also be IVI; I can only see the lower part of it." Brendan wrote it down as B went on. "There are five suits and two chicks with Captain K."

"Five lads and two lassies with the skipper," Brendan read his notes aloud and Kinosuke saw B smile. He guessed it was some kind of military lingo.

"The hard hats are plain, except for this fat guy's. It has a sticker on it that... I can't make out except for the ending LLC."

"Hmm. A private contractor," Brendan mused. "If it wasn't for the ladies, it'd look like your typical groundbreaking photo op."

"Except there's no ground—only 'low water'—and there're chicks," B said.

"Uh-huh. So I'd say congressional delegation plus constructor looking at a building to be renovated on some Navy facility."

"I can buy that," B conceded without lifting his eyes from the picture. "But why look at a building from a boat? Unless—"

"Unless it's one of those buildings you can launch ships from, which would make our Captain K a shipyard commander," Brendan said with a grin.

Kinosuke blinked. He had expected Brendan to see more into the picture than the boss and they had, but this was simply amazing, the sheer volume of information the two Americans had deduced from what seemed trifling little details. And they were far from finished.

"What I don't get is that thing about low water," Brendan said. "It can't be about depth since you can't launch ships into low waters, so what is it—"

"Wait," B cut in. "There's something else here."

"Where?"

"A reflection on the wheelhouse window. It goes 'T-A-B-1-8,' I think."

Brendan wrote it down. "TAB 18?"

"Yeah, that's it."

Kinosuke watched Brendan's forehead crease in thought, and he surprised himself by wanting to reach out and touch, as if that could help, or simply make Kinosuke part of what was going on and not some outsider watching from a prudent distance.

"TAB," Brendan repeated. "Tactical Air Base?"

B just shook his head, and Brendan agreed. "I know. This is obviously a naval shipyard, so no air base. What about Tactical Analysis... uh... Branch?"

Another head shake from B. "That'd be intelligence," he said. "They wouldn't advertise themselves on the front of a shipyard building."

Brendan groaned in frustration. "We should Google it." He fished his cell out of his pants pocket and started fiddling with it.

"Here it is," Brendan said after a moment. "TAB. Total Abstinence Brotherhood."

B snorted. "That's definitely not Navy."

"Yeah. We Navy boys are rather Tank of Ale Brothers," Brendan joked. "Thanks A Bunch won't cut it either. Here. This sounds better: Target Acquisition Battalion."

"Huh. What are we talking about here?" B asked. "Radar systems, target balloons? 'Cause if we're talking about drones, it wouldn't be Navy."

"Not unless they dipped under—Damn! That's it: *below water*. Fucking submarines."

B grinned from ear to ear. "You got it, Boss Man. There can't be that many shipyards building submarines on the mainland."

"Let's check it out," Brendan said, his fingers flying over the virtual keyboard. "It seems there are just two: Mare Island, California, and Kittery, Maine."

"Harris is a senator for New Hampshire," B said, "so it must be Kittery for proximity."

Kinosuke felt the expectation in the room grow as they watched Brendan type in the new data. They were all silent, as fascinated as Kinosuke was by the way the two Americans were making all the pieces of the puzzle fit.

Any other time Kinosuke knew he would have been annoyed, but now he felt foolishly proud, as if Brendan were still his student and his skills shone back on Kinosuke—and it didn't help that Brendan kept calling him *sensei* in that respectful tone.

"Huh?" Brendan grunted in confusion. "I keep typing Kittery Naval Shipyard, and it always comes back as Portsmouth Naval Shipyard."

"That's Virginia, not Maine," B said.

"I know. Besides, it's a damn museum; I don't think they build submarines in a museum's backyard."

Brendan kept scrolling down on the touch screen. "Oh, look at this." He grinned and read aloud, "*Keeping America below water*. There you have it."

B huddled closer to take a look, and Brendan must have realized the others couldn't see the image, because he lifted his head and explained. "It's a picture of—"

"*Vice Admiral Richard Z. Laws*," B read, "*tours Portsmouth Naval Shipyard facilities with Captain Kendall Barrows.* That'd be our Captain K showing the brass around."

Brendan's smile grew wider, and Kinosuke swallowed. Even though Brendan tried to include everyone each time he explained something, his gaze kept returning to Kinosuke and lingering there, green eyes eager, begging for Kinosuke's attention. It was driving him crazy, especially when Brendan smiled in the way Kinosuke had tried without much success to erase from his memory.

B's laughter turned everyone's attention to him. "I know what TAB 18 stands for."

Brendan took a peek and chuckled. "Man, we were waaay off the mark." He took the phone from B and passed it over to the boss, though he looked at Kinosuke as if apologizing for not showing it to him first. Shit. Kinosuke was going to lose it if Brendan kept that up.

When Shinya handed him the phone, Kinosuke's first thought was that he was touching something Brendan's fingers had touched, something Brendan's body had warmed, and the simple idea had blood rushing down to his cock. He almost cursed aloud. How could he be so stupid? How could Brendan still have that effect on him? Kinosuke had to tell himself that even though the man was apparently helping now, he was the one who had caused the whole fucking mess to begin with.

"A submarine," Tachibana said as he looked at the screen over Kinosuke's shoulder, and Kinosuke jumped as if he'd been caught jacking off to Internet porno. *Kuso.* He was going to kill either Tachibana or Brendan—or both, just for good measure.

He forced himself to focus on the damn photo to avoid meeting anybody's eyes.

There was a submarine there, all black and sleek where it emerged from the water, and two small red ships beside it, each one with a big white M on what appeared to be chimneys. The background showed a group of low brick buildings, and a taller, uglier one that looked like some sort of warehouse with its front doors directly over the water.

The top half of the building was painted blue, with big yellow letters reading "Portsmouth Naval Shipyard Estab. 1800."

Brendan was shaking his head. "Established in 1800, and not some crazy tactical battalion."

"That's the problem with block letters," B said. "It's difficult to know if you have the whole sentence."

"Yeah, but 'low water' should have been a clue. Anyway, what's with the M on the funnels?" Brendan asked.

Kinosuke gave back the phone and B started typing. "Let's check it out. Tugboat fleets in Maine. Yeah, got you: Marlan Marine Services."

"Good," Brendan said. "Now find out what the matter is with Kittery and Portsmouth."

"Aye, aye, sir."

Silence returned while B searched the net for clues, and Kinosuke's eyes drifted unconsciously to Brendan's bowed head. That was some color; even short as Brendan wore his hair, it shone red like a newly minted ten-yen coin.

Brendan lifted his head and Kinosuke couldn't look away. Those green eyes watched him wistfully, the yearning in them so strong, so sad, that Kinosuke felt his chest ache in a weird way. He knew he should be angry because Brendan had brought everything on himself, but it seemed the man was already chastising himself better than anyone else, and *that* did make Kinosuke angry, because the arrogant bastard was taking matters into his own hands as if, even when it came to punishment, he knew better. Self-important prick.

A low whistle made them all turn to look at B. "Small wonder you couldn't find anything as Kittery naval shipyard," he said. "The shipyard is on an island in the Piscataqua River, right between Kittery, Maine, and Portsmouth, New Hampshire. The island— Seavey's Island—is supposed to belong to Maine, but New Hampshire keeps claiming ownership because they don't agree with old King George II and his way of setting the border between the states in the middle of the main channel of navigation of the Piscataqua River. The last court decision is from 2002, and it dismissed New Hampshire's lawsuit against Maine, so even though the Navy named the shipyard after Portsmouth, Seavey's Island still belongs to Maine. And check this out: shipyard workers living in New Hampshire have to pay income taxes to Maine since that's where the shipyard is."

"Oh, I see," Brendan said. "The problem is not so much King George but the other George."

B nodded. "Yeah, the one on the dollar bill."

"Suppose you were a Republican senator," Brendan continued, "in a state that is lately electing Democrats for key posts; wouldn't you want that tax money returned, with the added benefit of gaining the support of all those discontented shipyard workers?"

"That's a no-brainer," B answered, "though he'd have to be creative to walk around that Supreme Court decision."

Brendan shrugged. "If the court's ruling doesn't mention it, he could say the location of the shipyard is still debatable."

The boss spoke for the first time. "Your conclusions are interesting, but they don't explain why Kenshin would go to the trouble of hiding that picture. Even if his father was doing what you suggest, there's nothing illegal to it, and Kenshin wouldn't point us in that direction unless it was something we could use against the senator."

Brendan nodded. "Or something that could suggest his actual location."

"I'm not so sure about that one," the boss said. "The picture had been in the box for some time, and Kenshin didn't know where those men would take him when he wrote the note."

"You knew about the picture before this?" Brendan asked, and Kinosuke saw Matsunaga-san's features harden. Brendan might not notice it, but he was touching a sore spot.

"Kenshin was naïve enough to believe we were too far from his father to be a nuisance, that he might forget we existed," the boss said, just this side of turning snarky.

"You discussed that?" Brendan kept pushing. Shit. Why did Americans believe everybody had to talk about everything all the fucking time? Kenshin might be American, but he wasn't a babbler, and the boss, well, he hadn't risen to wakagashira exactly by baring his soul.

Kinosuke could see the boss was about to chew Brendan a new one when Tachibana said in his most breezy style, "You don't know Kenshin-san, dude. That skinny gaijin acts like a daimyo reincarnate when it comes to obligation—he thinks he owes us for following him here, so even if he didn't believe his father would keep to his corner, he still wouldn't spoil our vacation in paradise with his worries."

There it was; simply put for even Americans to understand. Japanese men—or reincarnated daimyos—didn't need to put their intentions in block-lettered banners for everyone to see. They just acted on them. Didn't need to go to gay-friendly places as if they had something to hide or go shouting they were gay as if they had something to prove. Huh. Kinosuke wondered where that one had come from.

Brendan must have finally caught up with the hostility in the air, because his tone became more respectful now. "Look. I know Kenneth is a smart guy, so even if the puzzle box was apparently safe, he wouldn't have left behind an easy clue to fall in the wrong hands." He paused, fixing a pleading look on Kinosuke before turning to the boss. "I can go deeper into the matter, but I'll need to take that picture with me, make some phone calls, do some research. It might take a few days."

When the boss looked at Kinosuke, he felt all the men in the room turn as one to look at him too. Shit. Of course he knew Brendan better than the rest but, seeing what that had led to, it didn't seem like such an important decision should depend on his opinion.

Kinosuke didn't dare look at Brendan because the man had surely proven he could manipulate Kinosuke, and anyway he knew those eyes by heart. Yeah, he knew how the green changed when Brendan was mad, or amused, or horny—even knew the way the green darkened when the man came. And still he didn't know shit about the guy, except that he was a fucking traitor.

Could the arrogant bastard be trusted with Kenshin-san's security? Hell if he knew. And yet, somehow, Kinosuke could *feel* the answer, deep in his bones. He held Matsunaga-san's gaze for a moment, not saying anything, and the boss turned and said to Brendan, "I understand you might have been manipulated into acting like you did the first time, but if I find you are playing us again, I will take it personally, and I suppose I don't need to explain what 'personal' means to a yakuza."

CHAPTER 42

"HEY, KOTARŌ, my man. Can you point me in the direction of the sushi room?"

Kotarō blinked. There was a black man at the door, carrying a heavy computer bag and smiling at him as if he'd known Kotarō all his life, but before Kotarō could open his mouth, there came a low, hoarse voice from behind the man. "Otter, behave."

The black guy rolled his eyes at Kotarō. "What? I was just being friendly here. Ain't that right, Kotarō?"

The thrash-metal voice came back. "Kotarō doesn't know you."

The black man put his free hand on his hip dramatically. "And whose fault is that, huh? Now you tell me, kid, ain't that Irish mule told ya we were coming?"

Kotarō saw the black eyes shift slightly to his left side, but still he almost jumped out of his skin when Shinya spoke right beside him. Shit. Dude had this frigging habit of sneaking up on you. "Brendan-san told us he sent two men ahead," Shinya said.

"Brendan-san," the black guy repeated, his lips starting to twitch.

"Otter—" the voice warned, and Kotarō tried to get a look at the man speaking, but the guy named Otter was completely blocking his view until he bent forward, holding his belly with his hand and laughing like a madman.

Kotarō felt his mouth open in shock when he finally got to see the man behind Otter. There were guys with their hair bleached white—Kenshin-san for one—and then there were snowmen, real snowmen, looking nothing like those round, dorky figures with carrots for noses.

"Brendan-san," Otter wheezed, "the Irish samurai."

Light, almost transparent gray eyes met Kotarō's, and Kotarō stood there, fascinated. The guy looked as if someone had pulled him out of a cryogenic tank and left him half defrosted. Dude. Even his eyelashes were white, and Kotarō wondered if his body hair was everywhere the same silver white as the shaggy strands falling all over his face and not quite managing to hide his icy expression.

"Hi, my name is John," the snowman said with his scratchy voice, and Kotarō unconsciously looked down at his throat. He had a deep blue scarf wrapped around his neck in spite of the heat, so maybe he had the flu or something that explained the grating sound.

"Jesus, man," Otter said. "For a moment there, I thought you were gonna say 'My name is John Rambo.'"

Kotarō couldn't help giggling at Otter's impersonation of Stallone. The man was funny, and he wore this wide grin that seemed to compensate for his friend's stony expression.

"His name might be John," Otter said, "but we call him Burka."

"Burka?" Kotarō repeated. "Like that ugly thing Arab women wear?"

He grimaced when he realized John might feel offended, but the man's face didn't change when he spoke.

"Muslim, not Arab," John said.

Otter rolled his eyes. "Yeah, kid, just like you said." He pointed at the scarf around John's neck. "Though his burkas are not that ugly—mostly because I choose them; the man don't have an inch of style in his whole white bod."

It was difficult to see, but Kotarō thought he might have caught one of John's silver eyebrows rising.

"It's a hot bod, though, white and all," Otter said, and Kotarō had no problem seeing the up and down movement of Otter's eyebrows, and it sure as hell made Kotarō's cheeks heat with embarrassment. Otter winked at him and patted his shoulder. "Come on, show us to the origami room before I stick my flip-flopped foot in my big mouth."

Kotarō didn't have time to show his confusion before a pale hand smacked the top of Otter's head. "It's *tatami*, you dimwit," John said.

"That hurt, man," Otter groused. "Jesus; if I'd known languages, I'd be one of 'em dashing Green Berets and not this trained fat marine mammal with whiskers."

"Sorry to keep you waiting," John said, completely ignoring Otter. "Could you or Nakatani-san please show us the way?"

Kotarō gasped. How did he know Shinya's last name? That other friend of Brendan's, Big B, had removed all the cameras, hadn't he? Shinya fixed his gaze on John, and the man looked back, and they seemed to be talking even though neither of them moved a muscle or said a word. It was seriously weird.

Then Shinya turned and started walking away. Otter looked at Kotarō. "Seems like the tough guy wants us to follow, wouldn't you say?"

BRENDAN WAS almost beginning to feel at home in the empty room. Thanks to John Burka, he even knew it was called a tatami room—which seemed kind of obvious after the fact, seeing that the only things decorating the whole space were the tatami mats covering the floor and a hanging picture scroll.

John Burka. The man who knew too much and spoke too little even before Afghan shrapnel turned his voice into a rasp; the man whose icy stare never failed to return to Otter as if he needed to be sure of his location at all times; the man who made the strangest swim buddy, twin brother, and bedfellow someone like Otter could have chosen; the man Brendan never expected to see again.

And yet, there he was, his disturbingly light eyes resting on Brendan as if he knew his former CO was thinking about him. Brendan held the cold stare and shook his head. Geez. When you knew the man, that inexpressive face told you more than the whole repertoire of Otter's exuberant gestures.

"Hey, what're you two white boys up to?" Otter asked in a suspicious tone.

And when you knew the man, you could tell *Otter* was the jealous one of the pair.

"Go back to your presentation, Otter," Brendan answered. "You still have the attention span of a vinegar fly."

Otter murmured something about vinegar flies and mescal worms, and Brendan detected a flicker of amusement in Burka's eyes before he looked away to retrieve a thumb drive from the lanyard he wore around his neck and passed the small device to Otter.

"Thanks, cupcake," Otter said, his fingers touching Burka's far more than was strictly needed to get the flash drive.

Brendan almost cracked up. It turned out that Otter was not only the jealous type; he was also territorial, staking his claim over his lover in case any of the men in the room decided to take his chances with Burka. As if the man looked approachable anyway.

Of course that forbidding appearance didn't seem to work with the likes of Kotarō. The kid was obviously fascinated by Burka's looks, and he kept sneaking glances in his direction with all the subtlety of a mime. But even though the others were a little subtler, Brendan could tell both Burka and Otter intrigued the rest of the yakuza too.

Even in a place as colorful as Hawaii, his men still managed to stand out. On their own, they were both lookers, with handsome faces and triathlon-perfect bodies—Otter with his roguish, in-your-face manner; Burka with his quiet, cold intensity. Together, they made the strangest pair ever, strikingly beautiful in the extreme contrast of their complexions and personalities, yet as solid and harmonious as a yin-yang symbol.

And they were both there for Brendan. In spite of everything.

Brendan had delayed it for as long as he could, but he'd finally phoned Bobcat. The man had seemed honestly concerned about Kotarō—probably because his brother had been more or less Kotarō's age when he died—and Brendan thought he had a right to know.

It hadn't been pleasant. At first, Brendan had been selfishly relieved that the target of Bobcat's rage was Big B, but soon that rage had become an all-encompassing, paranoid fury that made no distinction between friend and foe, and Brendan hadn't been able to come up with arguments fast enough to answer the long list of accusations, so he'd finally just held the phone to his ear and bore the flagellation like a penitent purging his many sins.

His duty fulfilled, Brendan had forgotten all about Bobcat, his investigation taking all his time and mental space, but the man had phoned back two days later and asked about the investigation as if he'd never hung up on Brendan after a string of insults. And Brendan hadn't even hesitated before he told Bobcat everything he'd found out.

This time, too, Bobcat had hung up on him. He'd just asked, "You got a plan?" and when Brendan had told him that he did, Bobcat had said, "Okay. Count us in," and pushed the disconnect button. Just like that. And Brendan hadn't dared hope who the ones in Bobcat's *us* were until he'd gone to pick them up at Honolulu International.

When he'd seen the three men come through the gate, Brendan's spine had straightened unconsciously, needing to stand tall for his boat crew, what was left of the Islanders once again gathered under his command. The men had converged to where he stood with Big B—walking purposefully as if there was no one else in the crowded airport, discreetly scanning the place as they moved in a defensive formation—and settled in front of him in a half circle, not quite standing at attention but almost there, three pairs of eyes watching him expectantly, an assault element waiting for their orders.

And then Otter had said, "Don't you go all misty-eyed on us, Boss Man, 'cause you know I'm one of 'em HSPs and I'm gonna start bawling any moment now."

"You're a what?" Bobcat asked.

"A Highly Sensitive Person; that's me all right," Otter said seriously.

Bobcat only snorted, but Big B stage-whispered, "A High-Strung Popolo is what he is."

"Shut up, you Potagee mouth," Otter countered.

As the banter went on, Brendan's eyes met John Burka's icy stare, and he found that, after all this time, he could still read those apparently inexpressive gray eyes as if they were crinkling with laughter, and he allowed himself to grin so wide his mouth hurt.

"Here's the rest of your army, Brendan-san," Tachibana said, interrupting Brendan's reminiscence with his usual mocking tone.

Tachibana stepped aside to let Big B and Bobcat enter the already crowded room, and as Brendan looked around to see where they could sit, he caught Kinosuke's glare. Why on earth was his sensei glaring at Bobcat? Well, Bobcat might know why, because he sure was returning the glare with his own bad-mojo glower.

"Fucking Catman," Kinosuke murmured.

"Fucking *puto*," Bobcat spat, moving in Kinosuke's direction.

Oh right. Those two had met, and even though Kinosuke had been wearing his helmet at the time, Bobcat had heard the young man's voice frequently enough after that to know what he was talking about when he used the word *puto*.

Brendan closed his eyes. Up to that moment, he'd somehow managed to tiptoe around the issue of his relationship—or affair, or whatever the thing between them had been—with Kinosuke, since none of his men had asked about it nor mentioned the fact that he was gay. They'd talked about the Pech River Valley and Senator Harris until they were sick, but the rest had just been floating about like a big balloon in the shape of an elephant.

He couldn't just keep ignoring what shamed him, and he couldn't let his friend and his former lover engage in a fight because of him. He opened his eyes, ready to stand and put himself between the two men, just to find Burka already there, one pale hand on Bobcat's chest, his back to Kinosuke as if daring him to make a move on a defenseless man.

"Apologize to Yonekawa-sensei, Bobcat," Brendan said. "You can insult me to your heart's content, but he's not responsible for my misdeeds."

Two raven-haired heads whipped around so fast that Brendan almost heard their articulations creak.

"Is that what you call it now," Kinosuke shouted, "a fucking misdeed?"

Shit. Now he'd offended Kinosuke. How could this get any worse?

"Berto?" Kotarō's tentative voice called. The kid was standing too, looking at Bobcat as if he knew him.

B's eyes widened. "You are *that* Berto?"

Brendan looked from one to the other without getting it. Bobcat had tailed Kotarō for some time, but he'd never contacted him, and nothing in the conversations they'd recorded from the dojo suggested anyone there knew Bobcat. But then again, Brendan had only read Bobcat's translations of the Japanese conversations, while Big B had been having access to the full uncensored material.

"You were spying on Kenshin-san too?" Kotarō said, the hurt in his voice making Bobcat cringe.

Kinosuke cursed and tried to get to Bobcat, but John Burka kept blocking him and, as Brendan stood to help, he saw Kotarō dodge the two men and send his fist flying in Bobcat's direction. And Bobcat never moved a single inch.

CHAPTER 43

"NOW, LADDIES and gentlemen, if you can stop talking with your fists for a second, I got here some pretty pictures to show you," Otter said, a PowerPoint projector illuminating the wall in front of him. "Though you better close some of those onionskin doors if you wanna see something."

Kinosuke released the handful of Burka's T-shirt he'd been pulling at. Fuck. Had they chosen their nicknames so that they all started with a B? Bobcat, Burka, and, for good measure, Big B. Who was Brendan, then, Little B? At least Otter was Otter, though Kinosuke was sensing another theme there in Bobcat and Otter. Fucking crazy Americans.

He was moving in the direction of the shoji doors and as far from Brendan as he could get when a black hand grabbed his wrist like a carbon steel cuff.

"You touch my man again, and I'll rip your pretty head off your shoulders, *Sensei*," Otter whispered, a smile belying his words for the rest of the audience, hard eyes looking straight into Kinosuke's. Well, at least someone in the room was ready to fight for his lover and not consider what he had with him a mistake or—what was the word the bastard had used?—a *misdeed*, like something you might do when too drunk to know right from wrong.

"You touch me again and you'll get his frozen pieces in the mail—without the assembly instructions," Kinosuke whispered back, his eyes projecting all the anger Brendan inspired in him.

They stayed like that for a second, eyes and hands locked, and then the crackpot American started laughing, eyes crinkling and all, the iron grip on Kinosuke's arm loosening as the man let go to pat his shoulder as if they were fast friends. Fucking lunatic.

"Kotarō," the boss said, "is this the man who pulled you out of the water?"

Kinosuke turned around in shock. The Catman had rescued Kotarō? That psycho had plunged into the ocean to save a kid? He couldn't help noticing that Brendan looked just as startled as Kinosuke was, so it seemed none of his men had been doing what he was supposed to. Served the lying bastard right.

"He was following me," Kotarō whined. "That's why those men got that film they showed Kenshin-san and—"

"Enough, Kotarō," the boss cut his ranting with a gentle tone that took the sting out of the words. Then he turned to Bobcat and bowed deeply. "Thank you for saving Kotarō's life. I am in your debt."

Surprisingly enough, Bobcat bowed too, matching Matsunaga-san's angle. "I'm deeply sorry about that camera footage—it was never intended to be used against you. I am the one who is obliged to you."

"Don't apologize for something you didn't do," Big B growled. "I gave the senator the ammunition he needed, but I'm not going to apologize for doing my job. I'm just going to show that slimeball what happens when you fuck with a SEAL."

Otter whistled. "That's the spirit, Brudda," he said, and then the wacko patted Kinosuke's shoulder again. "Hey pretty sensei, would you mind closing that door now that we're done with all the punching and the groveling? I'd like to show you what we know before the senator dies on us from old age."

Kinosuke glared at the man, but Otter was already fiddling with his computer, so he just stomped to the shoji door and pressed the button in the wall to close down the storm shutter.

"Oh, cool. That's some sleek gizmo you got there, Sensei," Otter said, white teeth glinting in the projector's light.

Fucking madman. Now he was watching the uneven rectangle of light on the wall and clucking his tongue in disapproval. "That won't do. Can you guys lend me something to prop this thing up?" he said to no one in particular, and as Shinya got up, he added, "One of those sushi-cutting boards will do."

Kinosuke couldn't see very well in the darkened room, but he guessed the look Shinya gave Otter was one of his blood-curdling glares, and Kinosuke almost chuckled before he heard Otter say, "Just don't bring the sushi knife, dude. You look scary enough as it is."

The chuckle that sounded now wasn't Kinosuke's, and as he turned to look for its source, he was startled to see that even in the semidarkness of the room, Burka looked as if he was carrying a headlight. Shit. How did he manage to go on night missions without that silver hair giving his position away in the moonlight? Of course now he wondered what Brendan's red hair looked like in the shade, and his treacherous eyes moved on their own to find out.

He swallowed. Brendan was looking straight at him, the dim light reaching his eyes and making them glow in the greenish-yellow of fireflies, part of his short hair illuminated like a red flame, the intensity of his stare reaching Kinosuke like a physical touch that made him shiver. And he would've sworn those eyes caught his shudder, black pupils dilating just as they did when Brendan's arousal grew.

"Thanks, man," Otter said as Shinya deposited the living room coffee table—complete with its decorative ceramic bowl and Kenshin-san's puzzle box—in front of him. As Otter lifted the projector, Burka's pale hands picked up the bowl and box and placed them gently on the tatami, and Kinosuke wasn't surprised the two Americans were called *the Twins*, the way they didn't need to speak to move as a single person.

Somehow it made Kinosuke sad, knowing that he'd never experienced that kind of special connection with anyone, and even though he told himself it was probably just the result of the years these two men had been training, working, and living together, he couldn't shake the feeling until he saw pale fingers go back to the puzzle box, obviously intrigued. Then Kinosuke smiled wide; another mighty American soldier was about to be defeated in a battle of wits. Against a piece of wood.

"Now, finally, here's the slimeball in the flesh," Otter said, a picture of a man in his sixties appearing on the wall.

Kenshin-san's father didn't look anything like his son; he was a sturdy, square-jawed son of a bitch, and his small brown eyes looked calculating, though Kinosuke was probably reading too much in a gesture that might be just an instinctive reaction to the glare of a spotlight.

"Cedric A. Harris is a successful three-term Republican senator for New Hampshire, and he'll stand for reelection this fall, so everything likely to throw a monkey wrench into the campaign—like a queer son with yakuza connections—must be dealt with as swiftly and quietly as possible."

Otter paused, and the image on the wall changed to an enlarged version of the photo Kenshin-san had kept in the puzzle box.

"Of course Kenneth Harris knew his father well enough to imagine the senator might do just that, and so he steered you in the direction of one of his campaign assets— Portsmouth Naval Shipyard.

"The shipyard is a bone of contention between the two neighboring states because it means jobs, taxes, and millions in defense contracts. That's why you see so many smiling guys in this picture, because for every shipyard-related event, you get twice your money's worth in representatives—both from New Hampshire and Maine.

"It seems Senator Harris is very aware of the shipyard's importance, so you can find his name in every initiative concerning its ownership or, failing that, its location. He was behind the lawsuit New Hampshire filed with the Supreme Court in 2000 to claim ownership of the island where the yard is. When the court decided in 2001 that New Hampshire cannot say now that the border between the two states runs along the Maine shore of the Piscataqua River since the same state agreed in 1977 that the border lies in the middle of the river, Senator Harris changed his tune and said that the Supreme Court never decided the location of Portsmouth Naval Shipyard."

Brendan's voice came from the other side of the room. "All this may sound like balderdash to you, but it's the white-noise-generator strategy in action; politicians just repeat what they think their voters want to hear until those noises mask the rest of what they're really saying. And it works too. Come election time, you only remember they voiced all your concerns, as I'm sure all those shipyard workers who live in New Hampshire and still have to pay taxes in Maine will remember that Senator Harris kept calling it 'taxation without representation.'"

Kinosuke couldn't help feeling irritated at Brendan's lecturing tone. Did he think a PowerPoint presentation and a bunch of obtuse words were going to impress them? So far his man hadn't said anything new, and Kinosuke was starting to lose his patience. "Very interesting," he said. "But I don't think Kenshin-san left us that picture to give us a crash course in American politics."

Otter snorted. "Yeah; boss man here can't help sharing his Washington experience."

The slide on the wall changed to show another group of people in hard hats, some of them in uniform and all of them holding flashy golden shovels.

"What we believe your Kenshin-san wanted you to notice is this," Otter said. "Every time the shipyard renovates some building, or constructs a new one, or upgrades its facilities, you get this kind of picture."

Otter clicked on his mouse and the photo shrank to make room for a different one with more buildings in the background and no shovels this time, but there were again the men in uniform, the ones in suits, and two or three women, all with the usual hard hats.

"Look familiar?" Otter asked as other photos appeared, including the one Kenshin-san had kept hidden. "I'm sure by now you recognize the shipyard commander, the representatives from Maine and New Hampshire, and the guys from the construction company. And since you find politicians so boring, Sensei, let's take a closer look at the contractors."

Kinosuke didn't have time to reply before the images changed, a close-up of one of the hats filling the improvised screen.

"This corporation," Otter said, reading the name on the hat, "Spearman Engineers, LLC, seems pretty popular—can't figure out why when it sounds like all they do is diddle with sperm."

More images started to appear, more hard hats with the same corporation's name on them.

"The interesting thing about this contractor is that one of the corporation's major stakeholders is Marlan Marine Services, which you may remember from this."

Kenshin-san's picture reappeared, and Otter pointed at the big M painted on the ship.

"This company has a serious tugboat operation running in Portsmouth, and of course the shipyard is one of its clients. If you keep following the money trail, it turns out that Marlan's top shareholder is an Exeter-based telecom corporation called Fir Business Communications, whose largest single shareholder is none other than Campbell Harris."

Kinosuke observed the picture of a thirtysomething with a clear resemblance to Senator Harris. He had the same brown eyes, the square jaw, but he looked taller and less stocky than his father. And still he looked very different from Kenshin-san, as if their gaijin didn't come from the same family at all. Did he have a different mother? And why on earth didn't they know these things? It was true that Kenshin-san didn't like talking about his family, but it was also true none of them had asked too much about it. Did the boss know? Or had he, like the rest of them, found it too private a matter to pry into?

Americans didn't have the same concept of privacy, Kinosuke knew. Kenshin-san had sometimes asked about Kinosuke's family—very tactfully, never insisting when Kinosuke didn't say much, but he had asked, as Brendan had too. The redhead didn't have much tact to speak of, but his interest seemed more than simple curiosity; it seemed like he really cared—or cared too much about his investigation.

And now that Kinosuke thought about it, why was Otter telling them what Brendan had found out? Why didn't Brendan himself explain everything? Maybe it was too much effort to find words a bunch of Japanese goons would understand, or maybe... maybe Brendan knew that, whatever he said, they'd be too busy judging him to really listen to his words—just like Kinosuke was doing right now.

"The name Harris keeps popping up in everything shipyard-related. We have yet another Harris directing every construction project in the yard—Miles Harris, who is, as you've probably guessed, with Spearman Engineers."

This one seemed to be the eldest, a man about forty, with the Harris signature square jaw, mousy eyes, and a receding hairline. Like his brother, he looked taller and lighter-framed than the senator, but nothing close to Kenshin-san's bird-boned slender grace. They looked like a family of grizzlies who had adopted a flying squirrel.

"And since Papa Harris has every reason to be preoccupied with the shipyard, when the Base Realignment and Closure commission decided to close it, he threw himself into the fight and led an employee campaign that convinced the commission to keep the yard running.

"That was what gave him enough leverage with the Navy to force the goatfuck of a mission that got two of our friends killed. He used his political clout to lobby for the shipyard, and in exchange he expected a victory from our troops he could brag about.

"If the ops had been successful, the senator would have made sure everybody knew about his involvement in the matter—it would've been a nice campaign booster—but since it was completely FUBAR, there's nothing the good senator won't do to keep it buried.

"And here we are now, because Senator Harris has apparently decided he should go for a twofer and deal with the loose ends of Operation Disaster and the loose morals of his son at the same fucking time."

In the silence that followed, Kinosuke realized he'd stopped hearing the telltale sliding of wood panels that meant Burka was still working at opening the puzzle box. Most people didn't give up so soon, but maybe this weird guy was smart enough to realize at a quick glance when he'd been bested.

He looked at Burka and saw that the man was watching Otter with an unreadable expression on his face. Yeah. The white-haired guy had probably just stopped at the mention of his dead friends, or so Kinosuke thought until he lowered his eyes and saw Burka's hand. There, lightly grasped between pale fingers, was the box, the lid showing the empty space of the secret compartment where the picture had been hidden.

Shit. The man had opened the box in what? Five, ten minutes? It had taken Shinya the better part of an hour to find the compartment, and he was very good with all sorts of puzzles.

Matsunaga-san's voice brought Kinosuke back from his wide-eyed surprise. "Can you prove that the senator was behind the failed military operation?"

"No." It was Brendan who answered now, as if he felt the responsibility was all his when it came to failure. At least in that, he showed he might have been a good leader. "It's all classified material—he covered his tracks pretty well."

"Can you prove that he's been trying to silence you and your men?" the boss insisted, and to Kinosuke, who knew him, he sounded as if he didn't care much for Brendan's negations.

"No" came the simple, dispassionate answer. At least American rudeness had the advantage of clearing things right away. Now the boss could stop being courteous and ask the question that really mattered to them.

"Can we use any of the information you uncovered as leverage against the senator?"

There it was, the reason they had sought Brendan's help in the first place.

"No," Brendan answered, and Kinosuke had a hard time keeping his hands from reaching the redhead's throat. Why, then, had the smug bastard put on the show? Just to tell them nothing could be done, since he and his ultrasmart supersoldiers hadn't been able to do it? Why had Kinosuke ever believed Brendan could solve anything? He should have just trusted his own people, the people who got things done when it mattered. Shinya may have used one hour to open that fucking box, but he got the picture out when they needed it; Burka just got an empty compartment when nobody needed to know his brains were as bright as his hair.

"What I found out about the senator's sons doesn't make him look too good," Brendan explained, now that there wasn't anything to explain, "but since I can't prove there were irregularities in the adjudication of the contracts, it can be easily dismissed as the typical electoral campaign aspersion."

Kinosuke knew that if Brendan opened his mouth to add one more bit of codswallop of the same we-can't-do-shit-about-it species, Kinosuke was going to kill him. At long last.

And sure enough, there it came. "We can't use any of the information as leverage against the senator," he had the nerve to repeat, and Kinosuke was about to stand when Brendan added, "but I know where Ken is, and what to do to get him out of there while we kick some honorable ass in the process."

Kinosuke blinked. As he looked around, he could have sworn even the stoic Burka and the psycho Bobcat were baring their teeth in the same manic grin as the rest of their supersoldier buddies—their lunatic leader included. Fucking crazy Americans.

CHAPTER 44

AS BRENDAN had thought would happen, the guards didn't pay attention to the old pickup truck anymore. After two weeks of watching it take the dirt road to the coffee shack, they'd assumed the landowner had rented the place for the season.

"There goes the odd couple," Otter said beside him, and Brendan smiled without lowering his binoculars. Shinya and Burka did make a strange pair, but the funniest thing about it was noticing how protective Otter was of his swim buddy, now that Brendan knew the true extent of their mateship.

"Is it difficult?" Kinosuke asked, and both Otter and Brendan turned to look at him. Kinosuke seemed to cringe at the attention. "I mean, being, you know—"

"Black?" Otter said, and Brendan fought to keep a straight face. He knew exactly what Kinosuke was asking, but the little shit enjoyed embarrassing the *pretty sensei*—as he'd taken to calling him in spite of Kinosuke's obvious chagrin, or probably *because* of it.

Kinosuke huffed. "I mean being with Burka," he said.

"Well, the man is quieter than a school of abyssal fish, but seeing that I can't stop talking, we're sort of balanced. And you know all that claptrap about opposites and such."

"Otter…," Brendan chided, and the man rolled his eyes at him.

"Oh, you mean is it difficult being queer as military folk?" he said to Kinosuke. "Well, we used to keep it on the down low, if you know what I mean, and people didn't usually notice"—here he looked pointedly at Brendan—"but then they went and repealed the Don't-Ask-Don't-Tell bullshit—man, one of these days they're even going to let women get their rocks off in combat—and we thought it was time to stand up and shout our love to the world, you know?"

Brendan shook his head. He hadn't realized how much he'd missed Otter and his stories. He was the best to have near during the most boring of recon work. And, sure enough, he got Kinosuke's rapt attention.

"Problem is," Otter went on, "all my man can do is stand out and whisper in that sexy gravelly voice of his, and I'm not about to share his hotness with the world. Let them go find their own chemlight."

Brendan chuckled. "I'm surprised you didn't call him your glowstick—that was tame for you."

"No, dude," Otter countered. "That was *accurate*. His stick doesn't glow in the dark, especially since I like shaving all the hair he's got down there."

Kinosuke made a face, and Brendan laughed. "Now that's something we definitely didn't need to know."

"Don't tell me you never wondered if he was a natural blo… um… yeti," Otter said. "That's what got me hooked in the first place."

"What? His hair?"

"Curiosity, man. It got so bad that I couldn't sleep at night; I had to check." Otter made one of his dramatic pauses. "Of course after I checked, I couldn't sleep either, for entirely different reasons."

Otter wiggled his eyebrows, and Brendan snorted. "I can't believe I never caught a whiff of what was going on between the two of you."

"That's 'cause we're SEALs, not pigs; we wash—especially after, you know, strenuous activities. And, with all due respect, you can be awfully dense sometimes, Boss Man."

The noise of an engine saved him from having to answer or look at Kinosuke, because he was sure the yakuza agreed wholeheartedly with Otter's appraisal. They were all working together like a well-oiled war machine—in what Otter had christened Joint Special Operations Task Force *Karaoke*—but the daily interaction between Brendan and Kinosuke was nothing but the most complicated, narrow-eyed evasive maneuvering. And he had no clue how to fix it—just supposing there was anything left to fix.

"There they go, like clockwork," Otter said as they watched the black Explorer cross the outer gates of the property and turn north. "Man, don't they teach them at bruiser school to avoid being predictable?"

Every Friday the Explorer made the same route to the Costco near Kona Airport to resupply. Given the prices on the Big Island, and the number of people living in the mansion right now, it wasn't at all surprising that the owner was trying to economize— one didn't get this filthy rich without some pinching and scraping.

They were economizing on gas too—another luxury item on the island—by taking all those who had the weekend off to Kona on their way up, and probably also saving on antidepressants by blowing off some steam at the bars on Alii Drive on their way back.

"Let them be," Brendan said. "That gets a vehicle and about seven people out of our hair."

Otter shook his head. "I know, Boss Man. I'm just stating their obvious sloppiness."

"I suppose they believe they made a clever move by staying on the islands," Brendan said, "that nobody is going to find them—and much less attack them."

"They just don't think a bunch of Japanese gangbangers can be a serious threat," Kinosuke elaborated, his voice bitter.

"What I said," Otter insisted. "Sloppy."

Brendan saw Kinosuke stare at Otter to gauge if he was being sarcastic. Touchy Japanese. To be honest, though, before he had really interacted with them, Brendan didn't think much of the yakuza. Not because he thought they weren't dangerous, but rather because, to him, organized crime was not really all that organized when compared with your regular military unit.

Of course that was before he had met Matsunaga and his men. Even after leaving the gang structure, they still respected a clear chain of command, trained on a regular basis, and were resourceful enough that, even out of their turf as they were here, they had already gathered a lot of intelligence on their own before they asked for Brendan's help. In fact, it was the absence of Ken's name on the islands' plane and ferry passenger lists they had checked that told Brendan what to keep an eye open for. Otherwise he would still be canvassing the senator's mainland properties in search of Ken and wouldn't have paid any mind to the fact that one of the senator's cronies had a yacht—no passenger list required there—and a mansion in Hawaii.

"Oh man, there go Fido and Slobby-Doo," Otter said. "What on earth are we gonna do about them? I don't imagine pepper sprays work on monsters like those two."

Brendan trained his binoculars on the kitchen back door as a man in a white apron pushed it open, his hands full with a huge steel bowl that he carried to a toylike plastic table with two bowl-sized depressions on top. While the man fitted the bowl in place, one of the guards approached with two dogs on leashes. The cook cast worried glances toward the big animals and hurried back in. The guard, though, didn't set the eager dogs loose—maybe he was waiting for the cook to bring out another bowl so each dog would have its own.

A Rottweiler. Geez. One look at that column of a neck and you got a pretty good idea of the biting power of that jaw. The other dog was slightly bigger, its coat reddish brown, and had the dubious distinction of sporting an even blockier head than the Rottie.

"What did you say those wrinkly dogs were called?" Kinosuke asked.

"Mothers-in-law," Otter answered, and Brendan reached out to whack the man's head.

"Dogues de Bordeaux," Brendan corrected, though he had to admit that the animals' droopy eyes and mouths, plus all the loose skin around their necks, made them look like particularly ugly, overweight, judgmental in-laws.

"Whatever," Otter said. "I just don't wanna get any closer to that drool spout."

The cook came out with the other bowl and had barely placed it on the feeder when the guard released the dogs. The animals all but trampled over one another—and the cook—to get to their chow. In a repeat performance of the day before—and the day before that—the man in the apron gestured angrily at the guard while the big oaf just laughed at his own joke. It was like a Frank De Lima show, with the hot-tempered Filipino ready to pull a knife at the slightest offense, and the hulking, pea-brained Samoan bullying him. It didn't get any more badly stereotypical Hawaiian than that.

"Why are there only two dogs?" Kinosuke asked, and Brendan lowered his binoculars to look at him. His sensei obviously hadn't expected Brendan to face him, because he blinked, dark eyes almost looking away before Kinosuke made a clear effort to hold Brendan's stare. "I mean, this place is huge. Two dogs don't seem enough to keep watch."

Brendan fought to bring his attention back to what Kinosuke was actually saying and not the way those luscious lips moved. "They're just a deterrent. You see one of them and you imagine there's an army of dogs roaming about. But the real protection comes from that wraparound golf course."

The property had a horseshoe shape, the open side facing the ocean, the landlocked side neatly surrounded by a golf course that shone bright green in the middle of the black and dull browns of the lava desert around it.

"The course acts as a virtual moat," Brendan explained. "You can't cross it without being seen from miles away, so a bunch of cameras and ten guards are more than enough to keep it safe."

"That plus the electric fence," Otter said. "Against donkeys, I suppose, 'cause all that lawn sure must look yummy to a lava-starved burro."

Kinosuke smiled. He found it hilarious that they'd had to place "donkey crossing" signs along the highway to warn drivers against the descendants of the coffee-hauling pack animals that still roamed the country. And Brendan couldn't help smiling himself, because in those rare occasions, he could still see the mischievous youth Kinosuke really was.

"It might be against feral goats," Brendan added, knowing what Kinosuke would think of at the mention of goats. And sure enough, there came the yakuza's infrequent giggle.

"Are you laughing at what I think you're laughing?" Otter said, as susceptible as ever. "'Cause if you are, you better stop before I get mad, pretty Sensei."

"I'm not laughing." Kinosuke tried to sound serious, but his eyes were twinkling unmistakably.

"Good," Otter said. "He was only defending a cherished possession."

Kinosuke nodded.

"It took me hours to choose those boxer briefs for him, man."

Kinosuke nodded again, but Brendan could see his lips twitching.

"They got the green gator on them too," Otter added, unable to keep silent for more than a second. "Dude, you'd think a goat would be wiser than to go munching on gators."

First came the undignified snort, and then Kinosuke was cracking up, uselessly trying to smother the sound of his laughter behind his hand.

Brendan chuckled, remembering the picture Burka had made that night, trying to wrestle Otter's gift from a tenacious billy goat that had somehow found its way into their bedroom. The scene looked like the gay version of the Coppertone ad, with a pale Burka flashing an even paler ass at a black goat instead of the original Cocker Spaniel. And even the stoic Shinya had laughed when gathering an audience had stopped neither goat nor man from defending their cherished possession.

"Your man is a fierce goat wrestler," Brendan said, and Kinosuke's laughter was so loud that Otter and Brendan instinctively ducked their heads to hide behind the ridge they were watching the mansion from.

"You better stop laughing at my man and start planning how to extract our target from that fucking fortress down there," Otter groused.

His words sobered Brendan. The place was indeed a fortress, what with the electric fence, the golf course-cum-moat, the cameras, the guards, and the dogs on one side and the rugged cliff, the well-guarded dock, and the too-exposed beach on the other.

Then again, SEALs were trained for this kind of difficult ops, and stepping over a few legal boundaries if things went awry was not unusual for them. So nothing new here, not even the burden of having many people depending on Brendan's every decision. But it had never been this personal before.

Brendan might have always wanted to prove himself, but this time he felt he had too much to make up for, and the pressure was nearing the red, threatening to squeeze his brain flat. And Kinosuke's presence wasn't helping his concentration.

He closed his eyes and took a deep breath. He had to do this—there was nowhere for him to run to, nowhere for him to hide. He pictured himself in the middle of that blasted golf course, alone and exposed, wanting nothing but to howl his desperation to the moon.

And that was when the idea hit him.

"Crocodile," he said, smiling at the association.

"What?" Otter asked.

"The Lacoste logo on Burka's briefs—or what's left of them," he explained. "It's not an alligator, it's a crocodile."

Otter looked at him as if he'd lost his mind. "Shit, what are you now, a GQ editor?" Brendan laughed, and Otter shook his head. "Arguing about gators with a Floridian. Man, that's so wrong."

CHAPTER 45

KUSO. HOW could Brendan and his friends wear their hair that short and not itch constantly? Kinosuke's new haircut wasn't as short as their buzz cuts by far, but his fingers kept straying to his head to scratch here, touch there, and check for the umpteenth time that the tattoo on his scalp wasn't showing.

Not that he could actually tell by touch alone if the tattoo was still covered, but the way everybody stared, he couldn't help checking. The boss was glowering at him right now, and Kinosuke quickly lowered his hand to rest it on the folder that was supposed to make him look busy and attentive, which he obviously wasn't.

He could forgive the boss's shitty mood, though, because it must be killing him to have Kenshin-san so close and not be able to just storm that mansion and take the gaijin home, but Brendan was right. Kenshin-san's father had tried to lock his son up twice already, so maybe if they simply rescued the gaijin right now—as they were itching to do—the damn senator might start looking for more creative ways of putting Kenshin-san out of the way. They needed to stop the bastard forever, get their hands on something the senator would do anything to keep from hitting the headlines. Only then could they bring their gaijin back to safety with the confidence that he would remain safe.

So yeah, Kinosuke could forgive the boss's grouchiness, but he wasn't about to forgive the way Kitahara managed to look down on him in spite of being much shorter.

The man was a fucking sōkaiya, for crying out loud. He would hunt down companies that were not paying their due in taxes, or cooked their books, or offered kickbacks to government employees, or, generally speaking, fucked with the law. And then the guy would threaten to expose the company if they didn't pay—preferably in shares—his men doing a good job of throwing shareholders' meetings out of whack to prove Kitahara's power. That was the man's *profession.*

As far as Kinosuke was concerned, no matter how well he carried himself in the Armani suit and the fancy glasses, Kitahara was still a rat. And he wasn't half as imposing or elegant as the boss. Shit. Even Brendan looked smarter than Kitahara in that spiffy suit that kept dragging Kinosuke's eyes to him in spite of himself.

And sure enough, every time his treacherous eyes turned to the redhead, he found those laser-like, golf-course-green eyes trained on him. It made him mad, and fretful, and—fucking horny.

Shit. He wished they'd let him stay in the coffee shack with the goats. But Tachibana was their best marksman and Shinya looked too much like a yakuza even if they'd managed to hide his scar like they'd hidden Matsunaga-san's missing knuckle. And Kinosuke definitely didn't have their patience when it came to dealing with the weird local fauna—goats, donkeys, frogs, and Big B's cousins.

"Would you share the joke with us, Hidenori-kun?"

It took him too long to react to his new name, and of course that earned him more glowers from everyone around. It wasn't his fucking fault if he hadn't been there to rehearse things to death like the others, and anyway, why the hell did the Rat get to keep his own name?

"*Sumimasen*, Kitahara-san," he said, chewing on the *san* until it sounded far closer to *rat* than the proper honorific. The sōkaiya gave him a suspicious glare, but the man was always suspicious anyway, almost to the point that Kinosuke wasn't sure who'd be the winner if Bobcat and Kitahara competed for the title of Mr. Paranoia.

"All right, gentlemen," Kitahara finally said, "if you're ready, we'll go through the procedure one more time. I'm sure I don't need to remind you this might be our last chance to get it right, so please pay attention."

Oh, for fuck's sake. He was too old for this cram-school bullshit—and too nervous to pay attention. Kenshin-san's brothers would arrive in less than twenty-four hours, and they had to entertain the group for five days, keep them under their radar every second of those five days, and manage to convince them to close a deal before Friday evening.

It was both too much and too little time. Every loose end had to be tied up no later than Friday if their plan was to work out, but in so many days, there were too many things that could easily go wrong. They hadn't even started and there were hitches already—like the fucking lawyer.

The Harrises were supposed to bring some kind of legal advisor plus the wives and the swimming trunks, but you only had to look at Brendan's face when his Washington contact told him the man's name to know this wasn't a law student the brothers were bringing.

Brendan's face said other things when he talked to that friend on the phone too. Maybe Bobcat's paranoia was catching, but Kinosuke would bet that Craig guy had been something of Brendan's, and not exactly his lawyer.

He sounded like an asshole on speaker phone—a sleek, crafty asshole with a wry smile you could actually hear over the phone. And he sounded older than Brendan. That, in itself, made Kinosuke mad, because if that was the sort of man Brendan went for, what the fuck had he been doing with Kinosuke? Pumping him for information, of course, but seeing what he liked, he should have tried it with the boss instead—see how that one would have gone down.

While Kitahara turned to highlight something on his PowerPoint presentation with his flashy green laser pointer, Kinosuke took the chance to turn a little sideways and cast a furtive glance in Brendan's direction.

There he was by the conference room door, looking all professional bodyguard with his flaming buzz cut and his headset and the two-button, shoulder-hugging, leg-fitting suit that made him look taller and hunkier than ever. And, as usual, he seemed to always notice when Kinosuke was looking, his own green laser pointers immediately shifting to focus on him.

Fuck. Why did the bastard keep doing that? Why did he look at Kinosuke as if he were the most important thing around, more important even than this plan they'd all put so much effort into?

Kinosuke's pride was still smarting from Brendan's betrayal but, if he was honest, Brendan was more than making up for what he'd done by being here with his men, fighting a battle that wasn't his in the first place. And he was doing it as he seemed to do everything, burning his ships as he went, as if the word *halfway* had been banished from his vocabulary from the time he still had baby fat.

And yet, he'd already fucked Kinosuke—he could stop pretending he still wanted him. Why was he doing it anyway? It did him no good, it didn't help the mission, and he was failing miserably at it. Or was he?

Maybe that was the point, making it look like a lost cause so Kinosuke would fall for it, like the moron he was. But then again, in a week or two—supposing none of them ended up in jail or mauled by a Rottweiler or shot—Brendan was still going back home, probably to that Craig dude who sounded like he could offer far more than a make-believe kendo instructor. So what was Brendan's angle here?

Kinosuke frowned. Of all the bad things he could imagine concerning Brendan's motives, the worst was thinking the man was acting on that blasted American habit of striving to make people happy. If Brendan were just bolstering Kinosuke's self-confidence by proving the attraction had always been there in spite of everything, Kinosuke was going to kick his ass from here to the mainland.

A screeching noise interrupted Kinosuke's thinking in circles. Kitahara made the same face Naoko-chan used to make when Kinosuke raked his nails down the blackboard in first grade, and he had to look away to hide a smirk. And there it was, Brendan's answering smile, looking for all the world as if seeing Kinosuke having a ball was hotter than the lava from Kilauea volcano.

"Sorry, folks," Big B said, popping his head out of the technician's cabin. "That cardioid is interfering wildly with our own set of mics. We'll soon have it fixed."

Kitahara gave B a sour look. "That's what you said the other twenty times. Our guests are going to wonder what kind of crappy resort we've brought them to."

It was rich to hear Kitahara say *crappy* with that hideous accent. Not that Kinosuke didn't have an accent, but he wanted to believe it wasn't as thick—or as snooty as all that.

"Excuse me?" Big B said, leaving the cabin behind to approach Kitahara and loom over his scrawny figure.

"I said," Kitahara repeated, seemingly unfazed by B's thunderous expression or threatening bulk, "you never manage to solve that problem. Maybe we should hire some local talent to help us record what goes on in the room while I speak."

Uh-oh. This was going to get ugly fast.

"Listen, you fucking Jap—"

Because of course big Captain America would underestimate the short Japanese guy in the horn-rimmed glasses and, as soon as he pointed a finger at the sōkaiya, there came the classic aikido shoulder grab and the explosive sound of all those pounds of Hawaiian hitting the floor. And then of course the Rat would underestimate the big American oaf and lower his guard before the guy really hit the floor, not quite seeing the way B was moving his right leg even as he fell so as to send a vicious kick to Kitahara's ankles that swept his feet from under him and sent him crashing down onto the raised stage and—oh shit—tumbling over the edge.

CHAPTER 46

THIRD GRADERS. Brendan was working with third graders—not even amateurs, no, those would have been predictable to a certain degree. These people were walking liabilities.

"How long has he been in there?"

He glared at B. The man was a SEAL, for Christ's sake. He should have known better than to retaliate against a civilian, whether aikido practitioner or Shaolin master.

"One hour and a half," Matsunaga answered without looking at the wall clock, as if he'd been counting the minutes in his head to rein in the urge to strangle B.

At least B had apologized to all and sundry, and he now looked appropriately concerned and rueful—as well he should, having in mind that he'd probably made them lose their best asset in the business side of the plan.

"What if he can't walk?" B asked, shifting in the hard plastic chair like a restless kid.

"We'll cross that bridge when we come to it," Brendan said, glaring again for good measure.

"That's not the worst we can expect," Matsunaga offered in that calm voice Brendan knew to mean trouble.

"You think he might walk out on us?" Brendan asked, almost rolling his eyes at the unintended pun. "There's a lot of profit to be made here if everything goes as planned."

Matsunaga nodded. "Exactly; *if* everything goes as planned. That's a big risk considering the people involved."

Of course. From the Japanese point of view, Brendan and his men might as well have been circus clowns for all the credit they were given.

Matsunaga raised a hand as if to forestall Brendan's objections. "Don't get me wrong. I know you are professionals, and I'm certainly grateful for your help."

Yeah, right. He was grateful, but he'd die before admitting they wouldn't have made it without the Americans. Although if Brendan was honest, he really believed they might have tried anyway, given how bulldogged these guys were, and maybe even have succeeded in a do-or-die, reckless yakuza style. And it wasn't as if Brendan and his men had done anything but gather intel and plan like crazy, while Matsunaga had brought the financial resources and business savvy the Americans might have had some trouble finding in a pinch.

"But Kitahara doesn't agree with you on that," Brendan finished.

"Kitahara-san is used to working with his own team," Matsunaga said, as diplomatic as ever. "And he's got his pride too."

Brendan made a you-don't-say face and got a wry smile from Matsunaga. "If pride could be bottled," the yakuza added, "Japan would outsell Coca-Cola."

He chuckled and heard B's surprised laughter. Well now, who would have guessed the yakuza had a sense of humor? Maybe that was why Matsunaga wasn't a yakuza anymore. And as soon as Brendan thought that, another, more somber idea crossed his mind; what had it cost the man to get the Shinagawa-gumi, his former gang, involved in their scheme?

"Is someone here for Mr. Kitahara?"

The three of them stood, B and Brendan letting Matsunaga take the lead.

"I'm Nakazawa Shigure," the yakuza introduced himself, bowing to the doctor. "I'm Mr. Kitahara's business partner, and these men are in charge of our security."

Once again Brendan had to give Matsunaga his due. He was smart and, quite frankly, impossible to beat at the intricacies of Asian protocol. Seeing that the doctor was Asian himself—Chinese-American was Brendan's guess—Matsunaga had given his surname first, remembering to stay in character by keeping to the alias they'd agreed on and not bothering to introduce the other men, because here on the islands, a burly Kanaka Maoli and a military haole didn't amount to much in the occupational scale.

"Dr. Liu," the doctor said, shaking Matsunaga's hand and barely nodding to the others. "Mr. Kitahara's condition is not serious, but I'm afraid he's going to be bedridden for some time. He's fractured two ribs and his left tibia. Fortunately, this last one is a tibial shaft fracture and hasn't affected the articulation, but he'll need a close follow-up."

Matsunaga nodded, looking properly concerned. The doctor went on. "I wouldn't recommend a trip at this stage, but I understand he might prefer to return to Japan to be treated there. Can you contact his next of kin?"

"Yes, I'll talk to his family," Matsunaga answered. "And I'll try to convince him to stay here for a while at least, following your recommendation. Can I see him now?"

The doctor nodded. "He's in room D223, but don't visit for too long—it might be too taxing after both the trauma and the procedures."

"I won't stay long. Thank you, doctor."

Long enough to convince Kitahara to keep his end of the deal, Brendan hoped, though they'd had to improvise a way to make it happen without completely changing the plan fifteen hours and three minutes before the Harris brothers set foot on the island.

Well, what was that thing Brendan's BUD/S instructor used to say—when he wasn't yelling, "Drop and push 'em out"?

If an op goes baby-ass smooth, brace yourself for the imminent clusterfuck.

CHAPTER 47

KOTARŌ STOOD by the baggage carousel, looking stupid in his red-and-black bellhop uniform. With the hat. And the birdcage-like luggage cart. And still he had to be happy to have avoided the lei greeting team.

He straightened. This was for Kenshin-san. They were getting him home in a few days if everything went well, and Kotarō would make sure his part went frigging well.

"Hey, cuz!" he heard before a huge hand slapped his back and almost sent him headfirst onto the carousel. "You look sharp in da kine clothes."

Shit. The sheer size of B's relatives made Kotarō wonder if the *big* in his name shouldn't have been *humongous* instead.

"Wot? You no like yo clothes?"

Kotarō rolled his eyes. "Dude, have you seen my hat?"

"You want see mine?"

Kotarō grinned. "But at least you got to wear a black suit, man."

"You like?" Kawika said, moving his huge frame this way and that as if modeling for him.

He laughed and got a toothy grin in return. It was impossible to keep a straight face around these guys—or to stay nervous, which was, Kotarō thought, why Kawika was goofing on him. As if to confirm it, he blinked an eye. "No worry, cuz. You goin' stay killahz, I no kid you."

He was about to thank the man when Kawika whispered, "You bettah watch out now; heah come da lolo buggah."

Kotarō turned to see who Kawika was calling a "crazy dude" and let out a surprised giggle. Oh man, that was rich; a badass special operator dressed in the same stupid uniform Kotarō was wearing.

"Cut it out, kid," Otter said, wagging a finger at Kotarō. "And no bellboy jokes, okay?"

Now Otter stared right over Kotarō's shoulder and talked to no one in particular, and Kotarō watched in fascination as the man communicated with some other member of their team without changing his demeanor in the least. If Kotarō hadn't known Otter was wearing one of those tiny earpieces and a lapel mic, he would have never noticed there was something weird going on.

"Roger that," Otter said, his eyes focusing back on Kotarō and Kawika and narrowing in an unhappy expression. "Now guys, we got ourselves a Houston-we-have-a-problem moment here, so listen out. The lawyer is carrying an attaché case, so I'm gonna do my best to *unattach* him from it but, more important than that, I need him to touch something, so whatever oddball thing you see me doing, just act as if it was as fine as frog's hair, got it?"

"Fo' shua, brah."

"Hai."

Otter nodded. "Okay. Be back in a jiffy."

And just like that, he disappeared into the crowd, never mind the glaring red uniform.

"What was that he said about touching something?" Kotarō asked, his eyes still scanning the crowd in vain.

Kawika shrugged. "I no can tink like dat lolo, cuz."

The arrivals information panel did that fluttery thing that changed all the flights on display, and the plane they were waiting for was announced as landing right now. Shit. Otter hadn't explained what he was going to do, but it seemed likely that a delay in the flight would have come in handy.

Kotarō scanned the crowd once more, but there was no trace of the cakey red hat, and the airport was not on the big side—he could actually see the plane taxiing toward the terminal—so passengers would start spilling through the gate any minute now.

"*Kuso*," he cursed, pacing up and down for what seemed like a long while, not knowing what else to do.

"Check u'm out," Kawika said, nodding in the direction of the gate.

Kona International Airport had this cool design that allowed people to see everything going on because the terminals had no walls, so Kotarō looked at the gate and, even though they weren't close, he still could spot Brendan-san's red hair, and then the boss and Aniki guiding some strangers in the direction of their lei greeting team—B's cousins, all of them.

And still no sign of Otter.

The greeting team carried on with their antics—kiss on the cheek and all—but too frigging soon the party moved on toward the baggage claim.

Kawika lifted the sign with the resort logo and the name *Harris* in big block letters, and Kotarō straightened his jacket self-consciously. He was glad to have Kawika's solid presence by his side, because he couldn't help feeling anxious about the missing SEAL and intimidated by the group approaching them.

Kenshin-san's brothers didn't look anything like the gaijin. They were tall and fat and old and looked mean even in Hawaiian shirts—dude, Hawaiian shirts with slacks, way to go. Well, maybe they looked mean to Kotarō because he hated them already, for if you looked at Brendan-san, you got the perfect action-flick definition of mean, what with the dark suit, the dark glasses, the spy headset, and the badass attitude. Even Aniki looked not exactly mean but sharp and aloof in an I'm-all-business style, his new haircut making him more serious, his suit more on the salaryman side than his usual ones. And the boss, well the boss was always way out of everyone else's league of meanness. Now he looked more like a company *shachō* than a yakuza wakagashira, but still imposing even if he wore his shirt collar unbuttoned and smiled a little as he talked to one of the wives.

The wives were scary. Even more than the lawyer guy who looked constipated.

"That's us," Miles Harris said, pointing at the sign in Kawika's hands.

"*E komo mai*," Kawika welcomed them with a smile. "My name is Kawika, and I'll be your driver during your stay on the Big Island."

The Harrises seemed to have nothing to say to that, so Kawika went on, "If you'd be so kind as to point your luggage for us, we'll make sure it arrives to your accommodations before you do."

Kotarō bowed and smiled but got no reaction either, the wives just pushing ahead to stand as close as they could to the carousel. The younger one was dressed for a fashion safari in a tan jumpsuit and pumps that looked like they cost more than the boss's car. The older one tried to look younger in one of those white frilly dresses that were supposed to suggest freedom and white beaches, so she obviously didn't know many beaches on the Big Island had black or green sand.

"They're taking their sweet time," Miles said. "These tiny airports are the worst."

Kotarō tried not to glare. They'd just got here and were already complaining.

"And what's all that black rubble? Is the whole island this barren? I thought this was some kind of tropical paradise."

That was the younger brother, Campbell.

"The airport was built on a lava field," Matsunaga-san answered patiently. "This side of the Big Island may look a little barren because of the lava, but the weather here is perfect almost all year round, the beaches are spectacular, and those same black fields can give the landscape a special touch with the contrasting green vegetation. The other side of the island—the Hilo area—is more tropical, lusher if you want, but I don't think you'd appreciate the humidity there."

"According to our market research," Aniki said, "the most expensive resorts are located in this area. They offer the best big game fishing and snorkeling activities on the island, and have golf courses that are among the best in America."

Wow. Aniki sounded as if he had all that information in his head. Well, he had, in a way, because Kitahara-san was pouring it into Aniki's ear through the headset he wore, pretending it was one of those hands-free phone devices for busy people when it was actually a two-way radio like the ones special agents used in movies.

Big B had said they couldn't trust cell phone reception since they'd be moving around a lot, and Aniki had to be ready to supply the right answer anywhere, so Kitahara must hear what they were saying at all times. B and Bobcat also needed to record what was said, though they had a second device working just in case something went wrong with Aniki's one.

"At least that's what the statistics show, though I'm afraid I can't confirm them by personal experience," the boss said, waving his left hand with the brace—and the second microphone inside it. Big B had told him that this way he would have to be as careful as if he'd really broken some fingers in a surfing mishap and wasn't using the brace to hide his missing pinkie tip instead.

The brothers laughed, as the boss no doubt expected, because they looked like the kind of people who would crack up when someone did a pratfall. And then Miles went and patted the boss on his shoulder and Kotarō tried not to freak out.

"Tough luck, pal," Miles said. "Though, if you don't mind my saying, aren't you a bit old to try your hand at surfing?"

Oh shit. Calling the boss old. And the jerk was realizing now he'd made a joke with the hand thing and was laughing even more, in spite of the expression on Matsunaga-san's face.

"I think age is a question of attitude," one of the wives said, and it figured it should be the one trying to appear younger. "New things keep your spirit in good shape."

"And your body in the ER," Miles said, laughing again until the safari wife gave him a look of pure snake venom.

"You're right, darling," Campbell said, "Mr. Nakazawa's adventurous spirit will sure keep him young."

Kotarō realized with a shock that he had the wives mixed up, that the older one wasn't the elder brother's wife but the younger's. So Alice Harris—Campbell's wife—was the natural fake-blonde with the breezy dress, and Cynthia Harris—Miles's wife—was the safari version of Xena the Warrior Princess.

The lawyer seemed to be waiting for the lawyery stuff to open his mouth and, like Otter said, he was carrying a briefcase, a black leather box with some kind of latch that Kotarō had never seen before.

"Sir, we can carry that for you," Kawika said to the lawyer, pointing at the briefcase, but the man shook his head.

"No, I'll carry it myself," he answered, no thank-yous or anything.

"Those Prada suitcases are mine," said Cynthia, pointing at one of the very first heaps coming out of the flap-covered wall opening.

The cases hit the cart with a loud thunk and Kotarō watched them in consternation, trying to calculate how long it would take their team to go through their contents. What if the rest of the group had also packed for a year? Even if Kawika kept driving around in circles, they'd never inspect everything, plant the bugs and the tracers, put everything carefully back in place, and get to the resort before the Harrises did. And that was without counting the lawyer's briefcase.

When another couple of huge cases showed up not long after and Alice Harris pointed at them, Kotarō tried to convince himself that the women's cases were not likely to have anything important inside, since they were only on vacation here, so they could skim through them in a rush to check the men's luggage, but as the pile kept growing on the cart, he felt increasingly anxious.

And how on earth were they going to get the lawyer to let go of his briefcase? And where the fuck were the frigging SEALs when you needed them? Well, Brendan-san sure was there, but he wasn't even looking in Kotarō's direction; he just stood there waiting for the world's most dangerous terrorists to dare attack the Harrises, and Kotarō was about to be sick if Grumpy, Whiny, and Pouty had one more piece of brand-name luggage showing on the carousel.

CHAPTER 48

KOTARŌ LOOKED about to puke. Fortunately for them all, his Japanese complexion didn't really show how green around the gills he was, and it seemed the Harris brothers were the kind who grew up in a house with enough domestic workers to make them immune to contact with any service staff—to the senator's sons, they were simply invisible.

Brendan tried to ignore another of the Harrises' *ingratiating* features—their constant nagging about absolutely everything—because being around Washington types had showed him that these people considered approving of something a character flaw, so it wasn't as if their attitude would have any real weight in the final business decision. The Japanese, though, were no doubt used to quite a different style of interacting with people, something far more polite, if the long-suffering tone Matsunaga used to answer each stupid question was any indication.

Kinosuke's own tone was still weird in spite of all the rehearsing, but maybe Brendan found it so because he was used to his sensei's usual cocky speech. Now he was reduced to parroting Kitahara, and his efforts to not appear lame while he did it were more than a little cute. Geez. That plus the elegant suit plus the new haircut were giving Brendan a hard time—pun intended.

Yeah, with less hair hiding his features, Kinosuke looked both vulnerable and hot enough to eat, and maybe the young man wasn't even realizing it but his intense stare kept returning to Brendan as if he needed the reassurance that the ex-operator was still around to feel—well, Brendan didn't know exactly what, and not knowing was driving him crazy. He got anxious too, every time those black eyes landed on him, because now that their targets were with them, he couldn't look back, much less smile; he just had to stand there faking a professionally aloof look.

Oh my. Speaking of fake looks. Otter in a bellhop uniform.

Brendan had to focus on the palm trees outside the baggage claim to avoid cracking up, and still he could follow the approaching red spot from the corner of his eye as if it were a laser target designator. It would be a great help if NGO's in Afghanistan started giving away bellboy uniforms.

"Welcome, ladies and gentlemen," Otter said in the singsong way of PR reps and MCs when he reached their group. "Your transports are ready to take you and your prized possessions to your home away from home."

Geez. Trust Otter to overplay even a bit part. If the guy wasn't such a good grifter, they would always send Burka in his place—white hair or no—but right now, they were in need of Otter's skills.

With the Harrises came a Stewart Longchamp, who, according to Craig, was one of the top twenty corporate lawyers in the District. It meant the brothers were seriously considering doing business in Hawaii, but it also meant whatever move Matsunaga made would be closely watched.

They needed every advantage they could get, and knowing what Longchamp knew would definitely be an upside. The man didn't seem ready to let go of his briefcase, though, and Brendan had noticed it was one of those models with a biometric lock, which made Otter's intervention even more important, since they'd need a fingerprint if they were to crack it.

"Is this all your luggage?" Otter said, pointing at the cart. There were a few nods and grunts and Otter nodded in return, addressing the lawyer now. "We can carry that for you, sir."

"No, I'm fine."

It would have been too easy if Longchamp had conceded this second time after Kawika's attempt.

"If you're worried about safety, we can use our plastic protective packaging and specially designed security seal so you know the lock hasn't been tampered with, and we'll deposit it in the hotel safe for you to retrieve upon arrival. We haven't had any complaints in all the years our resort has been open, sir; it's perfectly safe and convenient."

Nice try, but the lawyer didn't seem at all convinced.

"No, I'd rather keep it with me."

"As you wish, sir," Otter said, and then flashed a smile at the group. "Now one last thing before you go. I'm going to check that we have the names right so there won't be any confusion."

He looked down at the stack of papers he carried and read aloud. "Miles and Cynthia Harris?"

"That's us," Miles said.

"Okay. Charles and Olivia Harris?"

Miles snorted. "That's close." The guy seemed to be this group's gagman, but the most comic thing at the moment was Otter's contrite expression.

"I'm so sorry. It seems we have a few Harrises staying with us," he said, starting to turn pages as if to confirm it, and read hesitantly, "Frank and Susan Harris, maybe?"

"Oh for Christ's sake," Campbell murmured as Miles laughed. "It's Campbell and Alice Harris. You think you can find that on your list?"

Otter looked completely at a loss, turning pages this way and that. "I hope so, sir. The assistant receptionist is on sick leave, and the temp replacing her doesn't know if she's coming or going, if you catch my drift." He kept turning pages until Campbell huffed and reached out to grab the stack of papers.

Brendan forced himself not to react. Those weren't the prints they wanted, but it would look weird if he tried to stop Campbell from touching the papers, and Otter was fast as lightning, jerking the stack out of Campbell's reach in a gesture that was masterfully disguised as eagerness to please. "Got it! Campbell and Alicia Harris, ain't that right?"

"Yes, that is right," Campbell said, stressing every word in an uppity, teacher's-pet tone that Otter pretended not to notice as he turned good-naturedly to his real target.

"Well, sir, that only leaves you," he said with a toothy grin. "Could you tell me your name, please?"

"Stewart Longchamp."

Otter's flustered expression was priceless. "Uh, is that French or something?"

The lawyer didn't take the bait, though—Brendan guessed he had to be a hell of a cold fish to make it to the top in his profession. He just repeated his name, spelling it for good measure.

Not that Otter would quit any time soon. He flipped through the pages anxiously, looking chagrined. "I'm so sorry, sir. This has never happened to me before." He flipped some more. "Lowenthal, Bradford—Jesus, the girl doesn't even know what alphabetical order is—she must think it's a call to room service for alphabet pasta."

Both Kotarō and Miles laughed at that, but the rest of the group only looked impatient, which was what Otter was aiming at. "I'm sorry to be delaying you, but I need to check this out. You wouldn't want your luggage to end up in Mr. Lowenthal's room, would you now? Or, worse, it could be *Mrs.* Lowenthal's 'cause it doesn't say here if it's a chick—imagine that."

The possibility of course amused Miles to no end, and the man palmed the lawyer's back in a congenial-drunk sort of way. "Now, Stewart, be a champ and help this poor fellow out, or we'll be here till sunset."

Bingo. It was obvious that Longchamp would have simply glared at Miles if Miles hadn't been his client, but it seemed lawyers tended to heed the adage about customers being always right—affluent customers at least—so he just put out his hand as if stretching his arm to grab the papers would be too much of an effort.

Brendan had to look away to avoid laughing at Otter's expression of abject gratitude as he passed the list to Longchamp. "Thank you so much, sir. You know how these things go," Otter said as the lawyer searched the list for his name. "They'd rip me a new one if I didn't check before you went, and they'd rip me a new one if I kept delaying you, so you just kind of saved my life."

"Here it is," Longchamp said, pointing at a line on one of the papers.

And before the lawyer would return the stack, Otter beamed and offered him a fluorescent green rollerball pen. "Highlight it for me, would you? I don't want to get it mixed up after you went to all this trouble."

Longchamp sighed audibly but took the pen and made a green circle around his name.

"Thank you very much, sir. Now Kawika will show you to your limo while we take your luggage to your rooms in a jiffy. Enjoy your stay on the Big Island."

"Please follow me," Kawika said.

And just as the group started moving, Otter turned to Longchamp and asked, "You sure you don't want us to carry your briefcase?"

Geez. Otter was like a dog after a bone, but this one bone seemed too hard to crack.

"No, thank you."

Well, at least he got a thank you this time—and a set of fresh prints as a lagniappe. All they needed now was to get their hands on the briefcase.

CHAPTER 49

SHIT. IF Kitahara didn't stop talking in his ear, Kinosuke was going to scream. Who'd have guessed the Rat was a windbag on top of everything else? Kinosuke had to pretend to keep taking calls for the boss, who was supposed to be some hotshot company CEO, but Kitahara was clearly overdoing it—and enjoying himself while he did it, the bastard.

"*Chikushō*," he cursed, hoping Brendan was right about none in the Harris party understanding Japanese. The boss, though, raised a brow at him.

"*Aitsu wa shaberimakuru*," Kinosuke explained, trying to look as if he was passing some momentous financial codswallop instead of insulting Kitahara.

"*Atarimae da*," the boss agreed on the same grave note and Kinosuke almost lost it, but he could always count on the Harris brothers to say something annoying to get his mirth back in check.

"Jesus! Don't these people know how to merge?" Campbell Harris grumbled on cue as the limo came to a shuddering halt.

Kinosuke schooled his face into a bland mask of indifference, though he'd already learned nobody paid him—the unimportant secretary—any attention unless he spoke up to repeat some of the data Kitahara kept pouring in his ear.

"Drivers here are friendly enough," the boss said, "but they never seem to be in a hurry, and most of the time they change lanes without signaling. It's quite different from the streets of Tokyo, let me tell you."

"Bunch of hicks" was Campbell's answer, and the boss gave him an innocent look that made Kinosuke bite the inside of his lip to avoid grinning in anticipation.

"I hear that you live in Exeter, Mr. Harris," Matsunaga said. "You'll have to excuse my ignorance, but isn't that a rather small town compared with Kailua-Kona?" And before Campbell could open his mouth, the boss added, "I would have thought you'd be used to this kind of relaxed driving."

Miles snorted. "You're right on the money, Nakazawa. Those provincial SUV drivers are the worst. They just slam on the brakes and signal *as* they turn."

Campbell glared at his brother uselessly, since the guy was too busy refilling his glass from the bar in front of their puffy seats. The limo was one of those ugly affairs, all leather and chromed surfaces, with a long curvy seat for about six people and two added individual seats facing the car rear.

The two married couples sat on the bench, facing large scenic windows and a well-stocked bar; the lawyer—who had yet to open his mouth to let out more than three words in a row—sat where the long seat took a bend, facing the car front and the two Japanese, who had the blessedly individual seats behind the driver's area.

"Is it always this cloudy?"

Everybody turned to look at Cynthia, Miles's wife. "I thought you said it was always spring here," she added, giving the boss an accusatory look.

Shit. Even the wives had caught the signature Harris whining.

"Yes, madam," the boss said, using an exaggerated foreign accent to make *madam* sound less than complimentary. "This side of the island almost always gets clear mornings, with clouds forming in the afternoon, and a few evening showers in the summer. These, and the mild temperatures, are what make people describe this weather as eternal springtime."

And before Cynthia could realize the answer was the polite equivalent of an eye-roll, Kitahara came to the rescue. "The average maximum and minimum temperatures in Kailua-Kona are eighty degrees and sixty-four degrees for February, and eighty-seven degrees and sixty-nine degrees for August, with humidity ranging between 50 and 80 percent."

Huh. It was kind of creepy for Kinosuke, blurting out figures as if he had a Big Island data bank in his head, but the Harrises didn't seem to find it strange, so maybe that was what corporate advisors usually did. All Cynthia did was pout to show her disappointment at not having twelve daily hours of blazing sunlight to keep up the dark tan she sported, though Kinosuke didn't peg New Hampshire for the kind of place where you could regularly sunbathe. But what did he know about the mainland, anyway?

The limo made a wide turn and merged seamlessly into the heavy traffic on Alii Drive. Big B's cousin number eighty—Kinosuke was starting to think the guy was related to every native Hawaiian on the islands—was a great driver and, so far, nobody had noticed he was bird-dogging traffic jams instead of avoiding them.

They desperately needed to make time for the home team to go through the tons of luggage the visiting team had flooded them with. Shit. Did they think this place was at the world's end? That there would be no Walmarts—or Guccis, for that matter? It would have been funny to watch the face Kotarō made as the suitcases kept piling up in his flashy cart if so much hadn't been at stake, but the most vital piece in this puzzle was information—or *intel*, as Brendan and his cronies called it in this weird-assed military jargon of theirs.

Kinosuke smothered the urge to turn his head to look at Brendan. The privacy partition was up anyway, so his eyes would have only met smoked glass, but he missed Brendan's reassuring presence. It was silly, but having the man around made Kinosuke feel safer, calmed him somehow, as if no matter how down the drain things went, with Brendan on their side everything would turn out okeydoke.

Maybe it was the SEAL nerve that did it, the kind of brassy swagger these guys showed even when standing still, and maybe it was easy for Kinosuke to catch it because yakuza soldiers—true yakuza, not bar-hopping slugs—tended to have a similar alertness to their stance, even the more easygoing like Tachibana. So when it came to Otter doing his monkeyshines, there was still a difference.

What had all that bellhop shit been about anyway? If Otter had been aiming for the lawyer's briefcase, the rest of the show he'd put on would have been useless. Had he been gaining time for some new development in their supercomplicated supersoldier schemes? He wouldn't be surprised if that had been the case; the way these guys planned even the exact length of their shoestrings meant there was always something not working exactly as they planned.

"Don't repeat this, Kinosuke."

Fuck. Speak of the devil. How on earth was Brendan talking through his headset? He just hoped he hadn't visibly flinched.

"Burka is going to approach the limo trunk, and we need a distraction to give him some cover."

Kinosuke had to acknowledge Brendan somehow, so he just blurted, "Hai."

"That's right, answer me in Japanese as if you were taking a call."

Shit. Wasn't that what he'd been doing with Kitahara for hours? Did Brendan think he was stupid?

"Ore wa baka ja nai," he said aloud, even though Brendan wouldn't get it, and the boss was giving him a what's-up look.

"Okay. We'll keep it simple, just discuss with them the activities we've planned, make them believe the resort is calling to confirm dates or reschedule new ones, but first tell Matsunaga what's going on so he can add to the conversation."

Great. So the boss could add to the conversation, but Kinosuke was not trusted to put a word in edgewise. Just ape Kitahara and he'd be fine—not that he was griping, they had more than their share of gripers in that ugly worm of a car. And at least Brendan hadn't reminded him to speak to the boss in Japanese so no one else would be any the wiser. Duh.

"Nakazawa-shachō?"

The boss turned to him and listened as he explained the situation, his expression never changing even when Kinosuke told him Burka was going to open the trunk and take the briefcase in front of everybody and his mother. Shit. Kinosuke was panicking just from imagining that blinding white hair popping up in the rear window.

"You're doing great, Sensei."

Oh. That was embarrassing, Brendan reading him like that, and it made his stomach feel funny on top of everything else. *"Arigatō,"* he murmured, and he would've sworn he could hear the smile at the other end of the whatever it was Brendan was using to talk to him.

"You're welcome. Um, okay, let's do this. Signal Matsunaga to address the Harrises, and Kitahara will read the schedule for you to repeat. If you hear any telltale noise, do whatever it takes to distract them. Don't be polite."

Noises. *Kuso.* He'd only been worried about the visuals. And what was that shit about not being polite? Did he have to sucker punch someone to call their attention?

Fuck. He had to stop thinking in circles like Kotarō. He could do this. Brendan said he was doing great, and he was the alpha SEAL of the pack; he should know.

"Hajimete kudasai," he said to the boss, asking him to start.

The boss nodded. "If I may have your attention, it seems our resort wants to confirm the activities we've chosen for you so that we can be sure the dates will be available. I take it all of you enjoy golf?"

"Sure," Miles said. "It's just my kind of sport—you don't have to squeeze yourself into a spandex suit, you don't break a sweat, and you're still allowed to call it a sport. It's the yoga of the business man."

Alice, Campbell's wife, gave Miles an outraged look. "Yoga is a good exercise; it tones your muscles and improves your balance, and some types of yoga can make you sweat a lot."

"Only because they put you in a sauna while you contort your body," Miles countered, and Kinosuke felt the limo pull to the right nice and easy, like a big sea creature swimming silently. Traffic on the right lane was heavier and slower, and they were soon crawling to a stop.

"It's not a sauna," Alice kept on, "Bikram yoga is done in a heated room to prevent injuries and get rid of toxins through the sweat."

"Yeah, well, it should be considered an extreme sport, since you risk dying of heatstroke while you salute the sun or some other bullshit like that," said Miles.

Kinosuke couldn't help looking at the rear window—it wasn't his fault if it was right in his line of vision—and he couldn't help seeing a moped approach the limo. Good thinking, that. Mopeds were all over the streets of Kona, and you needed to wear a crash helmet, so no white hair showing.

"There's no risk at all if you hydrate properly," Alice insisted peevishly.

As the motorbike drew closer, Kinosuke cast what he thought was a discreet look at the limo passengers, checking that none of them was looking back.

"Hydrate?" Miles repeated in a mocking tone. "Who have you been doing yoga with? Marines?"

Alice huffed in outrage, and Kinosuke could see that Brendan's advice about not being polite was solid, since everybody was watching Miles and Alice even though their conversation was the dumbest he'd come across in ages.

By now the moped driver was so close to the limo that he could have touched the trunk if he'd outstretched his arm, but the car was moving again, and Kinosuke imagined Burka was waiting for it to stop completely before trying anything.

"Miles—" Campbell scolded, then said to the boss, "Yes, Mr. Nakazawa, we all like golf, though the real expert here is Stewart. I believe you've even played here on the islands before, haven't you?"

Oh fuck. The limo had to come to a stop just when everybody turned their heads to look at the lawyer, whose fat head was smack-dab in front of the rear windshield.

"I was once invited to Waialae Country Club in Oahu," Longchamp answered, and of course the moped rider decided this was a good moment to touch the trunk. "But I've never played on the Big Island before, though I've heard Mauna Kea Golf Course is worth visiting. Laurence Rockefeller never did things halfway, and the course layout is said to be brilliant. Hole number 3...."

Shit. The guy hadn't opened his piehole more than three times before, and now he couldn't shut it. *Now*, with Burka's hand laying nonchalantly on the trunk, as if the man were just resting his weight while he waited for traffic to move on.

Everybody was looking at the lawyer, even though he sounded worse than Kitahara with his dumb statistics, and Kinosuke racked his brain for something to say to interrupt the man.

Fucking tinted windows. With everybody looking back, Kinosuke could have waved Burka to stop or, well, being a SEAL and all, Burka himself would have caught everybody looking in his direction and done a better job of pretending nonchalance, because that hand on the trunk was not exactly subtle. And suddenly Kinosuke's heart jumped in his chest. He realized he'd only been worried about the people *inside* the car seeing Burka, but what about all those other people stuck together in the heavy traffic with nothing to do but gawk at other cars? What would any of them do if a suspicious character on a motorbike lifted the trunk of a limo and took out a briefcase?

"It's a pity that Robert Trent Jones Sr. died in 2000, because you could trust the courses he designed to...."

And Longchamp kept going like the Energizer Bunny of golf. The Harrises were not yet bored out of their minds, but they soon would be, and then they'd surely notice the man lurking behind the limo.

Fuck. Where were Kitahara and Brendan now? At least the Rat had to be listening, so why wasn't he suggesting some lamebrained data on the proper lawn seeds for golf courses? Probably because Kitahara couldn't actually see what was going on; only Kinosuke and the boss had a clear view of the back of the car, and the boss couldn't well interrupt the lawyer without appearing too rude for a Japanese businessman.

So it all came down to Kinosuke; as a lowly, inexperienced secretary, he could afford to put his foot in it.

"And when Tiger finished, he said—"

"Sorry, sir, but our destination manager needs to know how many people will need to book lessons." There, impolite as all hell, by the looks he was receiving. Maybe even insulting, to suggest any of them might need lessons, but Kinosuke didn't know shit about golf, didn't know how you fucking went about booking golf courses—did you reserve holes like you did rooms?—so it was the only thing that came to his mind, and everybody was looking at him, so there, mission accomplished.

"Hidenori-kun," the boss called in his wakagashira voice and Kinosuke swallowed. "Our destination manager is at our service and the service of our guests, not the other way around, so we'll tell him what he needs to know when *we* are ready and not before. Am I making myself clear?"

"*Hai. Wakarimashita,*" Kinosuke answered automatically, and then felt his cheeks redden. He knew the boss was just helping, putting on a show, but Kinosuke had been on the other end of the boss's anger so many times that this felt like another of his usual blunders, as if, no matter what he did, he would always be the hopeless streetpunk.

"Now apologize properly to Mr. Longchamp."

That *properly* was the final nail in his coffin. It was as if Matsunaga were testing him, as if he expected Kinosuke not to know what was exactly proper in this case, as if he were sure Kinosuke would bend too little or go as far as assuming the *dogeza* on the carpeted floor of the limo.

He tried to convince himself that it was probably the other way around, that no company shachō would have to explain to his secretary what to do, that it was a way to assure everybody would look at him, but, as he half stood and bent forty-five degrees in the best *saikeirei* he could manage, he felt a rage out of all proportion.

Nothing was worth this humiliation. He shouldn't be doing this, not for the boss, not even for Kenshin-san, and much less for—

He realized with a pang that he didn't feel rage at having to humble himself in front of people he despised, or even because the boss had ordered him to; he couldn't stand it because Brendan was there, right behind a thin pane of tinted glass, and the remote chance that he might see Kinosuke like this made his stomach churn.

Fucking redhead. With his "sensei this" and "sensei that," he had made Kinosuke actually believe he could be the man he saw reflected in those foreign eyes, and now he couldn't resign himself to anything below those expectations.

The roof of the limo didn't allow Kinosuke to straighten back up with much grace, and he almost banged his noggin when his eyes came level with the rear window and he saw that the trunk lid was open.

He had to draw attention to himself, so he bowed awkwardly one more time, repeating his apology in Japanese for good measure, his thoughts running in ten directions at once, imagining the expression on the drivers' faces around the limo as they watched someone steal from the limo, imagining how many people would be dialing 911 right this moment and wondering how long it would take the cops to reach them.

Longchamp murmured something as Kinosuke straightened, and Kinosuke's eyes almost widened in shock when he looked out the rear window again.

The trunk lid was back down and Burka was right behind the limo, his white hair all but glowing in the overcast afternoon, no crash helmet or moped in sight, his thin frame encased in another of those glaring red bellhop uniforms as he carried the briefcase back to a van with the resort logo on its side, everything done in plain view, cool as you please, the guy just taking his time as if it were his everyday fucking boring job to pick up luggage from limo trunks.

Kinosuke sat back down with a thud as the car started moving again, and he saw from the corner of his eye how the van passed them, but it still took a few more minutes for his heart to slow down to a more or less normal rate. These guys were crazy—fucking brilliantly, hair-raising crazy—or had Xanax running through their veins to give them those nerves of steel.

"Haven't we passed that hotel before?"

He almost laughed hysterically. So someone had finally realized they were driving around in circles, and of course it had to be the lawyer—trust a shark to recognize a circling pattern—and of course it had to be right now, just when they got their hands on the briefcase.

Well, then; maybe beside bellboys, the SEALs were trained as picklocks too, and maybe they could open the briefcase, scan its contents, and put the briefcase back in the limo in the roughly ten minutes it would take the car to arrive at the resort now that they couldn't go on with the pretense of the scenic route. And who knew? Maybe Big B had enough cousins to have ended the inspection of the rest of the luggage by that time too.

CHAPTER 50

"AKA ONI to Maneki Neko, over" came the voice from the radio, and Kotarō was too nervous to even crack up at Brendan-san calling himself *Red Devil*. Aniki had been the one who had chosen the call signs and told the redhead they were all Japanese animals. Brendan-san had given him a suspicious look but used the call signs anyway, and only Big B had laughed like a fiend when Aniki told Bobcat to use the Maneki Neko call sign— guess he'd seen enough Asian businesses with the arm-swinging cat to know its name.

"Come in, Maneki Neko. Over."

Kotarō hurried to press the button. "This is Kakashi here, out. Um, I mean, over."

Shit, shit, shit. Bobcat was never going to trust him with the radio again.

"Tell the guys to move it. Be there in eight. You copy? Over."

"Hai, I mean, affirmative, I copy," he stammered and then remembered to add the *over* to let Brendan-san put a word in. Man, he was pathetic.

"Breathe, lad. It'll be fine. Out."

"Roger," he said, all satisfied with himself until he realized Brendan had said *out* and wouldn't be listening to his clever answer. Oh shit. Had he said eight? They only had eight frigging minutes?

Kotarō ran out of the room Bobcat called their "comm center" and into the organized bedlam of the living room, where fifteen people worked to beat each other in what looked like a contest for the fastest customs officer.

All the furniture had been pushed aside to make room for the seven suitcases that lay sprawled on the floor, two-people teams sifting through their contents and carefully placing everything on case-sized floor areas after taking a picture of each layer of packed stuff. Of course it had been Bobcat who'd come up with the idea to measure the cases and stick yellow tape onto the floor in their exact shape, but it was only when Bobcat said that they had to take photos and get a yellow-tape case for *every* layer of clothes and shit that Otter had shook his head and asked Kotarō if he'd ever met any other Catholic Methodist in his life—whatever that meant.

But no matter how much Otter mocked him, Kotarō could still see the respect behind the joke—as he could see it every time one of them called Brendan-san "boss" or "Mr. O." In fact, only Bobcat had been trusted to decide where to plant the devices to track the Harrises all the time.

"They're coming!" Kotarō squeaked into the busy silence of the room, and everybody stopped what they were doing to look up at him.

"How long?" Bobcat asked, his eyes immediately moving from Kotarō back to the fish tank.

"Eight minutes," Kotarō answered. "Though I suppose it's seven now; I came to tell you as fast as I could, but a minute is just these sixty seconds, and I guess—"

"Breathe, Kotarō," Big B cut him off, squeezing his shoulder reassuringly. "Okay everybody," he added for the rest of the room, "stop searching and put everything back in the cases. Be swift, but concentrate on placing each thing exactly where you found it."

Kotarō decided to follow the advice everyone was giving him and took a deep breath, though it didn't seem to do much for his nerves. "The briefcase is the most important, isn't it?"

"Seems like it," B said, then patted Kotarō's back. "Don't sweat it. A SEAL team can win a war in less than seven minutes."

Maybe a SEAL team could, but their team? With two ex-SEALs, four hotel maids, three waitresses, two maintenance guys, two taxi drivers, a bartender, and a construction worker? Dude, the most they could do was open their own resort.

The maids, though, were flying through the cases' contents now—and weirdly enough, so was the construction man, one of B's cousins—but the two extra members of their team, the ones supposed to bring the briefcase, were still missing.

"Six," B called to the room at large, and people seemed to rush even more as they transferred shirts and dresses and whatnots from the floor to the cases.

Kotarō turned in Bobcat's direction. Sitting at a cluttered table with all kinds of junk on it, the man looked like a wacko about to invent some crazy gizmo out of his garage.

Now he was carefully scanning one of the papers the lawyer had touched, which had the man's blackened fingerprints all over it. The way Bobcat had blackened the prints had been fun to watch too. Big B and he had cut a bunch of pencils open, then took out the black part in the middle and smashed it into a powder, and finally Bobcat had dusted the papers with this powder, using a brush Alma had lent him.

A knock at the door made Kotarō jump. Suddenly it seemed no one was in the room as everyone froze in place except B, who moved like a frigging ninja shadow across the littered floor, and Kotarō didn't even see him pull out the gun he lifted to point at the door.

"Stop pointing at my head and open the fucking door" came Otter's voice from the other side.

B chuckled and moved aside to open the door and let Otter and Burka in.

"Man, I need to take off the suit before they give me a VMA," Otter said, and Kotarō was so flabbergasted his head swiveled back and forth between Otter, who didn't seem to have a care in the world, and Burka, who crossed the room like one of those comets with red tails that only happen once in a zillion years, put the briefcase on the table, crouched in front of it so his scary eyes were level with the latches, and lifted a pale hand toward Bobcat without so much as a peep the whole frigging time.

"Five," B called, and the room was again filled with the noise of a lot of people moving a lot of stuff this way and that in more than your regular hurry.

"Come watch the experts work, kid," Otter said, throwing his arm around Kotarō's shoulders and pulling him out of the way of the repacking team. They stood behind Burka, and Kotarō watched as the man slid the central latch on the briefcase to expose a tiny window-like panel.

"That's the fingerprint sensor," Otter explained as Burka took the printout Bobcat handed him and pressed the image of one blackened fingerprint against the small sensor. "Now cross your fingers and—"

There came a red light and nothing happened. "And now we know it's not a cheap model," Otter said, cool as a frigging cucumber. Burka chose another fingerprint and pressed it again to another red light. "And that might be one of yours truly's fingerprints."

As Burka kept on going patiently through the fingerprints on the paper, Kotarō started to get anxious. "What if it doesn't work? What if we can't open it?"

"Then we implement plan B," Otter stated calmly.

The last fingerprint gave another red light, and Kotarō squeaked, "What plan B?"

"The one that comes before plan C, that's what plan."

Kotarō couldn't even blink before Big B called, "Four," and a timer went off somewhere.

"Cool. Our superglue pizza is ready. And just in time too."

"Open the window, Otter," Burka said over his shoulder and received an adoring smile in return.

"That's my man," Otter drawled, "looking after everybody's health even if the world is crumbling around us."

B snorted, but Burka didn't even look back from lifting the aquarium lid for Bobcat to turn off the lightbulb at the bottom and retrieve the pen Longchamp had used to highlight his name. Kotarō caught a whiff of something nasty even though the lid went back down quickly and Otter had already opened the window.

"Ugh," Otter grumbled on his way back to Kotarō. "That shit is foul enough without heating it, man. I wonder what kind of slob left superglue lying about on a heat source to discover the fumes were good to develop fingerprints." He leaned closer and stage-whispered, "I suspect the guy was just trying to get high and was a little bit hasty about it."

The pen looked almost the same, but it had this disgusting gray filmy stuff all over it, and Kotarō gaped when he saw two gray fingerprints clearly standing out.

"And we have a winner—or two—right here," Otter said. "Now, if we had the time, we'd make a beautiful model out of ballistics gel, but I don't think that sensor is so high-end as to need it."

Burka placed the pen against the sensor, and the light took a bit more to flash red, but it did, and only when Burka turned the pen to the other side with the other fingerprint did a green light finally appear. The problem was nothing else happened—the latches made no popping sound, and suddenly the light went back to red.

"Huh," Otter said. "So maybe the mofo is that high-end after all."

Kotarō looked from Otter to Burka to Bobcat and felt he was about to scream. Why weren't they freaking out?

"Wikiwiki, guys," B said. "We need the last two minutes to carry all this stuff to the rooms, so close every case right now."

Two minutes. Shit. Two frigging minutes, and Burka was just moving the pen this way and that as if deciding which side to eat first, and Bobcat and Otter were just watching him do it as if the pen was awesome or something, and Kotarō was about to bite his nails even though the boss had taught him out of that habit, and now Burka went and…. Oh shit. The crazy dude had just licked one of the fingerprints, just stuck his tongue out and frigging licked the gray stuff. Dude, that was—

Pop. The tiny light went green and the latches popped open when Burka put the slobbered print against it.

"Ain't my man badassically awesome or what?" Otter asked no one in particular, and Kotarō just looked at him in confusion. "Sweat, kid. People's hands are sweaty or greasy all the time, and my man here just fooled the sensor with some little fluid of his. That was disgusting, by the way; I'm not gonna kiss you in ages, man. What if I got superglued to you?"

"Time's up!" B shouted. "Otter, Kotarō, pick the ritzy cart and get moving. Now!"

Kotarō moved in a daze, holding the luggage cart as people threw the cases onto it as fast as they could, not daring to look back even though he still could hear the sound of the scanners working frantically behind him and B's voice as he used the radio to call Brendan-san. He wasn't going to try to figure out how long it would take to scan all the papers the lawyer dude was carrying, and he wasn't going to imagine how on earth Burka would take the briefcase back to the limo, and he wasn't even listening to B ask Brendan-san for more time. No way. Kotarō was just doing his part of the job and trying not to puke before they reached the rooms of Kenshin-san's brothers and Otter used the key card duplicates to let them in.

CHAPTER 51

"YOU GOT five, Dekai Kuma, over."

"Roger that, Aka Oni. We'll get it done. Out."

As simple as that. Because a SEAL would never say *I'll try* or even *I'll do my best*; SEALs were trained to go out there and get it done no matter what, and even if there was only one of them left, he would always use the collective "we" of the team.

Brendan hadn't realized how much he'd missed the reassuring simplicity of a special operator's life. Not that things didn't get complicated in the field—they always did—but the trouble you got into was always in stark relief against a solid background. If your chute didn't open, you knew exactly how many seconds of your life you had left to unfuck yourself.

Being around politicians, lawyers, and the rest of the District fauna, though, had been worse than being dunked into the pool, bound and blindfolded, in BUD/S training. Brendan had been lost moving through those murky waters, with so much out of his control and with no one to trust, not even Craig, who'd been a much-needed teacher, but contrary to Coronado instructors, Craig would manipulate Brendan for his own, very personal, benefit.

And that had been the worst to bear, living without at least a semblance of selflessness, without an ideal in sight, no matter how naïve or trite, and without a single person to rely on.

Brendan took a deep breath. He told himself one more time this was his second chance at getting it right; it might not be a fight to defend his country, but a flag was not needed to have an ideal or matching uniforms to have a team. Right now he was serving a righteous cause, and he was lucky enough to have an incredible team—ragtag as it may seem—who trusted him to lead. So as his instructors would say, "Pull your head out of your ass and lead."

"How long to the resort, Kawika?"

"Get deah in nutting, boss."

Brendan smiled. The GPS on his handheld Toughbook was telling him exactly the same but with much less local flavor. He checked the web on traffic conditions he'd been using to direct Kawika from one bumper-to-bumper traffic area to another and saw that the incident alert he'd spotted when B called was still on.

With Longchamp having noticed they weren't driving in a straight line to the resort, they couldn't change their route too much, but this was more or less in the right direction.

"I need you to take Palani Road in the next intersection," he told Kawika.

"Shua."

He checked the camera map Bobcat had provided. A blinking red dot appeared a little too close to their destination for Brendan's comfort, but he expected it would be far enough for him to get the promised five minutes without trouble.

The ease with which Bobcat hacked his way everywhere was amazing. It had taken him no time to get into the Hawaii County Public Works Traffic Division's system to allow them a constant update on the locations of the twenty cameras that provided video input to the department's command post—low resolution or not, they didn't need someone watching over their shoulders when they were about to engage in something, let's say, irregular.

The limo turned smoothly into Palani Road, traffic moving slowly but still moving. Brendan listened to Kinosuke repeating the list of spa treatments Kitahara read for him and found it difficult not to laugh. Poor Sensei. This must be so hard on his pride. And yet Kinosuke was doing it, even taking Brendan's suggestion to the letter and being rude to Longchamp.

Geez. That had been priceless, Kinosuke cutting the lawyer in the middle of his pontification to ask if they'd be needing lessons. *Lessons*. After the pompous bastard had been flaunting his arcane knowledge of golf.

Brendan had laughed then, imagining the scene behind the private partition, the look on Longchamp's face, but Matsunaga's rebuff had cut his mirth short. Of course the yakuza had only acted his role as a top company executive, but Brendan heard his own knuckles crack in response, he was clenching his fists so tight.

He couldn't stand Kinosuke being treated that way—like a misbehaving kid who was made to apologize to the grown-ups at his own birthday party. Yeah, his sensei could be a little brattish sometimes, and he sure was as cocky as they came, but he had a strength about him, a fundamental honesty that made him absolutely reliable, someone you could trust to guide you to safety even at his own expense. He would have made a good team leader.

Brendan had a more visceral reason for his reaction; he found it hard to keep still when someone attacked what was his. That Kinosuke had never been completely his didn't matter much to Brendan's stubborn instincts.

"Now wot?" Kawika asked when traffic stopped near the intersection of Palani Road and Queen Kaahumanu Highway. Workers were repairing a utility pole straight ahead, and they were causing the kind of short delay Brendan needed.

"Now we wreak havoc," Brendan said, flashing an evil grin.

The look on Kawika's face said this was some wacko he had riding shotgun, but Brendan ignored him to focus on his wreaking-havoc tool: a small MIRT that he plugged into the limo cigarette lighter before he stuck the suction cups to the dashboard. Simple and efficient, as all things should be.

"Wot's dat?"

"That, my friend, is a mobile infrared transmitter," Brendan said.

"Huh?"

"See that black thing on top of the traffic light, the one that looks like a designer tap?"

When Kawika nodded, Brendan explained, "It's a device that catches the signal coming from this transmitter. Emergency vehicles usually have one of these"—he patted the MIRT on the dashboard—"so they can emit a signal when they approach the traffic light. The sensor up there reacts to the signal and changes the light to green for the vehicle to pass safely. The device also activates a floodlight that changes from short flashes to a steady beam to indicate which direction the emergency vehicle is coming from."

Kawika's eyes widened. "Nevah went hear dat."

"Yeah, well, not many traffic lights have this equipment installed, but we've been lucky here. Wanna see it work?"

Now it was Kawika who flashed him a grin.

"Thought so," Brendan murmured as he gauged the distance to the traffic light and waited for it to turn red before he pressed the button to activate the transmitter.

As soon as he did, the floodlight on the traffic signal came on and Kawika pulled slowly to the right side of the road to make room for the emergency vehicle that was supposed to be approaching them. Brendan looked in the rearview mirror to check that most of the cars behind them were doing the same, the green light completely ignored while the other roads converging at the intersection got sudden red lights that made for a few screeching halts and more vehicles pulling to the side of the road responding to the flashing floodlights on their own signals.

"Ha, spock um out!" Kawika said, clearly amused by the situation.

Brendan turned off the MIRT, effectively shutting off all the floodlights, but drivers in every road were still waiting for an ambulance or fire truck to pass one way or the other, so no one reacted even though it took the lights a little more than usual to change. When they did change, Brendan reactivated the MIRT, and the cycle started all over again, floodlights warning of an approaching emergency vehicle and lights changing faster than usual, making some cars move forward into the intersection to stop there and wait for the ghost ambulance to finally show.

The workers repairing the pole were looking this way and that, no doubt searching for the emergency vehicle too, and it didn't take long for one of them to pull out a cell phone.

"Why is everyone pulling to the side?" Miles Harris was saying behind the partition.

"They're repairing the road," his wife answered, probably pointing at the workers.

"They don't look as if they're doing much of anything to me," Miles complained. *"Don't know what it is about islands, but they seem to breed lazy people; must be the climate."*

Brendan checked the location of the nearest traffic-monitoring camera and saw the dot on the map move toward them. His finger pressed the button on the MIRT to stop it from emitting its signal.

Kawika laughed as the lights turned to red. "Brah, I like do dat noddah time."

"Well, it might be as you say, Mr. Harris, but I've never heard anyone say that Japan was a lazy country—nor Great Britain, for that matter. Must be the climate."

Brendan smiled both at Matsunaga's retort and Kawika's eagerness, realizing for the first time that his new team was once again completely made up of islanders. He shook his head. Must be his fate.

"Go ahead," he told Kawika, watching as the Hawaiian pressed the button like a child with a new toy. Kawika laughed when the lights changed and not a single driver bothered to move, the big man amused to no end by the growing lines of cars in every direction.

The dot marking the position of the camera was getting closer, and there suddenly came the sound of an actual siren. Brendan checked his watch. "Time to wrap up," he said, unplugging the device; he then yanked it off the dashboard and shoved it inside the glove compartment.

"Dat went stay a good fun time, brah," Kawika summarized wistfully, and Brendan had to agree. "Plan simple and enjoy the ride" was his motto for a good mission.

CHAPTER 52

THE LIMO was moving once again, and Kinosuke didn't know whether to feel relieved or anxious. The sooner they arrived at the resort, the sooner he'd get rid of Kitahara and his weird activity schedule—whale watching he could understand, but whale watching on a champagne cruise? Maybe the intention behind the whole thing was for you to forget the size of whatever critter you saw after two or three glasses of the stuff. It might work too.

So getting to the resort would be fine, if it wasn't for that fucking white-haired bellboy never showing up to hand back the missing briefcase.

This traffic delay would have been the perfect moment to approach the limo, seeing that they didn't mind being obvious, but now there'd be few chances left before Longchamp was out the door and asking for his case.

How many times did traffic lights go crazy at a busy intersection anyway? A lucky coincidence, that, though Kinosuke had the nagging suspicion it was one of those spy-movie, ultracomplicated SEAL schemes, involving some remote computer hacking and a little breaking and entering at gunpoint into traffic-light control posts. Shit. If they could, these crazy Americans would force a volcano eruption just to create a small diversion. "The trickier and flashier, the better" seemed to be their motto.

"Kona is famous for its big-game fishing," Kitahara said through his ear piece.

Shit. There they went again. Kinosuke repeated the information wearily, but the men seemed to perk up at the sound of *fishing.* Golfers and fishers—a sporty lot, the whole bunch of them.

"What kind of catch can you get here?" Campbell asked.

Kinosuke parroted, "Mostly marlin, but also ono, mahi-mahi, ahi, and spearfish."

"Mahi-mahi? People here have nothing to do but make up hoity-toity names while they chug beer?" Miles whined, and Kinosuke was so tired and strung-up that he didn't even feel the urge to roll his eyes.

"Believe me, mahi-mahi is a rather simple name by Hawaiian standards," the boss said. "You should try pronouncing the name of the state fish in one go: *humuhumunukunukuapuaa.*"

That got a lot of oohing and aahing, and even some giggles from Alice Harris, and Kinosuke had to wonder how the fuck the boss had come up with that one.

"That humuhu... um, that fish is no longer the state fish," Kitahara said, and Kinosuke smiled. So the Rat was not so good with foreign languages, and it obviously irked him that the boss didn't need anyone murmuring in his ear to know a thing or two. Served Kitahara right for thinking sōkaiyas were in a different league than mere yakuza. *"The designation was limited to five years, and it's been controversial because that species is not unique to Hawaii and—"*

Yeah, right. As if he was going to repeat that flapdoodle just because Kitahara was jealous of the boss.

Kinosuke looked out the window while the others kept talking baloney and making *humuhumu* faces, and even though his seat was facing backward, he still could recognize the street heading to the resort.

Fuck. No sign of Burka, and they'd be arriving in a few minutes, maybe seconds. What the hell where they going to do? Tell Longchamp his briefcase had somehow gotten lost *after* it went into the limo trunk?

Kinosuke didn't think twice about it, he just turned a little to one side and murmured into his headset, "Brendan-san, *doko deska*, Burka-san *wa*?"

It was a sign of his agitation that calling Brendan first when he had the boss right there didn't feel at all weird, or that he wasn't even surprised when just hearing Brendan's voice made his anxiety come down a notch.

"It's okay, Sensei. Don't you worry about Burka. We got everything under control. Keep up the good work. Um, gambatte."

Kinosuke let out a surprised chuckle. It was difficult to recognize it as a Japanese word, the way Brendan smashed it against his teeth, but the man had taken the time to learn it. Fucking crazy redhead.

The limo came to a halt, and Kinosuke found everybody looking at him. He wiped the goofy smile off his face and almost shouted into the headset, *"Hai, hai, wakari mashita. Dewa mata."*

"Well, here we are," the boss said to cover him. "I hope you like the resort we've chosen for you. It's run by a famous Japanese hotel operator."

"Ah, the competition," Miles said, always the funny one.

The boss smiled politely. "I expect *we* will be *the* competition when we open up, Mr. Harris."

That received a few laughs, and the next thing they knew, the limo was stopping at the entrance to the luxury resort and a bellhop who *wasn't* Burka opened the car door for them.

Alice and Cynthia Harris climbed out first, and the boss motioned for Kenshin-san's brothers to exit before he did. That only left Kinosuke and the damned lawyer, and Kinosuke thought for a moment about being rude once again and climbing out before Longchamp to gain a little more time, but Brendan had told him they had everything covered, so he decided to trust Brendan and let the lawyer get out first while he pretended to be busy taking his headset off—not that the highfalutin bastard even considered letting a mere secretary precede him, anyway.

When Kinosuke stepped onto the tarmac driveway, Kawika was already there, making the Harrises laugh with some joke about Big Island traffic, but Kinosuke's eyes immediately went past the group in search of a particular redhead.

There he was, his sharp green eyes trained unfailingly on Kinosuke. Brendan gave him the smallest of smiles as he lifted his chin to point behind Kinosuke.

He turned to look in the direction Brendan pointed and did a double take. Burka had appeared from out of nowhere in his flashy red uniform and was simply strolling along the circular driveway with the fucking briefcase in his hand. Kinosuke's head whipped back to the group and then to Brendan, not daring to make any gesture but sure his eyes were screaming, *What the fuck is that idiot doing? Does he believe the white hair makes him invisible—the white hair under the flaming* red *hat?* But all Brendan did was smile a little wider, his head moving in the subtlest of nods, his eyes more or less saying, *Just you wait and see.*

So Kinosuke did; he waited and saw how Burka stepped out of the driveway and onto the sidewalk leading toward the hotel doors exactly when Longchamp spotted him.

"Hey, you there! Wait!" the lawyer called out, and Kinosuke resisted the urge to close his eyes.

"Sir?" Burka asked, all innocent and calm.

"I'll carry that myself," Longchamp said, pointing at the briefcase.

Kinosuke blinked. That was it? The man hadn't noticed Burka hadn't even touched the limo trunk?

"Of course, sir."

Burka offered the briefcase with his gloved hand and then raised it to his forehead in something that looked like a military salute gone bad and disguised as a hat tip.

The lawyer all but ignored Burka and turned to the group just as the boss said, "Shall we go in, then?"

Kinosuke stood there flabbergasted, breathing a little too fast, waiting for the group to disappear into the lobby before he sagged against the limo's body.

"*Chikushō*," he cursed aloud. "And that man is supposed to be a sharp lawyer?"

Brendan chuckled beside him. "That's only normal, Sensei. Most people don't notice much of their surroundings as a general rule."

"Yeah, well, I'm not talking about palm trees here, but fucking bellboy ghosts materializing out of thin air and magically extracting briefcases from a limo trunk without fucking opening it first. That was surreal, man."

Brendan laughed harder, and Kawika joined him. "Dat went stay trippy, brah."

Kinosuke shook his head, unable to keep his smile from showing, as it happened every single time Brendan laughed. It was a strange thing, but laughter seemed to wipe off all the military bullshit from Brendan's face to show an unusual openness instead, with something very gentle, almost unbearably sweet under its surface, like those hard lollipops that came with a soft, toothachingly sugary core.

Kawika said something that ended in "Shoots den," and Kinosuke nodded as if he'd caught it. Learning English had been enough of a bother that he did not want to go through it again just to understand the local variety, especially when Kinosuke had less retentive memory than fish—he was sure even that humuhumu guy had never dropped out of its school.

He straightened to lift his weight off the limo and waved back at Kawika as the man rounded the car's hood to get to the driver's seat. His eyes met a pair of amused green ones.

"What?" he said, not even managing to sound testy.

The limo moved smoothly along the hotel driveway, and Brendan watched it until its taillights disappeared in the distance, but Kinosuke kept his eyes trained on Brendan, waiting.

"What?" Brendan asked as he looked back at him.

Kinosuke rolled his eyes. "What are you now? A Potagee? Don't go answering me with another question."

That brought another peal of laughter from Brendan, and Kinosuke started to reconsider whether the effort to learn pidgin might be worth it after all, if just the one word had that effect. "So why were you looking at me that way?"

"What way?" Brendan asked, and Kinosuke just raised an eyebrow. "Okay, okay. I guess I was watching you smile."

Huh. Kinosuke hoped he hadn't been smiling in that goofy, I-look-like-a-dweeb kind of way.

"You don't smile that often, you know?"

Was it his imagination, or was Brendan blushing?

"And I kind of, um, like it."

Brendan was definitively blushing, his freckles standing out so much that they looked painted on. The fact that a captain, or commander, or admiral, or whatever fucking rank Brendan had held in the mighty SEALs could suddenly look like an embarrassed ten-year-old was more than Kinosuke could stand.

"Don't laugh at me," Brendan said, clearly amused anyway. "That's a bad sensei, making fun of his student."

When he wouldn't stop laughing, Brendan smacked his arm playfully, and Kinosuke found himself craving more contact. He searched the green eyes, seeing a matching longing there, and Brendan left his hand resting on Kinosuke's arm, the heat of his fingers searing through the light summer suit Kinosuke wore.

"You did a great job today, Sensei," Brendan said, no mirth left in his voice. "Matsunaga must be proud of you."

He didn't know why, but the mention of the boss angered him, so much so that his thoughts poured right out of him. "And you? Are *you* proud?"

Shit. Where had that come from? Now he was the one blushing, and the worst part was knowing that, embarrassed or not, he still needed to hear the answer; it was important—more important somehow than the boss approving of his performance.

"Sensei…." Brendan hesitated, and Kinosuke thought he wasn't going to answer. And damn if it didn't feel like a huge letdown. "Sensei, if I were prouder, I would be drooling all over the place like an Irish mutt."

Kinosuke burst out laughing. He was so embarrassed—and so pleased he must have looked like one of those puffed up globefish he hated but ate anyway just to show a yakuza wasn't afraid of a little fishy poison.

"There you go again, laughing at me," Brendan said, gently squeezing Kinosuke's arm.

"Yup. I'm an evil sensei."

"Yes, you are. But I love you anyway."

And there the world stopped. Kinosuke blinked and tried to force air into his lungs. He felt so many things at the same time that he didn't know which one to pick first to react to: his surprise at hearing the words—because Brendan had never said them before; his anger at the way they came in the middle of a joke—because maybe they were a joke too; the pain in his chest—because maybe the words weren't a joke at all, and it might be the first time he'd heard them from someone who wasn't a silly girl who drew lipstick hearts on her diary; or the stupid hope trying to turn his stomach upside down—because a man he couldn't help admiring despite himself had maybe seen something in Kinosuke worth loving.

He looked at Brendan, searching for a clue to understand what was going on, but Brendan looked everywhere except at Kinosuke. Brendan's expression turned blank with the easiness of long practice at hiding his feelings, and he loosened his fingers to let go of Kinosuke's arm.

So maybe a joke after all. And he was embarrassing Brendan by acting as if he gave a shit.

Kinosuke tried to force a nonchalant smile, to pull out a joke of his own, but Brendan chose that moment to look him in the eye, and Brendan's freckled face was back to that openness that Kinosuke somehow dreaded even more than the forced absence of feeling.

Brendan opened his mouth to say something and then flinched as if he'd been hit, his body turning slightly to the side as he recited flatly, "This is Aka Oni. Come in, Dekai Kuma. Over."

Ryōkai. They were in the middle of a complicated business here. Better to avoid getting personal when everything could turn into a great snafu from one moment to the next.

Kinosuke walked past Brendan without even looking at him and headed into the hotel lobby. He'd feel better after a long sleep in a luxurious bed. Probably.

Yeah, Red Demon was about right.

CHAPTER 53

THE SIGHT was impressive, Big Island style. Once you left Queen K Highway—as the locals called it—and drove into the property, there was nothing but black lava fields with astonishingly vivid green scrub, a few palm trees indicating the location of freshwater ponds, and, at the end of the dirt road, a jewel of a beach, small and pristine in the strange beauty of its fine black sand.

They had added a few personal touches: their Japanese corporation's nameplates on the fence surrounding the property, Big B's cousins looking appropriately imposing in their security guard uniforms—with every kind of family mutt acting as guard dog by their side—and the backhoe Kawika's brother had borrowed from the construction site where he worked.

All in all it looked like a place right about to be developed, not the neglected property some Japanese executive had spotted from a helicopter, bought without setting foot on it, and then left to rot while his company sorted the economic downturn back home.

The idea was to provide the Harrises with some physical evidence of the resort Matsunaga's corporation intended to build and to fill their heads with enough hype to convince them to invest in the project. Of course the economic offer would prove the most important part of the deal, but they couldn't neglect the project's overall presentation.

The SUV they had chosen for the occasion was now reaching one of the ponds, where they had set up the luxury equivalent of a chow tent. In that area Alma Tachibana and her numerous relatives who worked in any segment of the service industry had been an invaluable asset.

Kawika and Brendan climbed out of the car to open the back doors for their passengers. Alice and Cynthia came out with their contrasting fashion styles—Laura Ingalls versus Carrie Bradshaw—then the brothers in almost matching Hilfiger uniforms, then Matsunaga with his dignified samurai demeanor, always elegant even in casual clothes, and finally the more conventional suits, Longchamp and Kinosuke.

Brendan's eyes immediately went to Kinosuke, but his sensei ignored him, as Kinosuke had mostly done since Brendan inadvertently dropped the L bomb between them. That had been a major goatfuck. The rapport between them had been slowly building back to the time before the great divide, and maybe Kinosuke hadn't even realized it, but he'd been increasingly turning to Brendan for support.

And Brendan had acted like a man on a strict diet when allowed to indulge a little—he'd taken the one cookie and then finished the whole box in one second flat. As if exposing his feelings in a hackneyed joke didn't matter at all if he went back to his regimen of self-repression the following morning.

Maybe it wouldn't have mattered if Kinosuke hadn't cared one way or the other, but the fact that his sensei purposely avoided Brendan, when he'd been more or less seeking him out before, meant he was either angry or hurt or both—which Brendan deserved any way he looked at it.

"That's a lovely pond," Alice Harris said while the men dove straight for the lovely food and drinks and ignored the pond. "Is it safe to bathe in it?"

"It's not really deep, if that's what you're worried about," Matsunaga answered.

"No, I was worried about that leptospiralysis thing," Alice said, and Brendan was glad nobody looked at him, because his lips were surely twitching. Matsunaga blinked twice more than necessary. A pretty quandary Alice had created for him, because whatever he said now would sound as if he were correcting his guest, which was unthinkable to any polite Japanese—that is, to *any* Japanese.

"Only about one hundred people a year are diagnosed with leptospirosis in Hawaii, and in most cases it can be treated with antibiotics," Kinosuke recited, saving his boss from an inevitable faux pas. "The bacteria is only found in some of Hawaii's freshwater, and it can only enter the body through open cuts, the eyes, or by actually drinking the water."

"And why the hell would anyone want to drink brackish pond water?" Miles said in his usual charming style. "You should try this wine instead, Alice."

"I didn't expect Hawaii to have good wine," Campbell added on a more conciliatory note, "but this red is excellent, even though the name is still a mouthful— *Ulupalakua Red*. It's almost as bad as that fish you mentioned before."

Matsunaga smiled. "Local names are rather difficult, I agree, but they give everything a unique flavor. People wouldn't enjoy traveling far from home if they were to find exactly the same things they can buy in their mom-and-pop grocery store. They want some variety—new names, new tastes, new scents."

"Probably," Longchamp said, eyeing the food warily. "But if things get too exotic, some people may not want to take the risk at all."

The Harris brothers were getting a good run for their money with Longchamp, it seemed. From the moment they'd left the resort that morning, the lawyer had been alert, taking note of everything that might concern their budding investment opportunity, asking pointed questions, demanding detailed figures from Kinosuke, gainsaying Matsunaga as often as he could find anything arguable, and generally being a pain in the ass.

Brendan could see how the man made Kinosuke itchy—even though Kitahara never failed to provide him with the right answers to the impertinent questions—and that in turn put Brendan on edge. He wished it was Kitahara taking the brunt of the lawyer's attacks, since the Japanese extortionist very obviously enjoyed the most arcane arguments on abutting landowners' human-induced vegetation encroaching with beach transit corridors and public rights-of-way to the shoreline.

Kinosuke, though, was having a hard time repeating things he didn't understand while knowing how much depended on his performance. And Brendan desperately wanted to shelter him from it all, simply take his sensei with him to that other property not so far south from there and unleash Kinosuke's true skills in something as immediately satisfying as freeing Kenneth Harris.

In fact, if Matsunaga and his men had had their way, rescuing their beloved Kenshin-san would have been their first and only concern. But Brendan was sure the senator wouldn't stop until his son ceased to pose a threat to his political ambitions, and maybe the next time he wouldn't be content with locking Ken up.

They needed some insurance. Kenneth Harris deserved a future free from his father's looming shadow; he deserved a chance to be happy with the man he loved and the friends who cared about him.

Maybe Ken had always known it might someday come to this. The fact that he had kept those pictures from Portsmouth Naval Shipyard suggested it and, in a way, the pictures had shown Brendan where to start.

Gathering evidence on the Pech Valley op would have been all but impossible. The operation details were classified—as far as the public was concerned, it had never existed—and the senator had a personal interest in keeping it under wraps. So they had few chances at a frontal approach, but they could still attack the senator's flanks.

Ken's hidden pictures had revealed his brothers' greed and their father's lobbying to provide them with a few profitable contracts. What if this time the brothers signed with a Japanese corporation that Brendan's team could prove had yakuza connections?

"You're right about that," Matsunaga said, "and that's why our resort will offer enough local exoticism for the trip to be attractive, but also enough creature comforts for the experience never to be overwhelming."

Matsunaga was good; Brendan had to admit it. He showed the settled sedateness of a veteran negotiator, and he could be enthusiastic when needed, like right now, as he made a sweeping gesture with his hand to encompass every kind of food being displayed in front of them and used the mixture of tastes as a metaphor to explain the philosophy underlying the resort project.

Brendan zoned out of Matsunaga's sales pitch, remembering how much persuasion Brendan himself had needed to convince Matsunaga to be there making speeches when he could be storming the mansion where Ken was kept. But if the plan was to work, Matsunaga had to impersonate the Japanese corporation's CEO, because nobody else would have been credible in the role.

Brendan understood how hard it had been for Matsunaga to realize he probably wouldn't even be there when they actually stormed the mansion. The operation's success depended on perfect timing, because as soon as the senator learned of Ken's rescue, he would connect the dots and warn his sons about possible foul play in the deal they were trying to make. So the contract had to be signed immediately before the rescue, and Matsunaga needed to be there to conduct the negotiations.

If everything worked and the brothers signed the contract in two days—three at the most—Matsunaga would be free to join the rescue team the coming Friday, when part of the mansion staff would make their weekly trip to Kona.

That was supposing everything went according to plan, but an op wouldn't be an op without some serious glitch, as Longchamp's unexpected presence had already proved.

"The great thing about Hawaii," Matsunaga was saying now, "is that the mixture of cultures allows for a wide variety of food choices, so if you still find all these too exotic for you, Mr. Longchamp, we can offer you the tried-and-true sirloin steak."

Two waiters pushed a wheeled barbecue closer to them, and the crisp smell of grilled meat filled the air. The lawyer looked a little mollified by that, especially after the liquor tray came his way. He wasn't a heavy drinker like Miles Harris, but he did seem to enjoy fine alcohol.

"I thought Japanese people didn't eat meat," Cynthia said, and Brendan caught Kinosuke rolling his eyes. Good thing these people didn't pay too much attention to secretaries—or bodyguards, because Brendan couldn't help smirking.

"We usually eat more seafood than meat, that's true," Matsunaga answered, managing as always to avoid a direct negative answer. "But we do have quite a few meat dishes. In fact, you're about to taste our famous Kobe beef."

Brendan seemed to remember Kobe was a yakuza den—he'd heard earthquake relief had been most efficient there after the big earthquake in 1995 because the local gangs had *organized* it—so Brendan could guess how Matsunaga had been able to get the mouthwatering steaks that were now being served along with Hawaiian barbecue specialties such as rice balls filled with tuna or Chinese dough balls stuffed with pork.

And the yakuza didn't miss a marketing opportunity. As soon as his guests tried the steaks and expressed their appreciation one way or another, Matsunaga launched another campaign. "Bringing this beef to the Big Island hasn't been easy, and the same happened with other ingredients and seasonings that we had to bring directly from Japan. That's where your tugboat company would come in handy. Establishing a regular tugboat service between Japan and Hawaii would allow us to offer the highest quality products at a cost that would bring good profit margins."

Campbell Harris made an approving noise around a mouthful of steak, his gaze a little unfocused as if he was mentally doing a cost-benefit analysis on the spot.

"So the idea is basically to offer the best of both worlds?" Miles resumed.

"Exactly," Matsunaga answered. "A tasteful combination of Hawaiian ambience and Japanese comfort, with the best materials, design, and service available."

"But how will you mix the two cultures?" Alice asked. "I don't think pagodas and tipis match too well."

Oh my. Where had these men found their sweethearts? Brendan was glad neither Otter nor Tachibana were here, because those two would be rolling on their backs with laughter by now. Matsunaga, though, just smiled politely at Alice. "We'll go for a discreet mixture of the two traditions, Mrs. Harris. Our target market is quality tourists, so we'll avoid the theme-park style as much as possible."

"You said earlier that the resort is being planned as a private club. But how will that work exactly?" Miles asked.

"Much like an exclusive golf club," Matsunaga explained. "We'll have a limited number of members who will always have one of our private villas available to book throughout the year, while nonmembers will have access to our facilities by invitation alone. The market for cheap tourism is oversaturated right now," Matsunaga said, rounding off his argument, "and let's face it, the demand is steadily going down. The best opportunities now are those offered by luxury tourism, and the Big Island is very well equipped to cater to that segment."

"Membership fees," Kinosuke added, "are a quick way to recover part of the initial investment before construction is even completed, especially if fees are paid up front, as is commonly done."

"And speaking of construction," Matsunaga put in, "we're working with a Japanese company for the resort's design, but as you can see, this terrain poses some structural challenges that we are sure Spearman Engineers have the experience to resolve for us—and I expect we wouldn't be as difficult to work with as the Army must have been."

Miles laughed and slapped Matsunaga's back as if he was an old buddy, which Brendan suspected would have cost the clown a pinkie or two had the yakuza still been in active service. As things were, Matsunaga just faked a smile as Miles babbled. "I hope so, Nakazawa, because you have no idea how stupid those military types can be. You need a security clearance for just about everything, from digging a hole in the ground to taking a leak, and there's always one of their so-called engineers breathing down your neck and offering foolish suggestions you have a hard time convincing them are completely over the top or structurally unsafe—I guess they feel the need to show us ignorant civilians who's in charge before we start believing we don't need them."

Brendan clenched his teeth, thinking "ignorant civilians" was just about right.

"Well, Mr. Harris," Matsunaga said in mock horror, "I don't expect you'd want to take their place in combat anytime soon."

Miles chuckled. "Oh no, I'm too old to go swinging an M16 about just to impress some third-world country villager. Besides," he added in a conspiratorial manner, "what would we do with all these trigger-happy rednecks if there wasn't an army to let them blow off some steam safely away from home? Let me tell you, if we didn't have an army, we'd have twice the number of crackheads on our streets, but the military gathers all these ignorant souls together, puts them into lovely uniforms, and even makes them believe they can be heroes—so we all benefit in the end."

It had been a long time since Brendan had had trouble keeping his thoughts—and his fists—to himself. This was the son of an American senator speaking, and given Miles's brilliant intellect, Brendan wouldn't have been surprised if Miles was only repeating what he'd heard his father say a million times over dinner.

These were the kind of people his men had died to keep safe, or worse still, these were the kind of people whose incompetence and outright malfeasance had gotten his men killed.

He felt the weight of someone's gaze on him, and when he managed to tear his eyes away from Miles's pudgy face, he met a pair of black eyes straight on. Look at that. His sensei had all the reasons in the world to be angry at him, and yet the young man couldn't help being concerned and, yes, angry on Brendan's behalf.

This man understood duty, honor, and service far beyond the hackneyed slogans designed to manipulate ignorant rednecks into believing they could be heroes.

Kinosuke tilted his head like a curious puppy, an intrigued smile on his luscious lips, which made Brendan realize he himself must have been smiling too. Geez. How could he not fall for this guy? Next time he had the chance, he was going to throw caution to the wind and tell Kinosuke seriously that he loved him, consequences be damned.

"Don't be so harsh, Miles," his wife said. "You know all those poor soldiers are having a hard time fighting the Russians in Afghanistan."

The silence was suddenly so thick that the sound of the waves seemed deafening by contrast. And then an epidemic of coughing fits seemed to spread around them until Matsunaga deftly changed the topic of conversation.

"I believe you've worked with the Navy too," he said, "building a shipyard, wasn't it?"

Smart guy, pretending not to know exactly so he could flatter Miles's already bloated ego.

"Ah, you're talking about Portsmouth Naval Shipyard," Miles said, obviously pleased. "We didn't actually build the shipyard, but we gave some of its most remarkable buildings a good makeover. Did you know Portsmouth is one of the only two American shipyards still building submarines?"

The conversation went on along those lines, and Brendan could tell the Harrises were duly impressed. Kitahara had devised a solid business plan that offered attractive investment opportunities for each of the companies the brothers had a stake in, and Matsunaga and Kinosuke together gave off a very professional vibe, probably even better than Matsunaga and Kitahara would have, because Kitahara had too much business savvy for a simple secretary.

Of course the logistics also helped to create the right impression. Every detail, from the cars they drove to the expensive catering, had been carefully planned to show the Harrises that the Japanese investor had money to throw around.

Brendan wasn't privy to the financial side of their plan, but as far as he knew, Matsunaga and Kitahara were using more favors than real currency, in true don style—or politician style, if what Brendan had seen in the District was anything to go by.

Matsunaga had told the brothers the resort they were staying at belonged to a famous Japanese hotel operator, but he hadn't told them this operator had ties with a bank with so many yakuza connections that they'd let their group rent half a story for peanuts, no questions asked about the staff they'd brought with them to service those specific rooms. The very company they were supposed to be working for was one of the groups Kitahara "supervised"—that is, either extorted or advised on how to avoid extortion, which meant he had them in his pocket either way. The cars were courtesy of a Japanese-American who wanted to show his appreciation to Matsunaga for teaching his teenage son some discipline at the dojo. And the army of maids and waiters was living proof of that persistent Hawaiian fear of losing face, Alma's and Big B's relatives vying with each other for the title of Supporting Family of the Year.

All in all, Brendan believed they were doing a good job of stimulating the greedy gene that no doubt ran in the Harris family. Their problem now was how to smother the stymieing gene that ran in the Longchamp family.

CHAPTER 54

"WE HAVE a problem."

Kotarō swallowed. Brendan-san was as cool as the boss when it came to worrying about things going south, so if either of them used the word *problem*, it meant the shit was about to hit the fan.

Otter was silent too, no wisecrack or anything to break the ice, so maybe the shit had already hit the fan and they didn't know it yet.

They had all gathered in the biggest suite, the one the Americans called the command room, and were sitting around a coffee table that had its legs curved inward like a camel caught in the middle of folding his legs to sit down.

Today was activity day number two, and Kawika had taken Kenshin-san's brothers to an expensive golf course while Alma's niece took the wives shopping. The boss had excused himself, saying it would be painful for him to be in that fine golf course and not be able to practice his swing because of the finger he was supposed to have broken, and nobody had thought he had to excuse himself from shopping too, so all was good on that front for the time being.

"Is Longchamp trying to convince them not to sign the contract?" Aniki asked.

"Yeah," Brendan-san said, "but we already expected him to be difficult—that's what he was hired for in the first place—so we had our bases covered, left the right information lying around for him to find when he did the usual checks on the corporation we're using as a front. That wasn't much of a problem since the corporation Kitahara is working for is a solid one, but for some reason, Longchamp is going the extra mile and hasn't stopped at routine checks."

Three neat folders lay on the coffee table in colors that Kotarō was sure Bobcat had chosen following some secret code of his, and Brendan-san opened the green folder on top of the pile to take out a sheet of paper.

"We found this in Longchamp's briefcase," he said, passing it over to the boss. "It's a preliminary report on Kitahara's corporation."

Aniki moved closer to take a peek, and then the boss and he spoke almost at the same time.

"Who's this Yumoto guy?"

"Can this informer find out about Nakazawa?"

Kotarō tried not to giggle in a moment like this, but it was kind of funny to see Aniki and the boss acting like one of those aliens with two heads that appeared in video games. Aniki looked a little embarrassed, and then a little mad because Brendan-san was this side of smirking when he answered.

"This informer, Akira Yumoto," the redhead said, "is a freelance business journalist whose articles have appeared on the financial pages of the *Asahi Shimbun*, among others, and yes, being familiar with the inner workings of Japanese corporations, he might persevere long enough to discover that the actual Nakazawa is on a business trip in Thailand."

"And that he is a five-foot-two weenie," Otter mumbled.

Kotarō couldn't control the giggle this time, especially when Burka smacked Otter upside the head.

"What? Matsunaga looks like the Terminator on steroids compared to that dweeb," Otter said, before turning to the boss. "No offense intended, Matsu-san; the Terminator would never look that fine in a suit."

Matsu-san? Kotarō looked from Otter to the boss in horror, but the boss had his dealing-with-bugs face on, not his avenger-wakagashira one, so Kotarō took a deep breath and almost choked with laughter when the boss replied, "Thank you, I suppose, *Tanuki-kun.*"

Otter narrowed his eyes at the boss because he knew he was being made fun of but didn't have a clue how, because he sure as hell had never seen one of these awful tanuki figurines with the raccoon dog wearing a straw hat, carrying a sake bottle and sort of showing his big, um, pair of, you know, to everybody.

"Why do you think Longchamp has hired this journalist?" the boss asked Brendan-san. "I don't imagine the deal we're offering the brothers looks suspicious... unless Senator Harris is involved somehow."

Aniki whipped around to look at the boss, and Kotarō's eyes widened. Kenshin-san's father was involved? How could that be frigging possible? They'd planned everything so carefully, used Big B's contract to send the senator bullshit information, rehearsed every step a zillion times. Oh, wait. The senator had tricked Big B once into working for him against Brendan-san, so maybe—

Kotarō's eyes turned to the big Hawaiian of their own accord, as if he could simply tell if the man was snitching on them just by looking at his face, but now that he knew that face well, and the guy behind that face, there was no way for him to believe Big B could be a traitor—mostly because it would hurt too frigging much if any of these men happened to be working for Kenshin-san's father. For money.

"That's what I think too," Brendan-san said. "Longchamp hasn't contacted Senator Harris, but it might have been the senator who recommended him to his sons— they usually work with a different law firm. Whatever the relation between them, we still have to deal with the risk of exposure from this journalist Yumoto."

"The senator might decide to act on his suspicions too," Big B said, typing something on the laptop he had on the table. "We caught this conversation last night."

"Everything looks perfectly legit, Dad. And it can be a hell of a chance for us to expand into the Asian market."

Kotarō recognized Campbell's voice, and even though he knew it was normal in America, to hear someone as old as Campbell calling his father "Dad" was still a shock.

"Of course it looks legit. The Japanese are crafty little bastards, don't you forget that. And don't forget what happened to your brother."

"Oh, come on, Dad. You know we're nothing like Ken."

"Yeah, we're never going to get our panties wet at the sight of some tattooed goon, so stop worrying."

That fucker was Miles, and Kotarō wished he'd slipped some rat poison in the man's drink, and by the way the boss and Aniki were looking at the laptop, they probably wished Kotarō had.

"We're dealing with businessmen here, not gangsters, and you know Longchamp keeps double-checking everything for us too. We're safe, Dad. And probably about to get a little richer."

There came some nasty laughs, and then Miles said, *"You told us you had those goons watched, anyway. Are they up to something?"*

"No, they seem to be carrying on normally at that martial arts gym of theirs, but they could have sent someone your way. I don't trust them."

"Don't get paranoid. There's no way they'd know we were coming here, and even if they knew, Nakazawa has a good security detail—we'd be protected no matter what."

"Yeah, or you could send one of those basket-case soldiers you keep hiring, one of those killer SEALs to watch our backs."

"You don't say killer SEALs, *Miles; it's* killer whales.*"*

There came more stupid laughs from the laptop, but no one in the room was laughing. Kotarō looked around to see that all the Americans had their own version of the avenger face on—even Burka—and it was maybe a tad scarier than the avenger-yakuza face because it looked a little on the basket-case side of things.

"Just be careful, that's all I'm saying. I wouldn't want to have to send a rescue party to those backwoods islands this close to election time."

That was all, no good-bye or anything—the man had just hung up on his sons after more or less telling them he was only worried about the way their screwing up would hurt his career. And these were supposed to be the sons he approved of. How the hell had Kenshin-san managed to be such a cool guy having this douchebag of a father?

Nobody in the room spoke for a time until the boss said, "I'll talk to Kitahara. Maybe he can come up with a believable reason to speed things up, make these… *people* sign the damned contract so that we can get rid of them."

Brendan nodded. "Yeah. If the senator decides his sons are too dumb to notice when they're being conned, he might send someone to investigate or at least to make sure his other son is safely kept out of the way."

Shinya-san's ringtone with the taiko drums sounded a second before Big B's phone started ringing too.

"Moshi moshi."

"Wassa matta, cuz?"

Kotarō looked worriedly from the boss to Big B, trying to tell what was happening from their expressions.

After listening for a while, the boss told them, "A ship has arrived at the mansion this morning."

There were curses in two languages and Otter must have seen Kotarō's dumb face because he took the time to explain, "The fuckers will try to take your friend away, Kotarō."

Shit. How were they going to get Kenshin-san back if his father took him to the mainland? How would they manage to follow him? They had no ship of their own, what if they took a plane and then couldn't find the place the ship had landed? What if—

A hand rested on Kotarō's nape and squeezed gently. "Don't you worry, kid," Bobcat said. "We will stop them no matter what."

Maybe it was silly of him, but if Bobcat said it, Kotarō found it easier to believe they would, because Bobcat had a way of finding obstacles to every plan and every move they made, so if he said it could be done, it meant he had all the troubles already sorted out in his head, so maybe they had a chance even if the senator was a senator and had all these people ready to do whatever he said.

"What kind of ship?" asked Brendan-san, all business, and both the boss and B repeated the question into their phones.

"*Dekai fune*" came Shinya-san's voice when the boss activated his speakerphone.

When Big B did the same, his cousin said, "Cuz, I no kid you, I only wen see da kine boat wen I wen see dat movie about batunas deelahs an' da buggahs wen have bafetubs in da cabins an' a pool biggah dan auntie Alaula's—"

Big B turned off the speakerphone, but they all could still hear the voice of his cousin rambling away about the ship. "Looks like the kind of yacht that could make the whole trip to the mainland," B said with a smile, then told his cousin to call back if he saw any kind of cargo being loaded onto the ship.

The boss said something similar to Shinya-san before he hung up, so Kotarō guessed they were talking about food and the like being carried to the ship before they sailed away.

"But," he croaked, hating how his voice sounded when he was nervous, "if we wait until the ship is loaded, won't we be too late to rescue Kenshin-san?"

"We are not waiting, Kotarō," the boss said, looking Brendan-san in the eye as if he was challenging the man to argue. "We're rescuing Kenshin *tonight*. Kitahara will find a way to make the brothers sign the contract before that, but we need to know if they finish loading the ship before the papers are signed, because in that case we'll drop everything to get to Kenshin before he sets foot on that damned ship. I don't care if by doing so we lose the chance of getting evidence against the senator, because if something happens to Kenshin, I won't need any fucking papers to get back at his father."

Brendan-san held the boss's eyes until they looked like two rival yakuza *oyabun* in a *ninkyō* movie, and then Brendan-san just nodded once, his face dead serious.

"Hooyah!" Otter hollered. "We're gonna see some action at last!"

CHAPTER 55

BRENDAN WAS going out of his mind. "Don't pull this shit on me, Bobcat, not now."

"I won't blow this operation," Bobcat said again, and Brendan tried his best to rein in his temper.

Convincing Matsunaga to stay behind while they rescued Ken had been hell enough, especially because Brendan could relate; Matsunaga had left everything for the man he loved, and now he had to sit in a conference room and entrust his lover's safety to a group of men he barely knew.

Brendan felt like he had exploited Matsunaga's very Japanese trait of self-sacrifice, but Brendan knew he was right, and in the end Matsunaga had only been moved by Brendan's conviction that without some evidence to use against the senator, Ken would never be really safe.

Apparently, though, convincing Matsunaga to stay didn't count. He still needed to work on his persuasion skills by convincing Bobcat to go with them. "You'll blow this operation if you stay here," he said. "I need you out there with us."

Bobcat shook his head. "You need a SEAL, not a fucking coward who will freeze on you as soon as someone starts shooting."

"You're not a fucking coward," Brendan said, louder than he intended, but his patience was reaching its limits.

"Whatever you say, but I'm still going to freeze on you and fuck up."

Brendan couldn't take it anymore. "And you think you won't fuck up when you stride into that conference room looking for all the world like a junkie in desperate need of a fix? You think anyone in there will believe for a second that you're any kind of protection specialist?"

Bobcat flinched as if Brendan had hit him, but the words were already out there between them and there was no way for Brendan to soften the blow, so he didn't even try. It was the truth, anyway, and you couldn't run from the truth mere hours before a mission if you didn't want it to blow up in your face.

"Fine," Bobcat said. "Then I'll stay in my room so you can send someone who looks like a proper bodyguard."

And once started, Brendan couldn't be anything but brutally honest. "I'm already sending Keoni in my place, because all that job needs is someone with the right looks, but I don't need a poser in my assault element. What I need is another fucking special operator, and if all there's to choose from is a shell-shocked basket-case ex-SEAL, I'm still going to trust him with my life because no matter how far into mush his brain is gone, no one who survived Hell Week is going to suddenly turn into a fucking weekend warrior and faint at the sight of paintball blood. So pull your head out of your ass and start getting your gear ready. And don't make me waste any more spit on this bullshit."

Bobcat looked as if he were about to argue some more, but Brendan gave him the look—the kind of glare every CO had to have down pat before he could even think of ordering someone to tie his shoelaces—and Bobcat straightened and shouted, "Aye, aye, sir."

When the man disappeared into his room, Brendan let out the breath he'd been holding. He knew the risk was high, knew that even though the senator had managed to get Bobcat incapacitated on false grounds, his former crewman was still a textbook case of PTSD, and not even Bobcat could tell beforehand what would trigger a red light in his brain and render him useless; it could be something as simple and unpredictable as a noise or a smell, something as innocuous as the texture of some fabric that his memory had inextricably linked with the brutal death of his friends.

Still, Brendan knew he had to take the risk; he needed Bobcat, and Bobcat needed to face his demons if he ever wanted to heal. If something went wrong while Bobcat was holed up in his room, he would never forgive himself for not being out there, no matter how many times he tried to repeat he would have screwed the mission by actually being part of it. Of course if he did screw the mission, *Brendan* would never forgive himself for making the wrong assessment of his man's capabilities.

He shook his head. So many issues kept piling up that this op was about to become one of the most complicated he'd ever taken part in.

KEONI LOOKED imposing in his black suit, but he had nothing on Brendan.

Kinosuke had to admit that Brendan looked like the real thing, even though he was smaller than Big B's cousin, but he moved in a certain way and kept checking everything all the time, alert and ready, while Keoni was just standing there looking mean. Kinosuke hoped the Harrises couldn't tell the difference.

He missed the way Brendan kept checking Kinosuke too, but he wasn't going to admit that having Brendan there would have helped, so he'd rather think what he missed was being where the real action would take place while they played this American Monopoly game with Kenshin-san's brothers.

At least the Rat had been willing to help, and by the smug expression on his face, Kinosuke suspected the sōkaiya was enjoying himself at the prospect of springing his trap on the Harrises.

They'd been lucky that Kitahara's wounds were easy to conceal, and whatever Big B had done to the background looked for all the world like the guy would be participating in the meeting from his upscale office in Tokyo instead of the hospital room in Kona.

The boss nodded in the direction of the smoked glass hiding the tech room, where one of Alma's nephews was manning the controls. They were early on purpose, not just to get everything ready but to make sure Kenshin-san's brothers were late no matter the time they showed up.

It was a question of making the Harrises feel at a disadvantage from the start; that explained why the illumination of the conference room had been modified so the harshest light fell on the empty chairs, why those chairs had their backs to the rest of the room so their occupants would feel exposed, why all of them were wearing the most formal office clothes, and why there were five of them—six counting Kitahara—for the three in the Harris party.

They were aiming for intimidation, trying to impress the notion that this was some powerful corporation the Harrises were dealing with, a corporation that didn't particularly need to do business with insignificant American entrepreneurs like them.

Kinosuke glanced at the Filipinos and Hawaiians sitting at the table, looking all professionally spiffy in their suits and black dresses, and wondered for a moment why these beautiful people did nothing for him while a homely, pasty-skinned, freckled redhead made his stomach churn.

Fuck if he knew why he was so stupid, but he'd never been bright to begin with, and nobody said that moving from Japan to Hawaii was supposed to make you smarter. He wasn't intelligent like the boss—or even Kitahara—he wasn't as tough as Shinya, or as good a marksman as Tachibana. He was just a wild card, more or less like Kotarō, very good to be used as a gofer if he got step-by-step instructions and, in his case, very convenient for a holiday fling, easy to leave behind before moving on to more serious engagements in the mainland.

Whatever. If all he could do to help Kenshin-san was keep his mouth shut and look salaryman serious, he was going to nail it.

GOATS MUST be the meanest beasts on earth. Or so Kotarō thought after an hour of running in circles without catching a single one of the ornery critters. Wild boars were scary, but Tachibana-san had told him they were scared themselves, so Kotarō could forgive them for being aggressive since they were feeling trapped, but the goats, dude, they were frigging nuts, trying to jump over the fence and kicking the hell out of you if you were dumb enough to get near them.

The trap had been Burka's idea. It was simple once you saw it, but Kotarō wouldn't have come up with a way to catch wild goats even if he'd kept thinking till next *Obon*.

Burka had been tracking the goats until he found a place where they went for a drink, and then he and the others had built a high fence around the pond with only one entrance. This entrance was a tricky one, since it forced the goats to go through a corridor that ended in a ramp from which they had to jump down to get to the water, but since the ramp was standing on two high poles, there was no way for them to climb back up and get out.

Of course there was also a gate for people to go in—and shoo wild boars out—but so far, Kotarō hadn't managed to cross it with a goat he'd captured. Keawe and Kekoa made so much noise that the goats avoided them like the plague, and the two goofs couldn't stop laughing and naming the critters by the way each one looked. Tachibana-san had caught three goats already, and Burka held the record with five.

Since there were only another five of the beasts left, Kotarō thought they might—Burka might, that is—catch them all in time. After that, they still needed to load them into the old pickup truck and haul them all the way down the coffee shack dirt road. And then the crazy animals would be ready to act as a distraction. Dude, this might be the first time goats were part of an op. Way to go.

CHAPTER 56

THE MOON was in its waning quarter, the faint white light barely touching the dark rolling mass of the ocean. These were treacherous waters—the surf high, the undertow fierce, rip currents forming with no warning, rogue waves suddenly wreaking havoc in apparently calm seas. That explained why Hawaii had the first place in US drowning statistics and why it was a paradise for daredevil surfers—and SEALs.

Nobody in his sane mind would approach a property from the sea unless he owned a yacht or a runabout or an outrigger canoe and was entitled to steer into a well-protected dock like the one this mansion had at the end of the private beach. So no need to waste precious dollars building a fence around the rugged outcrop that made the golf course look as if it was spilling into the ocean, long, scarped fingers dipping into waters turned white by the strength of the surf crashing onto the rocks.

Approaching those rocks was far too dangerous, and even if someone managed to do it without capsizing or shattering his boat, there was no way to drop anchor and wait for someone else to make a run for the mansion, do their thing, and come trundling back to escape by sea. But SEALs were not just anyone, and they weren't going to drop anchor and wait for the surf to break them.

Brendan steered the F-470 Zodiac farther south to where the small peninsula would hide them from the mansion's view. Funny that Big B had bought what the teams called a "soft duck"—an IBS or Inflatable Boat Small—in a bout of nostalgia and kept it in his garage like so much clutter. Of course it would have been better if he'd bought two of the things, to keep up with the tried and true military adage that "one is none, two is one," but this was a sort of homebrewed, guerrilla incursion, and it had been difficult enough to transport one soft duck and a load of weapons to the Big Island to try their luck with two inflatable boats *small* enough to carry ten people.

Matsunaga's contacts had been invaluable in that area, and though they'd followed a strict don't-ask-don't-tell policy concerning all things yakuza, it was obvious that the gunrunning between the States and Japan through Hawaii was still profitable.

Big B pointed at the rocks ahead. This time Brendan was acting as coxswain, since they needed their bowline man to be the strongest among them, and nobody had to ask who that was.

"SORRY TO call you together with so little forewarning," the boss said after they'd all stood and bowed to the Harris brothers and Longchamp, the collective gesture underlining even more their late arrival and the difference in number between the two parties. "But something important has come up that we need to discuss."

"It's okay," Miles answered as he drew out one of the chairs. "We've been idling for too long; it's about time we got our hands dirty—so to speak."

The boss smiled politely and invited them to sit down. "Allow me to introduce our Senior Consultant and CPA, Kitahara Fumio." He then turned to the screen. "Kitahara-san, these are Mr. Miles Harris, Mr. Campbell Harris, and Mr. Longchamp."

They exchanged the customary pleasantries, and then the boss said, "Kitahara-san is part of our corporation's international acquisitions and development team, and he'll explain the practical dilemma we're facing right now."

"The Examination Department of the Taxation Bureau is about to conduct an investigation of our corporation's tax return," Kitahara said in his hideous accent. "And while preparing the books for inspection, our accounting department has discovered a small error in the calculation of our taxable income arising from a sale of property."

Miles clucked. "Someone forgot to make an entry for the sale in the books, huh?"

The Rat made an appropriately ratty face to counter the innuendo. "On the contrary, Mr. Harris. Our problem is that the sale was duly registered, but someone forgot to calculate the additional 10 percent tax on capital gains from sale of land that Japan's corporation tax regulation states."

"Ouch," Miles said, and Kinosuke wondered if the man behaved like this in every business meeting he attended or was just clowning about because it was Japanese businessmen he was dealing with.

"That's still a small percentage when compared to US capital gains tax rate," Longchamp said in his usual spoilsport style. "I don't expect a corporation like yours would have much trouble affording the fine."

"We are not concerned about any fine the Taxation Bureau might choose to impose," Kitahara answered primly, "but we don't want to set a precedent; we don't want our corporation to be regarded as prone to that kind of errors."

"In other words," Campbell resumed, "you don't want tax examiners forever breathing down your neck."

The boss nodded. "Exactly. And that's why Kitahara-san has come up with a solution that we wanted to run by you, since it implies some changes in our proposal."

There went the bait, and Kinosuke saw the change in the brothers' attitudes. Shit, if they'd been dogs, their ears would have perked right up, the money hounds immediately smelling some advantage to be gained from the Japanese's troubles.

The lawyer was the only one who kept an indifferent expression, probably because it wasn't his money they were gambling.

"As you know," Kitahara started in a professorial tone meant to suggest that his listeners knew shit and had better listen well, "Japan is very concerned with population problems and the efficient use of land. That's why, as part of the national land policy, the government has taken some special taxation measures for coping with urban problems and facilitating industrial zone planning.

"One particular measure is of interest to us: the special rule for replacement of business assets. This regulation states that if a corporation sells buildings or land, buys similar assets within the business year in which such a sale is made, and places the new assets in service within one year of the date of acquisition, 80 percent of the capital gains may be deferred by reducing the book value of the new assets."

Kinosuke couldn't have repeated a single sentence if his life had depended on it, but the Harrises were making "I see" faces, so he guessed they were getting the point.

"So you plan to treat the land purchase for the future resort as an asset replacement," Campbell said.

Kitahara nodded. "That way the miscalculation for the sale capital gains could be offset by the tax deferral from this land acquisition."

Whatever that meant, the brothers didn't seem to find any flaws in the argument, but Kitahara had warned them that the lawyer wouldn't have trouble pinpointing the too obvious, Tokyo-Tower-sized crack in the otherwise perfect scheme—in the Rat's own words. Since nobody else could come up with another brilliant idea in such little time, they just had to hope the brothers' greed blinded them to the small details while Kitahara put his snake tongue to good use.

And sure enough there it came, the Tokyo Tower. "If that is a special measure concerning land policy, doesn't the provision specify certain areas?" Longchamp said, adding with his lawyery nastiness, "I don't suppose your government would be preoccupied with the efficient use of *American* land."

Shit. For a rat, Kitahara had the cattiest smile Kinosuke had ever seen. "I don't know, Mr. Longchamp. My government has been suspected of aiming for world domination."

To Kinosuke's surprise, the Harrises cracked up, Miles even banging the table with his palm and saying, "That's a good one, man."

Longchamp looked about to open his mouth, but Kitahara seemed to be on a streak and overrode him. "The provision is meant to take the pressure out of urbanized, overpopulated areas, and that is exactly what we did by selling an office building in the Ginza district—it doesn't get any more urban and crowded than that—and relocating resources and personnel to a new area, since we intend to build, along with the resort, management facilities that may seat a future Hawaiian subsidiary of our corporation.

"The core problem, though, concerns our time schedule. The law establishes precise lapses of time between the original sale and the placing in service of the new assets, and, given the date of the particular sale I've mentioned, and the immediacy of the tax investigation, we find ourselves in the need to accelerate the proceedings.

"Of course this being our fault, our corporation is willing to improve the general conditions of your participation, should you wish to follow through with your investment and sign the pertinent agreement."

Kinosuke's eyes glazed over as Kitahara explained the benefits the Harrises would get if they signed, the figures being mentioned sounding as unreal to him as the ones they gave in documentaries about outer space. In front of him, though, the brothers were eyeing the screen with beady stares, the bastards probably used to handling that kind of money on a regular basis.

"We'll have to think it through," Campbell said. "How much time do we have?"

"For the conditions we're offering you to apply," the Rat said, pausing for effect, "you have until midnight to sign the contract."

CHAPTER 57

THE RADIO crackled and Burka's voice filled the cabin of the pickup truck. "Shiro Kitsune to Kakashi, over."

Burka always sounded as if he understood the joke of him being called White Fox and maybe even knew who Kakashi was and how Kotarō wished he was Naruto's unflappable instructor at times like these.

"Kakashi here, over," he remembered to whisper, since Burka and Tachibana-san were out there in the open and his voice might sound like thunder in the silence of the night.

"We're in position, out."

Burka always used as few words as humanly possible and it made Kotarō feel his brain wasn't fast enough to catch up with the guy.

"Ho, dat buggah stay killah," Keawe said, and Kekoa nodded his agreement.

Somehow Burka seemed invisible most of the time in spite of his white hair, but the Hawaiians had seen the way the man had moved to catch the goats that were now making crazy noises in the back of the truck, and they'd seen Burka handling that frigging killah sniper rifle. And once you saw him that way, there was no mistaking what the guy was.

Same shit happened with Tachibana-san. He might look like this goofy, uncool geezer who wore *tabi* socks with his flip-flops, but when he picked up a weapon, he got you pissing your pants in no time flat.

Burka and Tachibana-san had argued over what rifle their Shinagawa contact should bring, and they both sounded like one of those wacky magazines for gun freaks, spewing names like Accuracy International and Knight's Stoner, comparing model numbers and calibers until they'd had to visit a gun store in Kona to try all the rifles in their range and just see for themselves. And then Burka had admitted that Tachibana-san's British rifle was better than his American one. *Hah.* Problem was, with that super rifle, Burka was much better at hitting the targets, so Tachibana-san was going to do that spotter thing and sort of tell Burka where to point his gun.

Kotarō nodded to himself. So the two guys had found no trouble pretending to head for the beach outside the mansion's fence to do some night snorkeling and then stopping midway to hide among the bushes.

As soon as Brendan-san called, they'd start the animal show.

THEY WERE all paddling hard to beat the surf, all except Shinya, who was just clutching the gunwale rope and fighting to keep himself *inside* the boat.

There had been no way out of bringing the scarred yakuza—they needed someone Ken Harris would recognize, and choosing between him and Kotarō had been a no-brainer—but working as a well-coordinated team with a landlubber sitting there like a couch potato was a little awkward to say the least.

Waves kept crashing around them in a chaos of white foam, currents trying to throw the boat right out into the open ocean like a piece of flotsam, their paddles looking as weak as toothpicks against the strength of the surf.

Brendan shouted at B to get ready, and as soon as the bow hit the rocks, the big man jumped forward, carrying the strong mooring line—the painter—with him. He shot up the boulders like a huge panther and jammed himself between two rocks, firming the painter around his waist.

"Bowline man secure!" came the strong voice back to them.

Time was critical now since the Zodiac was glued to the rocks, unable to ride the surf, waves crashing at it as if trying to fill it to capacity. Brendan didn't bother with the cries of "Water!" that the situation begged for but shouted Otter's name instead.

Being the smallest man in the boat, Otter gathered the paddles and the rest of their gear and jumped over the bow, carrying it all onto the safety of the rocks without unbalancing the Zodiac.

So far so good. Now it was Bobcat's turn to disembark, and Brendan prayed this wouldn't be the moment his crewmate's PTSD chose to act out.

But no, the man moved swiftly over the bow, and maybe because Afghanistan had no sea, the only memory that seemed to come to him was the muscle memory imprinted on his body by dint of hard training, making it appear as if climbing out of a rocking, wave-hit, partially submerged boat was a walk in the park. Which of course it wasn't, as Shinya was about to discover.

To the yakuza's credit, he tried to move as fast as the others had since it was obvious the longer they kept under the constant pounding of the waves the worse they'd fare—not to mention Big B was still holding their weight—but Shinya was not in his element. He might have been fit, but he wasn't familiar with boats, and there'd been no time to properly rehearse this part of the plan.

So Shinya stood quickly, without having the precaution to stay a little hunched so his fingers had less distance to travel to reach the gunwale rope should he need it, and when the next wave crashed over the boat, he was there one second, arms flailing wildly, and the next second Brendan was alone in the boat.

"MIDNIGHT?" CAMPBELL squeaked. "You mean tonight?"

Kinosuke fought to keep his face blank. The wide-eyed surprise on the Americans' faces was not that funny, but he was so anxious that if he allowed himself to think about it, he would start laughing like a loon.

"I'm afraid so," the boss answered, looking appropriately rueful. "As your saying goes, time is money, and in this case especially so."

"That's unacceptable," Longchamp groused. "This is no minor transaction, and it involves the regulations of two different countries; just examining all the documents may take days."

Of course the lawyer was smelling something tricky. This was not the stock exchange, where you had to make decisions on the run—as far as Kinosuke understood it. If they signed the documents, they'd not only be investing a good sum of money but they'd also commit to delivering some stuff and services. It'd be a miracle if Longchamp agreed to go on with this—the deal had to be too sweet for the brothers to override the man's objections.

"We understand your position," the boss said, playing his role, "but we felt we owed you the chance to still participate in the project after all the trouble we've put you through by bringing you this far from your home."

Campbell waved a dismissive hand. "It's been no hassle; we've been enjoying ourselves here."

Miles was cruder about it. "Yeah, it's good to travel with all your expenses covered, and the wives have been having a ball with the slew of shopping and spa treatments. You people know how to entertain your guests."

"Well, Mr. Harris," the boss said, "that's to be expected when you own a few resorts."

The brothers chuckled, and Kinosuke wanted to scream. How could the boss be so calm? It all sounded like a polite closing of negotiations to him, and if they didn't hurry, Brendan was going to rescue Kenshin-san before they got the brothers' signatures on paper—if they did that at all.

He wanted to take a look at his watch, because Brendan had planned the whole thing to the second, but even though Brendan had never said a word, the Catman had mumbled under his breath about *aficionados* often enough for Kinosuke to understand the Japanese team was an unknown quantity for the Americans, the kind of third-world guerrillas you couldn't trust for shit. So maybe Brendan had plans B, C, and D ready in case they didn't deliver in time.

Fuck. He felt so useless. He wished he was out there with Brendan, there where people would be using real weapons instead of subtle misquotes of taxation laws, there where someone might get hurt and need real help.

As soon as he thought about someone getting hurt, his stomach did a little flip, and he cursed himself for his stupidity. Kotarō wouldn't be alone; Shinya, Tachibana, and Kenshin-san could fend for themselves, and the Americans were these fucking invincible SEALs—one stubborn, annoying, smug redhead included.

"Miss Akana will give you the documents with our offer," the boss said as the zaftig Hawaiian beauty sashayed around the table to hand out the folders. "If you don't want to retire to your rooms to study them, there's a small meeting room through that door on your right that you can use."

Shit. The brothers were hesitating too much, that wasn't a good sign.

The boss gave them a knowing smile. "Please, don't feel obliged. We felt we owed you a better offer under the circumstances, but we realize you'd rather not rush such an important decision."

"We wouldn't want to leave you hanging," Miles said, but the boss interrupted him.

"Oh, don't worry, Mr. Harris," he said, a rather smug smile on his lips. "I appreciate your concern, but Kitahara-san has already contacted two local investors who might be willing to take your place. Isn't that right, Kitahara-san?"

There. The brothers' ears perked right up at the mention of competitors.

The Rat's smile was predatory. "Yes, Nakazawa-san. They're seriously considering being part of our project, even under the original conditions."

The boss nodded. "Of course. Since they know the local market and are familiar with our work, they might easily anticipate the outcome of our project." He turned to the Harrises. "If you feel it would not be in your best interests at this time, we would be very disappointed to not be able to work with you on this project, but perhaps other opportunities may arise in the future."

Miss Exotic Beauty moved as if to retrieve the folders from the Harrises, and Kinosuke saw the brothers exchange a look. It was now or never, and he almost bit his nails waiting.

"Huh," Campbell said. "I guess there's no harm in studying your offer—after all, we still have two hours left until midnight."

"Yeah," Miles agreed. "It's not like we're in a hurry to go back to that hideous airport."

CHAPTER 58

BRENDAN DIDN'T even curse. He had no time. If he didn't act now, they'd lose Shinya or the Zodiac—or both, depending on how well he chose his next steps, but he had no time to choose. So he let his training kick in.

He scanned the roiling sea as he rushed toward the bow—confirming no visible sign of Shinya—and jumped onto the rocks, signaling for Big B to move.

Otter and Bobcat fell into place beside him, reaching out for the boat handles.

"Bowline man moving!" B shouted, and the three of them pulled as best they could until B shouted again, "Bowline man secure!"

Then they hauled with all their might, and when the Zodiac came out of the water they heaved it up over their heads like one of those paper dragons in a Chinese New Year celebration—only a hundred times heavier and much uglier.

As Brendan had expected, Shinya's head surfaced as soon as they lifted the boat, the strong currents having pushed him right under what suddenly must have turned into an impenetrable rubber barrier for him to come up for air.

Brendan left the boat in his men's hands and trundled down to the edge of the rocks. Shinya didn't seem to be moving his arms, and when the next wave retreated, Brendan could see why.

Shinya had a red line on the side of his head, the strong surf having probably sent him crashing against the rocks and leaving him unconscious.

"Fuck," Brendan cursed, his voice drowned by the waves. Only the lifejacket he'd insisted Shinya wear over his wetsuit kept him floating, but without a conscious effort to fight the strong undertow, Shinya's body would keep floating away into the open sea.

Brendan didn't allow his mind to consider the possibility that Shinya might already be dead. Whatever the case, he wasn't leaving Shinya there—among other reasons because Kinosuke would kill him if Brendan came back without his friend.

He turned around to yell a command, only to find Bobcat climbing down the rocks with a rope in his hands. Brendan followed the rope with his eyes up to where it rested around Big B's waist and shook his head. These men had been with him for so long, through so much, that they had no trouble reading his mind.

He lifted his arms for Bobcat to tie the rope around his own waist. As each knot was tied and carefully secured, Brendan felt as if he was being linked up to a lifeline that he had somehow lost along the way, his numbed mind not having realized that he'd been drowning without a purpose, far from the things that really mattered and the people he cared about.

Bobcat stood behind him and yanked, checking that the rope would hold, the pull as sudden and strong as a call to attention. And maybe it was—and maybe he'd been desperately in need of it.

"All set, Mr. O," Bobcat said, and Brendan didn't even have to turn to know that the line was secure, that it would hold his weight and Shinya's, that his men would be right there behind him as he jumped into the high surf.

"I THINK it's a setup. The whole tax investigation story sounds flimsy to me, and the proposed solution is dubious to say the least."

Of course that petulant voice belonged to the lawyer. As they'd expected, the Harrises hadn't wanted to use the meeting room nearby and had returned to Longchamp's room instead. Too bad that room, like the rest of their accommodations, was conveniently bugged.

"Yeah, well, but what's the point of it all? Why the hurry?" Campbell asked. *"You said the company is solid, so it shouldn't be a scam."*

They could almost hear the shrug. *"I think they're just trying to put some pressure on you, convince you that you'd only have the one chance to get these conditions."*

"And damn good conditions they are," Miles said. *"Hell, if this panned out, just having a regular tugboat line between Japan and Hawaii would make us filthy rich. Father wouldn't have to lose his ass after any more defense contracts."*

Kinosuke had to admit Kitahara had taken the brothers' measure from the start; he'd expected the idea of the tugboat line to be the major bait, since it didn't depend on the resort's success to work out and would begin paying dividends from the first trips— and he'd been obviously right.

"You should take your time to study the market on that area before you rush ahead blindly."

That was Longchamp, and Kinosuke groaned. Miles seemed eager to *rush ahead blindly*, but Campbell was less foolhardy and might listen to the old whiner.

"That namby-pamby secretary gave us the numbers. They look pretty promising to me."

Nanda to? What the hell had the stupid mofo just called him? By the blank faces everyone in the room tried to keep, Kinosuke deduced it was something in the pansy-assed range, and he felt the tip of his ears burn. *Kuso.* As soon as Kenshin-san was safe, he was going to give that bastard a piece of his mind.

"That's what I'm talking about. The numbers they've shown you might be too *promising."*

"Nah, I don't think so. Have you seen the prices around here? They wouldn't be so over the top if they had cheap, regular transport. I bet that makes smuggling very profitable too."

There was a small silence, as if the three of them were adding numbers in their heads, and then Campbell said, *"What worries me is the talk about local investors. If it isn't a bluff—"*

"Of course it is." Fucking Longchamp again. *"The Japanese are no good at bargaining; they think they lose face if they are forced to accept a lower counteroffer, so they're offering better conditions upfront and prodding* you *to accept it by all kinds of four-flushing. I don't think you should let them corner you into their time frame."*

There was another silence, and Kinosuke bit his nails; it was obvious the brothers wanted to sign, but if they listened to the lawyer and didn't do it that night as they were asked, it would be all for nothing.

KOTARŌ WAS about to puke. The two-way radio had been silent way past the time Brendan-san had said he'd call, and the goats kept kicking and stomping and sort of laughing hysterically in the back of the truck, and if Brendan-san didn't call soon, it looked like the crazy beasts would kill each other, climb their way out of the pickup, or kick a hole through its sides.

"You stay futless, brah," Keawe said, and Kotarō looked at him dumbly. Man, when he was so nervous he couldn't understand pidgin for shit.

Kekoa rolled his eyes. "Chill out, little cousin. You're too young to give yourself a heart attack."

That was frigging helpful, treating him like a baby. "I'm not little," he said, not exactly shouting or pouting but almost doing both just in case.

Keawe and Kekoa looked at him for one second before cracking up, and Kotarō blushed to the root of his hair. Shit. Telling any of Big B's relatives that he wasn't little was like the flea calling the dog a midget.

"Aka Oni to Kakashi. Do you copy? Over."

Nerves clawed at his stomach as he fumbled for the button. "Kakashi to Aka Oni. You're loud, um, I mean, I hear you loud and clear, over."

Shit. He just hoped the two Hawaiians would choke on their own laughter, the frigging turkeys.

"Are you good to go, over?"

He fought the urge to shout into the radio that they'd been good to go for more than a half hour already. "Affirmative, over."

"There's been a change of plans. You have to get the targets to turn off the fence, got it?"

"What!" he yelled into the radio.

"Get them to shut off the electricity, Kakashi. Need the surfer team inside."

Oh shit. How on earth was he going to pull that? And why did they need Burka and Tachibana-san to go into the mansion? What had gone wrong?

The radio crackled. "Kakashi, confirm. Over."

A big hand landed on his shoulder, and when he looked up from the radio, he met Keawe's eyes. The man nodded once, his face serious for the first time, and Kotarō remembered he was not alone in this. He had just met these guys, but no matter how happy-go-lucky they appeared all the time, they'd been ready to do anything to help Big B from the start, just because he was family. So the three of them had the same reason to do their best, and maybe that reason was all they needed to get it right.

"Roger that, Aka Oni. No electricity. We'll do it. Over."

"Roger, Kakashi. Be safe. Aka Oni out."

Damn. That *out* stuff always left him with one or two words on the tip of his tongue. He wanted to ask about the delay, wanted to know what had happened, wanted to ask why Brendan-san was telling him to be safe. Dude, that was definitely the wrong thing to say to someone who was about to puke.

The truck roared to life and Keawe drove it down the dirt road as if it were a racing car. At least no one was laughing now—except the frigging goats.

CHAPTER 59

THAT HAD to be the worst example of rock portage in the history of the SEAL corps. Fucking Pech Valley had no sea anywhere close, but it was impossible to take a single step in those god-awful mountains without being shot, and being shot meant bleeding, or watching others bleed, or anyway smelling blood whatever you did, and the problem with head wounds was that they never fucking stopped bleeding no matter how small they were.

Brendan had pulled Shinya to the rocks, and Bobcat and Otter had hauled the unmoving yakuza out of the water. And then Bobcat had seen the blood, or smelled it, or whatever the hell it was that had flooded his brain with first-rate, special-effects-realistic memories of being covered in someone else's gory remains.

When Brendan climbed out of the water, his team was suddenly two men short. Shinya was breathing slowly, but it was difficult to tell when—or if—he would recover consciousness. Standing by the prone yakuza, Bobcat was breathing too fast, his whole body shaking, his gaze lost in the effort not to see the nightmare replaying in his mind.

So Otter, B, and Brendan had had to carry more than six hundred pounds of rubber up the cliff, almost tumbling back into the water below more than twice, and then they'd had to go back down the rocks to gather the rest of their gear, haul Shinya's unresponsive body to a more or less safe spot, and drag Bobcat up the cliff as if he were stoned out his mind—which in a sense he was.

Not even in Coronado had they made worse time. And now they had to rely on three civilians—two hula dancers and a kid, to be more fucking specific—to get the fence turned off so Burka and Tachibana could climb it and join them, preferably *after* they'd shot out a few garden lights so the camera near their infiltration point didn't get a whole action flick on record.

And since it wasn't Friday as they'd initially planned, the whole security detail would be in the mansion, never mind the dogs, the cook, the maids, the gardeners, and any other fucking helper on earth and their mother.

Just as one of his instructors used to say: *if it doesn't suck, the teams won't do it.*

ONE HOUR left to midnight. The Harrises kept studying the contract with Longchamp, going through line after highfalutin line of legal babble in case they decided to sign anytime this millennium.

"Can't we offer anything else to make them change their minds?" Kinosuke asked to the room at large.

It was Kitahara who answered, the fact that his ratty face was simply projected on a screen not quite managing to douse his patronizing airs. "It would be too suspicious. We are supposed to have other people anxious to make the investment, so we should appear nonchalant."

Nonchalant. Fucking callous was what the man was. Because he didn't give a shit about Kenshin-san or Kotarō—and of course he didn't even acknowledge Brendan's existence.

"At least the senator hasn't called. That means the operation is going according to plan."

Kinosuke looked at the boss. He only *appeared* nonchalant, but Kinosuke knew the guy well enough to understand he was worried out of his mind.

He nodded. "I suppose if nobody has sounded the alarm, they must be doing fine."

Or they were doing so fucking badly that they hadn't even come near doing anything that could trigger any alarm, but Kinosuke kept that to himself and just went on biting his nails as nonchalantly as he could.

"I NO kid you, brah. You bettah keep da dogs out of heah if you no like da goats running all ovah," Keawe was saying.

Kotarō didn't need to puke anymore. One close look at the ginormous dogs barking their heads off behind the mansion's gates and he was about to piss his pants.

The fake accident had gone so well that the truck was probably useless now, one of the drive tires stuck in the ditch so badly they might need to tow the pickup out—not a very good thing if they had to run the hell out of there as soon as the others got Kenshin-san.

Keawe was talking to the guards who had followed the dogs to check what the ruckus was all about, while Kekoa and Kotarō pretended to be trying to round the scattered goats. They didn't really have to pretend much; the frigging crazy beasts were impossible to catch in an open space like this, but the two of them did their best to keep the animals moving as close to the fence as they could, to see if they could manage to make at least one try to climb it.

"The dogs are just doing their job," a guard said. He wasn't skinny or anything, but he looked small between the other two guards, two huge Samoans who looked amused by the situation. "And you better watch your animals, because this fence is electric."

"Wot!" Keawe was good. He and Kekoa did all kind of stuff at luaus, from hula dancing to fire breathing, so they were used to putting on a show.

"Yeah, brah," one of the Samoans said. "Da kine fence. Yo' animals come neah, we going have hulihuli goat fo' dinnah."

"Oh yeah no? Broke da mouth," the other big bully said before they all cracked up.

No good. No way these guys would give a shit about the animals, so how were they going to convince them to turn off the electricity?

"Wassamatta wit' you, brah?" Keawe said, faking indignation and not doing a good job of it this time. Kotarō frowned as he saw Keawe look at him and then quickly away. "Da poor beasties—"

What the hell? Had he decided the whole thing was hopeless and was just pretending for Kotarō's sake?

"Look, brah," Keawe sort of whispered now, "I no like da goats any kine bettah dan you, but see dat buddha-head kid ovah deah?"

The guards all looked his way, and Kotarō ducked his head, wondering what Keawe was doing calling him buddha-head and all. He was getting frigging mad.

"I no want talk stink, but his fadda got plenny attitude; tink his fut no smell."

The guards chuckled. "Plenny dollah?" one asked.—

"Yeah. He stays so tight even da pakes tink he tight."

The three guys laughed, and that only encouraged Keawe. "He want biggah dollah; 'ass why he wen buy da goats fo' make da kine yagi-someting an' den wen tell da kid to handle da beasts cuz he jus' coasting, an' den wen tell my cuz and me to handle da kid cuz we jus' lazy mokes."

"Bummah, man," one of the Samoans said, still laughing.

Keawe shook his head. "Yeah. Da kid no can handle da buckaloose goats."

"No shit," said the shorter guard, smirking, and it made Kotarō so mad he ran after the nearest goat so furiously that the animal felt cornered and tried to jump the fence. And it happened.

The goat ran for the fence and put its front legs on the wire as if to climb it. And the next moment it jumped back about half a mile, making a high-pitched crazy sound and limping about miserably after it landed back on the dirt.

The three guards were laughing their heads off.

"Did you see that? Never knew goats could fly."

Keawe looked contrite now. "Dat no fun, brah. His fadda going bus my ala alas."

The short guard shrugged. "Nothing we can do about it, man. Can't go out there help you and have *our* boss kick *our* ala alas—"

Keawe nodded. "I figga, brah. You no can try close da light but? The goats go bus someting up wit' da kine fayacracka."

The Samoans looked at the other guard, and Kotarō finally understood what Keawe had been all about; he knew the guys wouldn't give a shit about the goats, but they might sympathize with another local doing a shitty job for someone else.

"Brah, jus' fo' one second. No moa people round heah. Dey no can tell yo' boss."

The short guard seemed to hesitate. Kotarō swallowed. They had very little time left, and Brendan-san wouldn't have asked them to do this if he didn't really need Burka and Tachibana-san's help. Something was wrong, and a lot could depend on them; he had to do something.

"Keawe!" he shouted, trying to hide his fear behind a mighty glare. "Get over here! My father doesn't pay you to chat around!"

He put his hands on his hips and tried to do an impersonation of Aniki in one of his moods, though his heart was about to hop out of his mouth like a coqui frog.

"Shuah, bosu," Keawe shouted back, and then turned to the guards and whispered, "See wot I wen tell you? Try help me, brah. Jus' one second an' we go bag. You no can see us no moa."

"Come on, Pearson," one of the Samoans said. "The perimeter is clear; the road is empty. If anyone tries to come in here, we're gonna see the headlights for miles before they get here."

The short guard still hesitated.

"If someone tries to get to the house, they're gonna have to go through a bunch of goats first, and we're sure going to notice that," the other Samoan added.

One of the goats chose that moment to make a noise like some madman laughing, and the guards cracked up. The shorter guard shook his head and pulled a two-way radio out of his jacket.

"You have ten minutes," he told Keawe, and Kotarō tried very hard not to smile.

CHAPTER 60

THE BRILLIANT green circle around the garden light suddenly puffed out. There was only another green circle left along the path the camera covered, and Brendan watched it through his night vision goggles while he listened through his radio headset.

"Shuah, bosu," came B's cousin's voice as he talked to the guards. *"See wot I wen tell you? Try help me, brah. Jus' one second an' we go bag. You no can see us no moa."*

The last light went out, the sound of the bullet shattering glass muffled by the distance. It seemed the man watching the cameras was too distracted by the goats to notice the lights in that area of the garden, but if they didn't turn off the fence, Brendan would have to attempt the rescue with a three-man team.

"You have ten minutes," one of the guards finally said, and Brendan scanned the fence near the designated point. Barely two minutes later, a slender figure climbed the now dead wire and disappeared under some ornamental bushes seconds before the camera swept the area.

As soon as the camera swiveled the other way, a pudgier figure started climbing the fence, and Brendan groaned. Of all the yakuza, he had to be saddled with the only one who didn't teach kendo at the dojo, the one married to a Filipina who kept him on a diet of adobo.

"Come on," he whispered, watching Tachibana's slow progress.

The seconds kept ticking by, the camera started to turn, and the fence wobbled back and forth under Tachibana's weight, making his ascent something akin to a crawl.

Brendan could almost see the headlines—"Ex-SEALs and yakuza nabbed for attempted robbery"—supposing they got lucky and nobody started pulling the trigger.

Tachibana straddled the fence and awkwardly raised one leg, but no matter how fast he tried to climb down from there, it would be too late; the camera was about to get a perfect visual of a wet-suited intruder.

"Fuck," Brendan heard someone mumble beside him. Yeah, his thoughts exactly, but not even Burka, being so close, could do anything about it.

Brendan started running an alternative plan in his head, crossing out the surprise factor and just going for speed and violence, when the green image of Tachibana froze on top of the fence and then let go. Just like that. One moment he was there, the green elephant in the room, and the next, the camera swept over an empty landscape, not even a telltale bulk on the ground beside the fence.

"What the fuck?" B murmured.

The fence was high enough for an untrained civilian to take a bad fall and break something, but it seemed the apparently out-of-shape yakuza had even managed to roll out of sight like a pro.

"Fucking martial art freaks," Otter murmured, sounding rather amused.

Brendan shook his head, then shook it again when a pale green hand flashed a thumbs-up over a hibiscus bush.

THE HARRISES and their sidekick sat in the conference room discussing a limited liability clause—whatever the fuck that meant. Twenty-five minutes before midnight, they were still arguing about stupid details that would have probably saved them a slew of money, if the contracts had been fucking legit.

Kinosuke wasn't sure if the argument was simply a strategy to refuse over some technicality or if they really were interested and trying to make the best out of the deal. If they'd been Japanese, Kinosuke would have thought it was the polite way to say no, but seeing that they were dealing with Americans—and especially rude Americans at that— he wanted to believe it was the second reason.

Whatever the case, he was never going to razz Kitahara again. The guy knew what he was doing; he kept countering each and every argument Longchamp made, babbling about shit like indemnity clauses, damage caused by multiple parties, legal fees, nullified provisions, and even being able to cite Hawaii State law.

They could have never done it without the R... um, without Kitahara, never been able to understand most of the lawyer's questions, much less answer them, and they'd have probably found it difficult to convince the Shinagawa that this would be a profitable business for them.

But for it all to work, the Harrises had to sign before midnight, because right after midnight Brendan was going to make some noise, and the senator was going to hear about it, and being the paranoid son of a bitch that he was, Kenshin-san's father would probably make the connection between his son's rescue—or kidnap from his point of view—and the deal his other sons were making.

KOTARŌ ALMOST giggled when another goat started climbing the fence. Dude, they were like frigging circus animals, and they sure kept the monster dogs distracted, and the three guards had to be around to keep an eye on them—and laugh their heads off—so mission accomplished.

He felt good about it, but the possibility of being stuck here when all hell broke loose was starting to freak him out. The goats they could leave scattered about—they were wild goats to begin with—but if they couldn't pull the pickup out of the ditch, they would have to stay there waiting to be towed, and the guards weren't dumb enough to think they'd had a chance accident in front of the mansion's gates the same night the mansion was attacked.

Kotarō couldn't do anything about it now, so he just repeated in his head what Bobcat had told him many times, *"Don't worry about the future. Focus your energy in knocking out the target right in front of you, or you won't survive to have a future."*

CHAPTER 61

NO DOGS in sight. That was good, because Tachibana made more noise than Godzilla, and they had no time to go any slower. Geez. Even someone as hefty as Big B was able to move without a sound, but Tachibana just *looked* as if he were skulking.

Thank God these days anyone could carry the title of executive protection specialist. Though if Brendan was fair, he had to admit many guys in the profession were moderately good—vets or ex-cops—but the trappings of their new lives made them grow complacent. Living in this kind of mansion, in a place where nothing ever happened, could do that to the most disciplined. And maybe that was in Brendan's future too, if he kept doing what he did.

He signaled with his hand for the team to stop, the gesture a little brisker than he intended, but he needed to put a stop to the ramblings of his mind. He needed to focus on the here and now, acquire their primary target and exfiltrate safely. That was what he'd been trained for, and he had to stop thinking he had to prove he hadn't lost his edge, because the moment his goal changed into proving something, his priorities would get all mixed up and someone might suffer because of him.

He moved his hand in the air again, and Burka jogged noiselessly ahead to flatten himself on the ground behind a thick bush, his rifle pointed at the lanai of the thatched villa immediately below their position.

The villa was one of the two smaller constructions located some distance away from the mansion but on the same side of the property. The areas for the owner and his guests were clearly separated from the staff residences that were discreetly hidden behind a cluster of palm trees, farther away from the main building.

The vistas were breathtaking here—green vegetation enveloping the dark wooden villas and contrasting sharply with the black lava of the ground, gas tiki torches illuminating the way to a lagoon that appeared to have no end, seamlessly connecting with the ocean beyond, a clever design of terraces hiding the beach from view until you were literally stepping onto the sand.

They had no cameras here, to preserve the privacy of the guests, but the residing guest was a special one this time, and the guards circled the perimeter of the villa on their rounds. That was why Brendan checked his watch before he lifted a single finger. One minute to go before the guard appeared, and then they'd have fifteen to enter the house, get Ken Harris, and get the hell out of Dodge.

The loud crunch of approaching boots drew Brendan's attention. The guard had no reason to be stealthy, so his steps were sure as he walked right up to the lanai. There he stopped, facing the darkened rooms of the villa, and Brendan frowned.

In all the days they'd watched the mansion, the guards had never actually entered the villa where Ken was staying, so why did this one look as if he was convincing himself to do it in the middle of the night?

Geez. Of all the fucking days in the month, the guy had to choose this one to try to steal whatever it was he wanted to steal from the Harris kid. Fucking copacetic.

Brendan made a signal for his men to sit tight. With a little bit of luck, the impromptu cat burglar would be in and out in a few minutes and leave them enough time to do their thing without triggering any alarms.

The man finally entered the villa, and the unmistakable sound of something big hitting the floor reached them. The moron had stumbled over some piece of furniture. Wouldn't it be great if the very guy they'd come to rescue was the one to raise the alarm? Over a petty theft?

A muffled cry came from the villa, and before Brendan could decide what to do, Tachibana leapt to his feet and ran to the lanai.

Brendan followed behind, signaling madly for Otter and B to spread out and for Burka to cover them. He stormed into the house, his Glock at the ready, his night-vision goggles giving him a clear view of what was happening.

The guard was on the floor, or rather would have been if Ken Harris hadn't been right under him, pinned by the man's heavier weight, fighting to get the guard off him, both of them too engrossed in wrestling each other to notice Tachibana standing by the lanai doors and aiming his gun.

Had it been anyone other than Tachibana, Brendan would have tried to disarm him, but the yakuza was too fast with a gun, and even as Brendan moved, he knew Tachibana's finger was already squeezing the trigger, so he just struck Tachibana's extended forearms with his own.

The silencer muffled the sound of the shot, the bullet going high over the head of the guard who looked in their direction in wide-eyed surprise. Brendan moved forward, but the guard had already reached for his gun, and this time the sound of the shot was loud enough to be heard in Kona. Even the guard seemed startled by the sudden blast, and Brendan's fist connected with a satisfying crunch. The man's limp body collapsed on top of Ken.

KINOSUKE LOOKED from Campbell to Miles Harris. They sat in silence, mulling over Kitahara's words. Even Longchamp seemed to have run out of questions, and he was just rereading the contract for the millionth time.

So far so good. They looked ready to make a decision, and they still had ten minutes left to midnight, more than enough for a team of superwarriors to—

Miles's phone started ringing, and everybody in the room—his brother and his lawyer included—scowled at him until he fished it out of his pants pocket and disconnected it.

"Sorry," he mumbled, and hearing him apologize was so unexpected that Kinosuke took it as a good omen. That is, until Campbell pulled his own vibrating phone from his pocket to check the caller ID.

Campbell didn't say anything, but he rolled his eyes at his brother, and Kinosuke almost cursed aloud. *Shit.* That was a universal gesture between siblings, and right now, it could only mean that something had gone very wrong with Brendan.

"Well, gentlemen," the boss said, "I'm afraid we can't wait any longer if we want to give our other investors a chance."

Miles and Campbell exchanged a concerned look, and Kinosuke tried hard not to smile. They had them. The bastards were going to leave their signature on paper, and they were going to nail them.

"Senator Harris?"

Kinosuke almost jumped off his chair. He'd been so busy watching the brothers that he hadn't seen Longchamp take the call. The call from Kenshin-san's father.

THE SHORT guard stopped laughing when his radio made a crackling sound. He took a few steps away from the gates, far enough that Kotarō couldn't hear what he was saying since the Rottweiler was still barking his head off at the goats that came near.

When the guard returned to the gates, he had a thunderous expression on his face, and the two Samoans looked like two kids about to get a tongue-lashing.

"Ulu, come with me," he ordered. "Toa, you take the dogs and round these jokers up."

Kotarō exchanged a glance with Keawe and Kekoa. This was it; someone had discovered Kenshin-san was missing—or worse, someone had discovered Brendan-san—and even if the short guard meant the goats when he'd told the Samoan to round them up, Kotarō didn't want to stay there long enough to find out.

Even before the gates started opening, Kotarō and Big B's cousins were running for the pickup. The truck doors slammed closed not a second too early as the dogs threw themselves at the windows with their jaws open, drool trickling down the glass, and their barking so loud Kotarō almost couldn't hear the sound of the engine.

Kekoa stamped on the gas pedal, but the truck just made this lame attempt at moving forward and then stopped; the front wheel on the right side was firmly stuck in the ditch. That gave the guard time to approach them and shout something, and even though Kotarō could barely hear him over the racket the dogs and the engine were making, his meaning was too frigging obvious anyway.

"Put it in reverse!" Keawe shouted. When his cousin did and stepped on the pedal, the pickup lurched backward for a moment, but the pull wasn't enough to get them out of the ditch.

Kotarō looked up, and his whole world froze for one terrifying second. The big Samoan was out there, right in front of the hood, both his arms raised as he pointed a gun at the windshield.

CHAPTER 62

"*DAIJŌBU KA?*"

Tachibana had shoved the unconscious guard off Ken as if he were nothing but a man-sized garbage bag, and now that Brendan took in the little details, he understood why. He couldn't be 100 percent sure, but the way Ken's sleeping shorts had almost been torn off his thin hips strongly suggested it wasn't petty theft the guard had been aiming at.

"Tachibana-san?"

The naked hope in those weird eyes was painful to witness. Brendan felt tempted to take his goggles off, but now more than ever, he needed clear vision after the gunshot had alerted the whole property of their presence.

"We have to get out of here!" he said urgently, and got matching glares from Tachibana and Ken.

"Who the fuck are you?" Ken spat, and Brendan was reminded once again of the reasons why a guy like Matsunaga would risk everything for this pale, skinny American. Yeah, the man could be small and fragile-looking, but he had attitude in spades. Someone had tried to rape him, someone had shot a gun near him, an alien-looking armed stranger was giving him orders, and he still had the presence of mind to act like a king—a half-naked, tattooed king—deciding whether to grant an audience or throw the intruder headfirst out of his palace.

Brendan lifted the goggles for a moment, a wry smile on his lips. "Brendan O'Farrihy at your service"—he almost added *Your Majesty*, but he didn't want Ken to think he was being mocked—"and that service is gonna be really short if we don't get the hell out of here."

He slipped the goggles back on in time to catch the look of recognition on Ken's face and the glower that followed.

"*Koitsu wa nakama da*, Kenshin-san," Tachibana said. "He's helping us."

Geez. It sounded as if Brendan was carrying their luggage, but still it made Ken stand and dash for the closet, the amazing tattoo on his back distracting Brendan for a second, even though he was seeing it in weird shades of green.

"There's no time to get dressed," Brendan finally managed, only to be completely ignored.

He cursed under his breath and started for the closet, ready to grab Ken and carry him if need be, but the man turned around and thrust a pair of running shoes in his face. "Have you ever tried to walk barefoot on *a'a'* lava?"

Brendan bit back a nasty comeback because Ken was right and because the man got the shoes on in no time and went to stand beside Tachibana, the two of them looking at him as if *Brendan* was the one making them wait.

Fuck. If he made it out of here alive, he was never teaming up with civilians again.

"YES, SIR," Longchamp repeated. "I'll put you through."

He passed the phone to Campbell, who said to the boss, "Sorry about this," before he pressed the cell to his ear. "Dad?"

Kinosuke watched as the man listened, watched the surprise registering on his face, and felt like grabbing the fucking phone and smashing it against the wall. He was so angry he could hardly breathe—or rather, he was so *worried* he couldn't breathe, which made him so mad he almost felt dizzy. Fucking stupid, numbskull redhead and his fucking dim-witted, supersoldier plans.

"That's awful," Campbell said, "but I don't see…. Yes, of course we have…. But, Dad, we have a chance to…."

Miles tapped his fingers on the table impatiently while his brother tried to put a word in edgewise, until it seemed Miles couldn't take it anymore and snatched the phone from Campbell.

"We're in a business meeting here, Dad," he said testily. "You can't—"

Of course the son of a bitch could—he was the fucking one and only Senator Harris, and Kinosuke didn't see his favorite sons growing a pair and telling him to go fuck himself anytime soon. So maybe the only intelligent thing to do right now was to ditch the bastards and go help Brendan. And Kenshin-san.

It scared him shitless that his first thought had been for Brendan, and his eyes sought the boss as if he expected the man to have caught him forgetting their real target. *Shit.* Now he even used the same jargon as Brendan. But the boss was too busy listening to Miles and—fucking fretting. Yeah, the boss might fool the others, but Kinosuke knew that pinched look and knew he had to do something about it, because it didn't matter if Kinosuke was about to be sick with worry, since his brain didn't know his ass from his elbow under the best circumstances, but if worry froze Matsunaga-san, they'd be up to their eyes in shit.

"Um, Nakazawa-san," he said tentatively, and when the boss focused his high-octane glower on him, Kinosuke pointed at his watch. He hadn't the foggiest idea what he was trying to convey, but it seemed the least stupid or eye-catching thing to do. And it seemed to work too—that or Miles's next sentence did the trick.

"Sure, send us the pictures of these goons, and we'll let you know if we've seen them around," he said with a long-suffering gesture aimed at his brother.

Fuck. If Miles and Campbell saw those photos, they'd be screwed.

The boss was speaking urgently into his own phone in Japanese, and Kinosuke frowned when he caught wind of the meaningless babble coming out of his mouth. Was his cell even on?

"*Nani ka?*"

"What? Dad, you still there?"

Suddenly, there seemed to be some problem with the phone signal.

"*Hidenori-san,*" the boss said to Kinosuke, "would you please go talk to the technician and see what the problem with the phone reception might be?"

"*Hai*."

As Kinosuke stood, the boss addressed the Harrises, "I'm sorry for this inconvenience, but it might come as a blessing in disguise."

Kinosuke walked slowly toward the tech room, wanting to hear what the boss was up to. "I was contacting our central offices in Tokyo, asking them for more time, but they told me the conditions for this contract couldn't stand past the time margin we'd settled, so maybe it's a good thing that the signal has gone off."

Kinosuke knocked softly on the tinted glass and opened the door to the tech room as Campbell Harris asked, "Are you saying we still have time to sign?"

"Yes, Mr. Harris, for as long as it takes them to fix the problem, which I'm sure won't be too long anyway, but maybe long enough for you?"

So the ball was back in their court, and even if they suspected foul play, they might attribute it to some kind of power play between Nakazawa and his colleagues in Tokyo, and not to anything related with their father's paranoia.

Still, it didn't solve the problem of how the fuck they were going to help Mr. Don't- try-to-contact-me-while-I'm-doing-my-SEAL-shit.

"RAISE YO' hands, cuz," Keawe said, and Kotarō raised his shaking hands for the guard to see. The Samoan waved the gun to one side, urging them to come out, but Kotarō couldn't decide which was worse, waiting for the man to shoot them and hope he missed or going out there to get eaten by a mastodonic dog.

"He mento or wot?" Kekoa said aloud what Kotarō was thinking, and the Hawaiian carefully moved his raised hands to point at the Rottweiler outside his door, but the Samoan waved his gun again and shouted at them to get out.

Keawe looked at the animal barking on his side of the truck. "Dis kine looks bettah," he said, and Kotarō's eyes widened even more. Yeah, maybe this dog didn't look as manic as the black one on the other side, but dude, the size of that mouth. This beast could use a longboard as a chew toy.

Keawe took a deep breath and turned slightly toward Kotarō. He must have seen how frightened Kotarō was, because he made an effort to avoid his usual pidgin. "Now, little cousin. I'm going to open this door and try to keep the doggy calm. You stay right behind me all the time, yes?"

Kotarō nodded because that was what he always did when someone asked anything of him, but as soon as Keawe pulled the handle and the door opened just a crack, the dog tried to thrust his massive head into the opening, and Kotarō couldn't help his reaction. He lunged himself at Keawe, grabbed his arm, and pulled him back, yelling "No!" at the top of his voice. And that was when the gunshot rang out.

CHAPTER 63

THEY HAD barely set foot on the black lava when a myriad of artfully concealed garden lights came on at once and turned the night into a dazzling green day.

"Fuck," Brendan cursed, pulling at his goggles and pointing blindly at the place he remembered the nearest bushes to be. "Take cover!"

His eyes adjusted as he flattened himself on the ground behind some ornamental shrub, Ken and Tachibana lying close to him, slightly better protected by the low branches of a koa tree. He saw no visible movement around them, but they could hear running footsteps and voices.

Brendan looked at the path that led back to the rocks, weighing their options. The way the villas were located, with the lagoon up front and the golf course to their left, the guards had to come from the right side, from the staff buildings—the only guard who had been doing a perimeter check was now unconscious inside Ken's room. If the guards tried to come at the intruders from both flanks, they had a long way to go with Otter and B hiding somewhere along their path, prepared to intercept them, and Burka waiting with his sniper rifle at the ready.

There had to be nine guards left, nothing four SEALs and a yakuza couldn't deal with, but having Ken with them, Brendan didn't want to risk him getting wounded in the crossfire. So they had to run for it, and do it now, before the mansion staff got any closer.

He flashed a hand signal for Burka to cover them, then whispered, "Ken, you stay right behind me; keep your head down, and run as fast as you can. Tachibana, you follow behind and cover his back." He met two pairs of unimpressed eyes and couldn't help a smile. "Yeah, well, forgive me for being obvious. Now run!"

He shot out from behind the shrub and took the path marked with smoothed-out lava slabs. He could hear more noises and shouts, but he didn't bother looking back. They were running in the open, and his first priority was to get Ken to a safe place; he trusted his men to stop the guards from following too close.

The manicured path gave way to the loose, spiky clinkers of *a'a'* lava when the first gunshots started ringing, not far enough for Brendan's comfort, but at least all of the shots came from behind and did not ricochet often. The reassuring report of two SIG-Sauer pistols and an Accuracy International sniper rifle let him know the guards wouldn't be able to follow the three of them into the now garishly illuminated golf course.

There was a soft hill hiding the rocks where they'd left the Zodiac, and Brendan decided to go around it so as not to offer an even clearer target. He looked over his shoulder to make sure Ken and Tachibana were following.

Ken was right behind him, looking as weird as they come in an almost full-body tattoo, dark silk shorts, white running shoes, and the most wildly cropped mop of bleached hair. Brendan had no time to shake his head, though, his eyes jumping to

Tachibana and doing a double take, because the yakuza's eyes had gone cold, and his arms were slowly raising his gun to point it at Brendan.

KOTARŌ WAS alive. He only felt pain in his hand, but as he looked down at it, he discovered he was squeezing Keawe's arm to death and immediately let go.

"You all right, kid?"

Kotarō nodded and followed Keawe's look to where Kekoa sat. "I jus' wen piss my pants," Kekoa said sheepishly, and Kotarō felt an irrepressible urge to giggle like a fool, and he might have giggled if the dogs hadn't chosen that moment to leave the pickup doors and run barking their heads off toward the back of the truck.

Kotarō looked up to see the guard sprawled on the ground, holding his hand as if it hurt like hell, and then there came another shot and a whimper, and when Kotarō looked through the pickup's rear window, he saw the black dog lying on the asphalt and the brown dog lunging at a man in a wetsuit.

It happened so fast that Kotarō wasn't sure he was seeing right. One moment the dog was flying, big jaws open as if to swallow the man whole, and the next the big animal jerked as if struck by lightning. The dog's huge body smashed against the road with a loud thump, and when Kotarō raised his eyes, he met a familiar haunted look.

"Bobcat!" he shouted, and those eyes sort of softened a little and almost smiled at him before Bobcat shouted back, "Stay there!"

As skinny as he was, Bobcat looked all spindly legs and arms in the black suit, but he moved like the animal he was named after as he walked to the front of the pickup and approached the guard.

The big Samoan acted like one of those lame characters in action flicks, the ones who think they're being all crafty when they look at their guns out of the corner of their eyes as if the rest of the world wasn't seeing them look at the gun lying on the ground three feet away. And Bobcat simply reached out and hit the man in the head with the butt of his rifle while the Samoan was looking away and pretending he wasn't and not really seeing shit except the gun that he couldn't reach anyway. Dude, how awesome was that?

As soon as Keawe climbed down, Kotarō couldn't help himself. He jumped out of the truck, dashed to where Bobcat was standing, and lunged at him like another crazy dog. Bobcat looked startled for all of a second, but then he just hugged Kotarō and petted his head as if he really was some crazy dog.

Kotarō felt the heat in his cheeks and hid his face in Bobcat's neoprene covered chest. He wasn't this silly and touchy-feely most of the time, but dude, those had been the worst moments of his life, what with the guard pointing the gun at them and those frigging ginormous dogs wanting to eat them, and—and this was Bobcat, and he was a real Navy SEAL, and he had saved his life once already, and now he'd left the others and Kenshin-san just to save him again because somehow he'd learned Kotarō was in trouble.

"How did you...?" he said, looking up into those big brown eyes.

"Your radio was still transmitting," Bobcat explained.

Of course. He'd had to leave it that way for Burka and Tachibana to learn when the fence would be switched off, since Kotarō couldn't use the radio openly in front of the guards, and then he'd forgotten the whole thing.

"Ho, brah," Kekoa said, "we go help yo' buddies or wot?"

Bobcat shook his head. "We'll help them better if they don't have to worry about us, so let's get the pickup out of that ditch and scram."

"Suah, brah," Kekoa said. "I no can tink of a bestest way."

"You nevah can tink nutting, cuz," Keawe said, and Kotarō finally giggled, because maybe now that Bobcat was with them, everything would be fine.

CHAPTER 64

BRENDAN WAS always surprised at how fast his wetware processed information when someone pointed a gun at him, the strange time bubble that combat never failed to generate somehow expanding and accelerating his ability to think, while every movement around him slowed to a point where he could catch the smallest detail.

That was why he saw the barrel of Tachibana's gun move slightly to Brendan's right side, as if the man wasn't sure where his heart could be. But this was Tachibana, and the yakuza was nothing if not accurate with a gun, and even though none of Matsunaga's men liked Brendan much, all of them had a fierce loyalty to the American running behind in his underwear.

Killing Brendan would only reduce the chances of getting Ken out of his father's clutches, and only someone working for the senator would want that. It was true that Tachibana had a family now, and families—especially Filipino extended ones—were expensive, but the guy was a yakuza, one of those old-school yakuza who were still in the business of chopping knuckles off and doing time for their bosses' crimes.

So Brendan shoved his survival instinct down and turned his head in the direction the gun would point when Tachibana finished raising it over Brendan's shoulder, Brendan's own gun mimicking the yakuza's movement to aim at the real threat he hadn't yet seen.

And there it was—three armed men standing in their path no more than ten feet away.

Fuck. Where had they come from? In his adrenaline-enhanced thinking, Brendan had time to realize he'd forgotten about the yacht that had expedited the rescue in the first place, forgotten a yacht of those dimensions would have a big crew, forgotten any friend of the senator would not travel without a security detail, even though there would be one already waiting for him when he landed.

"Freeze!"

And this security detail was made up of the kind of morons who would yell "freeze."

This was bad. Brendan took a look at their weapons—submachine guns—gauged their churlish cowboy stances and their waist circumferences, and understood the *Three Stooges* had probably never seen a picture of Ken Harris. And since they didn't look like the kind trained to think on their feet but rather *with* their feet, they would probably assume the son of a senator would look more like an Ivy League escapee than some relative of Marilyn Manson.

That meant Ken would be in danger even if Tachibana and Brendan dropped their weapons.

"Drop your weapons!"

Geez. These guys were so slow, they needed a commercial break between one thought and the next. The problem was, this kind of *bright* people usually did a slipshod job of following the basic rules of executive protection, and their sloppiness made them dangerously unpredictable.

Brendan knew he could rely on Tachibana's accuracy to take out the three hostiles, but Tachibana wasn't a SEAL, hadn't gone through the same training as Brendan, didn't have the concept of teamwork fire-branded into his very soul, so Brendan couldn't predict his reactions either.

If it'd been any of Brendan's men, he would have read Brendan's subtle changes in stance to guess which target he would try to disable first, and his crewman would go unerringly for the other two. Tachibana, well, he might choose to ignore Brendan or simply use him as a human shield while he shot the three bodyguards in the order that best suited him, not especially caring about casualties.

One thing Brendan knew for certain: neither he nor Tachibana would drop their weapons. Bullets were going to fly, and Ken had nowhere to take cover.

So Brendan cast his eyes over the scene in front of him one more time, looked at the men and their guns, followed the direction of their stares, and scanned the landscape to their sides and behind them, catching every single change in the still life of the golf course and replaying in his head all that he'd learned about the yakuza in the last few months. Then he decided on a course of action and prayed that his guesstimates would prove accurate. If they weren't, he'd be screwed—painfully, even mortally, screwed.

The instant he caught movement in front of him, he turned around and threw himself on top of Ken, shoved him down onto the ground, and covered the thin tattooed body with his own just a split second before the guns started their blasting chorus.

"SHIRO KITSUNE to Kakashi. Do you copy? Over."

Kotarō pressed the button, feeling he might be finally getting the hang of it. "Kakashi here. I read you loud and clear, over."

Listen to him. A whole frigging sentence without blowing it.

"Kakashi, confirm location, over."

Oh shit. Did he have to give coordinates and all? He looked at Bobcat for help, but the man was kind of busy pulling at a rope that went around a utility post, then formed some sort of complicated double triangle with a lot of knots and these things called carabiners, and then another thick knot tied to a tow hook on the pickup bumper so Kekoa and Bobcat could pull the truck—with Keawe inside, dude—out of the ditch.

"Kakashi? Are you on the road to Kona? Over."

Kotarō looked at the road, then at the truck, and then pushed the button. "Um, we are sort of on the road, but one wheel is almost out of it, right by the ditch on the side of the road, and the other is inside the ditch, so I don't think you can say we are completely on the road, though Keawe and Bob... um, I mean, Maneki Neko, they are pulling at the truck with a rope so that we can get it out and really be on the road. The road to Kona, that is. Um, over."

He was trying to be precise and all, but, dude, that just sounded frigging lame.

"Kakashi, confirm Maneki Neko is with you, over."

Huh? Burka didn't know Bobcat was with them? Weird. "He is, I mean, affirmative."

He hadn't said *over* or anything, but Burka asked right away, "You all okay?"

"Affirmative," he said, smiling until the thought popped into his mind that they might be fine but Burka and the others might not, and that could mean that Kenshin-san—"Are you... is Kensh... um... is the...."

Shit, he couldn't even remember what the code name for Kenshin-san was.

"The parcel is wrapped and ready to deliver. Don't you worry about anything, Kakashi."

Those were way too many words for Burka to say in one breath, and Kotarō got a very bad feeling. "Um, are you all okay there, Shiro Kitsune?"

And those were way too many seconds of silence, so many that Bobcat and Kekoa had time to give the rope a final heave that pulled the tire out of the ditch and onto the tarmac, and still there was time for Bobcat to run to Kotarō, take the radio from him and say, "Shiro Kitsune, location and status."

And finally Burka answered, "Maneki Neko. Exfiltrating now. Two casualties. Move it. Out."

CHAPTER 65

YAKUZA WERE not SEALs, but, as Brendan had deduced from watching Matsunaga's entourage, they had their own sense of teamwork. And their tough reputation was not just an urban legend.

Tachibana had appraised the situation as calmly and in as much detail as Brendan, it seemed. And Shinya, who Brendan had thought would still be lying unconscious by the Zodiac, had trudged all the way to them when he had caught sight of the new threat coming their way.

They'd acted in perfect coordination, Tachibana and Shinya, with the cool determination of trained soldiers, somehow knowing which hostile the other would disable and making short work of the three bodyguards without—to Brendan's relief—killing them.

Of course they probably hadn't counted on Brendan lunging at Ken to shield him, but they hadn't even looked startled; they'd just taken their cue and, as soon as Brendan and Ken were out of the equation, moved forward to neutralize the threat.

The only problem was that Shinya might have been a good shot under normal circumstances, but nobody with a concussion could expect his aim to be true—it was a miracle he'd managed to bird-dog the guards after getting his noggin banged like a bell clapper—and the only thing on earth that could be worse than a moron with a submachine gun was a *wounded* moron with a submachine gun.

Bullets sprayed in a crazy arc as one of the knuckleheads flailed, lost his balance, and fell with his finger still on the trigger. It took another shot from Tachibana to rip the gun off the guy's hand and stop the barrage. By then, though, the moron's buddies weren't the only ones to receive a lagniappe of stray bullets.

Brendan rolled off Ken. "Are you okay?" he asked with a grimace, checking the lithe body for signs of blood.

"Yeah," Ken said, but his eyes followed Brendan's to a telltale red spot on the tattoo-free area of his thigh.

Those weird, mismatched eyes zeroed in on Brendan's leg. With the extra illumination that would have allowed them to practice night golf if they'd been in less of a hurry, Ken had no trouble locating the bullet wound.

"It's just—" Brendan started, but Ken was having none of it.

"Don't fucking tell me it's a flesh wound, because I'm clearly seeing bone, you asshole," he hissed.

Shit. Brendan did *not* need to know that. Laughter bubbled out of him in an undignified snort.

"Geez. Nobody's ever let me pull that line. It's frustrating," he said, his laughter dying down as he watched Shinya approach them. The scarred yakuza had ripped off the too-white bandage Otter had put around his head, allowing a trickle of blood to run from his hairline down to his jaw.

"*Buji ka*?" Shinya asked and, by the way Ken glowered, Brendan supposed that was the yakuza equivalent of his flesh-wound line.

Ken let out a string of angry Japanese words, *baka* and *kodomo* repeated often enough for Brendan to pinpoint them, but in spite of the tone, Ken's eyes had a suspicious glint, while Shinya's stony face was changing from granite to limestone.

"Sorry to interrupt the family reunion, but we have a bunch of angry goons hot on our heels" came a deep voice from behind them.

Brendan smiled. His men had arrived, and seeing them as he'd done so many times—in formfitting wet suits, guns at the ready, looking cool and efficient—was Brendan's own family reunion. And damned if it wasn't making him get all emotional.

"Shit, boss," Otter drawled, "what'cha doing down there? Got one of those golf handicaps or something?"

He chuckled. So much for emotional reunions. "Yeah, or something. Now shut your fucking cock holster and help me stand."

"Hooyah, Mr. O." Otter held his arm, Burka moving in sync to grab Brendan's other arm as if he really was Otter's far-from-identical, mute twin. They helped Brendan to his feet, and he tested his wounded leg, cursing a blue streak when it wobbled under his weight and pain ratcheted to a dizzying point.

It turned out Shinya wasn't too steady on his feet either, so they made a rather lame—in every unfortunate sense of the word—procession toward the boat, Big B now helping Brendan while Shinya leaned on Ken.

Burka, Otter, and Tachibana covered their backs, though there wasn't much movement behind them now. Tachibana had properly disarmed the three men from the yacht, and the rest of the hostiles weren't literally "on their heels" as B had put it.

When they made it to the Zodiac, though, they found a little surprise waiting for them—or rather, very much *not* waiting for them.

"Where's Bobcat?"

They all looked at Shinya, but the yakuza shrugged. "He wasn't here when I woke."

Brendan closed his eyes for a second. Damn PTSD. Watching Shinya lie unconscious must have been too much for Bobcat, and there was no telling where he'd gone to hide. Or maybe Brendan was being unfair, maybe Bobcat had simply felt ashamed of his initial reaction and had tried to help them somehow.

Whatever he'd done, he hadn't left Brendan many options. Probably every other military corps had the same motto about not leaving any buddy behind, but the SEALs had actually lived up to the slogan throughout their history, and even though Brendan had left the corps, he wasn't going to start breaking the tradition.

They were going to find Bobcat, but they had to secure their primary target first.

"Okay lads," Brendan finally said in the way he used to address his men before an op. "Tachibana and Shinya are coming with me in the duck; we'll get Ken out of here. You three go find Bobcat. Avoid the west path to the villas, because that's where the yacht crew can come from, and we don't know how many armed men they've got left. You'll have to use one of the staff vehicles to exfiltrate. In case that fails, make for the sea and contact me; I'll come back for you as soon as I take Ken to safety. You still have your radio?"

Burka nodded. "Yes, Mr. O."

And wasn't it nice, being addressed like that with no trace of mockery, as if his authority was taken at face value, his commands respected because he was believed to know what he was doing? And why shouldn't it be so? He'd been trained by the best; he'd gained his stripes by dint of hard work; he had the skills and the combat experience. His pride had been wounded, yes, and he'd been holed up trying to hide from his own nightmares, sure, but he was here now, and he wasn't letting anybody down. Not ever again.

A thought suddenly crossed his mind. Bobcat might be suffering from PTSD, and maybe he would have let himself go, knowing his crewmen could manage without him even if he lost it. But there were other people in this op, civilians who hadn't been trained to fend for themselves, and one particular civilian Bobcat would never allow to come to harm.

"Burka," Brendan said. "Try to contact Kotarō. Find out where his team is."

CHAPTER 66

THE ROAD was dark, and there was no traffic in either direction, so Kotarō's mind had nothing to distract it from the same thoughts and images.

He was worried about the others, but somehow he was even more worried about the images that kept replaying in his head. Or not exactly worried but kind of freaked out by them.

It wasn't like he'd grown up in a shielded atmosphere. Shit, the boss had practically raised him, and the boss was a yakuza wakagashira. So violence was nothing he found strange, or surprising, or whatever, but maybe, in a way, it had never been this bad.

He'd been in some fights, ended up in the hospital when members of a rival gang had beaten him for crossing their territory, but he'd lived all his life without facing the barrel of a gun. Until today, that is.

It had scared him shitless, having that pistol pointed at him, but it had also surprised the hell out of him because of the look in that man's eyes. He knew that look very well; the men he'd grown up with had it, but exactly because of that, he'd learned to trust it, to tell the difference, to feel safe around the men whose eyes were hard around the edges, because he knew it meant they wouldn't hesitate to do whatever it took to protect their own.

The man in the mansion, he'd been *paid* to watch some rich dude's house, and yet Kotarō had been sure he would have pulled the trigger and shot Kotarō just for being there. It made no frigging sense. Or it made too much frigging sense, meaning you could have what it took to use a gun even if you didn't need to do it for any important reason.

Yeah, well, he guessed toddlers knew that, but somehow Kotarō hadn't actually believed it until now. He'd just thought bullies were full of shit, but as it'd turned out, bullies could sometimes cross the line into the world of big guns and real death.

And what kept nagging at Kotarō's thoughts was the notion that if some nitwit could cross that line, maybe it wasn't that hard to do, so what kept someone like the boss or Aniki from crossing it in any direction? What had kept Bobcat from killing the guard? Had he simply missed? He had killed the dogs, so he probably knew what he was doing, but what if he went crazy and started shooting everyone? What if he thought Kotarō and Big B's cousins were the enemy?

"Wot you tinkin', brah?"

He turned to Keawe. He and Kekoa didn't have the look; their eyes were somehow softer, more open, more full of laughter. Kotarō was sure they'd never shot a gun, but they'd risked their lives because their cousin had asked them to. It was all so frigging confusing.

He shrugged. "Just thinking sh… um, things."

Keawe nodded as if Kotarō had said some important shit. He kept silent for a moment and then turned to look through the rear window. Kotarō followed his look to where Bobcat sat on the bed of the pickup, his rifle within easy reach but hidden from the view of any other car that might go by, his eyes scanning the road tirelessly.

"Nahele gets li' dat too," Keawe said.

Kotarō frowned. "Nahele?"

"Our cousin, Big B," he said, dropping the pidgin for Kotarō's sake. "He's like your friend back there; he can be laughing at your jokes, but you can tell his eyes are watching everything, like, you know, really watching, as if someone was going to attack us any moment or something."

"Has he ever—" Kotarō shut his big mouth. Big B was Keawe's cousin; he didn't want the man to think he was insulting his family.

"Went mento an' shoot fo' nutting?" Kekoa supplied nonchalantly. "Nah. He stays solid."

Keawe shook his head, smiling. "Yeah, like he says."

"I didn't mean—" Kotarō tried to apologize, but Keawe waved a dismissive hand at him.

"I know, brah," he said. "You're just worried about that guy back there. He your friend?"

Kotarō nodded. "He saved my life. Before tonight, I mean."

"There you have it. He's saved your life twice. That kind of man isn't going to start shooting around just because he can, like that Samoan mofo back there."

"Yeah, but...." Kotarō hesitated. He didn't want to imply that Bobcat was a little crazy, but the man did act funny sometimes, and now that Kotarō had actually seen what he was capable of, he couldn't stop worrying. "He had some bad shit happen to him in Afghanistan, and now he gets all weird when there are loud noises or too many people or someone goes and moves something from one place to another."

"I hear you, brah," Keawe said. "Nahele did that too. He would shout at his little girl just because she'd taken one of his pencils, and then he would feel so ashamed he had to leave the house."

"'Ass right," Kekoa confirmed, "An' he nevah went to da mall."

"Yeah," Keawe said. "I guess there are things you can't unlearn, like Kekoa and me with the hula, you know? You watch a bunch of people with grass skirts and you probably think they're doing a great job, but Kekoa and I, brah, we've been dancing since we were kids. We can't stop seeing who's got the moves and who's faking it. Know what I mean?"

Kotarō wasn't sure what hula had to do with anything, but Kekoa explained it even better. "You no can train a dog fo' smell pakalolo an' den want him no bark at you wen you go smoke some, brah."

"You mean they can't stop being soldiers?" Kotarō asked.

"Warriors," Keawe said. "I'm sure soldiers can forget all about these idiots yelling drill commands at them, but they go to war, they come back all changed."

They kept silent for a moment, and Kotarō thought he was never going to forget that man pointing a gun at him, so he figured it would be impossible for Bobcat to let go of all the lousy shit that had happened to him.

"But your cousin Big B seems normal now," Kotarō said, "I mean—"

Keawe patted his arm. "I know what you mean. Your friend out there still acts a little out of it, but he'll get over it. Might need some help, though."

"You mean a shrink?" Kotarō asked, a little wide-eyed.

"Nah. Just something to let go of the anger, you know? Big B used to go ride some badass waves—Banzai Pipeline, Sunset Beach, the works—and there nobody heard him shout his head off."

They were silent again, and probably because of that, Kotarō heard the sound of another engine for the first time.

"Brah, I tink dat cah stays too close," Kekoa said, and when Kotarō turned to look, his eyes almost bulged out of their sockets when he saw Bobcat pointing his rifle at a big black SUV running behind them. And that was when the shooting started.

CHAPTER 67

"NICE OUTFIT. What's that, Dior nude?"

Brendan couldn't help chuckling, especially when Ken flipped Otter the bird. As it turned out, the senator's son could behave more like a punk than even Kinosuke. But the man could carry his weight too—literally.

Putting the Zodiac back in the water hadn't been easy, and Brendan had felt like a useless lump watching the others haul the rubber behemoth down the rocks under the harsh illumination of the golf course. Ken's "outfit" showcased the play of muscles needed to lift and control all that weight, the incredible tattoo on his back moving in a way that made the lion cub look as if it was actually climbing the inked ravine walls.

Brendan could count the man's ribs too. Mansion or no, Ken had been a prisoner and probably had been trying to come to terms with the fact that he might never see his lover or his friends again.

"Now Mr. O, don't glare at me. You know that leg won't hold you," Big B said, mistaking his anger on Ken's behalf for wounded pride at having to be carried onto the boat.

"Yeah, well, thanks for reminding me that I'm a damsel in distress," he said, actually feeling a little humiliated as B lifted him and hopped over the prow with Brendan in his strong arms. His only puerile comfort was that it took the big man some effort to do it.

Then came the fun part of distributing the weight of seven men over the madly rocking boat to avoid capsizing. Big B took the coxswain place, and Brendan and Otter straddled the gunwale—port and starboard—to show the others what they should do, Brendan's leg finding some relief in the rubber cushion under it.

Otter looked over his shoulder at Burka. "C'mere babe," he called, patting his own ass. "Check if I have panty lines."

Burka rolled his eyes but went dutifully to take his place right behind Otter, lying flat so that his body would not stand out against the wind, his head resting on his lover's hip. Of course Burka had no trouble doing that, but the look on the yakuza's faces when they understood that was the position they had to assume was outright comical.

Shinya looked from Brendan to Ken's almost naked body and hesitated.

"Hey guys," B shouted over the sound of the waves, "remember what Instructor Ellis used to say?"

Brendan met Otter's eyes, and they chorused, "This would be a lot more fun if we were all gay!"

They laughed like loons, the situation so familiar—the wetsuits, the rocking boat, the reckless laughter, even the pain from his wound—that Brendan felt right at home.

Shinya and Tachibana weren't laughing, though. They were doing what they excelled at: pretending the rude Americans didn't exist while they mentally debated the exact protocol for a yakuza captain's spouse when traveling by sea with a bunch of foreign devils.

To Brendan's surprise, Ken acted the part, his commanding voice clear as he looked at Tachibana. "*Ike!*" he shouted, and whatever that meant, Tachibana didn't hesitate; he jumped onto the boat, crouched low to avoid falling overboard, and turned carefully to help the next man.

Brendan was fascinated by Ken's knowledge of yakuza psychology. The logical thing given Shinya's head wound would have been for Tachibana and Ken to help him board next, but Brendan was sure there was no way Shinya would leave his cherished Kenshin-san alone on the rocks, and Ken knew it too, so the senator's son hopped gracefully over the bow and sat riding the gunwale behind Brendan with the dignity he would ride a tall horse, leaving Tachibana to help Shinya so he wouldn't lose face.

Geez. The intricacies of the Japanese mind. Ken taking the place behind Brendan had its meaning too, he guessed, because after Ken bent lower to mimic Burka's position, Tachibana and Shinya had no problem occupying the two places left, Tachibana behind Burka and Shinya behind Ken.

And right on time too, because no sooner had B recovered the painter and started the outboard engine than a group of men appeared on top of the rocks. Brendan wasn't worried about their guns, since the Zodiac would soon put enough distance between them to prevent bullets from doing any harm, but he'd seen one of the guys using his radio, and that could only mean one thing.

They left the cover of the rock promontory, and Brendan saw what he had expected—a fucking fast runabout heading straight at them from the mansion's dock.

THE PICKUP swerved a little, but Kekoa soon regained control of the wheel and floored the gas pedal, making Kotarō and Keawe swing in their seats as if they were in a bumper car. This was no fun, though, the sound of the bullets hitting metal too scarily close for Kotarō to pretend they were fake.

And Bobcat was out there without even the flimsy protection of the cabin walls. Kotarō supposed Bobcat must at least have flung himself down onto the floor of the truck's bed for cover, but Kotarō was too frightened to turn and check.

Then, the next time he flinched at a bullet hitting the cabin, his eyes caught a glimpse of something in the rearview mirror and he had to look up in shock.

"*Masaka!*" he exclaimed, and he and Keawe turned at the same time to look through the rear window.

Bobcat was there all right, but he wasn't lying flat on the floor. He was frigging kneeling on the bed of the truck, the left knee up to rest the arm holding the barrel of the rifle while he sat on his right foot, cool as you please, taking his time to aim while bullets flew everywhere.

"Aiyah!" Keawe shouted. "Wassamatta wit' dat mento buggah?"

Kekoa looked at the mirror, and the pickup swerved again, sending Bobcat against one of the side panels just as a bullet hit the rear window, shattering the glass in a zillion pieces that showered them with little sparkling blocks.

Kotarō couldn't help crying out, even though the glass pieces were not sharp, but he was scared to death, his hands shaking as he pressed himself against the door trying to disappear from view.

"You okay in there?" came Bobcat's voice from behind, but Kotarō couldn't answer for shit.

"Yeah, man," Keawe shouted back. "You do your thing; we're fine."

"Roger that," Bobcat replied. "Keep the truck steady."

"Easy fo' da buggah to say," Kekoa mumbled, and Kotarō felt as if everything was happening a very long distance away. He was frozen in place, trembling like a leaf, his mind drawing a blank, completely unable to process even the shame of acting like a chickenshit.

Keawe said something to him, but he couldn't understand it. He just burrowed himself farther against the passenger door, his position offering a clear view of the back that he certainly didn't need, but he couldn't move again, much less now that he could see Bobcat reassuming his kneeling position on the truck bed like a big, unmoving bull's-eye.

Bobcat's rifle went off, his body rearing back a little and then moving forward again to the same exact position, the sound of screeching tires forcing Kotarō to look at the SUV.

The big car swerved and slowed, its windshield suddenly decorated with a huge spider web of broken glass. Then the glass bulged for a moment as a booted foot kicked through it, pushing large blocks of material out of the way.

And then the car was closing in on them as if nothing had happened. Kotarō could see four men in the SUV, three of them armed with guns and shooting at the old piece of junk that was their pickup.

Bobcat was slow pulling the trigger, but every time he did, something happened. He ignored the bullets whistling all around him and first blew the black car's headlights out, one after the other, and then sent the gun of one of the men flying.

The road wasn't illuminated in this area and, without its headlights, the SUV driver could only see by the faint light reaching them from the pickup's own headlights. It didn't stop the big car, but it probably mucked up the shooters' aim, though Kotarō was too addled to tell the difference.

All he could see were the flashes of yellow light coming out of the muzzles of two guns and the now darker shape of Bobcat kneeling out there, his thin body recoiling briefly when his rifle did, his face lit for seconds at a time as if by those crazy-making strobe lights that froze people in the middle of their dancing, though nobody was dancing here. The explosions that came with every gunshot felt even unbearably louder than club music, and the shrill of the ricocheting bullets had Kotarō so wigged-out that he had to cover his ears with his hands to be able to breathe, and when he still couldn't pull air into his lungs, he opened his mouth like a dying fish and screamed.

He barely noticed it when Keawe pried his hands from his ears. He was shouting something, but Kotarō wasn't even looking in his general direction, he was looking out the rear window, looking at Bobcat, because Bobcat was looking straight at him and even though there wasn't much light to see his expression, Kotarō could still feel it like a pressure against his chest.

Only then did Kotarō realize that he'd been screaming for what felt like hours and shut his mouth abruptly.

"He's not hurt," Keawe said, and when Bobcat nodded, Kotarō heard once again the sound of bullets flying everywhere.

He blinked. Nothing had changed. He'd just managed to disconnect from it all for a few seconds. He shifted in his seat, too aware of his own body now, and looked up to find Bobcat was still looking at him as if he didn't quite believe Keawe.

It gave him a funny feeling, like the one time he'd watched a video about a mother cougar defending her cub against a huge grizzly bear and he'd wished he was as lucky as the cub to have someone who would chase the bears away. Only now it seemed he had a bobcat doing that for him.

"I'm fine," he croaked, then saw Bobcat nod and finally turn around to face the SUV.

He forced himself to at least watch in silence. It wasn't much compared to what Bobcat was doing, but it was all he could do—being as he was the frigging helpless, stupidly scared, wide-eyed little cub.

Bobcat lifted the rifle once again, aimed, and let both seconds and bullets pass by him unnoticed until he found what he wanted. And then he fired.

CHAPTER 68

"HOLD ON tight and keep your heads down!" shouted B for the three civilians' benefit, and Brendan hoped they understood it wasn't just an advice to keep them safe. They needed all the advantage they could get, and melding into the streamlined design of the boat would offer less resistance to the wind.

The runabout was one of those flashy affairs equipped with on-board LED lighting that gave the deck a bluish aura and the sort of underwater illumination that created a pool of green light around the stern.

They were so close to the sport boat now that Brendan could see the two men riding with the skipper. Thanks to the garish illumination, he could also see the weapons they were packing, and he guessed the senator's friend must have been at some submachine gun sale—either that or his men were all ex-Secret Service who'd been allowed to keep their old Uzis.

He turned and shouted at B, "Keep the distance!"

B gave him the okay sign. Not that he could go any faster with so many people on board, but he could avoid any maneuver that brought them closer to the runabout and its weapons.

The morons on the runabout must have been the other morons' cousins, because they started spraying the ocean with bullets and kept on shooting even when it was obvious they weren't hitting anything but ugly Hawaiian fishes with unpronounceable names. Maybe their Uzis came without the instruction manual that clearly stated they weren't effective at more than 200 yards.

He signaled Burka to take a look at the two hostiles. Burka lifted his finger to point at his own chest, then made a tunnel with his hand and raised it to his eye. Brendan gave back an affirmative sign. The rocking of the Zodiac made it difficult to hit anything, but if anyone could do it, it was Burka with his brand-new Accuracy International L115A3 sniper rifle—the same model that had been used recently in Afghanistan to establish the new world record for the longest sniper kill at 1.54 miles.

At the speed they were cruising, they were soon much closer than that fabled distance in a course that would end in collision if neither of the boats veered.

The runabout was positively faster, and even if B tried to steer wide, the sport boat would have no trouble intercepting them. And that was about to happen in a minute or three.

Still, Burka took his time to set the rifle, leaning on Otter's back for support, and Brendan had to smile at the look Burka received from his partner. Even in the poor light that managed to reach them, Brendan could almost touch the schmaltz.

Geez. Those two made the most weirdly cute couple he'd ever seen—followed very closely by the Matsunaga-Harris pair and their tattoos in matching yakuza style.

Tachibana had his head a little raised to watch Burka with professional curiosity, and Brendan noticed that he had drawn his pistol just in case. Unlike the runabout morons, though, he wasn't even trying to take aim yet. Good man.

Brendan turned to check how Ken and Shinya were doing and met two pairs of cool eyes in rapid succession. Ken pointed at Brendan's leg, and Brendan looked down to see a dark trail of blood running down the rubbery surface and into the sea.

Shit. It seemed Ken had a flair for highlighting things Brendan wanted to ignore. He couldn't focus on his wound right now, and it wasn't like they needed to walk anywhere anytime soon, so he was about to make a dismissive gesture when Ken pointed at his own chest and then mimed tying a knot.

Brendan had a hard time holding back a chuckle. This guy was amazing. Any other person without military training would be scared to death with all the shooting and the imminent danger of collision, but Ken Harris was trying to make a tourniquet for him, and the guy might even manage to find something to use when they were all wearing neoprene wetsuits and… silk boxers.

Bullets hit the water dangerously near the duck, the runabout closing the distance between them fast, even though B kept slightly changing their course to avoid interception. Brendan looked back to meet B's eyes, and B nodded.

"Hold on tight!" he shouted to Ken a second before Burka's rifle went off and the Zodiac did a one-eighty to head back to the rocks they'd started from.

Brendan looked over his shoulder and checked that nobody had fallen overboard. Burka shook his head at him, meaning that he hadn't hit his target, but when Brendan looked at the runabout, he could see that the windshield was all cracked. Close enough for a shot in those conditions, anyway, and it meant the skipper had to steer standing now. That, added to the wake B's maneuver had sent their way, created havoc inside the pursuing boat for the few more precious minutes it took the skipper and the accompanying morons to find their balance and reset the course.

Burka set his rifle again on its improvised human tripod, but the conditions were even worse now. The closer they got to the promontory ahead, the stronger the surf. B was expertly taking the high waves bow on, but since they were going at full throttle, they kept leaping over the crests and slamming down into troughs in their own fancy-rubber roller-coaster.

The runabout wasn't doing much better. In fact, it traveled beam on to the waves, and that made the sport boat roll like a bad DUI case.

They kept approaching the shoreline, so Brendan guessed what B was trying to do. During the days they'd spent conducting their recon, they'd used an outrigger canoe to map ocean conditions around the promontory to find the safest infiltration point. They had found the safest point all right, but they'd also found a little surprise under the surface—what their Aussie counterparts in the International Security Assistance Force in Afghanistan called a *bommie*.

It looked innocent enough on the surface, especially in good weather when it didn't even sport breaking waves, but you suddenly found yourself in a unexpected shallow area created by a submerged reef—or in this case a rock shelf—with the most dastardly dangerous eddies over it. And it was all but invisible at night.

Burka squeezed the trigger once again, with no result that Brendan could tell. The man was nothing if not patient, though, and he didn't even move from his position to prepare for the next shot in case he could inflict some damage.

The runabout was again closing the distance, the morons once again wasting bullets, but the skipper must not be a relation of theirs because he was steering smartly, coming at the Zodiac from their starboard, even though it was taking him longer to intercept them that way, but assuring that, when he did, the duck would be trapped between his boat and the shoreline with no room for evasive maneuvers.

That meant B had very little time left, but if he veered too soon, they'd only get a temporary relief since they couldn't outrun the sport boat forever. Their only hope was to outmaneuver it and pray that the skipper was not familiar with this area and didn't know where the bommie was—or was too distracted by the chase and the trigger-happy morons to remember it at this time of night.

To contribute his own distraction to the cause, Burka sent a shot their way and another in close succession, and then he went on a rampage and kept shooting until the morons started trying to duck out of the way.

When Tachibana began shooting too, Brendan realized they were close enough for short-range weapons to cause damage, which meant the submachine guns could now reach them and the vulnerable rubber keeping them afloat.

He narrowed his eyes to look over the prow, but he couldn't see a damn thing indicating where the bommie was—he would have to trust B to know exactly where they were and to veer before *they* hit the shallows themselves.

Bullets splashed ocean water right below the boot Brendan had hanging over the gunwale, so he drew his Glock from its holster. He was a worse marksman than either Burka or Tachibana, but he could add to the noise, make the morons ease up on their triggers until B did his thing, which was about to happen in—

"Hang on!"

That was all the warning they got before the Zodiac veered abruptly, crossed the runabout bow and ran down the other side like a half-witted pilot fish that couldn't quite make heads or tails of its host shark.

His hands still holding the pistol, Brendan made the mistake of using his legs to anchor him as the boat made the savage U-turn.

"Fuck!" he cursed as his wound pressed against the rubber, the pain so sharp that he lost his balance and was thrown into the middle of the Zodiac. He looked back over his shoulder, trying to check everyone else's positions, but his eyes were immediately drawn farther back to the point where the runabout rocked madly in the wake that B's maneuver had sent crashing at them from three sides, and before the skipper could regain a semblance of control, the sport boat was right on the eddy line of the bommie and caught in the strong current that hurled it against the treacherous rock shelf hidden under the surface.

"Tachibana-san!"

Brendan barely heard Ken's shout over the sound of the runabout crash, but he did see the man trying to stand and cross to starboard, where Tachibana had been before the duck changed direction.

His leg didn't allow him to act fast enough, but fortunately, Shinya's head wound had not addled his reflexes, and the scarred yakuza threw his weight down on Ken, effectively holding him against the gunwale. Yeah, these people had very good bodyguard instincts.

Brendan signaled at B to stop. The runabout wasn't going anywhere, and their occupants would now be too busy swimming their sorry asses to safety to cause any more trouble for the time being.

Otter nodded toward the sea, and Brendan gave the affirmative sign. They called him *Otter* for a reason, obvious in the fluid motion that brought his slim body into the dark waters—the man was as much in his element as the furry creatures, even at night and even if the ocean was a roiling mass of opposing currents this near to the shoreline. If someone could find Tachibana, it would be Otter.

The yakuza must have fallen overboard when B made the Zodiac veer. Burka and Tachibana had both been busy shooting, both hands on their guns, but Burka had been trained for this kind of combat and had held his position on the gunwale.

Tachibana hadn't found his sea legs in time, and Brendan could only hope the man had learned to swim.

CHAPTER 69

HOSPITALS WERE the same sorry affairs everywhere, but nurses treated people far more politely in Japan. This nurse was looking at the boss as if the man was offending her by blocking the view from her desk.

"Could you please tell me where to find Brendan O'Farrihy?" the boss repeated patiently.

Kinosuke was glad it wasn't him doing the asking, because by now he would have shouted something awful and been thrown out the door.

"You family?"

Yeah. Fucking Irish the whole lot of them.

"As I explained before," the boss said, his tone almost reaching the I'm-about-to-get-mad pitch, "he is a close friend, and he was in a fishing accident with a group among which we have family members—this lady's husband for one—who may be injured too."

The nurse looked wearily from the boss to Alma's anxious face.

"She the wife?"

Kuso. No wonder she worked the night shift, with that sharp wit of hers.

"Yes," the boss said, not bothering to clarify things further. And of course she reacted better to that than to all the previous explanations—maybe she couldn't process more than one word at a time. Go figure.

She checked her desktop for an eternity, and Kinosuke's leg started bouncing wildly. Shit. Brendan would be out of there before she found his damned name, and the worst part was not knowing if his condition would let him leave the place in anything but a body bag. Fucking closemouthed Burka and his fucking cryptic message.

"He's in Trauma," the nurse finally said, looking at them as if Trauma was a landmark as famous as Iolani Palace or some shit like that. When it was obvious no one was moving away from her precious desk, she added. "One floor down. Waiting room B5."

Kinosuke didn't wait for the boss to thank her before he was dashing for the elevator. A waiting room. That meant Brendan still didn't have a room, and that could only mean one thing Kinosuke didn't even want to consider.

"The blond man didn't say anything about Yoshinori being wounded, did he?" Alma asked for the hundredth time as they rode down to the basement.

Kinosuke snorted. The blond man. Transparent was what the fucker was—besides mute, that is. "Don't worry, Alma-san. Tachibana can defend himself. I'm sure we'll find him telling bad jokes in the waiting room."

It said something that the boss didn't add a single word to Kinosuke's this time. He must be worried to death about Kenshin-san, because the tongue-tied albino bastard had only said they had *secured the package*, which only meant they'd grabbed their gaijin and run for their lives. Kenshin-san's condition was anybody's guess.

As they poured out of the elevator and followed the signs on the green walls, Kinosuke found he was both anxious to get to the waiting room and scared to reach it.

Fuck. He was going to kill Brendan for turning him into a wet noodle. And what for? The asshole would give him a smug smile about rescuing Kenshin-san and then catch the first plane for the mainland—just supposing he was well enough to smile, and supposing Kenshin-san was well enough for the boss not to kill Brendan, and even supposing Tachibana was well enough for Alma not to stab the redhead with a cane knife.

"He got nervous, brah. You know how the big fuckers can look to someone who's never seen a shark before."

Kinosuke almost stopped short at the next corner. That was Big B's voice all right, but what the hell was he saying about sharks? Nobody had mentioned sharks. Burka hadn't mentioned sharks. Had Brendan been attacked by a shark?

He exchanged a look with the boss before they rushed ahead as fast as they could without actually running, not even bothering to look back to check if Alma was following. She couldn't get lost anyway.

"Well, yeah, but your friend shouldn't have been packing heat in the first place, man. This is a fucking mess."

He didn't recognize that voice. As the boss and he turned the corner and faced the open waiting room, the first thing that met their eyes was the broad back of a uniformed policeman.

Shit. It hadn't occurred to them that the police would have already caught wind of their little escapade.

Big B looked their way over the cop's shoulder, and the cop and his partner turned to follow the direction of his eyes. The two officers, a man and a woman, were native Hawaiian too, and almost as big as B, but rather on the chunky side, unlike B who was all muscled and athletic.

Movement out of the corner of his eye made Kinosuke turn to the left, and he almost gasped. Those mismatched eyes he would recognize anywhere, but the rest of the figure watching them intently was difficult to connect with the Kenshin-san he knew.

Someone had done a messy job of cutting the bleached strands the gaijin used to wear gelled into spiked points, and the short, disheveled mop only accentuated the dark lines under his eyes and the hollow cheeks.

Fuck. The man was so skinny it hurt to look at him. And why the fuck was he wearing green scrubs and flip-flops? The scrubs and B's wetsuit made it look as if they'd just left a costume party turned bad.

"Shigure...."

Oh shit. It was barely a whisper, but it sounded so broken that Kinosuke wanted to run and hug the silly gaijin to death even though it wasn't his name Kenshin-san was calling, so he couldn't begin to imagine what the boss was feeling.

The cops kept swiveling their heads to look from Kenshin-san to them, and the boss was frozen in place, looking angry, frustrated, and... in pain. Yeah. He looked for all the world as if seeing Kenshin-san like that was killing him.

And of course Kenshin-san knew all about wakagashiras and their fucking pride, so they just stood there with suffering expressions like Noh masks hanging on a wall.

"*Mattaku*," Kinosuke groused under his breath before he crossed the distance to Kenshin-san and gathered the scrawny body in his arms.

Screw it all. Wasn't this America, where everybody was touchy-feely and in-your-face? And weren't they trying to fit in? Well, that was what Kinosuke was doing, and by the way Kenshin-san half sobbed, half laughed against him, it was the damn right thing to do. The boss and his pride could go to hell.

"Where is my husband?"

Shit. He'd forgotten about Alma, and now that he thought about it, Kinosuke could see there was nobody else in the room, no sign of either Tachibana, or Shinya, or even Burka or Otter. Were they all wounded? Burka at least had made the call, so he must be all right; maybe he was just fetching coffee from the cafeteria or something.

"I'm sorry, Alma," B said, "I should have explained when I called, but I had to use the front desk phone, so I couldn't make it long." He added for the cops, "She's Tachibana's wife."

What the fuck? Burka had made the call, not B. Why was he lying?

"Tachibana?" The male cop asked. "The one who fell overboard?"

Alma gasped loudly, raising a trembling hand to her mouth. *Kuso*. Tachibana was not exactly a strong swimmer.

"He is—" B started, but there was a commotion in the aisle, and they all turned to see what was happening.

Kinosuke's glance met a pair of narrowed eyes scanning the room. The fucking Catman. At least that one was safe and sound, though *sound* was probably stretching it, given the way the man appraised them as if they were all enemies.

"Kenshin-san!"

A human missile darted across the waiting room and flung himself at Kenshin-san, Kinosuke's arms tightening instinctively around the gaijin until he realized there was no harm in the attack. It was just that hurricane Kotarō had finally arrived.

"*KUSO GAKI*," Aniki mumbled, but he didn't look mad, and Kotarō couldn't have stopped smiling even if he'd been ordered to by the cops in the room.

Wait. Cops? He disentangled himself from Kenshin-san.

"Why are these—" He stopped short when he took a good look at their gaijin. "Why are you wearing scrubs? You cut your hair? Man, you look like sh—Are you all right? You aren't wounded, are you?"

"More friends from the dojo?" the policewoman asked with a smile.

Big B chuckled. "Yeah. And this is my buddy, Roberto Catalán."

"Oh, another tough SEAL," the woman said as she shook Bobcat's hand without letting go, and Kotarō rolled his eyes. Dude, she was a frigging cop; she should know better than to go flirting like that. She was making Bobcat uncomfortable.

"Ex-SEAL, ma'am," Bobcat said, blinking.

"Ho, cuz!"

"Hey, Rodney, brah. Wot you doin' heah?"

Those were Keawe and Kekoa and they seemed to know the cop from the way they were slapping his back and all—if they'd done that in Japan, they would have ended up in jail for assaulting a police officer.

"You know these guys?" the policeman asked, waving a hand to include everybody in the room.

"Shuah," Kekoa said. "Dass my cuz Nahele, an' Nahele-dem go stay wit' us fo' da kine days."

The cop turned to B, giving him a serious look. "Since these two are your cousins, and I know where they live, we're going to let it run for now. But be warned that there'll be a follow-up, so don't leave the island before talking to us."

"Yeah," the woman added, "let us know when we can question your other friends."

She wrote down something on her notebook, tore the page, and handed it to Bobcat. "Call me if anything comes up," she said, and Kotarō couldn't tell why it sounded somehow dirty. Bobcat was blushing, so it must have sounded that way to him too.

"Yes, ma'am," Bobcat said, raising a hand halfway to his forehead before he realized what he was doing and dropping it—must have been the uniforms confusing him or something. The woman, though, she looked as if she liked Bobcat even more for almost saluting her.

Everybody watched in silence as the cops left, and then everybody was asking about everybody else because only Big B and Kenshin-san were there in the waiting room.

B lifted a hand for them to be quiet. "Let me explain," he said. "First of all, Alma, Tachibana is all right, they just have him in observation in case he still has some water in his lungs."

Alma's eyes filled with tears of relief, and Kotarō smiled at her. "They did that to me too. You don't have to worry, Alma-san. They run a slew of tests to make sure you aren't going to leave the hospital looking good and then sit watching TV and suddenly drown as if you were under water, because that's what happens if—"

Kenshin-san squeezed his shoulder, and he realized Alma was giving him a wide-eyed stare. "What Kotarō means," Kenshin-san said, "is that they're making sure nothing bad happens to your husband, Alma. Kotarō didn't suffer any consequences after he nearly drowned because they made sure at the hospital that he really was all right before sending him home."

"Yeah, his dumbness has nothing to do with swallowing salty water," Aniki said, and Kotarō couldn't even get mad because that was the kind of thing Aniki used to say before this mess started, and it felt good to have him back.

Now Aniki was looking at B. "What was that about a shark? I thought Brendan had been shot. And where're the others?"

"Is Shinya all right?" the boss asked, and Kotarō did a double take. Why was the boss over there when Kenshin-san was over here?

Kenshin-san was looking at the boss and biting his lip like he used to do when one of his drawings didn't come out right, Aniki was looking at the boss as if he wanted to hit him upside the head, the boss was glaring at B as if he was responsible for all the mess, and Kotarō didn't understand a single thing.

Big B lifted his hand again to calm everyone. "Shinya's got a concussion and has to be in observation for some more hours, but the doctors said he seems to be doing fine. As for Brendan, you know hospitals have to report gunshot wounds. Since Brendan and I are the only ones here with firearm licenses, we made up a story about inviting our Japanese friends to do some night snorkeling and one of them getting so nervous about a shark that he tried to shoot the animal with Brendan's gun, accidentally shooting Brendan instead. Also, I sent Otter and Burka out before the cops arrived. They're still active military. They can't get involved in a police investigation."

Kotarō felt even more confused than before. Why wasn't anybody asking more about Brendan-san?

"Is the boss man out of surgery yet?" came a voice from behind them all, and Kotarō turned to see Otter standing there with Burka. Man, they were so sneaky someone should hire them for one of those *Mission: Impossible* movies.

"Surgery?" Aniki repeated.

"Yeah, pretty Sensei," Otter said. "That's when they come at you with this sharp knife and cut you open to remove whatever strange stuff you've managed to put where it doesn't belong. You copy?"

"Otter—" Burka, B, and Bobcat called at the same time.

"You see, Kotarō?" Otter asked him. "That's an example of the white men's conspiracy that has kept our brothers under the yoke for centuries."

Kotarō didn't know what to say, but fortunately Aniki spoke before Kotarō could open his mouth and say something lame.

"How long has he been in there?"

Kenshin-san looked at him in an odd way. "Forty-five minutes give or take. He was shot in his leg, and the bullet was still inside his thigh. It looked as if it had broken bone too, and there was really no time to stop the bleeding because we were being chased."

Maybe Kotarō was imagining things, but Aniki seemed to be getting a little pale, and maybe Kenshin-san was seeing it too, because he hurried to add, "Still, he was conscious when we arrived, and his friends say he's survived much worse, so he's probably going to be all right. You know these things take time because they have to reset the bones and extract the bullet without causing more damage. It doesn't mean anything is going wrong, don't worry."

"Yeah, Sensei, don't you worry," Otter said. "Mr. O is a tough son of a bitch; he's gonna make it just fine. And by the way, Bobcat, boss man's gonna tear you a new one for that disappearing act you pulled on us. That was a serious goatfuck, buddy."

The way Otter said *buddy* sounded like an insult, but Bobcat just stood there without defending himself, simply glaring at Otter, and Kotarō couldn't bear it after everything the man had done for them.

"He came to help us!" Kotarō almost shouted. "We could have died if he hadn't come! That big guard was going to shoot us, and we couldn't leave the pickup because the two frigging dogs were outside barking their heads off, and we couldn't drive out of there because that piece of junk that Brendan-san made us drive with the goats was stuck in the ditch, and Bobcat heard it all over the radio and came as fast as he could and killed the dogs and took the gun from the Samoan and even showed us how to pull the pickup out of the ditch, and if he hadn't been there we would be frigging dead anyway because they followed us in a SUV that was ten times faster than the rusty pickup, and they were shooting at us all the time, and they sure would have killed us if Bobcat hadn't just kneeled there on the bed of the truck under all those bullets and shot out their windshield, their headlights, and then hit one of the tires when we were taking a sharp bend so the SUV started skidding and then rolled over, and still Bobcat made us stop to check that the guards were not dead before we could leave. So he didn't do that shit you said he did; he was just saving our frigging lives—just so you know."

Kotarō shut his mouth and found that everybody was staring at him.

"Jesus, Bobcat," Otter finally said, "are you gonna adopt this kid or what?"

B laughed, but Aniki threw one arm around Kotarō's shoulders and pulled him close.

"He already has a family," Aniki said, and he didn't exactly sound like he was joking.

"Now don't be like that, Sensei," Otter scolded him. "The more family one has, the better. And speaking of family, isn't that your man over there, Matsu-san? The man you haven't seen in… how many months? I don't know about him, but if it was me standing there after going through some traumatic kidnapping-plus-rescue experience, and you kept standing there as if someone had put a restraining order on you, I'd be mighty pissed off. But, hey, don't mind me. I'm just an ignorant American."

Oh shit. The boss was giving Otter one of his dangerous glares, but it was Kenshin-san who spoke instead of him.

"Yeah, you're an ignorant American with a big fucking mouth. And maybe if you and your SEAL cronies hadn't made such a production of rescuing the helpless hostage, Shigure and I wouldn't have to meet in a hospital waiting room without any trace of privacy. And I don't know about you, but if I'd made such a mess out of a simple operation against a bunch of civilian bodyguards and two fucking dogs—if I'd made such a clusterfuck out of it that my CO had to be taken to the ER with a bullet in him—I'd be mighty pissed off with my own fucking self."

The room was so silent that Kotarō thought even people on the first floor would hear him swallow. And before anybody could think of something to say, Kenshin-san was crossing the room in big strides and stopping right in front of the boss.

And dude, they scowled at each other as if they were both *mighty pissed off*, and then Kenshin-san went and said, "You look like shit."

Oh man. After so much time without him, Kotarō had forgotten how frigging reckless Kenshin-san could be. He was the first guy Kotarō knew who had stood up to the boss when the boss was a scary yakuza wakagashira.

Not that the boss wasn't still scary as he looked down at the skinny American in green scrubs and a crazy hairdo standing in front of him with his hands on his hips, but Kotarō noticed that the man's lips were twitching slightly, and when he finally opened his mouth, what came out was a hoot of laughter that Kotarō hadn't heard coming from Matsunaga-san in ages.

"Kuso gaijin," he said, and then he grabbed Kenshin-san and lifted him off the floor, he was hugging him so hard.

Otter shook his head. "Man, sometimes I just talk too much."

Burka gave him a blank stare. "Sometimes."

"Well, it can't be helped," Otter said seriously. "It's as much a part of me as my curly black hair. You take out the words, I might turn into a completely different person."

"Yeah. Your hair might come out white and straight," Burka agreed.

"Yeah, imagine that."

Burka nodded sagely. And his lips weren't even twitching.

CHAPTER 70

"GO HOME," Kinosuke said, though he knew the hotel was not exactly home, but Kenshin-san needed to rest. And to eat properly. And to put on normal clothes—or not exactly normal but at least not so obviously borrowed in a pinch.

The stubborn gaijin was already shaking his head. "We won't leave you and Shinya alone."

Tachibana had been allowed to leave with a teary-eyed Alma, and the Hawaiian bunch had taken Kotarō and Bobcat with them, but Shinya still needed to be in observation. And Brendan... Brendan was another fucking story. The bastard had managed to spend two hours in surgery and then been sent straight to ICU, because, hey, you know these simple thigh wounds? Well, it seems they can kill you if you take too fucking long to get to a hospital. Surprise, surprise.

"I can keep an eye on Shinya," Kinosuke insisted. "And the boss is gonna burst something if he doesn't take you home soon."

Kenshin-san chuckled. The boss had been pacing like a caged, grumpy old lion, and the gaijin had sent him to the cafeteria only two minutes ago.

"Nah," Kenshin-san said. "You know Shigure; if we leave here, he's going to worry about you and Shinya all the time."

Kinosuke didn't know about the boss, but Kenshin-san would sure worry about the whole lot of them, even about Brendan, though he barely knew the guy. Kinosuke hadn't realized how much he'd missed Kenshin-san's comforting presence until now.

He reached out and touched a ratty strand of bleached hair. He wanted to say so much, but it was all tangled up in this heavy skein inside his chest he didn't know how to disentangle. "Who cut your hair?" he asked lamely, and Kenshin-san's face softened as if he understood. Shit. He loved this damned gaijin.

"They wouldn't let me around anything sharp, so the cook took the fish scissors to my head," Kenshin-san explained.

"Figures. Kotarō would have done better."

"Well, yeah, but I'm not sure I could have escaped the mohawk."

He smiled. The mohawk was one of Kotarō's all-time fascinations, especially because the boss had never allowed him to get one.

"That guy Bobcat," Kenshin-san asked, his face going serious. "Is Kotarō safe with him? He seems a little bit... intense."

Kinosuke couldn't help snorting at the choice of words. "Intense? The fucking Catman is a serious whackadoodle. They say he's got this traumatic disorder shit from Afghanistan, but I bet he was one of those crackpot hillbillies who sleep with their rifles even before he joined this gang of military crackpots who sleep with their rifles."

Kenshin-san laughed, and Kinosuke found himself smirking. "You know what I mean," he said, waving a dismissive hand.

"Yeah. It's pretty obvious what you mean," Kenshin-san said. "But you didn't speak up when the *Catman* left with Kotarō, so I guess you trust him to take care of the kid in spite of the wackiness."

Kinosuke nodded. "I don't know why, but with Kotarō he's like a man on a mission—and not just because he keeps pulling him out of trouble. He's always looking out for him, helping him with his studies, trying to teach him things—I don't know, just being there in case Kotarō needs him."

He flushed a little. Those were exactly the things Kinosuke had stopped doing for Kotarō, so, in a way, he had to be thankful for the Catman's presence. And if that was absolutely fucked-up, only Kinosuke was to blame.

"Kinosuke...."

He looked into those weird eyes. He'd nearly forgotten how disquieting that gaze could be, especially because those eyes seemed able to see further and deeper than the ordinary, dull-colored ones.

"It's not your fault, Kinosuke. We've all been out of sorts since we came here, trying to adapt and not doing a great job of it. It's been a big change, and we've all made mistakes."

Oh, that was rich, coming from the man their mistakes kept putting in danger. "Yeah? And what mistakes have *you* made?" he said, his voice rising out of his control.

"You want the whole list?" the gaijin answered, his voice rising too, his long fingers lifted to count out. "It was me who forced you to leave everything you knew to bring you to a foreign country, me who put you all on my father's radar without taking any steps to protect you, me who enrolled Kotarō in a school where he was bullied, me who gave you a job you probably hate, me who made Shigure throw his whole life to the wind, me who forced you to risk your lives and your futures to get me out of my father's clutches, me who's got someone you care about shot, me who—"

Kinosuke reached out and caught the pale hand in his. "Stop it, damn you," he said in a whisper, because it fucking hurt too much to feel all that guilt, all that pain Kenshin-san had been carrying around, and not have the words to get through to him how wrong it all was. "We fucked up your life, and in exchange you gave us a home, so yeah, I guess you made a big mistake."

The gaijin shook his head furiously. "You didn't fuck up my life; you saved it. You gave me a family, and believe me when I tell you that's something I never had."

"No shit."

It just came out that way, his mouth simply blurting it out as if he had no brain to speak of, and Kenshin-san was giving him a wide-eyed stare. Fuck. How stupid could he be? Kinosuke was about to apologize when the crazy gaijin started laughing, and he found it so hard not to join him that soon they were both hooting like lunatics in the silent hospital aisle.

"I forgot you've met my brothers," the gaijin said, still laughing.

"Yeah, it was fucking instructive." And he couldn't suppress the urge to add, "I especially liked Miles. He's such a people person."

That got them going again, until they both seemed to remember where they were and sobered fast. The silence that followed was comfortable, and even though Kinosuke knew some day he'd have to apologize formally to Kenshin-san, he felt he was already forgiven, maybe had been from the beginning, but he hadn't been able to see it because, well, because he was as stubborn and stupid as they came.

"Can I ask you something?" he said tentatively and had to smirk when the gaijin rolled his eyes. "Okay. It's just that... I was wondering...."

Fuck. He could blurt out the most inconvenient things, but he couldn't even mention what was driving him mad.

"You want to know how I knew?" Kenshin-san asked, and Kinosuke tried to pretend he didn't understand. "How I knew about Shigure being *it* for me?"

Kinosuke couldn't find his voice, so he just nodded, and the gaijin got a smile going as if he was suddenly in a faraway place or in a time long past.

"I knew it when just being in the same room was enough for me." Kenshin-san's focus was back on Kinosuke, and he hurried to explain. "Don't get me wrong—I don't mean I'd just be happy standing there looking at him from a distance, but it was as if my whole body relaxed when he was around. He made me feel safe, made me feel I was in the right place; just the way you feel when you open the window to a stuffy room and find you can breathe again. Know what I mean?"

Yeah. He fucking knew. When Brendan was around, Kinosuke couldn't stop cursing him for one thing or another, but it was worse when he wasn't even there, because then all Kinosuke got was this ache he couldn't dull whatever he did.

"You...?" Kenshin-san didn't finish the sentence, but it didn't really matter.

"Yeah," he answered, a blush creeping up his cheeks and making him as angry as everything else in this fucked-up situation. "But as soon as he opens one eye, he's gonna hightail it back to his fucking upscale Washington life. If the stubborn bastard makes it out of ICU, that is."

A pale hand touched his, and he realized his own knuckles were as white as Kenshin-san's, he was squeezing his fists so hard. He loosened his fingers, and the gaijin petted them as if rewarding a good doggie.

Kinosuke smiled. "Sorry. I'm being silly."

"Don't apologize. It comes with the territory."

He frowned. "What territory?"

"I mean that you're supposed to act silly when you're in love," Kenshin-san said, and Kinosuke's eyes widened. That was what they'd been talking about, he guessed, but to actually hear the words made his stomach lurch. He was in love? With that smug, pigheaded, homely American? The man had freckles, for crying out loud. And was a fucking supersoldier to boot. Well, had been, but nobody seemed to have told him he wasn't anymore—they wouldn't be waiting here for him to make up his mind between living and dying if someone had.

"Kinosuke?"

He looked up to find the gaijin watching him with amusement, and he blushed again. "I thought you were just asking me if I liked him, not, you know, the other... shit," he stammered.

"Uh-huh." Kenshin-san was fighting back a smirk, the bastard. "So I take it he doesn't know about your, um, feelings?"

"My feelings?" Kinosuke snorted. "He doesn't even know my fucking name—"

"Is there a Yonekawa-sensei here?" a man in a white lab coat asked, and Kinosuke raised his hand. "Okay. Follow me. The patient is asking for you."

He followed in a daze, vaguely hearing Kenshin-san's laughter over the din his heart was making.

CHAPTER 71

BRENDAN FOUGHT back the urge to close his eyes and surrender to the drug-induced drowsiness. Or was it a result of blood loss? No, most likely of outright idiocy.

He should have known better. He was a highly trained SEAL officer, for Christ's sake; he should have taken the time to treat his wound. Just as Ken had suggested. Ken Harris, a civilian who had only seen combat wounds on TV.

The doctors had told Brendan he almost didn't make it off the surgical table, that only his age and his level of fitness had kept him alive. He supposed the fact that he would have made a busy ghost might have helped too—the list of things he still needed to get done was so long that he could restock a wallpaper store with it. And at the top of that list was a serious conversation he'd been delaying until it almost had been too fucking late.

The green curtain around his bed wouldn't offer much privacy, but when the doctors had tried to convince him to wait until he was moved to a room to receive visitors, he'd used as much as he could pull of his command voice and told them it was a matter of life and death. Yeah, well, it seemed he wasn't going to die from the leg wound, but it had been a close call, and it certainly had put the rest of his life in perspective.

"No more than ten minutes," the nurse said to someone outside, pushing the curtain open. "He'll be taken to a room very soon, and you can stay with him there if you want to."

"Thank you," a familiar voice answered.

The curtain was pulled back into place, but Brendan couldn't have cared less. Even if the whole Bolshoi Company had decided to perform in front of his bed, all he would have seen was the young man standing there glaring at the cast on Brendan's leg.

Look at that. Kinosuke was wearing his suit, and the fact that he had come running straight away, without taking the time to change, made Brendan feel even warmer in the already warm hospital.

His sensei looked drop-dead gorgeous in that suit, too, his usual cockiness replaced by a sedate elegance that made him appear more mature. It failed to give Kinosuke the sensei solemnity he was always after, though Brendan would die before revealing that it put Kinosuke more on the runway model side of things than the Zen master one.

"Sensei," he started, his voice still so weak and raw that he had to swallow hard to be able to go on, and that second was all it took for Kinosuke to fix him with a fiery stare and burst into a tightly controlled explosion of angry words.

"You stupid fuck. You had to be the only one who got shot in the whole fucking bunch—a pair of old yakuza who don't even know how to spell Zodiac did better than the almighty SEAL. Who the hell trained you? Homer Simpson? And did he tell you that supersoldiers didn't fucking bleed, or was it one of the five clever-clogs ideas a day your water-shrunk brain comes up with? No, I suppose it's just that you're too fucking tough to stoop to getting a tourniquet—that's only for staff weenies, not for beyond-compare-special special operators descended from a long line of reckless Irish warriors."

It was almost funny to hear all that rage delivered in a barely more than whispered tirade. Kinosuke's ingrained politeness wouldn't let him disturb the other patients, and the way he shook with the effort to control himself was so fucking adorable that Brendan's heart was about to trigger the pulse monitor's alarm.

"Sensei…," he murmured, reaching out a hand and making all the wires and IV lines rattle in the process.

Kinosuke watched the hand as if it would bite him, and Brendan waited patiently for him to acknowledge the peace offering. Finally, strong fingers closed over his, but Kinosuke still wouldn't meet his eyes.

Brendan pulled at the hand holding his. "C'mere," he said softly, his voice choked with all the contradictory emotions that threatened to drown him, the need to wrap that beautiful man in his arms the most overwhelming of his feelings.

Kinosuke looked up, pain and anger still making those black eyes burn fiercely, but Brendan saw other things there, things he couldn't very much sort they were so fused, things that made his strong, defiant sensei look as lost and vulnerable as a little child.

"God, Sensei," he rasped, pulling so hard at Kinosuke's hand that the young man lost his balance and crashed halfway on top of Brendan.

Brendan welcomed the weight on his chest; it seemed to give a rational cause to the pain he felt there, his arms immediately rising to encircle Kinosuke in a protective cocoon, his fingers moving restlessly to stroke the soft black hair, the long arms, the tense back that slowly relaxed in his grip until powerful sobs racked the lean body.

"Shhhhh. It's okay, baby," he hushed. "Everything is going to be fine."

"I thought you…," Kinosuke mumbled against Brendan's shoulder.

"I know," Brendan said, never stopping the soothing motions of his hands. "I'm sorry I frightened you. I was stupidly careless."

"You bet you fucking were, you blockhead" came the muffled reply.

He couldn't help smiling. "I'm sorry, Sensei."

Kinosuke lifted his head, watching him closely as he wiped his eyes. "Don't you *sensei* me, you fucking schmuck."

"All right, Kinosuke-san."

God, how he loved teasing this sexy man.

"Are you fucking with me?" his sensei asked, suspicious as hell but not making much effort to remove himself from the support of his human cushion.

"Nope," Brendan said, trying to sound serious. "But I can only wish."

The look in those eyes when Kinosuke realized what he'd said was priceless, a blush trying to show under the golden skin, and right after the blush, the swift anger of the streetwise kid who reached out and smacked Brendan a good one upside the head.

"*Aho.*"

"Ouch." Brendan made a show of rubbing his head. "It's not fair to take advantage of the wounded. And what's that you just called me?"

"Look it up, you nitwit," Kinosuke said, then added under his breath, "It's about time you learned some fucking Japanese words."

Brendan smiled like a fool. His sensei wanted him to learn his language, and that was the closest to a long-term commitment either of them had ever dared to mention. Still, he didn't want to further embarrass Kinosuke by showing that he'd caught his meaning, so he tried to go for a light tone. "I'd love to learn fucking Japanese words."

Kinosuke huffed, his blush trying to come back with a vengeance, and that obviously irritated him so much that he raised his hand as if to smack Brendan again. "You—"

And of course that was the moment the orderly chose to pull the curtain open and push a gurney inside.

Kinosuke shot to his feet, almost crashing against the IV pole in his haste to put distance between him and the bed. Under other circumstances Brendan might have found it funny, but now he just felt he had let time slip and failed to say what he wanted— needed—to say.

"You'll have to wait outside, sir," the orderly said in a surly tone meant to show Kinosuke wasn't letting him do his job.

Brendan cringed at the way Kinosuke just nodded, his shame so powerful he couldn't even find his voice, his whole posture cowed as he retreated without even looking back at Brendan. And for once Brendan understood how selfish he had been every time he would get angry at the thought that this shame was all about him, about Kinosuke and him being seen together.

No, his sensei was not ashamed of the bond between them; he was ashamed of himself in the way only kids growing up without means and education are, the way that meant they were painfully aware of their own inadequacy.

Brendan could relate to that feeling because he'd experienced it firsthand when he had started operating in the District's elitist circles. Craig had helped him navigate those waters, but still, deep inside, he'd always felt way out of his depth.

He couldn't even begin to imagine how that would have felt if he'd been a newcomer in this country, having to keep his past a secret, his only source of pride a new occupation that hadn't yet proved to be even mildly successful.

Brendan understood, and because he understood and this was Kinosuke, the man he loved, he wasn't going to let it run, wasn't going to let some disgruntled orderly make that strong, smart, capable man feel ashamed.

"Yonekawa-sensei!" he called, startling the orderly in his fumbling with monitor wires and drip tubes, but Brendan could tell with grim satisfaction that the man had heard the honorific attached to Kinosuke's name and was discreetly looking up when Kinosuke reappeared by the pulled curtain. Yeah, this was Hawaii, and the Japanese here had a high status—probably many of the doctors the orderly worked under were of Japanese descent, so the man knew *sensei* meant much more than idiosyncratic martial arts teachers.

"Sensei," Brendan said in his best no-bullshit voice, "there are still some important matters I need your advice on. Would you please come visit me later?"

The change in Kinosuke was immediate. He straightened his spine, his suit adding weight to his seriously professional persona. "Of course. I'll be back after you rest some."

Brendan felt warmed deep inside. Kinosuke was dying to get out of here, but still he worried about Brendan's health. "Arigatō, Sensei."

The small, almost private smile on those luscious lips was all the reward Brendan needed. Nobody looked down on his sensei. Not on his watch. Not ever again.

CHAPTER 72

BRENDAN LET his lips curve in a wry smile. Craig preceded him as they both followed the senator's assistant, and Brendan could tell Craig's eyes had drifted down to the assistant's backside.

The amusement Brendan felt was a little surprising. Before his trip to Hawaii, he would have been fuming in silence every time Craig checked out another man's ass, and the consequent raised eyebrow from Craig would have ashamed him, sure that his *primitive* jealousy made him a military cad.

Now he didn't care much how Craig acted, and Craig's opinions on the outdated concepts of fidelity and monogamy slid down Brendan's skin like rain water. He even understood how Craig had manipulated his ex-soldier insecurities, but Brendan couldn't seem to care enough to feel resentment.

Craig had used him but, in a way, Brendan had used Craig too. The refined lawyer had helped him navigate the District's murky waters, and Brendan had learned a lot at his side. Ultimately Craig wasn't what Brendan wanted or needed and, with his newfound confidence, Brendan knew he couldn't blame Craig for being aloof—you didn't blame a shark for being cold-blooded.

Confidence felt as unfamiliar as his new suit, and not in bad way. He had chosen the olive-green suit without thinking and had been pleasantly surprised when Craig had praised it. But he would have worn it even if Craig hadn't liked it, and that made all the difference in the world.

Now that Brendan knew exactly what he wanted, he couldn't care less what people thought. The needle in his compass had stopped moving wildly, no more swayed by the magnetic pull of a myriad of different forces around Brendan. Now the needle pointed steadily in one direction—toward a place far warmer than the North Pole.

With that destination in mind, it was easy to steer clear of obstacles. He had even accepted Craig's invitation to stay in his apartment for as long as it took Brendan to tie all the loose ends of his life in the District. For all his advocacy of open relationships, Craig understood clearly what Brendan meant when he said he had someone in his life now.

And for all his detached nonchalance, Craig had realized how important it was for Brendan to tie this particular loose end and had surprised Brendan with his offer to help.

They passed the third cheap print of what Craig would no doubt consider a deplorable hunting scene. It was pompously framed like a baroque still life, and Brendan watched Craig give the print a glance and make a disgusted face. Yeah, it seemed Senator Harris was a philistine on top of everything else.

Brendan let his smile turn predatory. He was going to enjoy this. He would have done it any way he could—he owed Matsunaga the insurance he and his men had fought so hard for, and Brendan's own men deserved to get their long overdue payback. But this was no doubt Craig's area of expertise, and Brendan was more than content to simply watch the lawyer work his magic.

"Senator? Mr. Kalbson is here."

The assistant motioned them inside and closed the door without a noise, but the senator didn't even look up from the papers on his desk as he said, "Take a seat, Mr. Kalbson. I'll be with you in a moment."

So that was how things stood. Brendan wasn't impressed, and Craig showed no sign that he cared—the lawyer was an old dog at this game, not easily intimidated by the likes of Senator Harris.

Instead of taking the obvious seat in front of the tall desk, Craig ambled back to the couch and armchairs around the coffee table and sat in the biggest chair, taking his time to extract his Netbook from his Armani briefcase.

Brendan stood behind Craig's chair, easily slipping into his usual bodyguard role. He hid his smile when he saw Craig was typing a grocery list.

"Mr. Kalbson?"

That half-annoyed tone was very satisfactory and, as usual with District types, the senator ignored Brendan's presence—any kind of protection specialist was for them like the cheap prints on the wall, an often misguided attempt at decoration.

Craig turned in his seat. "Please call me Craig, Senator."

"Well, Craig, what can I do for you?"

The senator was taking a defensive position behind his desk, and that would put them at a strategic disadvantage. Craig had to lure him out.

Craig put on his most innocent expression. "Wouldn't you be more comfortable here? I'm sure this couch looks inviting after the long desk hours your constituency must extract from you," he said with an ingratiating smile.

The senator grunted as he stood, his annoyance clearly smoothed away by the flattery.

Harris was a rather pudgy man, his square jaw giving him an air of determination that could have inspired trust if it hadn't been for his narrow, calculating eyes.

His dressing style was conservative—the old-fashioned navy suits—but he'd chosen some kind of tablecloth pattern for his tie that Brendan knew no self-respecting image consultant would have suggested. Which meant his wife probably chose his clothes for him. No surprise there since the senator was a confirmed tightwad.

The leather couch made an undignified hissing sound when all that political weight landed on its surface, and the senator found himself having to look up at Craig, his genial expression not quite managing to hide his aggravation. Point for Craig.

"How can I be of help?" Harris asked, folding his hands in his lap like a staid, attentive teacher.

"Well, Senator, I hope *I* can be of help in this case."

Harris studied Craig, probably trying to anticipate where the conversation was going.

"You see," Craig went on, "I learned by chance that your sons had been negotiating a deal with Hanseiki Corporation."

The senator straightened at the mention of his sons, but Brendan could tell he was mostly expecting to be asked for some favor, so he wasn't overly concerned yet.

"For some reason," Craig said, "that company sounded familiar to me, so I did a bit of research out of curiosity, and I soon found out why the name had rung a bell." Craig paused for effect. "The data I unearthed made me remember that corporation's name had come up in a case concerning yakuza activity in our country."

That surely got the senator's attention. Craig added with a candid face, "I suppose you've heard of the yakuza, the Japanese Mafia?"

Now Harris felt insulted, and that put him enough off-balance to blurt, "Of course I know who the yakuza are. I had a very close encounter with those bast... gangsters."

A sore spot, no doubt. One that Craig would exploit. "How awful. I had no idea they'd become so bold as to attack a US senator. How did that happen?"

Harris was obviously torn between the need to express his frustration and the mistrust ingrained from his years in office. And obviously he wouldn't have come this far if he'd taken lawyers at face value.

The senator waved an impatient hand at Craig. "Never mind that. You are mistaken about that company's yakuza connections. My sons' legal consultants made sure everything was legitimate in this deal; Hanseiki Corporation is a perfectly respectable resort management firm."

If Brendan hadn't known about the senator's suspicions concerning the deal, he still would have guessed Harris had his doubts by the heated way he argued on the contrary. A truly innocent party—or someone with more self-control—would have shrugged or directed Craig to his sons for answers. Harris was no fool, though, and he seemed to have realized his mistake. He was now quickly backpedaling into the tried and true I-look-after-my-family excuse.

"I followed the negotiations closely—after my previous experience with the Japanese, I wanted to protect my sons—but you should talk to Miles or Campbell. They'll be happy to dispel your concerns."

Craig smiled. "Oh, I'm sure they'll be happy to *try*, Senator, but I'm afraid my concerns spring from solid evidence they'll never be able to gainsay."

"My sons have nothing to hide, Mr. Kalbson."

So it was back to Mr. Kalbson. Craig lifted both hands in the classic placating gesture. "Of course, sir. It was never my intention to suggest any foul play on your sons' part. If I'm here, it is because I'm sure they don't even know who the Shinagawa-gumi are, much less suspect they have any connection with the hospitality company they've been dealing with."

But of course the senator did know about the Shinagawa-gumi, as well he should after the gang had allegedly kidnapped the son Harris never seemed to include when he said "my sons."

"You mentioned you had evidence that Hanseiki Corporation has yakuza connections," Harris said, his tone dry but not yet hostile—he seemed to be playing it safe, testing the waters before plunging in headfirst.

"Let me show you," Craig said, retrieving a thick folder from his case. "This is Hanseiki Corporation's financial report. I'm sure this is more or less what your sons' consultants provided, and it shows that the company is not only legitimate but pretty solid too."

Harris took his time checking the documents. "What's the problem, then?" he finally asked.

"The problem is well hidden," Craig said. "So much so that I wouldn't have found anything if that case I mentioned earlier hadn't been such an eye-opener."

He offered the senator another document. "I'm sure you've noticed this Heiwa Bank is mentioned several times in Hanseiki Corporation's report as cofinancier in many of its projects." When Harris nodded, Craig went on. "The bank profile is unobjectionable, but you'll see on page three that another bank appears as a frequent strategic partner, Fukueki Finance Corporation."

Craig waited for the senator to flip to the page in question. "As it turns out," he explained, "Fukueki Finance is not properly a bank, but what the Japanese call a *sarakin*. Simply put, sarakin are loan companies that cater primarily to wage earners. Before the government limited the interest rates they could charge through the Sarakin Regulation Law of 1983, those interests were much higher than the ones banks charged, which made it a profitable business for the yakuza—who had their own means of enforcing debt collection, as you can imagine.

"After the law was passed, though, many banks stopped financing the sarakin companies, causing a lot of the loan sharks to go bankrupt. Fukueki Finance is one of the survivors, and, as you may have already guessed, it is owned by the Shinagawa-gumi, one of the two most powerful yakuza gangs in Japan."

A tense silence filled the room, and Brendan could almost hear the senator's mind gears working at top speed.

"I take it you have evidence that this Fukueki Company belongs to the yakuza," Harris finally said, trying to find a weak point in Craig's exposition.

"Of course." Craig handed over more documents. "Here is the original Japanese text, and here you have the translation. The Shinagawa have enough business acumen to use front companies for most of their operations, so this sarakin is an affiliate of their Ebisu Group, as you can see here."

Brendan had been amused to see Craig's surprise at exactly how business-savvy the yakuza were. Craig and Kitahara's videoconferences had been priceless—the cool District lawyer exchanging financial subtleties with a gangster who spoke like a Harvard business graduate and wore Gucci glasses.

"Well, you must admit these are really faint connections," Harris said, sounding too relieved for Brendan's purposes. "Even if the Shinagawa own Fukueki, this company is no more than an infrequent strategic partner to a bank that only appears to finance Hanseiki Corporation's projects on occasion. I don't think my sons need to be concerned about this."

The senator was almost smug, but Brendan had no doubt Craig would do something about it.

"I might have agreed with you," Craig said nonchalantly, "if I hadn't found this."

Craig produced yet another document, a property deed this time. Brendan had been nothing if not thorough in his evidence gathering, and Harris was looking satisfactorily worried again, even though he tried to stall for time.

"What does this prove?" Harris asked in a defensive tone. "Fukueki purchased some land in Hawaii—so what? Many Japanese companies do."

"Not so much these days, I'm afraid," Craig answered, "not after the investment boom of the 1980s. That's why this particular acquisition drew my attention. If you're not familiar with the terms of the agreement presented to your sons, the location of this property won't mean anything to you, but these 19,000 acres Fukueki bought are to be developed into a luxury resort by Hanseiki Corporation, the very resort your sons were offered the chance to invest in."

Before Harris could open his mouth to argue, Craig added, "And yes, Senator, I can prove it."

Craig produced a bulging folder with a copy of the contract Brendan had given him and pushed it across the table to the senator. "You'll find the exact location of the property on page fourteen."

Harris didn't go further than the first page. "How did you get your hands on this?" he asked indignantly.

"I'm not about to reveal my sources, as you can imagine," Craig said, waving an impatient hand. "And in any case, that's not what is at stake here. Your main concern now is that, for all purposes, your sons have just signed a contract with the yakuza."

CHAPTER 73

IT WASN'T a pretty sight, Harris's pudgy face all flushed with righteous indignation, and for the first time, the senator looked directly at Brendan.

For a moment Brendan thought Harris would recognize him. Brendan knew he'd lost some weight during his convalescence, and both his longish hair and slightly tanned skin gave him a different look, but any observant person would have no trouble identifying his freckled face. He put on his best bored bodyguard expression and waited.

"You're taking this too far, Kalbson," the senator finally said to Craig. "And I'm not sure we should have this conversation in front of your...." He made an impatient gesture, as if not finding the right word irritated him. "Why have you brought him anyway?"

So the senator didn't remember Brendan. Not surprising, but slightly disappointing. It would have been worthwhile watching the senator's expression if he'd remembered, because at this point Harris could not reveal he knew Brendan was anything other than a security consultant the senator had hired for some minor surveillance job.

Craig waved a dismissive hand. "Never mind him. One of my clients has managed to acquire a few enemies, and my partners at the law firm thought I should have constant protection. He's signed a nondisclosure agreement, so please ignore he's even here."

The senator looked from Craig to Brendan and back, then said peevishly, "My sons would never deal with gangsters."

"Not willingly, they wouldn't," Craig replied in a soothing tone. "I didn't come here to insult your family, Senator. I came to relay this information so you can make a decision about it—I shudder to imagine what some unscrupulous elements out there could do with this now that election time approaches."

The threat was out in the open, and the senator caught up quickly enough. "Well, if that's your concern, Mr. Kalbson, you can rest assured that I'll deal with any unscrupulous elements as they appear."

"And how will you do that—if I may be so bold?" Craig asked, and Brendan noticed Craig was trying not to sound too smug about the recovered "Mr."

"Well, it's quite simple," Harris said. "If what you say is true, my sons' lawyers have ample grounds for rescinding the contract."

This was exactly the turning point Brendan had been eager to reach, and Craig didn't disappoint. "Oh, I wouldn't do that, if I were them."

Harris tilted his head like a big, ugly dog. He was smelling danger, but he couldn't be sure of what kind yet. "Why not?"

"As I told you, I'm sure your sons had no idea they were dealing with the Shinagawa, but they did sign the contract, and you know how those Japanese types can get. If your sons try to rescind their agreement, the Shinagawa will consider it not only a breach of contract but a breach of honor too."

Craig paused, seemingly enjoying the tense silence before dropping another less-than-subtle hint. "I suppose I don't need to tell you how the yakuza can react if they feel insulted."

But of course Cedric Aloysius Harris was not the kind of man who would let a bunch of Asian ruffians intimidate him, and so he did what most self-important men do under similar circumstances—he reverted to anger to cover his fear. "Miles and Campbell are the sons of a US senator. They are well protected against scum like that. No yakuza could get close enough to lay a finger on them—just let them try to set foot on the mainland and see how we deal with trash around here."

"As far as I know, Senator," Craig said slowly, "the Shinagawa don't even need to try to reach the mainland. They are already well established here, and when I say well established, I'm talking about solid business networks—solid enough that they could hire others to do the dirty work for them. And now that you mention it, didn't you tell me you've had some bad experience with them? As a US senator, aren't you supposed to be protected?"

Harris gestured impatiently. "That was not me. It was Kenneth—my youngest— and he brought that upon himself."

Brendan clenched his teeth. He hated all these righteous bastards who'd never suffered any kind of violence and still had the nerve to claim victims brought violence upon themselves. And the senator was talking about his own son, even though he had carefully avoided using the word.

Kenneth, he'd said—not Ken, or Kenny, or something that might have indicated a bit of affection—was *his youngest*. He might as well have been talking about one of his pet horses.

Now more than ever Brendan willed his plan to work, because Ken deserved to be free from this sorry excuse for a father.

"Excuse me if I put it bluntly, Senator," Craig said, not hiding a good dose of sarcasm, "but you seem to have this quaint notion about the yakuza being a bunch of sword-brandishing, mindless thugs that any bodyguard could protect you from."

Harris looked about to sputter some inanity, so Craig added, "The Shinagawa are not going to show on your doorstep with shiny katanas; those times are long gone. Now the yakuza use lawyers, financial consultants, MBA graduates, and even hackers to get the job done."

The senator was frowning mightily, as if he couldn't decide whether to believe Craig or go back to his righteous anger. With an impeccable timing Brendan couldn't help but admire, Craig dropped a little improvised explosive device. "Have you given any thought to the fact that your sons' trip to Hawaii was entirely paid by the Shinagawa?"

"What are you talking about?" So righteous anger it was. "All the expenses were covered by Hanseiki Corporation. The damn Shinagawa had nothing to do with it!"

"Uh-huh," Craig said, lifting an eyebrow. "I take it you've seen the receipts, then?"

"No, but—"

"Well, sir, as it happens, *I* have."

Brendan almost smiled. He knew Craig's expression meant he'd tired of circling his prey; it was time to move in for the kill.

"You? How—"

The senator was many things, but stupid was not one of them. His small puffy eyes shone with intelligence as he came to the obvious conclusion. "Oh. So this is what you meant when you said the Shinagawa would use lawyers against my family."

"Not exactly, sir." Brendan understood Craig had to protect his own reputation. Unlike Brendan, Craig would still be working in the District when this was over. "Let's just say my little investigation into Shinagawa business interests didn't go unnoticed. And let me tell you, they can be very persuasive."

Harris shook his head. "So what do they have against my sons, apart from a few receipts?"

Craig retrieved yet another folder bulging with documents. His briefcase seemed bottomless, like some kind of Mary Poppins carpet bag—if the good nanny had been into blackmail.

"As a matter of fact," Craig said, handing the folder over, "there're more than a few receipts, ranging from the obvious plane tickets and resort stays to luaus, yacht trips, and spa treatments, all paid by the Ebisu Group."

The senator studied the receipts with a clenched jaw, the amounts consigned in them probably insulting to a frugal spirit like his. "Corporations are known to throw away this kind of money on a regular basis to attract investors," Harris finally said, disgust clear on his face. "It may be an objectionable practice, but it's by no means illegal."

As if anyone was going to believe that the senator himself hadn't benefited from those "objectionable practices" often enough. "Of course," Craig said in an understanding tone. "The contract your sons signed is perfectly legal too, but you must agree that, when you put all the information together, it does look a little disreputable. And disreputable is not a word you want attached to your family name come election time."

Harris shrugged. "You never know how voters will react. Some may even applaud my sons for scoring one on the Japanese."

So the senator was willing to take the risk. It was time to raise the stakes.

"That they may," Craig agreed with a smile, "but I doubt you'll find many voters ready to applaud a cocaine habit in your family."

The fraction of a second it took Harris to find his indignation told Brendan he wasn't much surprised about that little fact. "What are you trying to imply? No one in my family has ever—"

Craig cut the tirade short by producing a few close-ups of the contents of a suitcase, Campbell's wife's passport clearly displayed on top. "Well, this very much looks like a cocaine stash to me—not that I'm an expert in the matter, mind you."

The senator watched the pictures with clear disdain. "This is a crude fabrication. No court would admit it as evidence."

It was Craig's turn to shrug. "Probably not. But most papers would publish it if the source was the very corporation that paid for that room."

The senator didn't seem overly worried; in fact, the bastard seemed to be calculating how many voters would sympathize with the burden his son had to carry. Brendan could only hope Craig pulled the big guns now.

He reached for his Netbook. "I told you the Ebisu Group owned the resort your sons stayed at," he said as he retrieved a sound file. "That means it wasn't only their luggage the yakuza had access to."

Craig clicked the file open, making sure the loudspeakers were on. Campbell's voice filled the room.

"We've been enjoying ourselves here."

A grave, accented voice that Brendan recognized as Matsunaga's asked, *"I take it you're happy with the services the Shinagawa have provided?"*

The answer came from Miles this time. *"Yeah, it's good to travel with all your expenses covered, and the wives have been having a ball with the slew of shopping and spa treatments. You people know how to entertain your guests."*

The senator's face looked flushed again, and Craig paused the reproduction.

"That's a hoax!" Harris barely waited for the sound to stop. "You yourself said my sons didn't even know who the Shinagawa were!"

Craig shrugged. "It was just an assumption, but if their brother had some trouble with the yakuza—"

"It was an ugly business," the senator said with finality, "and I did my best to keep Miles and Campbell from getting mixed up in it."

Craig shrugged again. "I don't know how these recordings came to be, Senator. I'm just showing you what the Shinagawa have against your sons, as you asked."

Harris was beginning to look worried, and that was distinctively good.

"Is there more than that snippet?" he asked.

"A lot more, I'm afraid," Craig said, doing his best to look grim.

Harris made an impatient gesture for Craig to go on, as if Craig was a particularly dumb member of the senator's own staff, and Brendan smiled inwardly, because Craig would surely find a way to make the senator pay for the slight. Now Craig simply clicked on the play button.

"It can be a hell of a chance for us to expand into the Asian market," Campbell's voice said on the recording.

"Yeah," Miles agreed, *"Have you seen the prices around here? I bet that makes smuggling very profitable."*

"Exactly," Matsunaga said. *"The Shinagawa are behind most of the crystal meth business in Hawaii, and that's why we're so interested in your tugboat operation. Of course we are ready to compensate you for your troubles, as you've seen in the conditions we've offered you."*

"And damn good conditions they are," Miles said. *"Hell, if this panned out, just having a regular tugboat line between Japan and Hawaii would make us filthy rich. Father wouldn't have to lose his ass after any more defense contracts after this."*

It was hard for Brendan to keep a smirk from his lips as the senator went from flushed to almost livid, but he'd been trained to keep a blank face, and he saw with amusement how Craig even managed a sympathetic expression. As a lawyer—and a successful one at that—Craig was by necessity a well-trained actor.

Craig hit pause. "I'm sorry, sir, but there can be no doubt these are your sons speaking."

The senator seemed to recover a bit. "Anyone can tamper with that kind of tape, cut and paste until Miles and Campbell seem to be saying what they never said."

"I suppose," Craig said, not even trying to hide his skepticism. "And I guess a good sound engineer could detect any fraudulent tampering, but then again, I doubt many news media would go to the trouble once they hear what your sons *seem* to be saying."

It was a sign of the senator's agitation that he didn't even reach for his anger this time. "Is there more?" he asked, visibly troubled.

Brendan guessed it had been Miles's mention of his father that had put the fear of God into the man. His family he could disentangle himself from, if worst came to worst, but direct references that implicated him were a different matter altogether.

When Craig pressed the play button again, the senator's eldest said, *"Ah, you're talking about Portsmouth Naval Shipyard. You're right on the money—we sure got our hands dirty on that one."*

CHAPTER 74

BRENDAN COULD tell Craig was having a ball. So was Brendan, but watching the senator as he rubbed a now mostly pale face with his chubby fingers didn't quite manage to balance the scales.

Miles was still talking on the tape. *"We didn't actually build the shipyard, but we gave some of its most remarkable buildings a good makeover."*

Campbell added, *"And got a little richer."*

There came a nasty laugh then, and after that, Miles again. *"Someone forgot to make an entry in the books, huh?"*

"Yeah," Campbell said. *"You don't want tax examiners forever breathing down your neck."*

Matsunaga's voice sounded somewhat reproachful on the next bit. *"Getting richer is good, but now that your country is at war, is it wise to trick the military?"*

"Tough luck, pal." That was, of course, Miles. The man seemed to have no self-censorship to speak of. *"You have no idea how stupid those military types can be. Why the hell would anyone want to help them?"*

"Well, at least I always hear good things about your Marines," Matsunaga said.

"Marines?" Miles asked with a lot of sarcasm. *"They are the worst. They have nothing to do but chug beer and then go swinging an M16 about just to impress some third-world country villager. Besides, what's with all that black rabble? The idea is basically to offer the best of both worlds? Or some other bullshit like that, I guess."*

"Bunch of hicks," Campbell put in.

The senator was no doubt imagining how all that would go down on an electorate with so many parents and spouses of veterans and war heroes. And Harris hadn't yet heard the *pièce de résistance*.

This was Miles at his best—and without even the need to edit random sentences into a meaningful speech. *"Though, if you don't mind my saying, what would we do with all these trigger-happy rednecks if there wasn't an Army to let them blow off some steam safely away from home? Let me tell you, if we didn't have an Army, we'd have twice the number of crackheads on our streets, but the military gathers all these ignorant souls together, puts them into lovely uniforms, and even makes them believe they can be heroes—so we all benefit in the end."*

As the recording ended, Harris let out a resigned sigh. He probably thought things couldn't get any worse, and Brendan was happy to hear Craig disabuse him of that notion.

"These are all the sound files they gave me, but I can't guarantee they are all the Shinagawa have in their possession."

The senator snorted. "Of course not. I'm sure the bastards are well covered."

If the man still had the presence to be sarcastic, he wasn't frightened enough. Craig needed to switch to plan B.

"As a matter of fact," Craig said as if he was just remembering something inconsequential, "they did suggest they had some evidence implicating you in some failed military exercise, or something of that ilk—I figured it was just a big put-on, since defense policy falls outside your jurisdiction."

It seemed they had struck pay dirt. For a moment a look of pure, unadulterated panic crossed the senator's eyes, and even though he recovered quickly, there was no denying it had been there.

Harris shook his head, pretending to be disgusted. "They sure are ambitious, trying to implicate a US Senator."

As if his sons' babbling hadn't already implicated him.

"Yeah, that's the problem. These people respect nothing," Craig said, as if humoring him.

Harris nodded and asked with false nonchalance, "Did they mention where that alleged operation had taken place? Was it Iraq?"

Oh, man, that was rich, the way Craig frowned in fake concentration. The lawyer was definitely having a ball, no two ways about it. "Hmm. Let me think. I believe they said Afghanistan, though I didn't pay much attention." Craig paused, looking at the ceiling for inspiration, and then snapped his fingers. "Yes, Afghanistan, I remember now. They specifically mentioned Pech Valley, which struck me as funny at the moment—I thought they'd watched CNN to get their references straight."

They both laughed at that, but Brendan could almost smell the fear that oozed from the senator's every pore. And that, somehow, changed everything for Brendan. Up until this moment, he'd been enjoying Craig's performance, but hearing the words *Pech Valley* and sensing the senator's apprehension turned everything too personal to even consider smiling.

Harris tried for a light joke and failed miserably. "And what was it that I did, send a marine platoon to catch a herd of camels?"

Craig chuckled. "Oh no—I told you these guys watch CNN. They said—" Craig smirked, as if he could barely contain his hilarity. "They said you more or less sent a SEAL team on a suicide mission and got a few of them killed. A SEAL team, imagine that."

Brendan's hands clenched into fists. He had wanted to be here for this moment alone, to watch the senator's face the instant Harris realized someone knew of his blunder, someone knew his incompetence had almost wiped out an entire SEAL assault element. And now Brendan could only regret being in this fusty office, because now, for the first time in his life, he felt an irrepressible desire to kill a noncombatant.

The senator sat there sweating, abject fear widening his narrow eyes, and Brendan wanted to shake him by the lapels of his ugly suit and yell in his face, "What are you afraid of, you lousy motherfucker? What have you got to lose, huh? Money? Influence? Power? Fuck you! My friends lost their lives. Their lives, you stupid son of a bitch!"

Brendan's limbs began to shake, his hatred so intense that no amount of military training seemed enough to contain it. He had promised Craig he'd simply be the fly on the wall, stand there like a lead soldier and listen as Craig spun his web, but finally having proof that this man had murdered his friends made his blood boil, and the lead of his armor was melting to expose the naked core of his anger, the rage of finally meeting his lethal enemy only to discover he was this spineless coward—this greedy, selfish bastard that some fool had entrusted with a morsel of power.

Brendan started to move. Somewhere in the back of his mind he knew he was going to break a few promises, but he couldn't even remember what they were about. Nothing existed in this moment except Brendan's hands and the hostile that was still breathing after having killed Brendan's men.

He took one step numbly, then took another, and then the hostile's eyes met his and Brendan's vision tunneled. He could only see those wild, frightened eyes, and as he watched, the eyes seemed to grow bigger, turn darker, the face around them suddenly covered in blood, and Brendan found himself watching Bobcat's face.

"Senator?"

Brendan blinked. Bobcat was not there. Only Craig and Senator Harris.

Brendan studied the senator. This was the man who had killed two of his friends and tried to put the rest of Brendan's men out of commission. This man had hired Brendan because he knew who Brendan was, but now he had seen the murderous hatred in Brendan's eyes and had looked away without noticing it or recognizing Brendan, because this man, this elected representative of the people, had only looked around to check no one of consequence would see the incriminating fear in his eyes.

"Senator, I'm really sorry you have to go through this," Craig said.

Brendan gritted his teeth. He knew Craig was not sorry, but Craig was doing his job and doing it to the best of his ability. Brendan wasn't. All Brendan wanted to do was kill the senator, because the bastard owed Brendan, and nothing short of murder would be payback enough. Yes, this was fucking personal.

Realization hit Brendan like a howitzer blast. He felt dizzy. Had he gone through all this trouble just to get back at the senator? Had he put his own men and Matsunaga's at risk because the senator had wounded Brendan's pride as a commanding officer?

Maybe he had. Brendan had ignored Matsunaga's arguments for rescuing Ken first and worrying about the senator after Ken was safe. And the reason had to be that, without Matsunaga's yakuza connections, Brendan would have never managed a ruse big enough to bring himself here, to this very office where he had the senator finally sweating.

Everything about the Pech Valley op was classified information. Brendan would have never gathered enough evidence to confront the senator with it, but he could easily go around it, gather evidence on another matter cutting close to home but not close enough for the senator to do something, just to show him Brendan could produce evidence if he wanted to. And then it would be easy to have Craig casually mention Pech Valley, because by then the senator would have been ready to believe that Brendan could prove this too.

"This yakuza business is really ugly, and let me tell you the legal consultants your sons hired should have done a better job."

Brendan almost laughed. Craig was taking advantage of the situation to disparage Longchamp? Maybe, but as selfish as Craig was, Craig hadn't planned this complicated strategy just to get back at some colleague, while Brendan….

He closed his eyes and visualized Kinosuke's face. Brendan had offered his help to search for Ken, and Matsunaga had refused. But when Ken had pointed them to the pictures in the box, Kinosuke had called Brendan. *Kinosuke* had asked for Brendan's help, because the case seemed too complicated for them since they were newcomers in this country.

And Brendan hadn't called Burka and Otter, not even Bobcat. *B* had. Because they trusted Brendan. Because even after Pech Valley, they knew Brendan would do the right thing.

And the right thing now was to swallow his pride and disappear into the background, forget how much he needed to kill Harris and just stand there looking dumb while Craig secured the target they'd come to acquire.

"Since I'm sure we both want this ugly business to end as quickly and painlessly as possible," Craig said, "I'm going to relay to you what the Shinagawa demand in exchange for their silence."

Harris nodded curtly, no trace of his righteous ways left in sight, and Brendan knew the moment of danger had passed. He was not going to kill the senator, and the notion left him deflated, in the type of ugly down that followed an adrenaline rush.

"I was led to believe that the Shinagawa can be very reasonable if their suggestions are met in good faith," Craig explained, "and they are aware that, under the present conditions, fulfilling the contract they signed would be too much to require of your sons. So the Ebisu Group itself will rescind the contract, alleging some legal problem with the land permits."

The senator seemed relieved to hear that. Obviously having his stupid sons tied to the yakuza by a five-year contract would have been hard on his nerves.

"In exchange, what they ask of you," Craig said, "is your written word that you will never interfere in the life of one of their captains, a Shigure Matsunaga—I believe you are familiar with that name?"

Harris nodded again, his gesture one of utter disgust, bordering on hatred. Yeah, it seemed the man was familiar with the name of his son's yakuza lover.

Craig pretended ignorance as he handed the senator the document Craig himself had carefully phrased to prevent any ambiguity. "This is the document they want you to sign."

The document was a sort of restraining order by which the senator agreed to never come near or take action against Matsunaga *and* the people closest to him, including of course Kenneth Harris.

The senator lifted his narrowed eyes from the piece of paper. "I suppose they understand this has no legal value whatsoever."

So the senator was still trying to appear clever. Brendan would have laughed if he hadn't felt so exhausted.

"Of course. It's just a symbol of your good faith." Craig smiled nastily. "They wouldn't expect you to cut off your little finger, would they now?"

It seemed Craig had hit a nerve, because the senator almost tore his suit pocket in his haste to take out the pen he carried there. He put the document on the table and signed it with brisk strokes. "There they have it. Tell them my sons will be expecting all the documents concerning the canceled contract no later than next week."

Craig took the piece of paper from Harris and put it carefully inside his case. "I'll be sure to tell them, though I can't guarantee they'll comply."

Harris was trying desperately to recover some leverage, but it was already too late. "What about the initial investment my sons have transferred to Hanseiki Corporation?"

"Oh, that," Craig said with indifference. "I'm afraid the Shinagawa intend to keep it as a compensation for the exorbitant expenses your sons incurred."

It wasn't very far from the truth too. The Shinagawa had really paid for everything, but it hadn't amounted to that much; the money was simply the payment Matsunaga had promised his former yakuza group for their participation in the business.

Craig slowly put away his Netbook and the folders he had spread all over the coffee table, obviously enjoying the angry vibes coming from the now silent senator.

Craig stood, not bothering to offer his hand. "Well, Senator, it's been a pleasure doing business with you, in spite of the circumstances."

Harris stood and grunted at him, apparently not having any sneaky remarks left to offer in exchange. Brendan didn't care much either way; he focused his energy on following Craig out of the fucking office. They got what they came here for, and that was all that mattered.

As they reached the door, though, Craig turned as if an idea had just struck him. "Silly me. It's so ludicrous that I was forgetting to tell you." He rolled his eyes. "Following with that Pech Valley yarn of theirs, the Shinagawa wanted me to tell you that if you ever move a finger—their words, as you can imagine—against any of the soldiers who took part in this operation you ordered, they'll take it as a direct attack against the Shinagawa and act in consequence."

Craig gave the senator a brilliant smile. "Aren't they funny, these guys? Have a good day, Senator Harris."

Craig pulled Brendan out of there and didn't let go of Brendan's arm until they'd left a few corridors behind and entered the men's room. And then Brendan only reacted when Craig placed a chaste kiss on his lips.

He frowned. "What was that for?"

Craig grinned. "Easy, soldier. That was just my way of thanking you. I haven't enjoyed myself so much in forever."

"Hmm."

Craig sobered. "You probably don't care about my opinion, but I think your plan was brilliant. You've managed to grant Kenneth and his lover a safe future, and nobody but the enemies they make on their own is going to try to harm your buddies now."

Brendan roused himself enough to speak. "I'm the one who has to thank you. I couldn't have done it without you."

Craig snorted. "Don't flatter me. You would have done it perfectly fine." He paused. "With less style, that goes without saying."

Brendan found a smile for Craig, but Craig patted his arm and turned to leave. He'd never been one for sentimentality.

"Let's go, Bren. We both need a nap in the worst way. Not killing a rat when you spot one is really exhausting."

Brendan froze. Of course Craig had noticed. The man was nothing if not sharp. Craig's voice came now from the open door to the corridor. "Don't worry. I knew you wouldn't do it. You are one of the good guys."

Brendan clenched his jaw. Was he?

Craig's form reappeared in the doorway. "And the fact that you doubt yourself only proves my point." He waved a finger at Brendan. "Believe me, I know the score. And if I thought you'd care, I'd tell you that I'm proud of you. But I know you don't, so don't stand there like a ficus; this place is killing my taste buds."

Brendan's smile was easier this time. Yeah, this place was killing him too. But all he needed to do was leave it behind.

CHAPTER 75

"SHOOTS DEN, Sensei!" the last of the students waved at him, and Kinosuke waved back, shaking his head. Now he had a class full of hulking Hawaiians, Samoans, and the occasional white, and even though every one of them was much taller—and wider—than Kinosuke, they all treated him with a respect he'd never received from his previous class of self-absorbed executives.

Kinosuke snorted. Kotarō would say that this bunch of overdeveloped third graders were executives too, since they studied *executive* protection. And maybe after a few more PR classes from Alma and Miss Long-legs Akana, they would even look the part.

The truth was that opening a bodyguard school had been a great idea. The problem was the pea-brained dumbfuck who had come up with the idea had barely stayed long enough to lay out the plan others had to put to work without him. In typical super-SEAL-team-leader chickenshit style.

He retrieved his *zōri* sandals from the wacky *getabako* Kenshin-san had given them—trust the gaijin to find a shoe cupboard that looked fine even brimming with carved turtles. Now there was an American you had to kidnap to keep him away from the people he cared about.

The turtles blurred a little as he stopped to process that thought. Maybe he'd found the real root of the problem, the shitty truth at the bottom of the present snafu. Yeah. Maybe Brendan didn't really care—maybe he just needed to lead a bunch of clueless people until they were properly set on their path and then move on in search of someone else to rescue.

Right. As if that snake Craig needed to be rescued.

"Kinosuke?"

He smiled. Kenshin-san was about the only person he was happy to see right now.

"Hey, Kensh—"

Shit. After all this time, the gaijin still managed to surprise the hell out of him with the clothes he put on his skinny frame.

"What the fuck are you wearing?" he asked, not even trying to hide his horror.

Kenshin-san all but pouted. "It's Christmas!"

"In Zombieland?"

"What?" the gaijin asked in outrage. "These are classic Christmas red-and-white colors!"

Well, his knee-length tight-fitting pants and matching shirt were truly red and white, but the colors had been sort of splashed all over, as if Kenshin-san was covered in gore, the fabric ripped here and there as if to confirm the outfit was the product of some accident.

"Man, you look like an axe murderer's groupie," Kinosuke said, and the crazy gaijin glowered at him for all of a second before cracking up.

"You say that because you don't pay attention to details," Kenshin-san said, pointing at his leather choker. "I'm wearing Christmas stars—"

Sure. On a closer look, the metal spikes on the choker were star-shaped. Sharp enough to cut your skin to shreds, but star-shaped.

"And a Christmas bauble," he finished, pointing at a little shiny red ball hanging from his left earlobe.

Kinosuke blinked. He had no idea what a bauble was, but anything attached to a skull by a chain couldn't be very Christmassy in his book.

"Never mind," the gaijin said, and then he suddenly looked embarrassed. "Were you going home?"

Home. The SEAL guys all loved what Kenshin-san had done to the dojo, the way he'd transformed the old warehouse into a great living and teaching space, so they'd searched the neighborhood until they found a similar property and renovated the old buildings with that model in mind. Of course with them being who they were, the result was more like a huddle of military barracks with a paved patio in the middle—they weren't the gardening type either, this bunch.

Brendan had asked Kinosuke to be a partner in their business and to teach in the bodyguard school, and Kinosuke had moved there when the renovations ended, but it still didn't feel like home.

He couldn't have gone on living in the dojo after all the things he'd said and done, and teaching in the new place was great, but there was still something missing. Fuck. How could he call it home when he didn't even know what kind of bed to buy? One redheaded nitwit had forgotten to tell him if he intended to come back in this century and, in case he ever did return, if he wanted to share a house with an ex-yakuza. So he didn't even know if he was going to need a dog for company or what.

Kenshin-san was looking at him with concern, so Kinosuke hurried to answer. "Yeah. I'm finished for the day." Then he noticed again how weird the gaijin was acting— for his already weird self. "Why? Is something wrong? Something happened to Kotarō?"

"No! Everything's fine. Kotarō is surfing with Bobcat, so he's safe."

Yeah. That was a sure thing. The Catman would die before letting Kotarō get a scratch on his little finger. Not that Kinosuke had anything to say about that. The guy had turned out to be more of a house cat than a bobcat, especially after Shinya had grabbed him by the scruff of his neck and dragged the scrawny soldier into the room with the taiko drums. One hour of banging the big drums to his heart's content and Bobcat looked almost relaxed for the first time since Kinosuke knew him.

Bobcat's presence around Kotarō had also allowed Kinosuke to move to the bodyguard school without feeling he was shirking his responsibility toward the kid. Now Kotarō had some kind of older brother there for him, someone who had never let Kotarō down the way Kinosuke had.

And Kotarō seemed to be suffering from a bad case of hero worship, so much so that the boss had felt obliged to have one of those what-are-your-intentions-toward-our-kid conversations with Bobcat. Shit. That had been fun, being there to see the tough SEAL blush to the root of his hair and protest that yes, he liked Kotarō because he reminded him of a brother he lost, and no, he would never even remotely think of Kotarō *that way* until Kotarō was of age, and only if Kotarō thought, you know, *that way*, about Bobcat too.

"So what's up?" Kinosuke asked Kenshin-san. "You look as if you'd eaten the last *mochi* in the house."

The gaijin chuckled and smacked Kinosuke's shoulder playfully. Being around so many Americans, Kinosuke was more used to their touchy-feeliness now, but there was still something special about Kenshin-san doing the touching because there was an affection there that all of Kinosuke's fuck-ups hadn't managed to kill.

"That's because I'm shy, you big lug."

Kinosuke made a show of looking the gaijin up and down. "Says the man who wears spikes on his flip-flops."

"There you have it," Kenshin deadpanned, "classic defensive fashion."

Kinosuke snorted. "Whatever. So what are you shy about and what does it have to do with me?"

"Jesus. You're too direct for a Japanese."

"That's because I'm a punk." Kinosuke put his hands on his hips. "Come on. Stop dodging my questions. What is this about? What have you been up to?"

A sudden thought crossed his mind. Did Kenshin-san know anything about Brendan? Had Brendan left a message for Kinosuke? He clenched his jaw and squashed the hope trying to make his heart race.

Kenshin-san wouldn't be embarrassed about that. And the redheaded fucktard had only contacted them—mostly the boss and the gaijin, and probably his men, and maybe the bakery selling malasadas on the corner; anyone in the whole of fucking Oahu but Kinosuke—to give them news about the op against Kenshin-san's family.

It was more than obvious that the dipshit was avoiding Kinosuke—4,834 miles between them was more than a subtle hint. That plus the almost four months without a phone call or a text message or an e-mail made for the typical see-you-later-alligator branch of breakup.

At least Kinosuke always went for the go-to-hell breakup and even decorated it with some "and-your-feet-stink" parting remark that left no doubt as to his intentions, but maybe that was just because he was a punk—maybe Rattlesnake Craig had shown Brendan how to jilt someone in style.

"Can we go to your place?" Kenshin-san asked awkwardly, and Kinosuke pushed Brendan out of his mind; if the bastard didn't want to be on the same continent as Kinosuke, he had no right to be in his thoughts.

"Sure," Kinosuke gestured toward the patio. "After you."

The gaijin turned earnestly and almost ran to the second building on the left side of the patio. Kinosuke had to laugh when he saw the skull with a Santa hat on the back of Kenshin-san's shirt.

That was what he loved most about the gaijin, the way he bounced back to his old crazy self after every shitty thing that happened to him. The man was a survivor, and he didn't hold on to pain or grudges; he acted just like one of those spongy cactus that were all spikes on the outside and all tender on the inside—he just soaked in affection as if it was rainwater and then sprouted spectacular flowers when the right time came.

Kinosuke saw the big parcel beside his door and looked at Kenshin-san with narrowed eyes. "What's that?"

The gaijin was practically bouncing. Small wonder he was still skinny even though the boss had focused all his scary determination on a campaign to fatten him. "You said I could paint something for that big empty wall in your bedroom."

Yeah. It was true. Kinosuke didn't have that much stuff and had never been one for interior decoration anyway, but Kenshin-san had been clearly salivating at the sight of all those empty walls. "You painted something for me?"

The gaijin nodded shyly, and Kinosuke felt warmth spreading all over his chest. Someone had wanted to do something special for him and, by the way Kenshin-san avoided meeting his eyes, Kinosuke's opinion on the matter was as important as the painting itself.

"You don't have to put it up if you don't like it," the gaijin said, as if reading his mind. "I'll just, um, let you take a look at it. Phone me later. Bye."

And with that, he was out of there in less time than any of the school trainees managed when they practiced evasive maneuvers.

"*Kurutteru ze*," he groused, shaking his head—though calling the gaijin "crazy" was more of a fair description than an instance of name-calling.

He had to carry the huge thing inside by himself. The front room was, like the rest of the apartment, mostly empty, so he didn't lack places to prop the behemoth against.

On instinct, he pushed the front door closed. If Kenshin-san hadn't waited for Christmas Day to give him the painting, it might be something he wouldn't want to share with their SEAL-enlarged family—even Burka and Otter would be on leave, so there might be some Japanese-American competition over who came up with the best wisecrack. And the joke would be on Kinosuke.

Shit. What if the gaijin had gone for some explicit man-on-man action? He wasn't exactly one of these abstract guys who just threw lines and colors about; Kenshin-san drew for children, and children had very clear opinions on what things should look like.

Kinosuke took a deep breath. He was usually in awe of anything that came out of Kenshin-san's hand, and he had no reason to expect it would be different this time. And even if he didn't like it, he would put it up anyway, because it wasn't every day that someone took the time to think and do something strictly for Kinosuke, and with their own hands too—hell, he couldn't remember any other time someone did; his mother hadn't even knitted a pair of socks for him as a child.

So he just nodded to himself and tore at the thick brown paper protecting the painting, not really looking until all the wrapping lay shredded on the floor. Then he took a few steps away, braced himself for impact, and turned.

CHAPTER 76

"*USO DA ro!*"

Kinosuke couldn't believe his eyes. He let out a shaky laugh. Why had he been afraid of Kenshin-san painting an outrageous sexy scene? This was ten, fifty, or one hundred times worse.

His knees buckled and he let them bring him down, unable to tear his eyes from the picture in front of him.

"Kuso gaijin," he murmured, his voice cracking, his vision blurring, his mind so blown that he didn't even hear the door slide before he heard a familiar voice.

"Kinosuke?"

Fuck. The last person he needed right now, he and his fucking concern getting so close that Kinosuke knew the man had to be kneeling beside him even though Kinosuke would die before turning to look the dipshit in the face.

"Sensei? Are you—Fuck me raw."

Kinosuke almost laughed, but it came out more like a sob. Yeah. The prodigal son of a bitch had just seen the painting.

"Shit, Sensei. That's fucking…." It seemed the all-knowing superhero SEAL had run out of words. "Is it Ken's?"

Anger filled him, and he held on to it like a lifeline because the last thing he wanted was to break in front of the asshole who thought he could stroll into Kinosuke's house as if he owned the place after four fucking months without a word.

"Yes, Kenshin-san painted it for me, you fucking, stupid moron. And the man has paid enough attention to know that I never liked mecha manga but I was a sucker for chanbara, and even though I've done nothing but hurt him every single time, he's never gone and left me until some fucker dragged him away kicking, and he is crazy enough that after all the shit that I've done to him, he still looks at me and doesn't see a worthless piece-of-shit, good-for-nothing, low-life *chinpira*, but that, that—"

Fuck. To his utter shame, after the tirade in perfect Kotarō fashion, his voice broke and he started bawling like a baby.

"Don't touch me, you asshole!" he half yelled, half sobbed into Brendan's chest, because that was what those strong arms had pulled him against, and he was powerless to move away.

"Shhh, Sensei, it's all right."

He sniffed. "The fuck it's all right, you ass hat. And don't you dare shush me— I'm not your fucking dog."

"No, you are not" came the serious reply. "*I* am your fucking dog or anything else you want me to be."

Kinosuke's head shot up so fast that he almost knocked off the ball cap Brendan was wearing.

Shit. Why did everyone who left have to lose weight? Brendan looked paler than ever, too, his green eyes a little dull, with dark circles under them.

"What happened to you? Rattlesnake Craig hasn't been feeding you?"

That surprised a laugh out of Brendan. "Rattlesnake—" He laughed a little more, then his face turned solemn, and the schmuck said in a highfalutin voice, "Craig is nothing of mine; feeding me is not his responsibility."

Kinosuke made a rude noise. "Have you filled in the right form to have your collar removed? 'Cause he doesn't seem the type to give up on the things he owns."

Anger flashed for a moment in those green eyes. "He's never owned me." And then the smug bastard was smirking again. "Are you jealous, Sensei?"

"Jealous?" Kinosuke snorted. "After the first month, I didn't even remember what color your eyes were, and after three more months, you were the last thing on my mind when I fucked other men." He felt a nasty satisfaction when he saw Brendan grimace. Yeah. Payback was nice.

Brendan shifted awkwardly, and Kinosuke almost smirked at him for trying to put distance between them, right until he realized that what Brendan was doing was trying to stretch his leg. His wounded leg. Fuck. Kinosuke was a ditz.

"Are you all right? Is your leg giving you trouble?"

Brendan looked up at him, his face softening. "Don't worry. It's mostly all right, but kneeling is still too hard on it."

Kinosuke looked away and met the eyes in the painting. He couldn't hold those eyes either, so he tried to look at the other wall until a hand caught his chin and made him turn his head.

"Why can't you look at it, Sensei?" Brendan asked neutrally.

"Stop calling me that. I'm not your sensei anymore." He tried for anger, but it came out childishly sullen instead.

Brendan shrugged. "You're still a sensei. Doctors are still doctors even though they don't treat you specifically."

That was infuriatingly logical, so Kinosuke kept on being childish. "Yeah, well, I may be a sensei, but I don't like you calling me that. Happy now?"

"No, but we'll discuss it later. Now tell me why you can't look at Ken's portrait of you."

Kinosuke couldn't help himself. "That's not my portrait!" he yelled.

And Brendan put on his military, no-bullshit face and went on mulishly. "It's a picture of a real person, so it is a portrait. And Ken is a fucking good artist, so there can be no doubt that the person depicted is you. So it is your portrait, whichever way you look at it."

"He got it all wrong," Kinosuke said under his breath.

"What was that? I can't hear you."

"I said that's not me in there, you annoying bastard!" he shouted, trying to move away, but Brendan's hands latched on to Kinosuke's biceps.

"It's you all right," the asshole said in a tone that seemed to imply Kinosuke was a deluded nitwit for not seeing the resemblance.

"That's not me! I'm not a fucking long-legged yaoi-pretty warrior hero!" he was yelling again, and the way Brendan's lips twitched, Kinosuke felt like slugging him a good one if he so much as grinned.

But Brendan didn't grin. He fixed Kinosuke with an almost stern look. "You think a warrior is a guy in fancy armor? Think again. Not even a weapon can turn you into a warrior just because you know how to use it. A warrior is someone who's ready to fight for what's important to him—or her—and don't tell me you're not one, because you know that's bullshit.

"You're loyal and brave, and you do whatever it is that needs to be done, never thinking about what it'll cost you. You left your country to follow a leader you believed in and to protect the people you'd come to think of as your family. And when a member of your family got into trouble, you did everything in your power to help him, even when it meant humiliating yourself to work with a man who had hurt you badly.

"If you hadn't been there, Matsunaga might have been too proud to even realize Ken was in trouble or to accept the help of my men. You never stopped looking for Ken even when it seemed hopeless, and when Kitahara had to stay in the hospital, you stepped up to take his place even though you hated doing it. And you may still think that your role was unimportant, but Matsunaga told me that you saved the day more than once, and if your team hadn't dealt with Ken's brothers the way you all did, we wouldn't have anything to pressure the senator with and Ken would be in danger for the rest of his life.

"So let me tell you that it's not only Ken who sees you as a hero. And for your information, you might not be pretty, but you're still fucking beautiful—and long-legged too, if you ask me. So deal with it."

Kinosuke didn't know where to look. He was blushing from head to toe and there was no safe place to hide, so he focused on a floor tile as if he had to draw its geometric pattern from memory. But then he saw Brendan shift again, and he looked up worriedly.

"Are you in pain?"

Brendan hesitated, as if he'd been about to answer in the affirmative, but then he smiled and pulled at Kinosuke's arms. "C'mere, Sensei."

He moved quickly, but only because Brendan wanted him to sit between his spread legs, which meant Kinosuke wouldn't have to look in his eyes.

He rested his back against Brendan's strong chest and felt the uncomfortable heat of his embarrassment change into something warm he didn't know he'd been missing so badly. Tenderness. He'd been surprised, what seemed like ages ago, that the tough soldier could be so gentle, so affectionate, and Kinosuke had never thought he had it in himself to appreciate it, but he couldn't help the contented sigh that left his lips when Brendan's arms wrapped around him. He felt happy to just be like this, and he didn't need to turn around to know how the plain face resting against Kinosuke's hair was all lit up by a bright grin. Yeah. In spite of what he'd said, he hadn't forgotten a single feature of that face, from the straight reddish brows, to the sprinkle of freckles over the cheeks and nose, down to the smiling lips he yearned to kiss.

"Sensei?"

"Hmm?"

"Open your eyes."

He was so distracted that he obeyed without thinking, only realizing his mistake when he met the eyes of his fucking *portrait* right on. And the bastard behind him had the nerve to laugh.

"Come on, Sensei. Ken painted it for you—the least you can do is look at it."

Fucker. Of course he was going to look at the painting Kenshin-san had done for him. Just for him. He might die of embarrassment, but he was no fucking coward.

CHAPTER 77

BRENDAN KEPT silent while Kinosuke took to studying the painting as if it were a hard but unavoidable duty. This was not simply a mirror he was looking into, but something much worse. Kinosuke's reflection had been captured by a man who knew how to see through all the defensive posturing and into the primal source of everything that Kinosuke was, and because this soul stealer was a true artist, the result was both beautiful and terrifyingly moving.

The background was a misty mountain landscape, done in soft strokes of black and gray that managed to appear distinctively Japanese, the ethereal, watercolor-like touches suddenly becoming bolder until the very mist seemed to congeal into the solid black lacquered pieces of iron that made the armor Kinosuke's image was wearing.

For a soldier like Brendan, observing the minute detail of that armor was a delight, each small metal plate tied to the next with red strings, the resulting pieces secured with yellow straps in precise, complex knots, the functional details like the sleeves of chain mail and the shin guards as slick and beautiful as the most ornamental items like the tasseled strings holding the chest plate or the engraved symbols on the upper plates of the shoulder guards.

But as eye-catching as the armor was, Brendan's attention kept drifting back to the man who wore it. There Kinosuke was, standing proud in the gloomy landscape, tall and powerful, his right arm extended to raise a katana in obvious challenge to an invisible enemy in front of him, the familiar features framed by long strands of black hair that moved in the wind, the look in those dark eyes fierce, the expression on his face one that managed to combine the glower Brendan had seen so often with the barely contained, defiant joy of someone who found pleasure in a good fight.

Ken had captured Kinosuke's cockiness, but he'd also uncovered the strength behind it, and the result was filled both with Kinosuke's exuberant youth and the grave, somewhat sad maturity his hard life had brought to his eyes.

The painting was beautiful and alluring, and Brendan thought he could look at it for hours and never stop discovering a new detail, something apparently trivial like the trickle of blood running along the left side of Kinosuke's face, from his hairline down to his jaw—a little red line that matched the one staining the katana blade to completely change the meaning of the scene, making the observer understand this was a desperate fight and Kinosuke might be the last man standing after a savage battle, the last warrior defending his home. And that was what made the picture so moving, the fact that Kinosuke was facing death with fearless determination, brave and beautiful as he defied an army only he could see, his features lit by the fiendish joy Brendan had seen many times in his fellow combatants.

"It's…," Kinosuke tried, his voice raspy.

Brendan took pity on him. "Awesome?" he supplied.

Kinosuke nodded eagerly, and Brendan thought his own smile couldn't get any wider.

"Ken is a genius," Brendan said, and he had to chuckle when Kinosuke nodded again.

Kinosuke turned a little to glare at him, so Brendan repeated it with a serious face. "I mean it—your friend is a genius."

His sensei seemed to believe Brendan was being honest, and he turned back to look at the painting.

"He did it for me," Kinosuke said after a while, the awe in his voice making Brendan wonder what kind of people Kinosuke had grown up around.

They were silent for a moment, and Brendan simply enjoyed having his sensei in his arms, remembering how good the lithe body felt against his, inhaling deeply to catch the unmistakably cedar scent coming off Kinosuke's warm skin.

And then, just as if an invisible snake had bitten him, Kinosuke shot up and away from Brendan, turning so fast to face him Brendan felt dizzy watching him.

"What are you doing here?" he asked, the glare back on his beautiful face. "That man got tired of your freckled face?"

Ouch. If he hadn't known it was jealousy fueling Kinosuke's anger, Brendan would have felt hurt—his freckles were not exactly his favorite feature.

He decided to ignore the second question. "I'm here because this is where my home is. You know I had to go to the mainland to make sure Senator Harris was dealt with and to settle my affairs so I could come back to stay."

Emotions flashed across Kinosuke's eyes too fast for Brendan to name them, but anger was still the winner in the mad race. "And how was I supposed to know this when you haven't even phoned once in four fucking months?"

It seemed Brendan's strategy of giving Kinosuke some space had not worked the way he had expected, but it wasn't entirely his fault—his sensei had been too proud to call him, even to yell at him, and it made Brendan's own anger surge. "I was only leaving you alone so you could decide what you wanted, and anyway you had my fucking number, so why didn't *you* call me?"

Kinosuke snorted. "Yeah, and catch the great SEAL warrior in the middle of an operation?"

Geez. It was the first time in Brendan's career someone had made *operation* sound sleazy. But Kinosuke wasn't finished yet.

"And what the fuck do you mean, leaving me alone to decide? What the fuck was there to decide? You think I'm a five-year-old to go changing my mind every ten seconds?"

Brendan frowned. "Well, it's not as if we'd talked much about us. I didn't dare assume anything, not on this matter."

"Us?" Kinosuke said, his temper forgotten for a cute moment of embarrassed confusion.

"Yeah, Sensei, us," Brendan said, trying not to smile. "I know you wanted to be part of the school project, and you've obviously chosen to live here, so the only doubt left is whether you'll let me be more than just a business partner. I didn't want to pressure you into a decision when I wasn't even around to discuss it with you."

"It would have been nice if you'd told me," Kinosuke grumbled, but he didn't sound angry like before; he sounded a little lost, and maybe even a tad hopeful. At least Brendan prayed he was hopeful because, in spite of what he'd said, he had very much assumed there would be a future for him and Kinosuke.

Brendan took a deep breath. He hadn't exactly rehearsed this speech, but he knew he owed it to Kinosuke to put his heart on the line and call things by their names, whatever the results. He also knew Kinosuke's pride wouldn't let him take the first step, so there was really no other way to go about it than to plunge in headfirst—that was what SEALs were trained to do, right?

"Kinosuke, this school is important to me because it means I'll get to work with the people I trust, under my own conditions, doing the job I'm more than good at."

Kinosuke's expression read "smug bastard" as clearly as if he'd mouthed it, but Brendan didn't care. He wasn't going to be self-effacing in the Japanese way, not about the only thing in his life he was proud of.

"This school is important," he went on, "but it won't mean much if you're not here to share it with—and I don't just mean to share the work with you. I want you in my life, Sensei.

"I know you feel like I betrayed your trust, but I never used what we had to get my job done; my feelings were there from day one—I never faked them or tried to manipulate you in any way. My only fault was not to tell you the entire truth, but I never lied to you."

Kinosuke seemed about to argue, so Brendan raised a hand to stop him. "I understand you still feel hurt, and I won't ask you to forgive me just yet. What I want you to know is that my feelings have never changed, or rather, they have, but to become stronger the more I get to know you.

"The man Ken painted? He is what I see every single time I look at you—an incredibly brave, strong, and beautiful warrior—and he is the man I want to share my life with. If he'll accept a plain, freckled redhead for a companion, that is."

Kinosuke glared at him, and Brendan's heart froze for a terrifyingly long second, until his sensei spat, "You're not plain, you stupid freckled redhead."

And then not even his most stern SEAL instructor would have stopped him from grinning like the fool in love he was. "I'm not?"

Kinosuke rolled his eyes. "No," he said in his characteristic un-Japanese, rude way, "you're not fucking plain, but you look like shit right now. What have you been eating? And why the fuck are you wearing a hat?"

Oh shit. He'd forgotten that little detail. Well, his sensei had pretty much accepted him even if he hadn't actually said the words, so how wrong could it go?

"Um, I sort of have to wear a hat until my hair grows back."

Kinosuke stared at him. "You shaved your head?"

Brendan was about to stammer some more, but his sensei was too fast for Brendan's jet-lagged self and knocked the ball cap off in a single move. So much for SEAL reflexes.

"You're hurt! When—"

He hurried to explain. "No, no, Sensei, I didn't get hurt. I'm fine."

Kinosuke didn't look convinced. "That's a fucking bandage you're wearing."

"It's just to protect it," Brendan said, but he knew he couldn't go on dodging the truth, so he just put it out there in the open. "It's a tattoo."

For once, Kinosuke was silent. He took his time processing the information, and Brendan didn't like the way his black eyes narrowed. "You got a tattoo on your head? What the fuck were you trying to prove? Wasn't it enough to get shot rescuing Kenshin-san while all I did was sit on my ass all day?"

Geez. Now his sensei was thinking he'd done it to prove he was tougher than Kinosuke because he could bear getting his scalp tattooed like the yakuza had. Brendan had never denied being a competitive bastard, but that was too much even for him. The problem was, not having taken part in Ken's rescue was a sore point for Kinosuke, and right now he didn't seem in the mood to believe anything Brendan might say, so Brendan realized he'd better just show Kinosuke and let him draw his own conclusions.

He lifted one corner of the bandage and ripped it off with a quick jerk of his hand. It hurt like hell anyway, but not as much as it hurt getting the symbols tattooed in the first place. That had been Hell Week compressed in a single fucking torture session.

Still, it might have been worth it just to see Kinosuke's eyes widen.

"What...?" His sensei couldn't even find words, and suddenly Brendan started to freak out.

Had he gotten it all wrong? It had taken him a lot just to find a truly Japanese tattoo artist, and the man had seemed a bit frustrated to have to ink simple kanji instead of one of those magnificent colorful designs, but he had drawn the two different set of characters confidently enough that Brendan thought he knew what he'd been talking about.

It was just his luck that the name Kinosuke could have two completely different meanings if it was either written *Kinosuke* or *Kinnosuke*. And, contrary to common sense, the first spelling had three characters while the second had only two.

What if Brendan had gotten the wrong name tattooed on his head? Wouldn't it be wonderful to have the name of a stranger on his scalp for fucking ever? He'd seen Kinosuke's name written on official documents, so he had thought it was the right spelling, but they were American documents, and maybe they hadn't paid much attention to a single floating letter.

Brendan had liked the meaning too; the other Kinnosuke was represented by characters that meant something about gold, while the three kanji in *his* Kinosuke meant something like taking pleasure in rescuing someone. That meaning seemed almost too fitting to be true, and Brendan had thought it was perfect.

And now his sensei was looking almost horrified, and Brendan thought this was his most embarrassing blunder since the day he'd peed his pants at a party—and he had been an eleven-month-old tyke then.

"What did you do?" Kinosuke finished the sentence in a whisper, and Brendan was ready to apologize and take the next plane to Australia, but he realized that his sensei had exactly the same look now as when he'd been trying to face his own image in Ken's mirror.

"I wanted to wear your name," Brendan tried, mentally crossing his fingers.

Kinosuke looked into his eyes. "You... you did this for me?"

If his chest hadn't constricted at the lost expression on Kinosuke's face, Brendan might have felt dizzy with relief. "Of course I did it for you. I wanted to do something more than say the words *I love you*; I wanted to show you that you are a part of me—" He smiled. "—wanted to show you that you're in my head all the time."

But Kinosuke wasn't smiling back. He wasn't exactly glaring, but it was a close thing. "*Mendō kusai na*," he said in a long-suffering tone. "What if you change your mind and hate my guts? What are you going to do with that? You know you can't erase a fucking tattoo, don't you?"

He shrugged. "Then I'll wear my hair long like a rock star."

"Yeah? And when you go all bald, you genius, what will you do then—wear a burka?"

Brendan laughed. "Well, then I suppose I'd better love you forever; it'll be easier on my handsome looks," he said, wiggling his brows and making Kinosuke snort.

But then, just as fast, Kinosuke went serious again, his expression a complicated mixture of surprise and insecurity. "You love me?"

Good lord. Such a speech and his sensei hadn't caught on to that *little* detail?

He couldn't help it; Brendan had to roll his eyes. "Geez, Sensei, you can be real dense sometimes."

Of course Kinosuke lunged forward to smack him upside the head, only to stop his hand mere inches from the still angry-red tattoo. Brendan's heart swelled with pride. That was his sensei, faster than lightning and as gentle as the Christmas snowflakes none of them would probably get to ever see again in the warm Oahu weather.

Brendan reached up to frame Kinosuke's gorgeous face with his hands. "I love you, my beautiful sensei—even though you're a little slow on the uptake."

Kinosuke tried to hide his smile behind a pout. "Shut up."

Brendan smiled wider. "Make me."

Kinosuke fixed him with a predatory gaze. He barely had time to chuckle before he had an armful of fierce Japanese warrior, his lips taken in an openmouthed kiss that felt more like being eaten alive, Kinosuke's momentum pushing Brendan back until he hit the tiled floor with a thud.

He was so drugged on the taste of those luscious lips he didn't even feel the impact, his hands too busy trying to reach warm skin to do anything but latch on to Kinosuke as the kisses went on and on, right until a wiry leg pressed against Brendan's and a painful moan escaped his throat.

His sensei tried to move away then, and Brendan tried to stop him, and they fought clumsily between kisses, both too starved of each other to let go even for that.

"*Yamero yo!*" Kinosuke finally yelled, pushing at Brendan's chest with both his arms to gain leverage. He looked even fiercer than before, his eyes shining black like the armor pieces on Ken's painting, his lips swollen and wet, his hair rumpled, looking down at Brendan as if he couldn't decide what to do with him, his voice managing to come out both stern and husky at the same time. "Stop it, damn you," he said. "You're hurt."

Brendan tried to pull him back down in vain. Had Kinosuke always been stronger than him? Surprisingly enough for his competitive nature, the thought that his sensei had no trouble overpowering him was a huge turn on. "I don't care. Come back here," Brendan said, almost choked by the need to have Kinosuke's powerful body flush against his, leg wound be damned.

But Kinosuke did not move. "I do, you stupid fool!" he yelled down at him. "I fucking care!"

Brendan looked up in shock, Kinosuke had sounded so close to tears. His sensei's arms were shaking, and Brendan knew it wasn't because his muscles had grown tired of holding his weight. No, Kinosuke was clearly upset, and Brendan felt his arousal change into something warm and pleasantly achy, as if his heart were getting sore after a long, good workout.

He stroked those trembling arms. "I know you do, Sensei," he said softly. "Just let me kiss you a little more. I'll be careful. Please, Sensei. I need you."

Kinosuke lowered himself to lie beside Brendan, and Brendan immediately turned to face him. His sensei shook his head, but his dark gaze was now soft with feeling, and he reached out to stroke Brendan's shaved head, carefully avoiding the tattoo lines.

"Kuso gaijin," he said fondly, and Brendan couldn't help the goofy smile, because the way his fierce warrior hero said it, Brendan knew it just meant "I love you."

EPILOGUE

KOTARŌ FELT like a kid on Christmas morning. He giggled at his own bad joke. He was not a kid anymore—in spite of what everybody else thought—but today was Christmas Day all right, even though it was frigging hard to tell here in Honolulu.

The bodyguard students had done a good job of decorating the patio with a weird mixture of reindeers, dolphins, and pineapples, a big plastic tree brimming with the craziest hibiscus and hula-dancer-angel ornaments, and stockings filled with candy canes and small shiny surfboards. There was a big banner too, with *Mele Kalikimaka* written in big letters in case someone was dumb enough not to remember this was not your usual Friday neighborhood luau.

And it wasn't. It wasn't your usual luau at all. This was the most friggingly cool luau the neighborhood had seen in frigging ever.

Kotarō looked at the improvised stage where Keawe and Kekoa were dancing with some friends and smiled. He had never imagined a group of dudes wearing skirts and flower necklaces and leaf garlands could move that way. Man, they were awesome.

Everybody was looking at the stage as if B's cousins were *aidoru*, so Kotarō guessed they weren't your common hula dancers—they must be pretty good if even the bunch of humongous native Hawaiian students couldn't take their eyes off the stage.

He discovered some other people *could* take their eyes off the dancers, and Kotarō couldn't help giggling at what he saw.

Shinya-san was looking slightly behind the dancers at the big potbellied Hawaiian drums being played to mark the rhythm, though Kotarō had the impression Shinya-san was specially looking at one, or more exactly, at the man playing one, a guy wearing a frigging amazing tattoo on his face that made him look as if he was wearing a cool warrior mask. Maybe Shinya-san was considering a tattoo like that to cover his scar, or maybe he was considering, um, other things.

Kotarō smiled. Tachibana-san wasn't even looking at the stage; he was looking at his wife as if she was the goddess Amaterasu herself, and she seemed to be at least psychic or something, because she took her husband's hand without even looking at him and placed it on her belly, and dude, the shock on Tachibana-san's face was frigging hilarious. The little one must have kicked his father for sure. Man, to think Kotarō had believed people as old as Tachibana-san couldn't have kids. He was frigging clueless.

Yeah, well, he wanted to think he'd grown up a little now and knew a thing or two more than before. Shit, not many people his age got to be tutored by ex-SEALs and ex-yakuza, so he sure had to be learning something.

For one thing, he wasn't ashamed of the way the boss looked at Kenshin-san anymore. Of course he was still embarrassed to look at them looking at each other that way, but that was because he knew it was rude of him to stare like he was doing right now. But dude, he couldn't help it.

Right now Kenshin-san was looking at the dancers with that face he wore when he was thinking about his next project, and the boss was looking at Kenshin-san with that laser-like look of his, and you could tell that he was itching to at least put his arm around the skinny shoulders but was too Japanese and too yakuza wakagashira to touch his guy in public. And Kenshin-san might be a space cadet most of the time—and dress like one too—but he sure noticed when the boss was being his stubborn self, because he moved just a little fraction but enough that their bodies were touching on one side, and then the boss seemed to be able to breathe again.

Kotarō giggled because not too far away from Kenshin-san and the boss stood another pair of stubborn guys, but Brendan-san had no trouble putting both his arms around Aniki in public, and even though Aniki seemed to be fuming at the PDA, Kotarō could tell his glare was more of the don't-even-look-at-my-man kind. And the smug grin on the redhead's face said he knew it too.

Movement in the corner of his eye made Kotarō turn his head in time to see Big B's daughter waving at him. He laughed and waved back. Dude, the girl looked tiny sitting on her father's broad shoulders. And that mountain of a man had eyes on the back of his head, because he frigging turned and winked at Kotarō as if he'd felt Kotarō had been staring. Man, you never got used to frigging SEAL skills.

And speaking of frigging SEALs, Kotarō's eyes were inevitably drawn to one glowing white head in the middle of so many black-haired people. There he was, the weirdest guy on earth—after Kenshin-san, that is—looking a little thinner after four months of doing SEAL shit in the back of Bumfuckistan and smiling the weirdest smile at the things Otter was whispering in his ear. Dude, those two were scary.

Kotarō got the strange feeling he was being watched himself, and when he turned, he caught Bobcat looking at him. Kotarō blushed and waved shyly at him. Bobcat smiled back. He was looking better these days, had gained a little weight, and his smile didn't look like someone had to pull a string to keep it stretched over his teeth. And Kotarō couldn't for the life of him imagine why the man liked to hang out with a clueless kid like him, but Bobcat was always offering to go surfing, or running, or even shopping with him—dude, he even looked almost relaxed in the mall now.

Bobcat turned to look at the stage, and Kotarō did too, but his smile had nothing to do with the dance. His smile was there because all the people in this crowd knew him. Most were friends, but many were family, and Kotarō had to wonder how did one go from being an unwanted child on one island to having so many people care about him on another.

He giggled. Dude, however it had come to be, it was frigging awesome.

H.J. BRUES lives in Spain, enjoying the hot weather, the brisk language, the warm-hearted people, and the thousands of books of the library she works in. She has a degree in medieval history and loves castles, knights in shining armor, and barbarian warriors with no armor at all. She practiced fencing till her knees started complaining, took archery till her elbow almost fell off, and then, wisely, switched to the less martial of the martial arts, tai chi.

You can contact H.J. Brues at hjbrues@gmail.com.

Also by H.J. Brues

http://www.dreamspinnerpress.com

Read more from this author in

A BRUSH OF WINGS

A Dreamspinner Press Anthology

http://www.dreamspinnerpress.com

Also from DREAMSPINNER PRESS

decision

Y.H. LIM

http://www.dreamspinnerpress.com

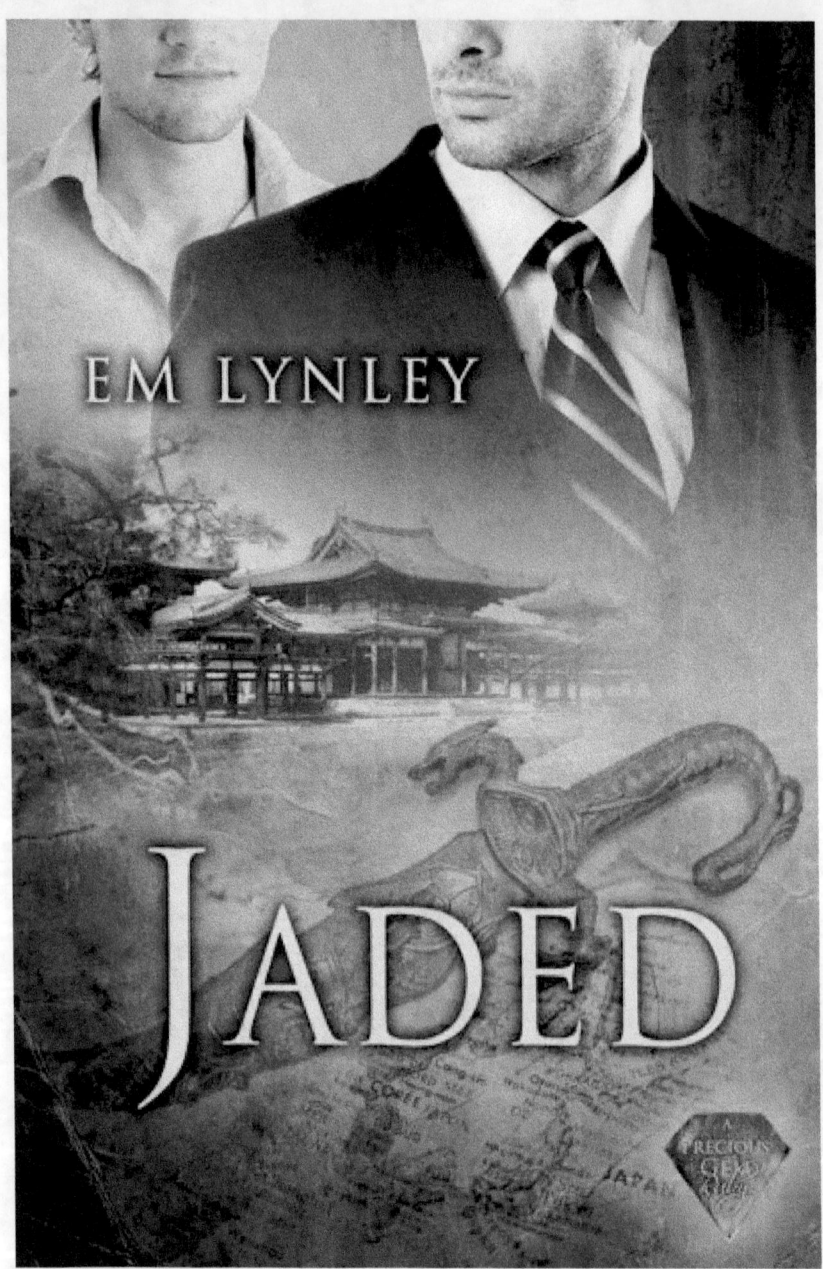

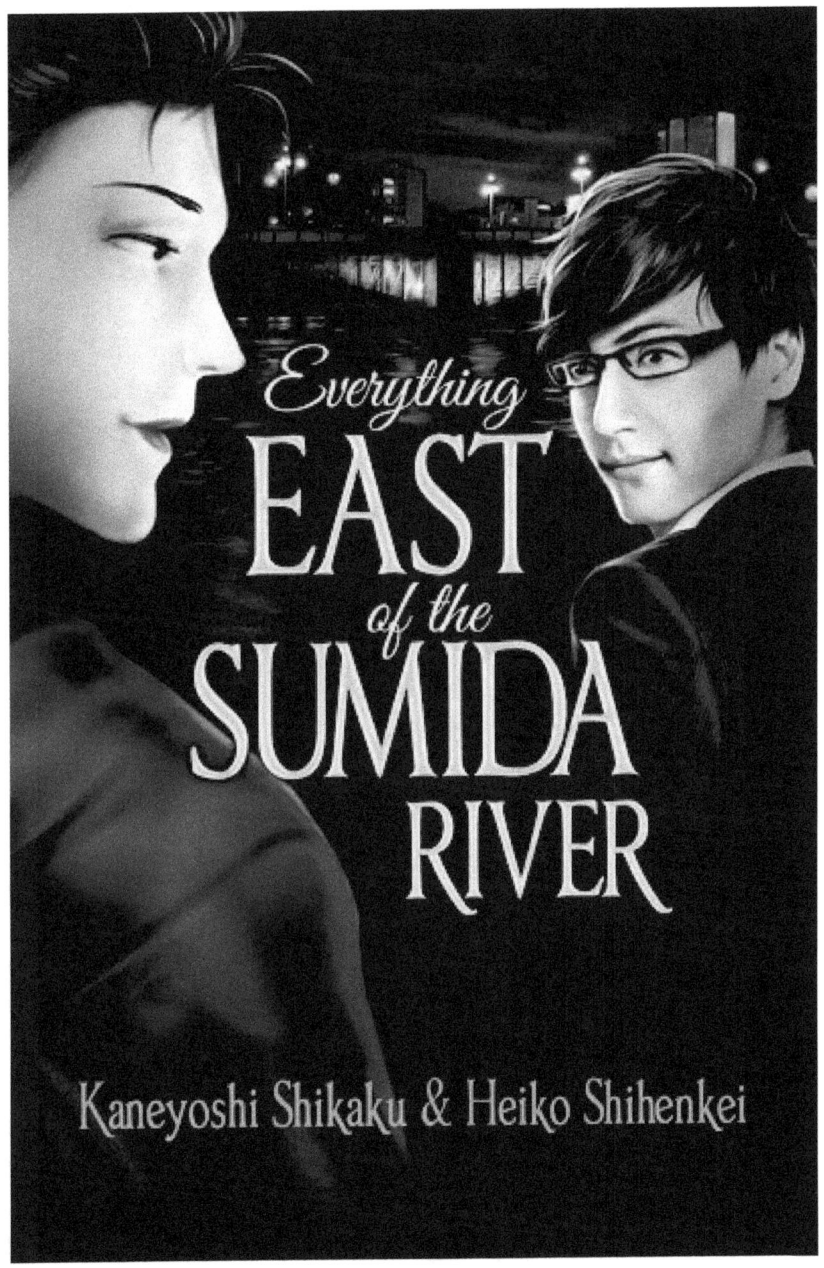

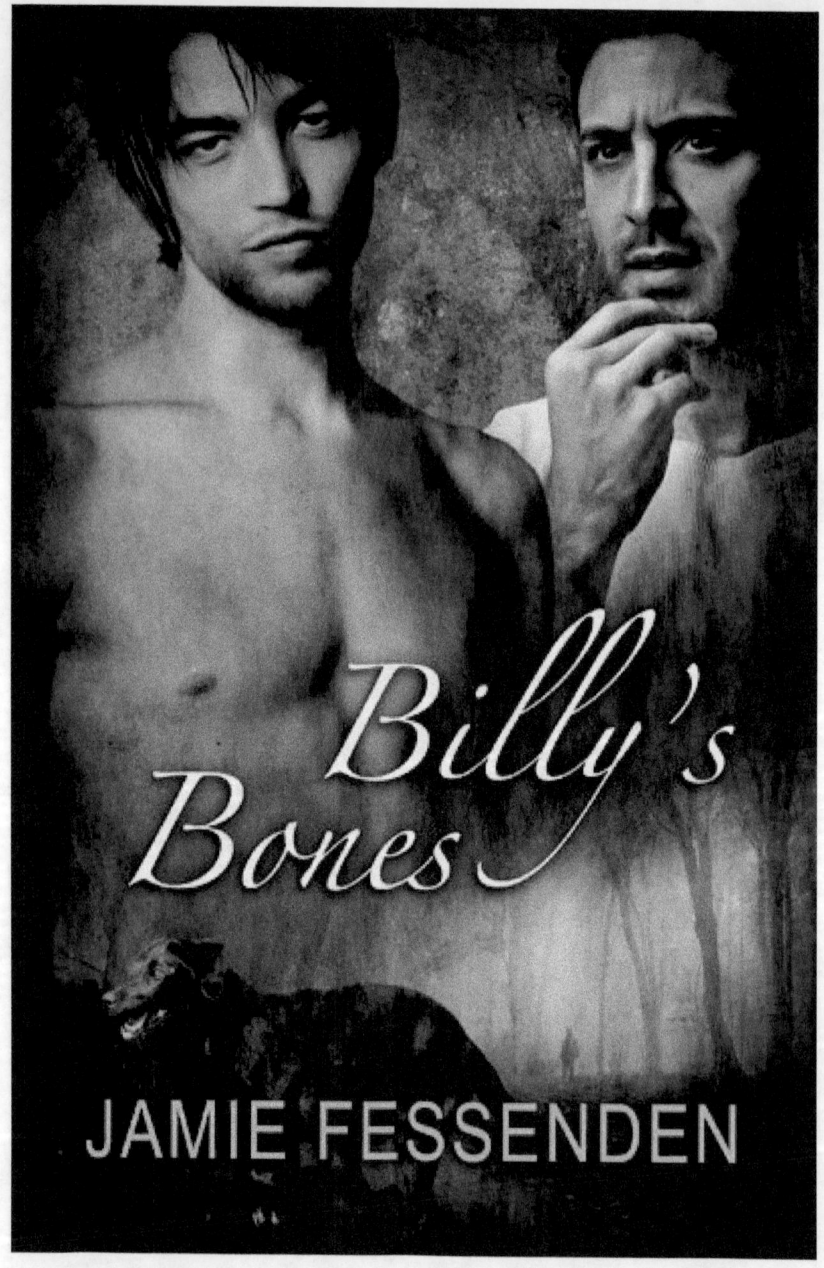

Billy's Bones

JAMIE FESSENDEN

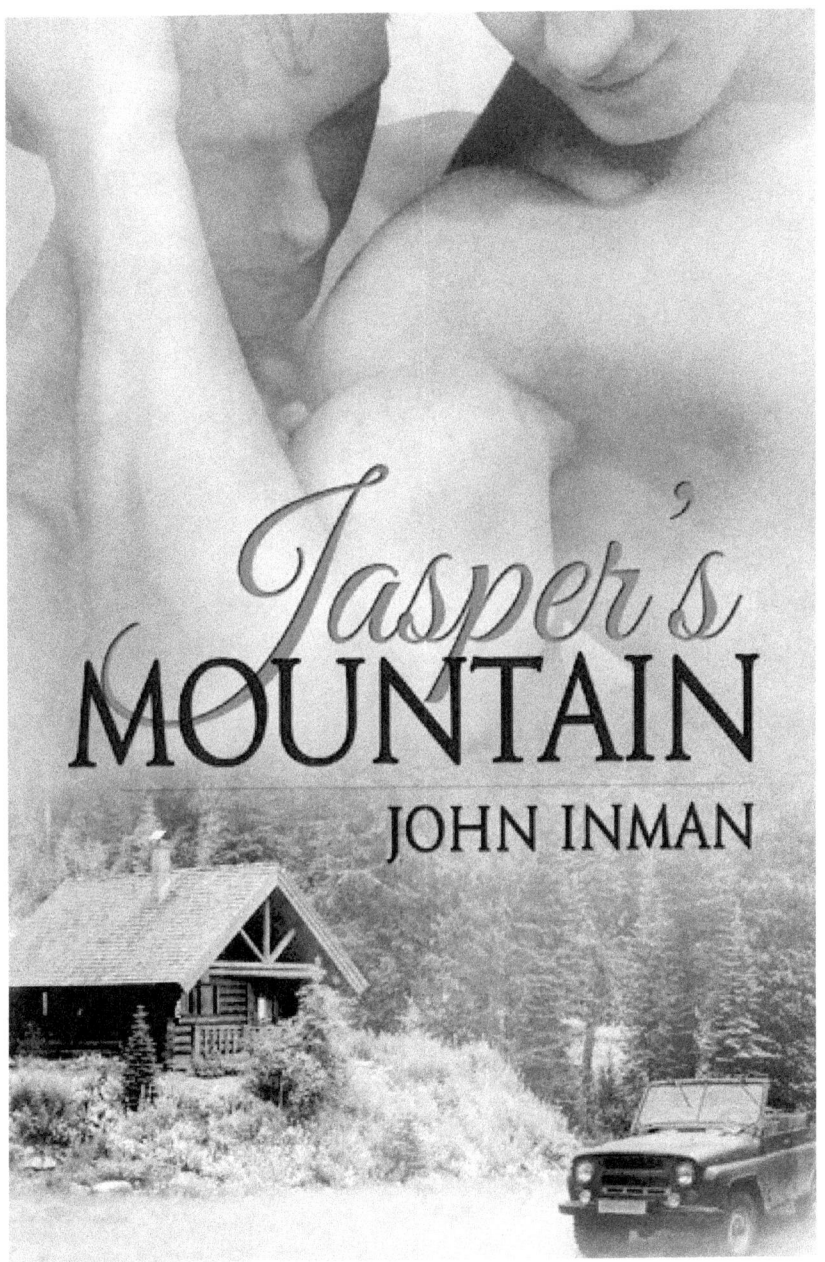

Jasper's
MOUNTAIN
JOHN INMAN

www.ingramcontent.com/pod-product-compliance
Lightning Source LLC
Chambersburg PA
CBHW070043030726
47506CB00002B/323